ON BOARD

PAINTED BAY 2

JAY HOGAN

SOUTHERN LIGHTS PUBLISHING

For my family who read everything I write and keep on saying they love it all, blushes included.

ACKNOWLEDGMENTS

As always, I thank my husband for his patience and for keeping the dog walked and out of my hair when I needed to work, and my daughter for her incredible support.

Getting a book finessed for release is a huge challenge that includes the help of beta readers, editing, proofing, cover artists and a tireless PA. It's a team effort, and includes all those author support networks and reader fans who rally around when you're ready to pull your hair out and throw away every first draft. Thanks to all of you.

CHAPTER ONE

Leroy

"What the hell are *you* doing here?" I dropped my damp duffle on the wide plank floor and glared at the man taking up space in my house. Fox bloody Carmody, looking handsome, annoying, and way too fucking comfortable in *my* kitchen. Wearing soft-faded jeans that hugged every hard curve, a navy-blue T-shirt, and bare feet, all six foot three of him looked utterly delicious. Except he didn't, of course. Because if I actually thought that was true, it might mean something, right? Which it didn't.

Had I mentioned that?

"Well, hello to you too, Leroy." Fox shot me an amused glance, green eyes dancing as a messy loose ponytail tried and failed to contain all those disobedient dark locks, their bleached-gold tips almost silver in the light. The man looked like a fucking angel—that is if you liked your angels tall, built, and irritating as fuck. A half-constructed chicken sandwich teetered on the butcher block in front of him, a steaming fresh espresso to the side.

What the actual fuck?

"Sorry, I'll just get this done. Then I'm all yours."

Don't tempt me.

He squished the bread lid on top of his super-sized sandwich, making me cringe. *Who the hell did that?* It wrecked the crusts and ruined the damn filling. May as well put the thing through a blender.

"From your reaction, I take it neither your mother nor mine told you I was coming?" He licked his fingers, and I absolutely did not watch. Then he eyed the enormous sandwich, looking thoroughly pleased with himself and with enough dimples popping to make me frown.

The Fox I remembered from his last few visits—four since the fateful lunch a year ago, but who's counting—didn't smile much at all, and I preferred it that way. Infinitely less appealing than this current chatty and relaxed version. And where the hell were the man's shoes or jandals or anything that didn't make him look so damn sexy?

We'd rubbed each other the wrong way from that very first meeting the year before, and it was a state of affairs I was more than happy to continue. Fox Carmody was an irritating thorn under my thick, grumpy skin and for reasons it didn't pay to dwell on for the sake of my sanity.

That I irritated him in equal measure was likely down to the fact that whenever we shared the same space, like within a small galaxy of each other, I tended to behave like an unmitigated prick. To that end we'd nestled into comfortable roles of mutual dislike, like bitchy teenagers, or at least I had. And I wasn't looking to change those rules of engagement in the next century or so if I could avoid it.

"No one said a word, but then I only live here, right?" I grumbled, my teeth grating at the bemused look on his face. Where was the blistering well-polished snark and bite he usually brought to our conversations? That's how it worked between us. I knew that man. Not this smiling Colgate version I wanted to punch in the throat.

The smile dropped and there was apology in his eyes. "I'm sorry about that, but it was actually *your* mother who invited me. I was going to grab a motel until I could organise something more long-term, but Cora insisted I stay here. I honestly thought you knew."

The interfering minx. I was going to have to scatter a few more retirement village pamphlets on my coffee table the next time she visited. *And also, long-term?*

"When exactly was all this decided?"

He raised a brow. "Sunday. I was supposed to get here Thursday, but I'm a day early. Surprise!" He gave me jazz hands which almost cracked a laugh from me, the bastard. "I did warn her I'd be early, and she said it was fine." He grinned my way. "Oops."

He carried his sandwich and coffee past where I stood—towering over me by a good five inches. I refused to look up at him, although I may have followed his back as he made his way to the giant twelve-seater, hundred-year-old dining table where he plonked himself down in a chair, *my* fucking chair.

My bloody mother. I was gonna kill her. I tore my gaze from the way his jeans stretched snug over those tight-muscled thighs as he made himself comfortable and crossed my arms solidly over my chest. To protect myself from what, I wasn't sure, other than whatever the hell it was, it was potent and too fucking dangerous to lift the lid on. Four times he'd visited, and I was still caught up in the power of the first one.

"And?" I may as well have tapped my feet.

With his sandwich halfway to his mouth, he paused and looked over. "I said, I'm sorry, Leroy. But it's not like I just turned up. I'm not sure what you want from me."

Neither did I. And he had a point.

He held up the monstrosity in his hand. "Would you like me to make you one? An apology of sorts."

I felt an almost irresistible urge to smack him on those red pouty lips. "No, I don't want you to make me a bloody sandwich."

He grinned. "That's probably for the best because I'm not sure there's actually enough chicken left, although I'd have given you some of mine. I'll buy more next time. I wasn't expecting you home just yet."

Home? This ain't your home, buddy. "Yeah, well we finished a bit earlier than—" Why was I explaining myself?

He smirked like he knew he'd caught me out, then ran a long-fingered hand over the smooth honeyed wood of the table in obvious appreciation. "This table has a beautiful patina."

I squirmed and ignored the urge to fling myself atop the damn thing. I'd really thought I was done with this stupid, stupid . . . whatever the fuck it was. *Get a grip.*

"What I *want*," I said testily, "is to know what the hell you're doing *here* in *my* kitchen, in *my* house, and not on Stewart Island at the other end of the damn country . . . where you live, or you used to, because I clearly missed the memo. And I'd appreciate the word *long-term* explained in a little more detail."

He held up a finger as he took a huge bite of his sandwich, and I absolutely did *not* watch his throat work as he chewed and swallowed it down, not even for a second, because that would be—*nope*, not going there, see the aforementioned statement. He followed the bite with a slow draw of hot coffee and then blew a sigh of utter contentment as he flicked a few of those dangling strands of hair back over his shoulder.

I was doing stupendously with the whole 'getting a grip' thing.

"Take your time." I rolled my eyes petulantly. "I've got *all* evening." I propped myself on a stool at the breakfast bar and waited.

"Sorry." He wiped the crumbs from his mouth and the rough scruff on his jaw while not looking the tiniest bit sorry at all. "I'm starving. I've been travelling for two days, the Cook Strait ferry was a bitch, my truck threw a flat tyre in Taupo along with an interesting rattle, and I missed lunch."

I stared, registering for the first time the weary look on his face and the fine lines around his eyes. He looked exhausted and I stifled the urge to fetch the man a bloody beer. "You still haven't explained why you're here in *my* kitchen."

He eyed me for a second, then wagged an annoying finger. "To be perfectly accurate, it's your *mother's* kitchen. The same mother who is currently shacked up with *my* mother. That detail aside, I *don't* live on Stewart Island anymore, as of a few days ago, and I believe you were present on one or two occasions where my possible move north was actually discussed at this table."

I shot him a look. "The operative word being *possible*, and *north* is hardly definitive. I don't recall Painted Bay ever being mentioned."

His mouth quirked. "It's a recent development." Then he shrugged. "Look, I'm not here to piss you off, Leroy. I'm here to spend a bit of time closer to Mum and to see if maybe I'd like to stay. Nothing is definite yet. All my stuff is still down south. I don't know where I'll end up. I might even go back. But that's kind of why I'm here, to think and make those decisions."

He took another bite of his sandwich and slouched in his chair, stretching his long, long legs out in front and crossing those naked feet. Then he gave an appreciative groan and swallowed . . . again. "Man, this bread is good." He took another mouthful.

I glanced at the carved loaf on the countertop and answered without thinking. "Rileys' Bakery make the best sourdough for miles. You should try their brioche and their cinnamon." *What was I doing?*

He sent me a wry smile and kept chewing.

"How long are you staying?" I pushed.

"Here with you, or up north?"

"Both."

He shrugged. "I sold my commercial fishing boat before I left, so timing is kind of a loose concept at the mom—"

"Stop." I tugged my phone from the pocket of my jeans and waved it at him. "I'm calling my mother. Not another word."

He snorted. "I'd say be my guest, but that would be three words. Oops, there's eleven right there—make that sixteen." He chuckled and took another bite as I rolled my eyes and walked out onto the deck, the heat of his gaze burning holes in my black Six6o T-shirt every step of the way.

I kept walking until I hit the steps to the lawn, which put me out of earshot. Then I leaned over the railing and sucked in a deep breath of salt-laden air as my heart ticked down. There was no point calling my mother while I was still pissing vinegar. She'd slay me in a couple of sentences, and I'd deserve it. Instead, I stared out across the bay and willed the spectacular view to weave its customary magic.

At the foot of the hill, Painted Bay lapped in placid calm, sheltered by the nature of its small, almost circular form. The wharf buzzed with locals pulling up their boats after a Saturday outing. We'd never enforced our private ownership, giving the community free access to the concrete boat ramp, although the pier space itself needed to be booked to ensure our mussel boats and actual paying customers always had a place to berth.

A movement at Jude . . . *Judah* and Morgan's converted boathouse next to the wharf caught my eye, and I half-expected to see my brother and his brand-new husband walking the cove and soaking up the last rays of the evening sun as they often did. But Judah and Morgan were currently on their honeymoon in Queenstown, Morgan having whisked his husband away with the ink barely dry on their marriage certificate.

It had been a simple ceremony, just the two immediate families and close friends, with a few extras invited to a barbecue at the homestead after. Judah asked me to be his best man which had floored me in the best possible way, and Morgan's brother stood up for him. Simple vows were exchanged under a clear blue sky on the sandy beach of Painted Bay and then it was a night of laughter, good food and far too much wine. All except for Judah who remained stone-cold sober and managed to silence the summer night and bring his new husband to tears with a beautiful dance he'd choreographed just for the occasion and performed on our back lawn under a starlit sky.

And so, instead of Judah and Morgan, it was the bouncing blond curls of Hannah that had caught my eye as she wielded her canes in a dance on the sand while her father, Terry, tended to Morgan's bazillion flowerpots. Terry glanced up and raised a hand, and Hannah stabbed her cane in the air, waving it madly.

I flourished my arm in reply, then refocused on the peaceful gleam of the bay and its almost mirror-perfect reflection of the bluffs that enclosed it on two sides. I loved this place. The caterwauling of the gulls; the clockwork roll of the tide that soothed my scratchy soul; the sharp brine in the air and the way it settled on my skin like a thin veil at the end of each day; the steadfast company of a fickle wind; and the lullaby call of those green-blue depths that rocked my heart like a baby in a damn cradle.

It was my home in every way that mattered.

I just needed to find a way to hang on to it.

I turned my face to the sky, the intense heat of the late February sun now mellowed by a gentle easterly fresh off the sea.

Why hadn't she told me about Fox?

It wasn't like I'd hidden how much the man irritated me. Perhaps not exactly fair, considering he was the son of Martha, my mother's girlfriend. But it wasn't like we saw much of him or that it mattered to them if we didn't see eye to eye on stuff. We were both adults. We didn't have to play together in the sandpit, for fuck's sake.

That first visit *had* kind of set the tone though, and it was mostly my fault. It had occasioned Mum and Martha's big coming out as a couple, aaaand I might not have handled that as well as I could've. It hadn't been my finest hour, but to be fair, I'd been a little stressed at the time. Judah was fresh home from Boston, his ballet career in tatters, and our relationship, which had never been easy, was tanking big time. Not to mention he'd started to date Morgan, one of my very few friends in Painted Bay, and the mussel business was in trouble. So yeah, I wasn't exactly on the top of my social game, which to be honest shot well below par even on a good day.

No excuse, of course, but then I wasn't exactly known for my subtlety. But then Fox had called me out on my bad behaviour, something that hadn't exactly improved my opinion of him. We had a bit of an argument where I'd shouted at him to keep his nose out of our family's business, and he'd calmly warned me that if I upset his mother, he'd rip my balls off and hang them from my mussel frames for the fish to feed on.

An excellent comeback, to be honest.

Still, I wasn't in that place anymore. I'd pulled my head out of my arse with my mother and Martha, Judah and I were getting along much better, and the mussel farm was doing . . . Well, two out of three wasn't bad, right? But my relationship with Fox remained . . . tense.

I avoided him as much as possible, which wasn't too difficult since he usually stayed with Martha and Cora, and the few times we met up over dinner with our mothers, and sometimes Judah and Morgan, I mostly ignored him or managed to hold up my end of the conversation without running my tongue up the side of his face, which I counted as a win.

To give the man credit, Fox *had* tried to smooth things. He ignored the worst of my icy politeness and even managed to sound interested in the farm. But he made me itch in my head, and the further away he stayed, the better. He was clearly a bit perplexed, but I was happy with perplexed. It was infinitely more acceptable than giving him any insight into how he really made me feel, which I wasn't thinking about anymore—not even a little.

Fox Carmody was a brooding, arrogant, self-righteous arsehole, and that's where he needed to stay pigeon-holed in my head. Which was why I was so monumentally pissed at his current apparent state of amiable affability.

Well, fuck that. I knew a freeloader when I saw one.

Two deep breaths and I pulled up my mother's number.

She answered on the second ring. "Leroy, before you say anything, I saw your boat berthed and I was just about to ring. I'm sorry." She took the indignant wind from my sails. "It's just that there isn't enough room in the cottage to have Fox for more than a few days at a time. We start falling all over each other. He takes up a lot of room." She chuckled. "Plus, I *was* going to tell you, today. But then

Fox called to say he'd decided to drive right through, and you were already out on the boat. When you didn't answer my call, I got his room ready and figured Martha would catch up with you when you got back. But then *she* had to leave early and didn't tell me. I tried again but you still didn't answer, so I figured, worst-case scenario, you'd call when you got home. And you have." She sounded flustered but not nearly apologetic enough for my taste.

I checked my phone, saw the missed calls, and swore under my breath. I'd switched it to silent. *Fuck.* I scrambled for a footing. "But you've known for three days, Mum. Why didn't you say something sooner, or I don't know, maybe even ask me first? Hey, there's a novel idea. I mean, it is my home. You don't actually live here anymore."

"Because you would've said no," she said flatly. "And Fox is *family*, Leroy. I wasn't going to have Martha's son staying in a motel when we have plenty of spare beds."

"He's not fam—" I stopped just in time.

"I'll pretend I didn't hear that." She sounded disappointed and I ran a frustrated hand down my face. "Fox has had a bit of a year, son."

And there it was. My mother had a soft spot for anyone in need. The mussel farm had a long history of Cora Madden's policy of employing local works-in-progress as she liked to put it. Most only stayed a few months, or in one or two cases, a couple of years, then went on to brighter futures.

I blew out a sigh. "I get you want to help people, Mum. But as I understand, from the *little,* read *practically nothing* you've told me, he had a relationship break-up a good while back. Sad, but hardly the end of the world. I like my space, Mum, you know that." Although I admit I was curious.

"It's not my story to tell, son. And he's Mattie's son. He just needs a place to stay while he figures out his next move. It's not even definite that he's staying up this way. He might head back down."

"And exactly how long is it going to take for him to decide?"

"As long as it takes," she shot back. "Don't force an issue about this, Leroy, because you'll lose. Fox is good people, and he offered to help you out on the farm if you want to put him to work. Earn his keep."

"He's said nothing to me."

"Did you give him a chance?"

Fair point. "I don't need his help."

She sighed. "Pick that damn bottom lip up off the floor and stop acting like a child. You *do* need the help. Especially if it's free."

"No one works for free."

"Fox offered in payment for the room. What's up with you, Leroy? I've never understood why you dislike him so much. Has he done something?"

Yes. Existed. Made me ask . . . questions. "No, I just like my privacy."

She sighed heavily. "I get that. But the house is big enough for both of you to get lost in without living on top of each other, so I suggest you deal with it and try to get on. I made up the bay room at the opposite end of the hall from you and stocked his bathroom. You can probably pretend he isn't even there if you try hard enough."

Fat chance.

"I'll see you tomorrow. You can yell at me then." She hung up before I could answer.

I shoved my phone in my pocket with a grunt and flicked a glance to the kitchen where Fox stood at the sink washing dishes and looking my way with a wary expression.

Fox Carmody in my house was the very last thing I needed, but it looked like I was stuck with him for the time being. Still, Mum was right about one thing. It *was* a big house.

I huffed my way inside only to be confronted by a long pink tongue attached to a knee-high, honey-coloured dog with black lopsided ears.

"Who the hell is this?"

"That's Mack," Fox said with obvious affection. "She's well trained. You won't even know she's here. Cora said it would be fine."

"Of course she bloody did." I shook my head, too exhausted to fight. Instead, I stared down at the dog who stared back as if I was some strange puzzle to solve. *Good luck with that.* I fought the urge to scratch her head. "Mack isn't the usual name for a female."

Fox shrugged. "She used to come on the boat with us, almost part of the crew, and she was always pestering the boys for a slice of fresh Mackerel, her favourite. Hence the name."

I shook my head. "Well, just keep her out from under my feet and off the furniture."

Fox appeared to swallow some no doubt waspish reply and the air grew thick between us. Then he gave an exhausted sigh and guilt pinged in my chest. "Look, Leroy, I'm sorry if we *both* came as a surprise. If I'd honestly thought you didn't know, I would've called you direct or stayed somewhere else or something. I just assumed—"

"Yeah, well, that was your first mistake." Mack nudged my hand, and I very deliberately folded my arms to keep from stroking her because fuck, she was cute. "My mother moves to her own weird and wonderful beat. And if she says you're staying, then you're staying. The best we can do is keep out of each other's way since we clearly don't like each other very much."

A crease ran the length of Fox's brow. "If that's the impression I gave, then I'm sorry for that too. We didn't get off to a good start, I know, but it was kind of a heavy weekend, right? And I wasn't in a good place for most of last year either. I'm sorry for my part. And with our mothers—" He gave a wry grin. "Well, I guess we'll be seeing a bit more of each other in the future, so maybe we can start again?" He wiped his hand down those butter-soft jeans, then offered it to me. "I'm Fox. Nice to meet you."

Oh no, no, no. I stared at those long, nimble fingers, tanned and calloused from hard work, and wondered what the hell I'd done for the universe to have it in for me so badly. I'd managed to avoid this for a whole year, but it wasn't like I could refuse now. I wasn't that much of an arsehole, mostly.

His grip was warm and dry, and when he squeezed, something hot pooled low in my belly. "Leroy," I croaked, clearing my throat.

"And likewise, I guess. But I'm not one for company, *anyone's* as it happens. So, I'm gonna leave you to it. I've got some, ah, paperwork to catch up on, in the study." I was about to leave when his hand landed on my forearm. I could only stare at it, feeling the burn on my skin like acid.

"Listen, I'd like to help out if I can? Earn my keep."

I raised a brow.

"With the mussel farm. I don't want to be a burden."

I pulled my arm free. "Thanks, but we're fine." *Liar.* "Now, if you'll excuse me—"

"I ran my own commercial fishing boat. I'm not entirely without skills. Let me help."

I looked him over. "Commercial fishing skills aren't exactly transferable to shellfish farming."

His jaw steeled because yes, I was being a total dick, but I couldn't seem to stop myself. Fox Carmody unsettled me like no one else.

"I'm good with *any* boat," he tried in a tone that dared me to argue. "I'm a hard worker and a quick learner."

"I'm sure you are." My gaze slid away. "And as I said, I'll let you know." I turned and headed for the study, wondering how many points you earned for being the biggest arsehole of the day. My cup runneth over.

Safely ensconced in the study halfway down the hall, I sat at my father's huge desk and bemoaned my stupidity. I didn't have *any* work to do that couldn't wait. I'd just wanted to escape the man taking up room in my kitchen and my head. Martha kept all the simple accounts in order, and the rest I managed on the one day a week I committed to paperwork, which wasn't today. After a long-arse day on my boat working the farm, my head was in no place to deal with figures, and to that end, I avoided late-night bookwork if at all possible.

End result? I'd just managed to shut myself away in a TV-less room in my own damn house for no bloody reason at all. What's more, I was going to look like a total dipshit and the liar that I was if I wandered back out after just a couple of minutes. Plus, it was too early to go to bed.

Fucking perfect.

My phone buzzed with a text and I pulled it from my pocket.

Judah: *Hey Leroy. Just checking in. Had an amazing picnic lunch at some vineyard in the Gibbston Valley. The scenery was gorgeous. And okay I had a drop attack last night. I wanted to tell you before Morgan dobbed me in. It was on the deck of our suite thank god and I recovered quick so don't worry. Tell Mum not to call me about it. Love you.*

I stared at the last two words, realised I was smiling, and blinked to clear my eyes. It was taking some adjusting to this new *thing* between Judah and me. We'd been less than we could've been as brothers for as long as I could remember, mostly my fault. But we were getting better.

I typed a reply. *Thanks for letting me know. I'll rein her in. You're in good hands.* I pressed send, then stared at my phone and quickly sent another. *I love you too*.

I threw the phone on my desk and scowled at it, a mix of sappy affection and jealousy curling in my gut. *Love you?*

Fuck. Me.

The wistful feeling caught me by surprise. I actually missed my brother. It was new and kind of nice. For all that it had been a bumpy road between Judah and me over the last year—forgiving old hurts and trying to forge a new relationship—we'd become a lot closer. Along with Cora and Martha and Morgan, we'd become this strange new family, feeling our way and treading carefully, but getting there.

And a picnic in a damn vineyard. I shook my head. I hadn't taken a break, let alone a holiday in as long as I could remember. The farm didn't shut down just because I needed time off, and my workers weren't up with the business enough to ask them to step up.

And whose fault was that?

Patrick was the first employee to stay with me long enough to even consider developing him. With my mother's inclination to run the business as a personal growth opportunity for local youth, we'd only ever really been used as a steppingstone. But Patrick had been with me for two years and professed to love his job. And he was good at it. Almost as good as me.

Maybe it was time. Maybe I needed a break. I thought of the man in my kitchen and sighed.

I logged on to Netflix on my computer to pass the time, but I'd been watching less than ten minutes when the door slowly squeaked open. Why did no one believe you when you said you wanted to be left alone? I summoned my best *put-upon* expression and looked up expecting to see Fox, but the doorway was empty.

Huh.

Something brushed my knee and I jumped in my seat as a pair of soulful brown eyes stared up at me from between my legs.

"This is not your room." I pointed sharply to the door. The eyes blinked slowly, and a hairy chin rested on my thigh.

Oh, for Pete's sake. "Where's your daddy?" *Your daddy?* I scratched Mack's warm velvet ears and she groaned in delight. "Where's Fox?"

Mack stared up at me, angling her jaw to get my fingers right where she wanted them.

She really was a pretty thing, just the sort of bitsa crossbreed I'd have loved as my own rather than having to share Dad's shepherd as I'd grown up. Judah had never been much into animals, just his dance. Mack was the sort of dog you saw in movies. The sort of dog that had started me thinking about Veterinary School way back when.

She sat on my foot, her hot butt covering my toes.

"Oh no." I wriggled my foot free. "Get up, you strumpet. I barely know you." I rolled my chair back and Mack made a beeline with her nose for my crotch, but I clamped my knees around her head just in time.

"Gotcha." I waggled my brows. "What's the password?"

Her gaze was endearingly hopeful as if I held the answer to every burning question that filled her small but convoluted doggy brain. I almost melted. The animal had way better game than me which, let's face it, wasn't hard to do.

"Don't look at me like that." I tapped a finger twice on the end of her wet nose. "Plus, you should really get that seen to." I wiped my fingers on my thigh. "Mucous doesn't rate high on one's Tinder profile unless you're into the kind of kink I want nothing to do with."

Mack leaned her full weight forward until her head rested in the groove between my thighs, the tip of that nose and the underlying teeth, just a warm breath away from my balls. Too fucking cute. I eyed her with an arched brow and tut-tutted.

"It's Mack, right?"

She cocked an ear.

"Well, Mack. I'll have you know, I'm not that kind of boy. I have high standards. Dinner first, at the very least."

"Good to know."

I startled at the deep voice, and my gaze jerked up to find Fox standing in the doorway with a wide grin plastered on his face. My cheeks flamed with a will of their own as we locked eyes.

Then his gaze broke to his dog. "Mack, come here."

She scooted to Fox's side, leaving a cold vacant spot on my thigh that I covered with my hand.

"Sorry about that." Fox looked genuinely apologetic. "Dogs, right? Can't keep their noses to themselves. I'll keep a better eye on her."

"It's, um, not a problem," I said, surprising myself.

He raised a brow. "I thought you didn't like dogs."

"I never said I didn't like them," I corrected tartly. "I like them very much . . . as it happens. I simply asked you to keep her from under my feet." *If she's not close, maybe you won't be either.*

"Right." He frowned, clearly unconvinced.

"And I'd prefer it if she slept in your room. But it's okay if she comes and says hello." I arched a brow at Mack. "Although your idea of hello has a wanton edge I'm not entirely sure I'm comfortable with." I couldn't help but smile.

Fox's lips quirked up. "Was that a joke, Leroy Madden, cos I think I might need a little more warning to mentally prepare myself?"

I rolled my eyes, unwilling to admit I found him in the least bit amusing. Mack was more than fine, but her owner had a long way to go.

Fox's smile disappeared. "Right, well, we'll leave you to it." He glanced at the Netflix logo on my screen, bit back a smile, and my face burned with the heat of a thousand suns. "Mack and I will hit the sack. It's been a long couple of days."

I turned my screen slightly. "Well, if you need anything—"

"I'll make sure to call your mother," he said with a wicked grin.

A thousand and fifty suns.

"Oh, I nearly forgot—" He reached behind into the hall where the sideboard stood and retrieved a plate loaded with a second doorstop sarnie. He took a careful step into the room and slid it onto my desk.

I stared at the sandwich dripping with deliciousness. "I told you I didn't—" My traitorous stomach grumbled to argue the lie I was about to make, and I shut my mouth.

"Jesus, Leroy." I was clearly stretching his patience. "I know my unexpected arrival has come as an . . . unwelcome surprise, and I get it, I do. But you have to eat *something*, and there was enough left to make this. Now, maybe you ate on the boat, in which case feel free to throw it away. But if you're anything like me, you wait until the work is done before you really tuck in, so . . ." He waved a hand at the plate. "Eat it or not, it's up to you."

I continued to stare at the plate. I wasn't this jerk, and I hated myself for it. "I guess I could eat something." I pushed my gaze up to meet his. "Thank you."

The smile was genuine and melted my toes. "Halle-fucking-lujah, you're welcome." He bowed dramatically. "See you tomorrow, Leroy." He pulled the door shut behind him and it was just me and the sandwich.

I lifted the generous slice of bread on top, relieved to see Fox hadn't squished this one, and salivated at the layers of chicken and cheese, tomatoes and lettuce, and some thick garlicky mayonnaise that I knew hadn't come from any staples of mine. Fox had been shopping.

I let the lid fall and stared at it again, a serviette tucked neatly and thoughtfully underneath. When was the last time *anyone* had done something nice for me like this other than my mother? And especially after I'd been such a prick.

Never.

I pushed aside the insistent voice that wanted me to simply bin the damn thing, somewhere Fox couldn't miss seeing it, and instead lifted the sandwich to my mouth and took a huge mouth-watering bite.

Oh. My. Fucking. God. I groaned in pleasure.

It tasted as good as it looked.

And yeah, wasn't that a fucking tease of a metaphor for my current life dilemma?

CHAPTER TWO

Fox

I heard Leroy rise just as the sun was brimming over the horizon and shooting warm light across my bed, but I decided to keep to my room and out of his way until I heard the back door slam.

As he moved around the kitchen, I indulged in a little fantasising about the shape of that tight body in those loose salt-crusted jeans he'd worn the previous night, the smell of the sea rolling off him in waves as sexy as any Tom Ford limited edition, at least to me. It set my blood thrumming in a way it had no right to.

More thickly muscled than his lithe dancer brother, he still moved with the same grace, as if the earth's crust carried him along on some eternal melody while the rest of us poor mugs had to settle for lumbering around in the backup percussion.

It was the first thing I'd noticed about him when we'd met the year before, how graceful he was for a guy. That, and the bluest eyes I'd ever seen, with cheekbones sharp enough to cut glass, although not as sharp as his tongue—something I'd realised the moment he'd opened his mouth and launched into the grumpiest, bullheaded commentary on anything and everything brought up in conversation that lunch.

The whole experience had left me shaking my head because I didn't get it. I'd watched him closely, for reasons that didn't bear too much scrutiny, and when the spotlight wasn't directly on him, I'd seen brief flickers of something I'd have sworn was closer to yearning or regret as it passed through those blue eyes. But then his gaze would land on me again, and a curtain of ice would shutter any warmth I thought I'd seen.

It was a shame he'd turned out to be such a dick, and apparently straight—all in all, a waste of all those moody good looks. Still, he'd surprised me in the study. I'd stolen a few moments to creep on the poor man as he'd chatted with Mack, and what I'd seen hardly fit with the grumpy guy I knew. He'd been tender and funny with my girl, soft, and even—I couldn't believe I was using the word—sweet.

And when I'd put the sandwich in front of him, he looked almost shocked. I might be a bit of a broody bastard myself at times, but my mumma raised me right, and I always pulled my weight. So, if Leroy thought he was just gonna brush my offer of help aside, he had another think coming. I knew what it was like to run your own business, especially one that had a fickle bottom line. I could at least help with some of the small stuff while I was here, and making an extra sandwich for a guy who was clearly lying about not being hungry was a no-brainer. Just *why* he felt he had to lie wasn't so clear, but I figured I was safe to run with ratty and thick-skulled.

Warm slices of sun cut across the sheet and up the wall behind, casting the room in a light morning gold. A chorus of seagulls signalled some activity down at the wharf, the familiar sound clawing at that bone-deep ache in my heart I wasn't sure I'd ever fill.

The minute I heard the back door slam, I rolled to my side and drew a deep breath rich in salt and the tang of seaweed. My inner seaman's clock said it had to be close to low tide, the new sun's warmth working on the exposed kelp. But the sharp smell was quickly overwhelmed by a suffocating fart let loose by Mack who was stretched out on her back beside me.

"Jesus, girl." I slapped her butt and shoved her to the far side of the mattress. "Our agreement explicitly stated you could sleep on the bed *if* you behaved. That insult to decent biology doesn't comply."

She sent me a disgruntled look, scrambled back to the centre, and settled in with a contented groan.

I ran my fingers through the dun-coloured scruff of her neck and pulled at the small nest of coarse hairs that sprouted like an old man's beard from her chin. "You get one more chance." She opened a single hopeful eye and I tapped her nose. "But only because you beat the last arsehole who occupied that position by about eleventy-billion points. And that's just on the loyalty factor alone."

She grunted and loosed another juddering fart.

"I couldn't have said it better." I patted her rump and threw the sheet off my legs, the light humidity of the morning wrapping a gentle warmth around my body—a welcome change from my home on the island.

Hanging thirty kilometres off the arse end of New Zealand, twelve hundred kilometres from my current bed, and the last stop before Antarctica, Stewart Island wouldn't know sub-tropical humidity if you slapped it in the face with a damp towel. But it was a staggeringly beautiful place to live. Rugged, remote, and mostly untouched—if you didn't have a freezing southerly straight off the Antarctic at some point on most days, you weren't living.

And I missed it like hell.

When I was sure Leroy had left for the day, I swung my feet to the floor and let the disappointment of his reaction to my arrival settle in my chest. I'd been delighted and relieved when Cora invited me to stay while I sorted out a new job and somewhere to live. Leaving my home and marriage had ripped me apart in ways I hadn't been ready for, and having some family around meant more than I was prepared to admit. But I wasn't about to stay where I wasn't wanted, and Leroy had made it patently obvious that he wasn't thrilled about the arrangement.

Which made me wonder why Cora *hadn't* told him. It made not a lick of sense and, frankly, didn't seem at all like her. We'd gotten close via Skype and the visits I'd made trying to escape the shitshow that my life had turned into down south, and I was thrilled my mother had found someone as bright and warm as Cora.

But there was no avoiding the fact that her son, Leroy, and I had started off on the wrong foot. He'd behaved like an arse at our mothers' mutual coming out, although to be fair, it was quickly apparent that his behaviour wasn't predicated on that development alone. Leroy was an equal-opportunity arsehole, at least judging by the tension between him and his brother. But with my own life teetering on the brink, I wasn't about to put up with his fuckery, especially where my mother was concerned, and the argument between us had sealed his opinion of me for good it seemed.

Was it the fact I was gay? I'd wondered about that for a while, but my mother reassured me it was more complicated. She wouldn't, however, explain those complications. *Whatever.* Things between them and Leroy had improved greatly and that was all that mattered. I had enough issues of my own without angsting over a grumpy fuck who couldn't get his head out of his arse.

Speaking of which . . .

I tapped the screen on my phone. Six thirty. I had a list of things to get through, not least of all booking my truck into a mechanic and talking to my lawyer and best friend, Tinny.

I jumped in the shower and washed off the travel grime I'd been too exhausted to deal with the night before, then pulled on a T-shirt and some old jeans and headed for the kitchen.

The sprawling nineteenth century weatherboard homestead—a rabbit warren of interconnecting rooms, high ceilings, generous hallways, and wide honey-coloured plank flooring worn smooth with age —was a pleasure to wander. Modernised to create a huge open-plan kitchen/dining/family space, it retained its original broad sash windows that flooded the rooms with light, while modern heating, insulation, new bathrooms, and a soft green and cream renovated kitchen kept it functional. Warm, comfortable décor—a little dated but cosy—invited you to curl up in a chair with a book and not worry too much about where you put your feet.

The soft pad of paws at my back let me know Mack was equally keen on breakfast. I fed her on the deck while the espresso machine warmed, then inspected the surplus of family photos that covered the walls of the large open family space.

The majority of images were, by a long shot, of Judah's dance career from toddler on—many, many more than of Leroy who showed up in the family candids, a couple of rugby action shots, and a few with his father working the mussel farm before Damien had died several years before. But Judah definitely dominated the display, enough to give me pause, and I wondered if that emphasis on the gifted son had been responsible in part for the tension I'd witnessed between them on that first visit? It was an interesting thought but one that wouldn't get an answer because there was no way I'd ever be asking that of Mr Grumpy Pants himself. Hell no.

The espresso machine pinged, and with a much-needed steaming mug of caffeine in hand, I threw some bread in the toaster and wandered outside to stare again at the beauty that was Painted Bay. Wide covered verandas flanked two sides of the house, but on this one, the open style family space was flanked by a wide sunny deck with the best view for miles.

I leaned on the railing, sucked the salt air deep into my lungs, and tried not to think of the home I'd left just three days before. A house I'd loved, a marriage, a business, a boat. A life I thought we'd have till we grew old and decrepit. A life I'd loved with a passion that had consumed me in the best possible way.

But there was no going back.

Mid-thirties and I was starting all over again.

"Quit complaining," I grumbled to myself. "You can build a new life."

Well, all except the marriage part. *Jesus Christ*. I didn't need that pain again.

The tide was on the turn—stealing slowly back over the sand, inching up the mix of old and new piles that kept the historic whaling wharf and its jetty afloat. The new steel roof on Judah and Morgan's boatshed home glowed in the sun, along with the matching one on the renovated old barn, now Judah's dance therapy studio.

I sniffed and then spun to find a thin dark trail of smoke bleeding through the open kitchen window. "Oh, shit." I hoofed it inside and popped the toaster just as the detector blared. "Goddammit." I chucked the charred remains out the window, threw open the patio doors, and waved a tea towel under the detector until it shut the fuck up.

"Hellooooo." My mother's voice rang through the house. "Burning down the homestead isn't going to win you any favours with Leroy." She strode into the family room in cut-off denim shorts and a white cotton shirt and screwed up her nose. "Holy shit, Fox." She headed for the opposite side and opened all those windows as well.

"Toaster," I explained, throwing the tea towel on the countertop so my mother could wrap all six foot three of me against her five-foot-six frame like I'd never left it. I curled over her like a big hairy giant, transported back to the million hugs she'd handed out like just so much confetti as I'd grown up.

At sixty-three, gruff and with an acerbic wit, Martha Carmody didn't suffer fools gladly, but she was always loving with me and anyone close to her. Having said that, bright and warm Cora Madden was my mother's perfect foil.

I tried to wriggle free, but she held on. "Stay a minute." She ran her hands up and down my back and I kissed the top of her head. "I haven't seen you in far too long. I hate that I couldn't be there for all the shit that went down, son."

"You were there plenty," I argued. "I always knew I could pick up the phone whenever I needed and you'd make time to talk. And the couple of times you flew me up here were a lifesaver, Mum."

She pulled back and glared at me with those shrewd grey eyes. "Yeah well, I knew if I didn't email you the actual damn ticket, you'd have found every reason under the sun why you couldn't come. Too stubborn for your own good."

"Wonder where I got that from?" I smiled, and she slapped me on the chest.

"Watch your mouth." Then her face grew serious. "You didn't deserve any of it, you know that, right? And what the hell is up with that settlement proposal? Van gets to fuck your marriage over and then gets half your business as well? I wanna slap that toad from here to next Sunday and back."

"It's the law, Mum." I buried my face once again in her hair, which seemed to always smell of lemons. "He's entitled to half."

"Stuff and nonsense. The little bastard wrecked your life. He shouldn't have gotten within a mile of your boat. Anyone with a lick of sense would've seen that. What the hell was Tinny thinking? I thought he was your best friend?" She pulled back, her eyes brimming in indignation.

"He is, but he's also a lawyer, Mum, and a damn good one. I was never gonna win that battle. Besides, it was my own fault. I should've insisted on a prenup. I—"

"Shhh. None of it was your fault. You loved that sodding idiot and you trusted him. The fact he didn't deserve any of it isn't on you. Just a lesson for the future."

I snorted. "No lesson needed. I'm done with that bullshit. Love 'em and leave 'em sounds pretty damn good for here on out."

She sent me a crooked smile. "But that's not you, is it?"

I rolled my eyes cos it was true. I'd never been the one-and-done kind. "I just wanted what you and Dad had, and I stupidly thought Van was it," I confessed, watching her expression soften at the words. "I liked being married. I liked having someone to come home to. I liked movie nights on the couch and fighting over whose turn it was to cook. And I hate that he took all that away from me." I hesitated over the words I'd barely begun to admit to myself. "I hate feeling like I wasn't . . . enough."

"Oh, son." Her eyes filled. "You were always more than enough. If Van couldn't see that—"

"I'm not so sure." My voice broke and I took a second. "I was away a lot. I thought Van was okay with it, like you and Dad when he was away all those months. But he wasn't, and I never knew."

Her hand landed on my shoulder. "It can be hard to be the partner of someone who works away, but it was Van's job to tell you how he was feeling, son, and he didn't. I also think he used it as an excuse."

I shrugged. "Maybe." Then I looked at her and the question came before I could stop it. "Did Dad know you were bi?"

Her eyes popped. "Wow, I didn't see that one coming."

"Oh god, I'm sorry. You don't have to answer."

"It's okay." She flustered a little, her gaze darting around the room before landing back on me. "No, he didn't, and maybe that's why I never told you either. I wish I had told him. I'm sure he'd have been fine, but it wasn't like with your generation. I didn't know anyone else like me until I was in my thirties, and by then I felt so bad about not telling him before we were married, I was scared, I guess. Scared he might not forgive me. Not for being bi, but for not telling him. Crazy, right? And then he was so good when you came out that I decided I'd just tell him anyway, and I was all set to do that when he died. After that I didn't even think about it for a long time until . . . well, until Cora."

"She's good for you," I said.

My mother smiled. "She is." Then she stepped back and regarded me with a critical eye. "You've lost weight." She slapped my stomach. "We need to feed you up."

Mack appeared from the deck, tongue lolling from a morning patrol of the homestead boundaries, and ran excitedly to my mother, who dropped to her knees for a cuddle.

I headed for the toaster and dialled down the setting before adding more bread. "I promise I'm eating better."

She grunted and followed me into the kitchen, Mack close at her heel. "So you say. Still, Cora and I are bringing lunch on Sunday."

I snorted. "Oh. My. God. Who's cooking?"

Her mouth quirked up. "Me. I wouldn't do that to you. We want to put weight on you, not put you off eating for life. Besides, I've been working on a plan."

I laughed. "Go on."

"I've convinced Cora she makes better desserts than I do. That ensures I cook the main course and everyone gets to eat at least one thing that's not gonna kill them. Cora's desserts are at least . . . palatable." She smiled fondly. "Sugar is a wonderful thing."

I laughed. "I'm betting she knows exactly what you're doing."

My mother chuckled. "Of course she bloody does. But she keeps trying, God love her. Only last week she took another of those online cooking classes. I'm just not sure how much longer my stomach can survive the homework she's given. But Sunday won't be the usual big crowd since Judah and Morgan are still away, but it'll give the four of us a chance to catch up. And yes, hello, beautiful girl." She bent over Mack who was still vying for attention and planted a kiss on her wrinkled forehead. "I was ignoring you, baby, wasn't I?"

Mack swiped a lazy tongue over her hand in tacit agreement.

"Well, I'm sure Leroy will be *thrilled* to have me to Sunday lunch," I said drily.

"Pfft." Martha wiped her hand down her denim shorts. "Leroy needs to take that damn mountain off his shoulder and lighten up. The man's as grumpy as a constipated bear."

I chuckled. "I'll let you tell him that. He's not happy about me being here, you know. Cora never told him?"

Martha pulled a face. "It's complicated. I wish she'd said something, but Cora is stubborn. She *was* going to tell him yesterday, but when you said you'd be here early, she decided to wait. And Leroy can be . . . bullish. Sometimes it's better to just do stuff and ask for forgiveness later. And this is still Cora's house, so . . ."

"I never presumed I'd be staying with any of you, Mum. I had a motel booked. This might be Cora's house, but Leroy is the one who lives here, and it's all a bit awkward now. I'll be finding somewhere new as soon as I can."

Her hand landed on my arm. "No, please. Cora would be devastated. She thinks it'll be good for Leroy to have some company. He's too . . . insular. Apart from his rugby, he hardly does anything outside of work."

"He runs a business, Mum. Whether it's mussels or cows, farming is demanding. He won't have a lot of spare time. I was the same."

"I know. I know. But I think she hopes it might help the two of you build a bridge or something?"

I stared her down. "Well, it might very well backfire. As long as she understands that as well."

My mother shrugged. "I'm well aware, but try telling her that. Will you at least give it another day or so, see what happens?"

I blew out a long sigh. "Okay, but the first sign of real trouble and I'm gone."

Her shoulders slumped. "Fair enough."

The toast popped, looking decidedly less charred this time around. "Want a cuppa or some toast?"

"Just coffee. I'll make it." She set to work with a speed born of familiarity. "Cora bought us a machine just like this and then spent two weeks schooling me how to get the damn foam just perfect. Let me wow you with my hearts."

I laughed. "So you two are still good?" I reached for the manuka honey I'd snagged at a farm stall just out of Oban, not far from my cottage.

My mother's expression softened. "Really good. For a woman who never cottoned on to her bisexuality until a little over a year ago,

Cora's kind of amazing . . . and hot." She sent me a wink and I almost choked on my toast.

"Dear God, no, Mum." I wiped my mouth. "Please. No sex stuff, promise me."

She grinned and waggled her eyebrows. "Take your toast outside and I'll meet you there. It's gonna be hot today."

"Promise?"

She pointed to the door with a spoon. "Out."

Shit.

I dragged a couple of the deck chairs together and set about demolishing my toast. The rich sweetness of the thick amber honey filled my mouth with a nostalgia I couldn't afford and too many wistful memories—countless breakfasts shared with a man I'd loved and who I'd thought had loved me.

I pushed the suffocating rise of anger and melancholy aside and concentrated on the view.

"Here." My mother handed me a mug of coffee and slipped into the deck chair alongside.

I stared at the foam and its beautiful heart. "Wow, you weren't kidding."

She laughed. "Cora's mad as hell. I'm way better than she is."

"Well, it smells incredible. When we were at sea, I was lucky if my spoon wasn't standing upright in the caffeine tar all the boys seemed to prefer. As soon as I got home, we always headed to the café for a latte before anything else." I hesitated. "At least we used to."

A deep crease formed on her forehead. "Killing is too good for that man."

I took her hand. "You're gonna have to teach me how to use the machine."

"Done." She forced a smile and squeezed my fingers. "And nice redirect."

She raised her coffee for us to clink our mugs and we sat in silence for a bit, watching the sun rise high enough to cast the large deck in a welcome pool of warmth. I wriggled my toes and soaked up the heat. "It's gonna be nice to have a summer actually warm enough to take your sweatshirt off."

She laid a hand on my forearm and left it there. "Any plans yet?"

I gave a half-shrug. "To be honest, I've been so focused on just getting off the island and up here that I haven't had time for much else. Figured I could work the rest out once I arrived. I still can't believe I've left. And when I think about not going back to my house, it . . . hurts, you know?"

She nodded. "Is that why you didn't sell it?"

I shrugged. "I love that place. I mean it's beautiful up here, but it's . . . more tame, I guess. Maybe too pretty. I love the ruggedness of the coasts down south. I still don't know if I did the right thing, Mum. Maybe when things settle down, I can go back."

"I can't tell you what to do, Fox. You're gonna have to work that out for yourself. In the meantime I have you up here with me, at least for a little bit, and you can be sure I'm gonna make the most of it."

I sent her a grin. "A definite upside. And in case you're wondering, I *did* offer to help Leroy on the boat today, but he turned me down flat."

She rolled her eyes. "No surprise there. The man is nothing if not a damn martyr. Keep pushing." Mack sidled closer to rest her head on my mother's thigh, and she stroked her fondly. "I'm glad you have her."

I chuckled at the adoring look on Mack's face as Martha tended to her. "So am I. I'm not sure what I would've done without her when things got a bit much." I sipped at my coffee and thought about the night before. "Can I ask how comfortable you think Leroy is about the whole gay thing? I know you think he's fine, but I don't know. He's really touchy with me, and I'm not putting up with any bullshit homophobia, low-key or not. He wasn't that great about you two last year."

Her gaze slid away. "It's not like he talks about the stuff with me, but to be honest, I don't think last year was so much about Cora and me as about him and Judah and the business. Morgan buying the two acres of land off Cora helped their cash flow, but I know Leroy is still concerned. The farm's keeping its head above water but it's a fine margin. And I think maybe Leroy saw you as some kind of threat last year."

"A threat? Why would he think that?"

"Well, Cora and I getting together and then you, *my son*, arriving and talking about moving up here? I think it got him worried."

I choked on a mouthful of coffee and spluttered it down the front of my T-shirt. "Jesus, Mum. What kind of guy does he think I am?" I leaned forward to brush the drips off my shirt. "I would never . . . what the hell?"

She shrugged. "I know. But remember, I might've worked with the Maddens for sixteen years, but we weren't family-style close. Leroy was a teen or in Auckland for most of that time, and you were off doing your thing down south. Before last year, you hadn't even met each other properly, other than to say hello in passing. And it's hard to know *what* goes on in that boy's head."

"Man," I corrected, then wished I hadn't when she fired me an appraising look.

"Yes, man," she agreed with an amused glint in her eye that I knew only too damn well. "I wondered if you'd noticed."

"Stop it." I wagged a finger. "I can appreciate a good-looking guy regardless of his orientation. Doesn't mean anything more."

She smirked. "Of course you can. But to answer your question, no, I don't think he's homophobic, just bad-tempered for one so young."

"He's thirty, right?"

She nodded, swirled the last of her coffee around her mug, and then swallowed it down. "Anyway, I have to go open up the office. I just wanted to check in and give my son a hug." She pushed to her feet and wandered to the edge of the deck to stare at the view. "So, what's on your list for today?"

Fox walked across to join her. "I've got a few calls to make, and then I'll unpack. I left pretty much everything in the house down south, bar any personal stuff which I threw in storage, so it's just clothes and essentials. But I need to get the truck to a mechanic for that rattle. Any recommendations?"

"I see you've brought the old blue Ford Explorer. I thought you'd replaced that a couple of years ago?"

I nodded. "Van took the new one. But the old girl still goes okay, held together with rust and good wishes." I avoided Mum's gaze. She's been less than subtle about her opinion on how soft I was, multiple times. She had a point, but I just wanted everything over with minimal drama.

She rolled her eyes. "Of course he bloody did. Try Henderson's, about five kilometres up the road. I can bring you back if you like, or the bus goes right past the door. You won't get a taxi or Uber around here."

I laughed. "Hell, a regular bus service is a step up from down south. I'll be fine."

"Well, let me or Cora know if you need anything. She aims to catch up with Leroy again to smooth any residual ruffled feathers. Hopefully that will settle things. I'll see myself out." She turned, then hesitated and spun back. "In case I haven't said it already, Fox, I'm really so damn happy to have you here. You've been too far away for too long, and I know that's mostly my fault for coming up here after your father died, once you were on your own, but he'd be damned proud of you if he was still alive."

Crap. Tears welled in my eyes and she brushed them away with her thumb.

"I hope he would," I said, clearing my throat. "Although I'm pretty sure he would've taken one look at Van back in the day and warned me right from the start."

She snorted. "True. He had a keen eye for waste-of-space people, that's for sure. I wish your move had been for better reasons, but I have every faith in you. You're a better man than Van ever was. I'm not gonna say I never liked him, but yeah, I never liked him." She sighed. "Too bad he lived up to my fears and ended up such a fucking disappointment all around. I just hope he doesn't scare you off trying again when the right guy comes along."

I pulled her into a tight hug. "Thanks, Mum, but I'm not remotely interested in dating right now, and certainly not in anything more, so no setting me up on blind dates, okay? I'm not sure I trust my instincts anymore, and that's gonna take a bit to remedy." *Maybe never.*

She pulled away. "Who me?" She patted my cheek and headed down the steps to the outside path. "It's like you don't even know me," she called over her shoulder, and my eyes rolled of their own accord.

I'd no sooner sat down when my phoned buzzed in my pocket.

I pulled it out and stared at the screen, a cold wave washing up my body.

Speak of the fucking devil.

With my gaze locked on Painted Bay as if willing some of that peace back into my heart, I answered. "What the hell do you want? We're done, Van. You're getting what you wanted, so just leave me the fuck alone."

"She's not yours."

"Like hell, she's not," I spat, my gaze shifting to Mack whose ears pricked up at my tone.

"I looked after her—"

"Oh puh-lease," I scoffed. "I had her way *before* you and I ever got together, and she's been with me on the boat for eight years, whether we went for a day or a week. You stayed at home, remember? Where you wanted to be, on your computer, while I earned the money to put you through your courses and fill our home with a million things we didn't need. And when I was back on land, *I* was the one who walked her and took her to her vet and every other damn thing. The most you ever did was throw some biscuits in her bowl and cuddle on the couch. How the hell does that make you the one who looked after her?"

"I love her too."

Jesus Christ. "You've never loved anyone but yourself, Van. A fact made patently clear in recent years."

"You've got no right to talk to me like that." His voice pitched high in the way he'd always done when he was trying to win me over, back in the days when I'd thought it was cute. Not anymore. I winced as he continued. "And who did what for Mack means nothing. She was *our* dog, Fox. You don't get to just take her away without even telling me. I only found out after you'd already gone. It's not right. My lawyer is petitioning for joint custody."

A cold wave fluttered in my belly. "Joint what?" I shouted down the line. "Well, good luck with that, arsehole. It wasn't like you didn't know I had to move. Hell, you made damn sure of that, didn't you? Screwed my business and then turned pretty much every friend I had in town against me with your lies."

Silence greeted the accusation which said it all. I carried on. "This is exactly why I *didn't* tell you. Share Ewan's old Labrador."

The silence continued for a moment. "I didn't lie. You were way too close with a couple of those guys on your boat. Why wouldn't I suspect—"

"Because they were my friends, you idiot. Because we both said we didn't want an open marriage. Because *I* didn't want anyone else. Because I'd fucking made that promise to you. We *both* had. Just because you didn't keep it in your pants doesn't mean that I couldn't."

"How could I trust you wouldn't—"

"Oh, for fuck's sake. Because I *said* I wouldn't, that's how." I rubbed at my eyes. "Stop trying to justify what you did. And I'd *really* appreciate it if you'd stop telling people you only went with Ewan because you thought I'd been unfaithful. I can't show my fucking face in Oban without getting a mountain of filthy looks."

"My family lives here. I had to—"

"Well, I lived there too, for ten years, in case you'd forgotten. Except I can't now, can I? Well done for making me the local fucking pariah."

He snorted, then continued, although a little less cocky than before. "You kept our house, didn't you? Nothing to stop you coming back whenever you want. You could've waited till things were finalised with the divorce, at least."

"*My* house, not ours. I bought you out, remember?"

"Whatever. That isn't what I called about. You should've told me about taking Mack, talked about it at least."

My heart jumped in my throat because he was right, legally, at least. But I'd suspected he might do just this. "Too bad. You're not taking anything else from me," I ground out. "And you can stop fucking calling me. Go through my lawyer."

I ended the call and threw the phone on the chair and walked away.

A few seconds later it buzzed with a text that I wanted to ignore but just couldn't. I tapped the screen and swore.

This isn't over.

Like hell it wasn't. I flicked through my contacts and dialled Tinny. We'd been best mates ever since I moved to the island and needed a lawyer to look over my first fishing contracts. He now called Invercargill home, a one-hour ferry or a quick flight away. He and his wife saved my hide when Van and I imploded, convincing me to spend a couple of weeks with them after the shitstorm hit, at least until I could feed myself without being at risk of pickling my liver in alcohol before I was even thirty-five.

"Are you dead already?" he answered. "Cos that's the only acceptable explanation for why you haven't called since you left the island. I suggested to Violet that maybe you'd been abducted by aliens, but she reminded me that no alien would stoop so low as to kidnap your sorry two-bit, ungrateful arse, and honestly, I couldn't fault her logic."

"Good morning to you too, sunshine." I smiled, which was kind of a miracle, all things considered. "Is that any way to speak to your best friend? Hell, your only friend since that little infection thing you had going on a while back."

"Fuck off, arsehole. What do you want?"

"I'm sorry, Tinny. I should've called. No excuse, but my head's been a bit woolly. The Explorer is a little worse for wear after all those kilometres, and I think I might need a new part or two, but otherwise, I got here yesterday and I'm good. As to the other reason for the call, Van phoned."

"Ah, shit. What's the fucker gone and done now?"

"He says he wants Mack. He can't do that, can he?"

There was silence at the other end. "Jesus, Fox. We talked about this. I specifically asked you if she needed to be put in the separation settlement. But you said Van was cool with you having her. If I'd known he wasn't, I would've warned you about leaving."

"I thought he was. He never once said he wanted her, and I've had her for the whole separation period. He can't do this, can he?"

"Technically, he has every right. Has he had *anything* to do with her since you guys split?"

I hesitated. *Fuck, fuck, fuck.* "A few times. He offered to look after her the times I came up to see Mum last year. It seemed the easiest solution . . . I didn't even think. And he sees her all the time around Oban. Hell, she used to wander to and from our places. You know what it's like down there. Fuck!"

"Calm down. We'll get it sorted, but under New Zealand law, pets are considered part of the chattels and property. That means he has a claim, Fox, whether you like it or not."

"But he signed that separation agreement when we first split. He should've said something then, right?" Anger mounted in my chest.

"Mack was never stipulated in that, and Van's entitled to change his mind or challenge the separation agreement before the formal divorce papers are finalized."

"Well, he's not taking her. I won't lose her too." My eyes squeezed shut as my voice broke.

"Come on, Fox." Tinny's voice softened. "You don't deserve this, and I'll do my best to sort it out. Leave it with me and I'll talk to his lawyer and see what the hell's going on in the idiot's head."

"Thanks. And I am sorry I didn't call."

"Doesn't matter, you know that. Maybe we can come north for a holiday when you get settled."

My heart caught in my throat. "I'd really like that."

We said nothing for a moment, the eleven hundred kilometres between us eating up my heart. "I miss you guys."

"We miss you too. I'll get back to you when I know something."

I ended the call wanting to do nothing more than crawl up the steps to my best friend's home and have him tell me face to face that everything was going to be okay.

Because somehow, I just fucking knew it wasn't.

CHAPTER THREE

Leroy

I THREW THE LAST OF THE ROPE INTO THE SHED AND POPPED MY head through the open door of the wharf office. "I'm done, Martha. Andrew's dropping off some more of those smaller floats tomorrow. I'll sort them out when I get back in the afternoon. Catch you then."

"Wait up." Martha threw up a hand. "I need an okay on these invoices I want to clear."

I leafed through the printouts. "Looks good. Go ahead." I passed them back and she filed them on her desk.

"And Colin Faulkner called again about what we still owe on the last harvest. I figure you'll be needing him again soon, so it might be smart not to let that one hang too long, even though it'll clean out our working account for a couple of weeks." She sent me a pointed look. It was no secret we were running tight.

I scrubbed a hand across my jaw. "I know, but it's not like we have a choice. We need those beds harvested then or we'll miss the half-shell shipment, and they'll be too big if we wait. If you need to transfer from the secondary account to cover, go ahead. I'm done for the day."

I turned to leave, anxious to get home and put my feet up with a beer.

"Leroy, wait a minute."

I spun back. "What can I do for you?"

Her gaze locked on mine. "Thanks for having Fox stay. He appreciates it, we *all* appreciate it. Did Cora get hold of you?"

I tried not to let my irritation show. "Yeah, and it's fine, I guess. I just wish she'd given me some warning, that's all."

"I get that." She nodded and ran a hand down my arm. "And I also know she's not always clued into you."

I hid my surprise. "Yeah, well, story of my life, right?" I stepped back from the doorway, but she followed.

"She loves you, Leroy." Her shrewd grey eyes tracked my expression.

"I know she does." And I did. "It's fine, Martha. I'll see you tomorrow." I turned away before she could add anything else and headed for my Hilux. I cast a look at Judah and Morgan's empty boathouse as I passed. No lights and no music. So very different from when they were home. An image of them picnicking in that damn vineyard sprang to mind, and an unexpected stab of loneliness struck me.

I threw my duffel in the back seat and then paused with my forearms on the steering wheel as I digested the strange feeling. I was genuinely happy for both of them, but I'd never really seen myself in the whole cutesy domestic thing. Hell, I'd only popped the lid on regular dating once or twice in my entire life, preferring one-and-done over catering to someone else's needs. And neither of *them* had lasted more than a few months.

I wasn't exactly the easiest guy to get on with, and the thought of a lifetime sharing every waking moment with another person was enough to send a shudder through my chakras. I liked my space. I liked quiet. I liked to work. What I didn't like was having to consider anyone else in that equation.

And I didn't need or want anyone looking after me, I never had. I didn't date or fuck anyone long enough to reach that point, and I'd never had the kind of friends you got invited to dinner with. A drink at the pub after rugby training was pretty much it. Not to mention, I didn't have the time. None of that fitted with a long-term relationship, and I didn't want to hurt anyone. If that meant staying single, so be it. I'd gotten used to the idea.

Or at least I thought I had.

I started the engine and cranked up the air conditioning, relishing the icy lick of air on my sweaty brow. But before I could throw the truck in gear, my phone buzzed with an incoming call. I grinned at the name on the screen and picked up.

"Jon boy. To what do I owe the pleasure of a call from our esteemed local police representative?"

"Our beloved coach has given me the job of making sure you get your sorry arse to rugby training this week, no excuses," Jon blared, rattling my eardrums. "With Morgan away, we're down a player, and I'm damned if we're gonna hand the cup to Kawhia again without a good fight. My counterpart up there was far too fucking smug for his own good last season. I need to shove a win down his throat to even the score. Don't make me come get you."

I chuckled. "I'll be there. But it's your turn to cough up for a beer."

"Yeah, yeah. Just turn the hell up and I'll be happy. And maybe bring Martha's son along. Fox, right? I heard he's in town and that he's a big boy. Does he play?"

Like I needed the reminder. "I don't think so."

"Excellent." Jon chuckled. "Then he'll fit right in."

"No, I don't think that's a good—"

"See you Saturday, Leroy, and bring Fox." And he was gone.

Fuck, fuck, fuck.

I glanced to the homestead on the top of the hill and squinted against the glint of the sun setting behind its iron roof. Bloody Fox Carmody had taken up way too much space in my head during the day as it was. And now I was supposed to invite him to rugby as well? Fucking Jon. There were few enough things I did in my life just for me, and rugby was . . . well, in all honesty, it was the *only* one. But if I didn't pass the message, Jon would just do it himself.

So much for cracking a beer and chilling on the deck as was my habit at the end of a heavy day. I'd grab a cheese toastie and lock myself in the bedroom instead. At least I had a TV in there.

I threw the car into gear and crawled up the hill, in no hurry to lay eyes on the irksome man who wandered somewhere within the walls of my home. Fox made my skin itch in ways I didn't under-stand. In ways I didn't want to examine. In ways that had come as a huge fucking surprise a year ago when I'd first laid eyes on him as an adult and which hadn't changed since. And in ways that had the potential to seriously fuck up my life.

I didn't get it, and I didn't want to. I just needed to get my head out of my arse and ignore it. I was ordinarily good at that—my personal superpower. Until he came along.

I pulled into the garage, grabbed my duffel from the back seat, and slid out of my truck, only to be set upon by twenty-five kilos of rippling, eager happiness. Pinned against the door of my car until Mack had licked every scrap of salt from any exposed skin she could lay her tongue to, I tried and failed to scrub the huge grin off my face.

"Are you done?" I gently pushed her with my knee so I could peel myself off the driver's door. She ran a couple of excited loops around my legs before bounding toward the long shadows of the back door. "Not yet, girl." I headed up the staircase on the side of the garage, and two seconds later, Mack's paws tapped up behind me. I smiled and pushed at the old wooden door, which had swollen tight in the recent rain, and almost fell into the room when it finally gave.

"Okay, so I admit the place could do with a clean." I coughed up my lungs as several years of gathered dust fell from the shelf above the door. The old bedsit had become little more than a dumping ground for the junk my mother refused to throw out on the basis it might come in useful one day. Much though it pained me to prove her right, I caught sight of the large tarp I was after for the boat and dug it free. I lugged it down the stairs and into the tray of my truck with Mack barking happily at the fun new game.

After checking Fox wasn't in sight, I crouched down and rubbed her ears, cooing silly things and feeling ridiculous at the subterfuge. I could like the man's damn dog without it meaning anything more than that.

"Okay, girl." I got to my feet and grabbed my duffel. "Let's head inside."

Mack launched herself along the veranda toward the back door, and this time I followed, toeing off my filthy boots on the top step before reaching for the door handle and taking a deep breath to steel myself.

The blistering vocals of Nine Inch Nails and "Closer" blasted through the open windows along with the mouth-watering aroma of —lamb?

Huh.

Mack nudged the door with her head to make a point, but I indulged a moment longer, smiling at Fox's voice doing an impressive and exceptionally loud job of ruining the most badass chorus ever written.

There was a sweet weirdness to the moment. Since Dad had died and Judah headed back to Boston, it had only ever been Mum and me in the homestead—rattling around like two mismatched peas in a pod —comfortable with each other but strangers to each other's depths. I loved her deeply, but we didn't necessarily understand each other, at all. Judah and she were much more alike.

I'd never been on the receiving end of my parents' concern the way Judah had. No one fussed over me or worried about my mental health. I wasn't gay and fabulous. I'd never been bullied. And I didn't fight stereotypes to make ballet a career.

I was just average Leroy who played rugby, did well in school, fitted in with the jocks and the popular kids, and who wanted to be a vet. Only I hadn't fitted in. Not really. And the misplaced dream of being a vet died with my father when I'd come home to run the family business.

But I had enjoyed sharing the house and working the farm with my mother—keeping Dad's legacy afloat and having her to myself for the first time ever, even if it meant suffering through those endless culinary experiments. Julia Child, she *wasn't*.

And in the space of a year, that had all changed. Mum was in love and living with Martha; Judah was home, happily married and living in the boatshed; and I was . . . well, I was back to being alone. Not that I didn't enjoy the solitude, because I did. But I couldn't deny coming home to a house that wasn't completely empty for a change felt . . . nice.

Fox's voice crescendoed a little flat on the final couple of lines, and I pushed the door open and stepped into the laundry—the air redolent with mouth-watering aromas. Mack raced past my legs while I dropped my duffel and washed the day's grime off my hands. Then I made my way into the airy open living space and froze.

Fox, who'd clearly not heard me enter, had Mack's front paws in his hands, singing and dancing barefoot in my kitchen to the words of "We're In This Together Now." It was an almost eye-roll-worthy, universe-kicking-my-arse metaphor. Mack was following as best she could, jumping up and down on her back legs, and I snorted softly and leaned on the door to watch. The late sea breeze kicking up through the wide-open sash windows cooled my face while the setting sun threw orange-gold splashes over the whole ridiculous scene.

If the music had been softer, Fox would've heard me laugh, but it was rattling the windows and he was completely oblivious. I watched for a few more seconds before my gaze landed on two plates set out on the breakfast bar, along with two glasses and a collection of shells that hadn't been there that morning.

A table for two.

My breath caught and something deep inside warmed at the thought. The rest of me broke out in a cold sweat, and with my socked feet rooted to the floor, my gaze slid back to Fox who was busy shimmying down in front of Mack. The move caused his soft green tee to pull free from yet another pair of threadbare jeans—could the man not afford to buy some decent clothes—revealing a strip of tanned skin and the beginning of butt crack.

My mouth ran to dust and my cock stirred.

Unaware of my presence, Fox bent to press a kiss to Mack's wrinkled brow, and those criminally thin jeans stretched even tighter, hugging that glorious arse as it swayed to the music and . . . I needed to get out of there, fast.

I wanted it to mean nothing. I really, really needed it to. But I was totally fucking transfixed to every bunch and swell and—

Move, you idiot.

In my haste, I stumbled over my feet and crashed into a dining chair, the sound spinning Fox in place.

"Oh, hey. I didn't hear you come in." He immediately dropped Mack's paws, those green eyes regarding me warily, no doubt wondering just how long I'd been creeping on him. And if my cheeks weren't flaming, I'd eat my fucking fisherman's hat.

"Hey. I, um, just got in. I should get out of these clothes." I pulled at my shirt, which frankly looked perfectly fine since I'd mostly just driven the boat today while Patrick worked the lines. Fox looked me over, his gaze lingering, and heat washed through my body.

"Of course." He shifted his attention to a pot on the stove and grabbed a large metal spoon from the utensil holder. "Dinner will be in about thirty minutes."

"Dinner?" I frowned, acting like I hadn't clocked the entire setup the minute I walked in.

"Yeah." He glanced back around to where I still stood like the fool that I was. "You know that thing where you put food in your mouth at the end of a busy day? I went to the supermarket and did a stock-up. I wasn't going to use your stuff without asking. Feel free to help yourself to anything you find. The butcher had lamb on special, so I thought, why not?"

My mouth watered at the thought, but *nothing* about sharing a meal with Fox Carmody of the soft jeans, tight body, and electric green eyes was remotely sensible. The man had the power to completely fuck with my head, and the last thing I needed was to get all friendly and cosy with him.

"You go ahead." I schooled my expression. "I already ate, but thanks."

He narrowed his gaze. "When?"

I hesitated. "When what?"

"When exactly did you eat?"

"That's none—"

"I asked Mum to call when your boat berthed so I'd know when to put the veggies in. She said you only ever eat lunch and half the time you skip that."

I bristled. "You asked your *mother* to let you know when I came in? You discussed my eating habits with her? What the hell?" I grabbed the stack of mail from the dining table, ignoring the question of how it had got there since the answer was obviously standing right in front of me. "I don't need you to keep tabs on me, Fox, and I certainly don't need—" I waved my free hand toward the kitchen. "—whatever the hell this is. I'm perfectly fine. Just keep out of my way and we'll be good."

"Leroy—" He took a step, then pulled up short as I turned my back and headed for my room, my face blazing. "Leroy, I'm sorry. I only wanted to help," he called after me. "Jesus Christ, Leroy, it's just a fucking meal. Don't be such an arse."

"Fuck you," I snapped back. "And make sure you clean up." I flipped him off over my shoulder and slammed my bedroom door to the clattering accompaniment of a metal spoon landing with force in the stainless sink in the kitchen.

Fuck. Fuck. Fuck.

I crashed onto my bed and waited for my pulse to stop pounding.

Could I have behaved more ludicrously? No. No, I couldn't. Would I apologise? Like fuck. If Fox thought I was an arrogant, thankless arse-hole, all the better. The further he stayed away from me, the safer things were.

Mack's claws scratched at my door and I yelled at her to go away, then winced. Like she had anything to do with me crushing over a fucking guy. Fox called her name and claws ticked back up the hall-way. It wasn't Mack's fault. Hell, it wasn't even Fox's. The fact he'd flipped some kind of switch in me wasn't on him. I just wanted it to go the fuck away. And him being so bloody thoughtful wasn't exactly helping.

I threw the spare pillow against the door and groaned.

Why now? Why did he have to turn up now?

The music dulled to a background hum, low enough for me to hear Fox talking to Mack but not enough for me to catch his words. The deep timbre of his voice tugged at that squirming niggle low in my belly. The niggle I'd first felt when I'd seen him standing all dark and broody in our house last year with a slash of hurt in his eyes from whatever misery was current in his life. His deep voice had resonated in my chest like a familiar echo I couldn't quite place. And when those gorgeous green eyes landed on me with undisguised interest, it stripped me raw. I'd never been studied quite so intently, and the memory alone had the power to kindle a heat and fear in my chest like nothing else.

I'd sat there like a total idiot that day as everyone chatted around me; Morgan finding his place for the first time at our table; Judah's eyes shining with his new love interest; my mother and Martha quietly together but not yet out. Hell, I couldn't tell you now what everyone talked about, I was so fucking captivated by Fox—his face, the sharp angle of his jaw, the way his brows sat heavy over pene-trating eyes, deep dimples in his cheeks, the sun-kissed ends of those lengthy dark locks falling to his shoulders, and the way he focused so intently whenever our eyes met.

I'd fumbled my way through the conversation, words jamming in my mouth like a tongue-tied teenager, a flush sitting high on my cheeks that I guessed most put down to anger, my cock stirring, every neuron in my body lit up. I put the attraction down to some kind of random reaction and did the only thing I knew how.

I'd been a total and unmitigated arsehole.

Shocker.

It should've worked. Most people didn't warm to me, and Fox was no different. Over the day his attitude cooled significantly, and I'd been able to put some much-needed distance between us. But later that evening he'd cornered me about my attitude to our mothers' relationship, and my breath had caught at his fierce protection and the fevered warning in his eyes, the low timbre of his voice. And in the middle of that heated discussion, I'd gotten . . . hard.

Me.

I'd been gobsmacked. I'd never felt the steam of sexual attraction to a man, ever. Played rugby all my life with brawny guys and never once wanted to climb into their pants. But then I'd never felt an attraction so immediate and intense with a woman either. And I *loved* women. Well, I liked fucking them. To be honest, I wasn't sure about anything more since I hadn't really ever had what you'd call a *proper* relationship.

I suspected they felt the same way about me. Okay in bed, but as for the rest? Words like hard work, cold, work-obsessed and distant tended to get peppered into conversations about how I wasn't there for them before they inevitably walked away. And so now the universe in its infinite wisdom had somehow decided that I needed to be shot down by the other half of the population as well? Well fuck that.

I wasn't homophobic. Judah would likely disagree, but he'd be wrong. My issues with him centred more around my parents than Judah's sexuality, although I'd been a total arsehole, for sure. I'd been absent when I should've had his back at school, at least as far as some of my very definitely homophobic friends were concerned. I shouldn't have been hanging around those losers anyway, and I'd go back and change it if I could. I'd had no idea how far things had gone, but I should have, and that was on me.

Irrespective of all that, I suspected this new development in my sexuality wouldn't go down well. What the fuck was I gonna say? 'Hey, bro, guess what?' I thought of tiny Painted Bay and rolled my eyes. They'd eat me for breakfast. They might be a lot more accepting than when Judah was a teenager, but I'd still be fodder for gossip for months, the target of wondering looks, probing questions, and hushed conversations—all in all my worst nightmare.

I wasn't ready for any of that shit, not yet. Maybe never. No woman had ever caught my eye for long, and there was no reason Fox should be any different. He'd be out of my house soon enough. Sooner if I could force the issue, and then things would calm down. I would calm down.

The lie sat sour on my tongue, but I chose to ignore it.

I remembered my mother's words and tried to think of Fox as family.

Fucking my stepbrother, huh? I paid attention to my body and waited for the ew factor to kick in, but nope, not the slightest moral wrinkle. *Dammit.* I was a sick puppy. But also, how in the hell had I suddenly made the leap from eyeing the man up to stripping him bare and fucking him?

I was in deep shit.

Fox Carmody was in my house, and just the thought of his long legs in those soft jeans or the way his T-shirt hugged his hard body, the tempting strip of soft skin at his waist, and the sexy curve of his mouth with those cute-as-fuck dimples had my wayward cock doing a happy dance as it rode off into the sunset, calling his name and leaving its torn and faded heterosexual flag lying in the dust.

And I was supposed to invite the man to rugby training as well? Thundering muscles and glistening skin and hot showers.

A plaintive groan rumbled from my throat.

I'm in so much fucking trouble.

CHAPTER FOUR

Fox

LEROY MADDEN WAS AN INFURIATING, UNGRATEFUL ARSEHOLE.
A sexy, intriguing, closed-off, infuriating, sexy, ungrateful, sexy
arsehole.

Well, fuck him.

I shoved a pair of spare socks, a windbreaker, my boardies, and a
breezy black singlet into my boat carry-bag and zipped it shut. Then I
grabbed my boots and tiptoed up the pitch-black hallway and into the
family room with Mack following quietly at my heels. I eased the
door closed behind her and made my way to the laundry, aided by the
weak grey light of daybreak washing through the huge sash windows.
I left my bag on the floor and dished a cup of biscuits into Mack's
food bowl on the back deck.

If Leroy fucking Madden thought he'd won the battle last night,
he had another think coming. What a jerk. He had no idea who he
was fucking with. Talk to any of my old crew and they'd have put him
straight in two sentences. I had the depth of patience gifted to all

serious fishermen, a compelling need to not be beholden to *anyone*, and I could be as obstinate and stubborn as he was.

I glanced at the clock on the wall. Five forty. Leroy would be up in another twenty minutes, if yesterday was anything to go by, and then out the door by the time the sun was fully up at six thirty.

Plenty of time.

My gaze swept the countertops that I'd made sure to leave spotless the night before. *'Make sure you clean up.'* *Fucker.* It landed on a knife and plate in the sink, and I smirked. *Someone* had been up for a midnight snack. I checked the bread bin, and the sourdough loaf had its end brutally hacked off. And when I opened the fridge to grab the container I'd prepared the night before, I almost laughed at the poorly rewrapped lamb leftovers sitting alongside. A late-night lamb sandwich, it would seem. No doubt he'd thought he'd be up before me to get rid of the incriminating evidence.

Good for you, dipshit. I hope you choked on it.

I tiptoed out the back door, feeling about twelve years old and wholly ridiculous, sat on the step to put my boots on, and then let Mack back inside. Leroy would likely just think I'd let her out from the bedroom. It would give him something else to complain about.

"Be good." I stroked her wrinkled brow. "Although, if you piss in *his* bed, I might just forgive you. I'll get your grandma to let you out later." I kissed the top of her head, closed the door, and headed for the wharf, adrenaline whooshing through my veins at the thought I'd finally got one over on Leroy Madden.

The man made me crazy.

When Leroy finally arrived and caught sight of me sitting on the pier next to his boat, with my legs dangling over the side, he froze. It took all I had not to burst out laughing at the shock on his face, although he quickly schooled it into a withering scowl. But it was too late. He knew he'd been had, and that was enough for me.

I got to my feet and simply waited. I knew enough not to set foot on a boat without the skipper's permission, and so I'd filled in the time chatting with Patrick who was already prepping the boat and loading supplies before I got there.

He'd practically beamed when he saw me, and I was reminded how tongue-tied he'd been around me at that lunch the previous year, his interest worn on his sleeve in bold rainbow colours. I wasn't sure if he was out or not, no one had said anything, but I'd gotten the message. I made a mental note not to encourage him. I didn't need the additional grief.

Leroy regarded my work clothing with a cool look. "What do you think you're doing?"

I brushed a non-existent piece of lint off my jeans. "I'm here to help, of course." I flashed him an innocent smile. "Now, don't get too excited. I know you've been waiting for this moment."

He shot a look to Patrick. "I want us out of here in five minutes, got it?" Patrick nodded, his gaze shifting between us. Then Leroy returned his attention to me. "I don't need any—"

"Just shut up and listen for once." I took a step toward him. "A novel idea, I know, but I'm sure you can make it work."

His gaze turned icy, but he said nothing.

Patrick glanced nervously between us. "I'll, um, go put the coffee on, boss."

Leroy nodded without looking, and Patrick scuttled into the galley like his tail was on fire. "So, you sneaked out before me. A little childish, don't you think?" Leroy muttered, throwing his duffle onto the boat.

He was calling *me* childish?

"I wondered why Mack was loose in the house," he added. "She'd better be well trained." He cast me a warning look and got the eye-roll he deserved in return.

Goddamn, but the guy was a piece of work. "Of course she bloody is. Do you think I'd leave her if I thought she'd wreck your place? Although to be honest, I might've been tempted if it was just yours, but it's your mother's house as well, and I happen to like Cora."

His lips twitched in an almost smile. So, he enjoyed a bit of push-back, did he? Good to know. I was more than happy to oblige.

I continued. "And Mum is going to check on Mack around lunch, so how about you back the fuck off? On the boat Mack had a sandbox she used without fail. She was more bloody meticulous than most of my crew. At least *she* never missed the tray."

That got a more definite smile before he suddenly remembered he was meant to be pissed with me and folded his arms.

I blew out a sigh. "For Christ's sake, Leroy, will you just let me help, you stubborn bastard? What do you have to lose? I might not know mussels, but I was born to helm and I can turn my hand to pretty much anything to do with a boat or marine work."

Leroy raised his chin defiantly. "You think it's that easy? You think *anyone* can just waltz in and do what we do? That we're just playing around here? We might not be deep-ocean fisherman, but we're still pretty damn skilled."

I threw my hands in the air. "*No*, Leroy. That's *not* what I'm saying, and you know it. What the fuck is wrong with you? Do you really dislike me that much?"

He glared in reply, and we stood there in some kind of a ridiculous stand-off.

"Boss?" Patrick interrupted, and Leroy's gaze reluctantly pulled away. "It's a big day, Boss." Patrick's gaze flicked to me. "We need to change out those floats *and* seed some new lines."

Leroy stared at his employee for a few seconds, his jaw ticking, and I just knew he wanted nothing more than to have the satisfaction of sending me back to the house. But I also saw the moment his common sense won out. It was kind of a relief to know he had some.

His shoulders sank and he turned a cool look my way. "All right. You can stow your gear. But you do as I say, Fox. *I'm* the boss on this vessel, not you. Understood?"

"Absolutely." I saluted, swallowing a grin. "Permission to come on board, skipper?"

He rolled his eyes. "Jesus Christ. Get the fuck down there."

I threw Patrick my bag and made my way down onto the deck. Leroy followed, muttering something about big mistakes and idiot fucking southerners.

I smiled to myself. Oh, sweetheart, you ain't seen nothing yet.

Game on.

Leroy

Much as it pained me to admit, accepting Fox's help had been the right call and meant we were headed for the wharf with nearly two hours trimmed off our day. And to be fair, he'd caught on quick, been respectful and interested in how everything worked, and followed every instruction I'd given to a T. Plus, he'd helmed the boat like the pro he was, which left Patrick and me to efficiently tick off our work list with very little wasted time.

All in all, I had zero to complain about, dammit.

With Patrick on his phone in the back of the boat, I stole a sideways glance to where Fox sat curled up in the seat next to the helm, eyes closed, arms crossed, a soft expression on his face. A few of those long golden-tipped waves had caught in the dark rough stubble of his jaw, and my fingers itched to set them free—a degree of touching that my dick was definitely not opposed to. But then it wasn't opposed to anything much when it came to Fox, and the day had proved . . . challenging.

When it warmed to an unseasonal thirty degrees centigrade, the man had stripped down to a loose black singlet highlighting the tanned skin of his broad shoulders and a pair of palm tree boardshorts that hung low on his hips and bunched around those long, muscled thighs—all of which turned my not-so-straight legs to fucking jelly and another not-so-straight part of my anatomy to attention.

I shook my gaze loose and focused on the shore and the rising swell that slapped at the boat's hull and sent it pitching. Not that any of it disturbed Fox who probably didn't open his eyes for anything less than a roaring forty.

I'd spent all damn day trying *not* to look at him, *not* watch all those muscles ripple and strain as he'd coiled rope, *not* linger over the way his shorts pulled tight over his arse, *not* wonder what it would feel like to be in those arms, and *not* fucking fantasise about those legs wrapped around me.

Tried and failed, epically.

Twice, Patrick had needed to shout to catch my attention to pick up slack in the ropes, something that never happened. The second time, he'd even come across to check I was feeling okay, and I'd snapped some churlish reply that sent him skittering away. I might be pissy with him, but he didn't deserve it, and I needed to make that right. My arsehole points were mounting up.

After all, I could hardly blame the poor guy for flirting shamelessly with Fox over lunch. I'd been pretty damn sure Patrick wasn't straight, but I could've done without twenty minutes of him fawning over the fisherman. Fox's response had been painfully friendly, making a point that even my clueless brain could understand, but it hadn't stopped my temper boiling. I'd left them to it before the urge to shove Patrick over the side of the boat became too strong to ignore.

And as for lunch—lamb sandwiches, for fuck's sake. I'd almost laughed when Fox handed them out with a knowing smirk aimed squarely at me. My midnight raid on the leftover roast clearly hadn't gone unnoticed. Still, the sandwiches beat the yoghurt and crackers I'd packed, and to be honest, I was grateful . . . and starving. Not that I told him that, although I did manage to cough up a thank you.

But they were all points on the mortification scale I was rapidly climbing. In under two days, I'd become this man I barely recognised, and anger rolled in my belly at the awareness. Why did it have to be *him*? It wasn't simply that I'd never been attracted to *guys* before. Hell, I'd never been attracted to *anyone* like this before, ever. My whole fucking world was arse-over-kite and I was holding on by my bloodied fingertips. And Fox fucking Carmody—

I stole another glance at the sleeping man—was completely oblivious.

Goddamn him.

And in that fashion, the afternoon had deteriorated. I barked orders at Fox like he was a clueless greenback, half expecting him to thump me at some point for the undisguised insults I threw his way. But he hadn't said a word, just did as he was told, albeit with the annoying hint of a smile on his lips which only served to infuriate me further. My fingernails were gone, the inside of my cheek was in shreds, and Fox was . . . fuck, Fox was cool as a fucking cucumber.

Another glance.

The man radiated peace—at home in a boat and on the ocean as much as anyone I'd ever known. The realisation sent a pang through my chest. In many ways he was a kindred spirit. Like I needed another reason to like the guy. For all that I'd thought I wanted to be a vet when I was a teenager, I fucking loved the ocean—

"You're creeping me out." He opened his eyes and caught me staring. "Is there something you forgot to yell at me about? Did you miss your quota for the day? I'm all ears. Have at it."

Heat raced up my neck and I turned away. "Don't be ridiculous."

He said nothing, but his gaze burned my skin.

"Okay, so I might've ridden you a bit hard," I admitted, thanking all the angels I remembered from Sunday school when Painted Bay came into view.

He snorted. "Trust me, I wouldn't be complaining if you had."

I frowned, replaying my words in my head until my cheeks blazed. "I didn't mean that . . . I wasn't . . . I just meant—"

"Calm down." He chuckled. "I know what you meant. And apology accepted."

I bristled. "It wasn't an apology."

"Was too."

I rolled my eyes and he waggled his eyebrows in reply. Then he faced forward to stare at the dull grey-green of the ocean heaving under the blanket of ash-coloured clouds. "So, are you going to let me help tomorrow without a fight, or do I have to stow away?"

I glanced his way. "You don't need to help me to make yourself feel better. Mum invited you to stay and that's that. It is what it is."

He sat a little more upright, yawned, and stretched his arms over his head, which drew his tank up over the flat line of his darkly haired belly and—no. I white-knuckled the throttle and trained my eyes on the wharf ahead.

"Well, be that as it may . . ." He dropped his arms and snagged his bag with an outstretched foot and pulled it over so he could drop the lunch boxes inside. "It helps me feel less of a prick for landing in your life uninvited. And in spite of your constant sniping, I actually enjoyed today. It's different from what I know, but it was still pretty cool. You've got a good operation going." He seized the grab rail as the boat hit a large wave and jolted hard. "I haven't been out on a boat in a while. It felt pretty damn good."

I frowned, trying not to feel good about the fact he'd complimented my business. "But you own a fishing boat. Last I heard you were thinking about moving the whole business north."

A flash of pain crossed behind his eyes and he looked away. "Yeah well, not any longer."

I waited but he didn't elaborate, and the rumble of the boat's motor filled the void. It was on the tip of my tongue to ask more, but I bit the words back and slowed the boat's approach to the wharf.

"So, tomorrow?" Those cool green eyes landed on me, and I sighed.

"Sure. I guess we could do with the help."

He cocked his head. "Wow. Just how badly did that suck coming out?"

I snorted. "You have no fucking idea." I eased the *Green Lip* alongside the pier as Fox laughed.

He got to his feet to help Patrick berth, slapping me on the shoulder none too softly as he passed—enough to leave a sizzle on my skin.

Cheeky sod.

I left the two of them to unpack and secure the boat while I wrote up my notes and then headed for Martha's office. My stomach dipped when I saw my mother there as well.

"Hey, Mum."

She glanced up from making heart eyes at Martha and smiled. "Hey, you. I see you had help today." She nodded to where Fox shouldered a coil of rope across to the store shed, all muscle and acres of sun-kissed skin.

I dragged my eyes away and planted a kiss on her cheek. "Yeah. We got done early."

"That was nice of him." She sent me a wry smile.

"Don't." I eyeballed her.

"Don't what?"

"Don't play your games."

"I have no idea what you're talking about." She blinked all wide-eyed and innocent, and Martha elbowed her pointedly. "All right, all right," Cora grimaced. "I apologise for not telling you about Fox staying." Another elbow and an even bigger grimace. "I should've asked first."

I glanced at Martha whose gaze darted away, the sneaky minx, then back to my mother. "Thank you. Maybe have a little more faith in me next time."

She actually flushed. "I guess I deserved that. But as it turns out, I have another favour to ask."

I rolled my eyes. "Why do I sense I'm going to like this one about as much as the last—hang on." I leaned out the office door as Fox walked past with his bag. "If you wait a minute, I'll give you a lift."

He hesitated. "It's fine, I can walk."

"Now who's being a stubborn arse? Give me five minutes."

He shrugged and veered toward my Hilux.

I stepped back inside. "So, what's this new favour, then?"

Mum's gaze flitted uncertainly to Martha, then back, and I

frowned. My mother was nothing if not forthright. It didn't bode well.

"You're a hand down since Sheena left for Auckland, right?"

I narrowed my gaze. "You know I am. It hasn't exactly been easy to find a replacement at this time of year, not at our rates."

"Well, I might have someone for you."

My gaze narrowed. "I'm gonna take a stab in the dark and assume this person is one of your pet projects and I'm not gonna like the idea."

She pursed her lips for a second. "Maybe. Probably. It's Kane Martin."

My jaw dropped. "Kane Martin?" I couldn't have been more shocked. "Why the hell does Kane need a job? He runs his dad's farm, doesn't he? That organic place they shifted to."

Her gaze slid over my shoulder. "Not anymore. Besides, farming wasn't something he ever really chose to do, and well, he finally decided to leave."

"Okaaaay? Good for him, but what's that got to do with us?" I stared hard at her. "You do remember he was one of Judah's high school bullies, right? Judah's hardly going to thank you for giving the man a job." I wondered if she knew about the kicking, but that was for Judah to tell, not me.

She nodded. "I know, and I fully intend to talk to your brother, but you need help and Kane needs a job. He's a good worker and he's reliable," she pressed. "He's not that thick-headed teen anymore, far from it, and for the moment this is still my business."

The reminder stung, and for a second, I was so shocked I couldn't get a reply out. Even Martha sat frozen in her seat.

But it was true, after all. Even if we both knew my mother's interest in the farm had to change if it was going to survive. It simply wasn't big enough to support us both. I just had no idea how on earth I was going to buy her out.

"Damn." My mother gave an apologetic wince. "I'm sorry, son.

That was uncalled for. This is your business, maybe even more than it's mine. Doesn't matter whose name is on the piece of paper."

"It's fine." It wasn't, but what could I say? "I'm just not sure that reasoning is gonna matter a scrap to Judah. What the hell is he going to think of me employing his schoolyard bully? Jesus, Mum. We're only just getting things between us back on track. You do realise this could screw everything."

She looked genuinely apologetic, which only increased my frustration. "I don't happen to agree, but I take your point. Regardless of that, Kane needs this job. It's only for a couple of months until he decides his next move. It could be good for everyone. And Kane *was* your friend."

I stared in disbelief. "That was over ten years ago, and he was only in my circle, not exactly a close friend. We've had nothing to do with each other since school. And if I'd known what he did to Judah, I'd have punched his fucking lights out."

Or I hoped I would've. I hadn't exactly been a shining example of brotherly love back then, too busy keeping my distance from my problematic, very gay sibling. An image of Fox sprang to mind, and shame hit like a blow to my chest.

My mother said nothing, just stared at me with that look perfected by mothers over the millennia. The one that came with a fuckton of guilt and the ability to make you feel about ten years old.

"All right, all right," I groaned. "Tell him to come see me at the house at four on Monday. I have to go to Whangarei for supplies, but I'll be back by then."

"I'd kind of told him he'd know something by the end of the weekend."

I stared at her. "Do I have a choice in this or are you just trying to make me feel like I do?"

She said nothing.

"Monday, Mum, that's my final word on it. And I'm not agreeing to *anything* until you okay this with Judah first. I don't even know what we can afford to pay Kane."

Her brow creased and I felt the heat of Martha's gaze. "I wasn't aware we were running that fine." Cora studied me closely.

I shrugged. "We're always a bit thin at this time of year, you know that." I looked to Martha. "What do *you* think about Kane?" I put her on the spot and watched her gaze flick to Cora.

"I agree that it's complicated," she said carefully. "But I was there when your mother bumped into Kane in Terry's store, and I think he's worth giving a chance. But unlike your mother—" Her gaze again flicked to Cora whose cheeks surprisingly pinked. "—I believe *you* need to have the final say, Leroy. You and Judah. And I'll encourage your mother to follow whatever that decision is."

The two women locked eyes for a moment before my mother's shoulders sagged and she turned back to me. "I'll do whatever you both decide."

You could've knocked me flat with a feather. My mother rarely if ever backed down. "Thank you. Get Judah to call me after you've spoken to him. If he says no, I'm not even going to speak with Kane, understand?" We hugged a little stiffly, then I grabbed my bag and headed for my vehicle and the brooding man leaning against the passenger door with his phone in his hand and a frown on his face.

"Get in." I popped the locks and threw my bag in the tray. "I need a beer like fucking yesterday."

CHAPTER FIVE

Leroy

THE CALL CAME LESS THAN THIRTY MINUTES LATER AS I WAS sitting on the toilet. One glance at my phone and my stomach sank. My mother didn't muck around. I leaned sideways against the wall and mentally steeled myself.

"What the actual fuck, Leroy?"

I sighed. "Hello, Judah. Nice to hear from you. You sound so relaxed. The mussel farm is doing just nicely, thank you for asking. How's the honeymoon going?"

Silence bled thick from the other end. "Leroy." Judah practically growled my name.

"Just let him talk, baby." Morgan's softer voice of reason came from somewhere in the background and I could picture his hand on my brother's shoulder or maybe cupping his cheek.

They were nauseatingly tactile, something I tried very hard to ignore. Judah had been dealt a savage blow, but he'd found a new direction and a man who loved him deeply. I was both proud and, of late, increasingly envious. There'd always been a touch of gold to my brother, like a weighted toy that wobbled but always found its way right side up. Not that he didn't work his arse off to make those chances happen, but the kid in me hadn't wanted to see that, and it hadn't helped things between us growing up.

"It wasn't my idea," I reminded him. "And I've told her I won't even consider agreeing unless you're okay with it."

"Okay with it? Okay?" He snorted derisively. "Kane Martin is . . . *was* an arsehole to me, Leroy. You know damn well what he did. Hell, you stood back and watched most of it hap—"

"Judah," Morgan cut his husband off softly, and Judah's sigh fell heavy with the weight of those years of fear behind it.

I said nothing, because Judah was right.

"I'm sorry," he said quietly. "I shouldn't have brought that up again. It's just that sometimes—"

"I know." I swallowed hard. "And I deserve it. I might not have known the details of what they did, but I knew they were hassling you. I should've put a stop to it and I didn't. I'm so fucking sorry for that, and I'll say it as often as I need to, as often as you need to hear it."

He sighed. "Jesus, this mess is so fucked up. And where in the hell are you? You're all . . . echoey."

"I'm sitting on the bloody toilet. You have the worst damn timing."

He snorted. "It's kind of appropriate if you ask me. Just don't fall in. I want the pleasure of shoving your head down it myself when I get home."

"Oh, charming."

He chuckled, a significant improvement on yelling at me. "What the hell is Mum thinking? And FYI, you are so *not* this arrogant arse-hole you make yourself out to be, you know that, right?"

"Keep your voice down. I have a reputation to maintain." I thought of Fox and almost smiled. "Anyway, just say the word and I'll tell Mum, no. Martha's made it clear she'll back me up."

"Really?" The surprise in Judah's voice was unmistakable.

"Yeah." I chuckled. "Shocked me as well. But not as much as Mum agreeing she'd toe the line."

"Holy shit." Judah laughed. "Must be true love."

My chest tightened at the throwaway comment. "You know, I think maybe it is."

We were both silent for a moment as that sank in.

"What do *you* think about Kane?" Judah finally asked. "I'm not exactly on board with the idea, but I'm also hardly objective in the matter."

"And there's no reason you should be. All I know is Mum says he needs a job. That he's left the farm and that he's maybe . . . struggling, whatever that means. But she wasn't any clearer than that."

Judah sighed. "Goddamn, our mother. It's just like her, trying to save the lost bloody sheep. I get why, even if I hate the idea. It's not just Kane she's thinking about. She hopes it will help me . . . move on."

"That's none of her business or her decision to make."

"I know," he said somewhat wistfully. "And thanks for not automatically taking her side."

"I wouldn't do that to you."

Judah went quiet for a moment, and it went unspoken how I'd done exactly that to him in the past. I couldn't have loved him more for not reminding me.

He continued. "Last year Terry told me that Kane wasn't the same guy he'd been at school, and if I'm honest, I guess I felt some of that when he tried to apologise to me. Maybe I should take the higher moral ground."

"There's nothing that says you have to do that," I reminded him. "I don't care whether Kane's had a divine revelation and turned his whole fucking life around, he did what he did to you, and you don't have to make anything easier for him."

"I know," he said flatly. "But I've talked about it with a couple of my dance therapy teachers over the last six months, and the crazy thing is, I'm not angry or fearful about Kane anymore. I don't really feel *anything* about him, or if I do, it's more like pity. Having said that, I don't know if I'm ready to forgive him or if I'll ever give him the satisfaction of hearing those words even if I do get to that point."

"No one says you have to do either."

"Thanks. But maybe Mum does have a point here, and it's just a couple of months. After the high of telling him to fuck off last year, I kind of settled into an emotional stalemate about the whole thing. Jesus, maybe this *is* the next step for me to close that circle for good."

And not for the first time, I thought Judah was by far the better man of the two of us. I'd have struggled to give Kane a second chance had I been in his shoes. "You don't have to do *anything*, Judah. You were pretty angry when you called."

"I was, I *am*. But more about Mum's manipulations, no matter how well-intended they are. She really is a lone wolf." He went quiet, but I could hear him breathing, feel him wrestling with the decision, and I kept silent.

"Okay," he said finally. "*If* I agree to Kane working with you, just for a bit, I want to be really clear about a couple of things."

"I'm listening."

"I don't want to see him or have anything to do with him unless I choose to. He goes to work with you and goes home, that's it. No talking to me, no saying hello, no coming anywhere near the boathouse or the studio, not even a wave my direction unless I do it first. You need to be really clear with him about that. If he's in the office and I come in, he leaves, got it?"

"And I'm with Judah one hundred percent on this, Leroy," Morgan made his feelings clear. "It's the only way this is going to happen, and Cora needs to understand that too. If she so much as tries to initiate *anything* between Kane and Judah whatever her good intentions might be, I'll be paying her a decidedly pissed-off son-in-law visit."

"I absolutely get it," I readily agreed. "And don't worry, that's exactly what I intend to say. By the time you're both home, the rules will be well-established. Hell, Kane might not even make the grade yet."

"Yeah, well, the bar isn't exactly set high. You took me, after all," Judah teased, then added in a softer tone. "I'm trusting you on this, Leroy."

I blew out a sigh. "You do remember our mother, right?"

Judah chuckled. "Love you."

I stumbled as I always did when he said those words, my tongue tangling hopelessly in my mouth like it knew I wasn't worthy of them. "Love you too, bro."

After a few seconds of mutual silence, he hung up.

Family.

One hour and four beers later, I was in my favourite lounger on the deck, gazing at the evening sun reflecting off the smooth skin of water that stretched across the bay and listening to Fox pottering in the kitchen doing God knew what. Whatever it was, it smelled delicious. His deck chair sat next to mine, two empty bottles alongside my four.

We apparently needed something to soak up the alcohol, or so he said. I was pretty sure that was a bad idea. The whole situation was terrifyingly domestic, but with every beer that slid down my throat, it seemed less problematic and that seemed a good enough reason to keep drinking.

The wind had dropped to a whisper and the occasional zing of a mosquito braving the brief calm had necessitated a hasty grab for the repellent, and I was soaking in a veil of insecticidal fumes. I only caught a couple of barefooted steps before a plate of food and a fresh beer appeared in front of me.

I startled, almost sending both flying. "Jesus, warn a guy next time." I scrambled to a sit and took the plate and bottle on offer. "You're ninja quiet." I opened the beer and took a long swallow, aware of his gaze on me and liking it. I glanced up and he quickly looked away which set me to wondering. Did he feel it too?

"I think your hearing's pickled," he remarked, collapsing into his chair, and popping the cap on his bottle.

"Do you ever wear shoes?" I glanced at his feet, tanned and inviting. Why the hell I found it so sexy watching him pad around my house that way, I had no idea, but I did.

"Not if I can help it."

Mack lifted her head from the end of the deck where she was sprawled, soaking up the last of the sun, and gave an interested sniff at our food. Fox had been right. She *was* well behaved. The house was just as I'd left it that morning, and she'd greeted the two of us like we'd been gone six months on an Antarctic expedition while simultaneously managing to convey just how very annoyed she was at being left behind.

"You can bring her tomorrow if you want." The words were out before I could haul them back.

Fox paused with his bottle halfway to his mouth and frowned. "Are you sure? I mean, she'd love it, of course, and she'd be no problem, but you don't have to."

I fired him a look. "I'm well aware I don't have to. Let's just see how she goes. She's . . . cool."

"She is." He relaxed back on the lounger, his beaming smile burning all the way to my balls. "And thank you. Now, let's eat before it gets cold."

I stared at the mound of bubble-n-squeak and let out a hungry groan. Roast potatoes, pumpkin, kumera, lamb, peas, all bound up with our neighbour's free-range eggs. Damn, I was starving. "This looks amazing." I grabbed the fork and tucked in. "Oh. My. God. It's awesome," I said through the first mouthful of food.

"Better than a lamb sandwich?" He gave a crooked smile.

I had to swallow quickly before I spat my mouthful of food out on a laugh. "All right. So, I might have been hungrier than I said last night."

"You were being petulant for the hell of it, admit it." He spoke around a mouthful of potato.

"I wasn't being—" I couldn't help a small smile. "Okay, I was. But that's all you're gonna get." I forked another mound of food into my mouth.

He gave a broad grin and went back to his plate. "Fair enough. I added a ton of garlic and some chilli you had in the fridge, by the way. Figured if you bought the stuff, you must like it. Hope it's not too spicy?"

"Nope. Perfect," I answered, relishing the sizzle on my tongue. "I like it hot." The words were out before I thought about them, and I was pretty sure my ears were glowing. *Whatever.* I took another slug of beer.

A soft snort was the only indication Fox even heard, then we went back to attacking our food like ravenous dogs. It wasn't long before I was scraping my fork over my empty plate to get the last of the crumbs, and once that mission was accomplished, I slid the plate to the deck with a contented groan. "That was amazing, thank you."

"You're welcome." Fox worked on his last few mouthfuls while I finished my beer.

When he was done, I pushed to my feet, collected his empty plate on top of mine, and headed to the kitchen. "Another beer?" I called through the open window.

"Nah, I'll sit on this one." He scooted down in his chair, his singlet riding up to yet again expose that smooth line of skin and smattering of dark hair that dipped into the jeans he'd changed into. He crossed his hands on top of his head, the gold tips of his dark waves like a Klimt painting in the setting sun. But it was the rich pocket of shadowy curls in his underarms that stole all my attention.

Huh. I paused with water running over the plate in my hands. Since when was that shit sexy?

I shook my head, left the plate in the sink, and turned for the fridge. With a fresh beer in hand, I ran the cold glass across my forehead, then popped the cap and took a long swallow. Much better. I made my way back out to the deck and the lengthening shadows stealing across the lawn.

"Thanks for your help today." I slid back onto the lounger as Fox spritzed his feet with repellent.

He looked up with an arched brow and a smile. "Wow, that beer must be stronger than I thought."

"Fuck off," I grumbled. "I know I was a dick. I'm just not used to people offering to do shit for nothing. And we didn't exactly start off on the right foot with you sneaking off this morning."

He huffed. "When have we ever been on the right foot? But I think this time was down to me. I had no idea Cora hadn't asked you—"

"*Asked* me?" I rolled my eyes till they rattled against my spine. "Mum doesn't ask, she simply decides and then waits for everyone else to agree." I slugged back a mouthful of beer.

He frowned and went quiet. "You really don't like me, do you?" He fell back against his cushion and studied me. "Is it because of that argument last year? I know we didn't—"

"No." I looked away, worried he might see exactly how far from the truth that actually was. "Well, maybe a little. I was out of line that day, but it wasn't what you thought, and I didn't appreciate being called on it, even if I deserved it. I had a lot going on."

His gaze remained steady. "Okaaaay, I'll buy that. So what am I missing?"

Nope, not going there. Instead, I said, "Judah and I were in each other's faces back then, and things were . . . difficult. Then Mum and Martha came out, which kind of floored me, and I was worried about the business as well. I think you and our . . . misunderstanding were simply a convenient target."

We locked eyes for a minute until finally he nodded. "Well, I wasn't in such a great space either, so maybe it was all just a perfect storm."

"Maybe." I finished my beer and turned slightly on my hip so I could better see those captivating green eyes washed with gold in the dipping sun. "The *mothers* did mention something about a bad break-up."

He rolled those eyes, breaking the spell. "Oh, they did, did they? Personally, I like the *gruesome twosome*."

I snorted.

"And break-up makes it sound like we were a couple of teenagers. Van and I were married. When you and I met last year, we'd separated, but I guess I was still coming to terms with it. The divorce is set to go through soon, as long as I can get Van to agree on a few final points."

"Married?" I didn't even try to hide my surprise. "I'd assumed a . . . boyfriend the way Mum and Martha talked. If anyone mentioned you were married, it didn't register. I can't believe I missed that."

He shrugged. "You were still at uni when Van and I married. It was all very low-key, no big wedding, just signed papers. And let's face it, up until last year, I'd only visited a couple of times and you and I hardly met. No reason you should pay attention to something like that. Mum never really liked Van and so we never came to stay as a couple. She's still pretty goddamn angry about the whole thing. She can barely say his name."

Fox had been married? I still couldn't process it. Not to mention I felt like an arse for the way I'd brushed it off with my mother. "How long were you two together?"

"Five years. Until the day I came back from a fishing trip to find he'd moved his stuff out of our place and in with the owner of another commercial boat. Ewan, who also happened to be a friend and business competitor. They'd apparently been fucking for a year, a not so minor detail I didn't discover until much later." He raised his bottle in salute and downed the last of it.

"Holy shit. You had no idea?"

He shook his head, a flush sweeping his cheeks. "I should've, right? Stewart Island is a tiny place, a few hundred people. Nowhere to hide, really. But no, I had my head well and truly buried up my arse. Sure, we'd had our moments, but every marriage does. I thought we were solid in the parts that really mattered. I thought he was the one. Turns out, not so much."

"Wow. I guess I can understand wanting a fresh start in a new place, then."

He stared at me for a minute. "Funny thing is, I didn't. I was happy to stay and tough it out. I love it down there. We had good friends, and I had an amazing crew—none of them local, but all good southern boys who lived part-time on the island so they could work my boat. I appreciated every single one of them and told them as often as I could. We were a family, albeit a rowdy, disreputable one. But we had each other's backs. And if I had to tear one of them a new arsehole every now and then, we still got along afterward. I made sure of it." He ran a weary hand down his face. "I miss them like hell."

My heart went out to him. I had the feeling he was a great skipper, a natural leader. Had I ever let Patrick or anyone who'd worked for me really know just how much I appreciated them? The answer was uncomfortable. I needed to do better.

"At first, I thought it would be okay, that things would settle," he said. "It's my home, always will be, and having to leave cut me up like you wouldn't believe. I'd go back at the drop of a hat if it weren't for all the pitying stares and the whispers and the not-so-subtle comments. Maybe one day I can."

I frowned. "But he cheated on you. Wouldn't people be on your side?"

He snorted. "You'd think, right? But Van's a local boy, and he started bullshitting about how I'd been fucking one of my crew and practically pushed him into Ewan's arms. After that, things went from being awkward to me becoming the local fucking pariah. Van even half-convinced Ewan who I think was just happy to shrug some guilt off. It wasn't true, of course, but Van's local and I'm not. And down there, local trumps everything." A flash of pain passed behind his eyes and I wanted to reach for him.

I sat on my hands. "What a bastard. How the hell did you end up with someone like that?"

He looked up, surprise in his eyes. "When Van and I first met, he'd just returned to the island following a few years overseas, and he was this sweet, slightly airheaded but funny and sexy young man. Worldly, attentive, and seemingly smitten with me. It was flattering. I can't lie. Anyway, we were married three months later."

"Three mon—"

"Believe me, I know." He threw up a hand. "Don't even say it. But he didn't change overnight. Those early years were good. I still don't know when everything went wrong. I think that's what's shaken me the most. How do I trust anyone again? For that matter, how do I trust myself?"

I snorted. "Don't look at me. I'm the last person to ask about relationships. But you miss it down there, I can tell."

"Like my arm's been cut off, but I needed to escape, at least for a bit. The place is a tiny pressure cooker of gossip. Things got uncomfortable really quick. Still, I never dreamed Van would go for the *Blue Swell* itself in addition to a payout from the business. I'd had it years before I met him, and it was my whole damn livelihood. I used the small inheritance I'd gotten from Dad along with a huge loan from the bank. I'd been first mate on a similar boat for a while by then, and I was so damn excited to have my own. But when Tinny said Van had a legitimate claim, I simply couldn't afford to buy him out and so I sold it."

My mouth dropped open in utter disbelief. "What? But . . . why, that little . . . it was him who . . . fucking hell." My stomach dropped. "Couldn't you fight it?"

He gave a half-shrug. "I could've tried, but it's unlikely I'd win. Legally, he's fully entitled to half the entire business, and fighting him on it would tie up the divorce settlement for months, if not years. I just wanted to be free of him. In fact, that's been my driver the whole way through, much to my mother's disgust. She thinks I've been too soft."

Damn right. "Have you?"

He shrugged. "Maybe. But I couldn't see me living on the island the way things were, and I'd been having unsettling thoughts about the whole fishing industry even before Van fucked off. I thought maybe it was a sign." He quirked his lips. "Anyway, with Van's legal agreement, I found a buyer and put the meagre profit from the sale with the lawyer. Bean, my first mate on the *Blue Swell*, actually joined forces with his parents and bought me out. It meant the crew stuck together and that helped. They keep in touch, although the hours of work don't make it easy. But the sale freed me to come up here and try something new, so there's that."

He was putting a brave face on it, but I felt gutted for him. I couldn't imagine losing the farm to a relationship gone wrong and being forced to sell. "Did you two have a house together?"

He nodded. "Yes, but I *did* buy him out of that. We've signed all the papers, so that's done. I'll rent it as soon as I decide what I'm doing. Or maybe I'll move back down when things settle. Who knows? I just wanted to keep a foot on the island." He looked to the deepening shadows on the lawn, seemingly lost in thought.

I gave him a moment before asking, "So, what will you do?"

"I'm not sure yet. Once the settlement goes through, I'll have some cash to invest in something new. I just don't know what. I'd be shit working for someone else, so it would have to be my own business again or at least be working toward it even if I have to get an interim job. But I've got enough money to see me through for a little bit while I think."

"Still, it has to be tough."

He shrugged. "I'm trying to see it as a chance to do something different, not just fall into the first thing that happens along. An acquaintance of mine, Jeff, runs a game fishing charter in the Bay of Islands not far from here. He used to run a boat down south for his dad, but he was always complaining about the weather and got out of there as soon as he could."

"What's the business called?"

"Deep Charters."

I nodded. "Yeah, I know the name. Pretty pricey if I remember."

He shrugged. "Anyway, he's looking to take on a partner and asked if I was interested. Commercial fishing isn't a job to grow old in, and it was tough being gone for weeks at a time. I keep wondering if I'd had regular hours, maybe things would've been different for Van and me. Maybe we could've saved what we had."

"Fuck that," I barked angrily, and his head snapped up. "Sorry. I just mean that the guy cheated on you. Maybe I'm too black and white, but I think you either have that in you or you don't. Then he compounded it with a horrendous lie to save his own skin. He stripped you of a home and a fucking living while he was at it. I don't see why you should offer him even the tiniest benefit of the doubt. If you're not feeling it anymore with someone, then I'd think the right thing is to talk about it and get things squared away before jumping into someone else's bed. There's no fucking excuse for that."

He stared at me wide-eyed, and I swallowed hard. "Sorry. I know practically nothing about either of you. Not to mention I haven't ever had a long-term relationship, and I mean *ever*. I should just keep my mouth shut. Ignore me."

He smiled, reached across and squeezed my hand briefly before letting it go. I almost grabbed it back without thinking but stopped myself in time.

"No, thank *you*," he said softly. "For a guy who's never had a long-term relationship, you're surprisingly perceptive. And you're right, but it's hard to see all that when you're in the middle of it. All I felt for a long time was cold anger. Now I feel . . . numb, I guess, and relieved. I consider that an improvement."

Things fell quiet between us and I mulled over his words, feeling even more of a dick for the shitty reception I'd given him two days before. But there was also a weird outrage simmering in my chest on his behalf.

I didn't know Fox well, but no one deserved to be treated like that, and I wanted five minutes alone with this Van guy to press the point home. I also hadn't missed the irony that a large part of my pissiness toward him last year had centred around my own concern that he might've had designs on the mussel farm. I couldn't have been more wrong about the man.

"Anyway, enough about me. What about you?" He faced me. "Any girl in the picture in *any* capacity?"

Fox

"Nope." Leroy's gaze lifted to the thick blue-black sky resting over the homestead. "Relationship avoidant, remember?"

"I remember." The sparse dusting of stars shed just enough light to drink in the sexy stubble that lined his jaw, which had the gravitational pull of a black hole as far as my dick was concerned. I spent an embarrassing amount of time imagining the scrape of it against my throat, my chest, between my—*enough*.

"I need plenty of space and women are rarely okay with that," Leroy explained. "You sure aren't missing anything there, let me tell you." He turned and flashed a devastating smile that sent my stomach scrambling.

The man was a conundrum. Pissy, I was well acquainted with. But this coy, grinning version was seriously fucking addictive.

He continued. "Having said that, I'm not entirely without experience. I *have* actually dated as long as six months, so I guess you'd call those girlfriends. But they all eventually came to their senses and dumped me. No foul. I'm one hundred percent positive I deserved it. But it means I prefer to keep things . . . simple."

No need to clarify. "Well, I'm hardly the poster boy for a successful relationship myself," I said with a wry grin. "I think I'll try it your way for a while." I raised my bottle and clinked it with his. "Cheers to being happily single."

"Yeah, happily single," he said softly, pausing for a second or two before finishing his beer in one long guzzle.

The conversation lulled and we slid down in our respective

loungers and stared aloft. The stars vied for my attention with a dozen uncomfortable feelings that circled my gut. The last thing I needed was a little crush on straight Mr Grumpy Pants. Fucking hell. Someone needed to take my taste in men and bin it, pronto, before it got me into another shitload of trouble I could do without.

But that thick, choppy dark hair and tight muscular build had my fingers itching to touch. And when he dropped that pissy, guarded expression he wore like armour and those bright blue eyes came alive with a promise of so very much more, I found myself enthralled.

I sneaked another glance. Leroy was maybe not as pretty as Judah, but he was equally captivating in an entirely different way. I was usually drawn to arty types, full of sass, lean, waifish, mouthy, and excruciatingly high maintenance. Cue Van Davies. Intense, ruggedly handsome, buttoned-up, broody chip-on-my-shoulder types didn't usually get the time of day from me, until this one. Go figure.

The upside? The annoying attraction was somewhat of a relief after a long dry spell of feeling nothing much of anything. When Van moved out, my dick had packed its dusty bags and gone with him. Not that we'd exactly been setting our bed on fire for a long while before that. He'd clearly got what he needed in Ewan's bed, and sex with me was just going through the motions. It still fucking hurt in that humiliating way the cheated party always feels.

I kept my sigh quiet. I'd said altogether too much about the sad state of my love life as it was while Leroy had said pretty much zip.

I rolled to one hip and faced him again. "Do you have a type?"

His forehead drew down in a deep frown. "In women?"

"No, in fucking fish. Yes, in women."

His laugh broke between us like a warm swell, and I liked the clear sound of it far more than I should. Grumpy Leroy was a blast, but this soft, open version was truly something special, and I reminded myself it was the beer that was responsible, not me.

"I'm not sure I do." He swung his legs over the side and pushed to a sit, his expression softly lit from the kitchen. "Quiet?" His eyes twinkled. "Yes, that would definitely be high on the list. And also . . .

curvy, or strong. I like to feel I actually have something in my arms, not just the sniff of a breeze. Stick figures are definitely not my thing."

My turn to laugh and to wonder what it would be like to hold Leroy Madden for a minute, or a year. To wrap my arms around all those prickles until they lay flat and let me in. That would be something.

His cheeks pinked. "Maybe someone who has their own thing going on. Independent, I guess. I don't want to be someone's *every-thing* if you get what I mean? I couldn't stand the pressure and I seriously doubt I'd be able to deliver. The thought of being responsible for someone else's happiness freaks me the hell out. I figure everyone has to sort that one out for themselves."

His gaze slid to Mack who'd wandered over to rest her head on his knee. He idly stroked the wrinkles on her brow. "I don't think it's fair to expect someone else to do that *for* you. Watching Judah taught me that much."

Jesus. The simple words hit like a punch to my chest, and I thought of my first conversation with Van after he'd moved out. He'd been so fucking angry.

"What did you expect me to do? Hang around and wait for you? You're never here, Fox. And when you are, you're always so damn tired. I was bored out of my tree. Bored with our life. With being stuck on this fucking island alone half the time. Bored . . . with us. There was no fun anymore. At least Ewan runs his boat and crew from a desk. He doesn't go out himself. He has time for me. We actually go out. He takes me to the mainland, to clubs. We have friends over. But that boat of yours was way more important than I ever was."

Which was a lie. Yes, I'd loved my boat *and* my job, but I'd loved Van too. And I didn't have the money that Ewan had. He'd been left his boat by his father. Van had always known it would be years before I'd get my business to that level. I thought he'd been okay with that. Not so much as it turned out.

I swallowed hard. "I think that's exactly what Van expected. For me to make him happy. And I couldn't do it. Or rather, maybe we had different ideas about what that meant. For me it was sharing a life together, talking, planning, just being with each other, even if my job took me away for a few days at a time. Looking back, I can see that he needed my life to centre around him and what he wanted. He was never comfortable being on his own. Why hadn't I seen that?"

Leroy groaned. "See, that's why I don't do the whole long-term thing." He swayed to his feet and reached a hand toward me. "It's too fucking complicated. Who writes the rules on that shit anyway?"

"Fucked if I know." I clasped his hand and let him pull me up, the firm warmth of his grip shooting low into my belly. His gaze caught on mine for a blistering second and then he frowned and dropped my hand like he'd been burned. "Let's clean up." He headed inside, leaving an icy wind in his wake.

What the hell just happened?

I frowned and patted my thigh for Mack to follow. She slipped past my leg and sent the empty bottles flying. I grumbled and bent down to pick them up. When I straightened again, Leroy was watching me through the kitchen window, that frown still in place. We locked eyes for another strange, long second before his gaze dropped to the sink and the moment was broken.

But that look. I shook my head, not willing to even go there, and joined him in the kitchen. He was practically scrubbing the glaze off the plates like he didn't have a dishwasher two steps to the side. I wasn't going to ask. He had *stay the hell away* written in neon fucking capitals on his back, tension rolling off his body in palpable waves.

Mack positioned herself under the dining table, her curious gaze darting between us. I shrugged her way. '*Your guess is as good as mine.*' I'd swear she nodded.

Ignoring the glacial chill that had settled between us, I grabbed a tea towel from the pantry and waited at Leroy's side. The charming man I'd been talking with on the deck had well and truly left the building. We did the dishes in silence, moving around each other in a domestic dance that was achingly familiar to my foolish, wounded heart. It was strange the things you missed. I'd have thought sex might've come high on the list before Van left, but instead I missed doing the fucking dishes, go figure.

Leroy cleaned the countertops while I made our lunch for the next day—colossal ham salad sandwiches and crisp apples from my excursion to Terry's store the day before. Leroy's brow creased when he laid eyes on the food separated into two distinct piles.

"You don't need to—"

"Shut up. I'm doing it."

It was like the last day hadn't even happened. Out on the deck, I'd thought we were finally getting somewhere, but that had all disappeared in a puff of awkward smoke the second we'd clasped hands. Had he seen something in my face? Had I let my attraction to him show, dammit? Whatever it was, Leroy had closed up like a fucking clam, the space between us chilly and growing colder by the minute.

With our sandwiches made and boxed in the fridge, I turned to the sink for a damp cloth to clean the last crumbs and caught an unsuspecting Leroy as he turned at the same time to hang the fry pan on the pot rack suspended from the ceiling. We collided, my front into his side, and I automatically grabbed his hip to steady myself.

"Shit!" He leapt back, almost arseing out on a puddle of water on the floor before saving himself at the last minute, spinning to grab the edge of the countertop to steady himself.

But the sudden turn had caught me off balance and I practically fell against his back, my groin hard on his hip, my dick a little too happy to get acquainted, though I doubt he would've noticed it.

He grunted and froze, his entire body coiled and tense like he might just explode. "Get. Off. Me," he ground out.

"Fuck, I'm sorry." I pushed away, putting some space between us. Maybe it had been more obvious than I thought.

He didn't move.

"Look, I didn't mean to . . ." *Fuck. Fuck. Fuck.*

"It's fine." Leroy pulled the plug in the sink and leaned against the counter, staring at the dirty water circling the drain like he wished he could join it. "I'll finish here."

The message was pretty clear. *Leave me alone.* Twice we'd touched and both times he'd reacted, well, less than happy about it. And yet on the deck he'd been relaxed enough talking about Van, so what the hell?

"Is there a problem, Leroy?" I pressed.

He shrugged. "I said it's fine. It was my fault. I'll finish up. You go to bed."

It seemed an order more than a suggestion and I sighed. "Sure. Fine. I'll see you in the morning."

"Yeah." Still with his back to me, he said, "And, well, Jon wanted me to ask you to rugby training tomorrow, if you were interested."

He'd made a point of letting me know it had been Jon who'd invited me, not him. *Well, fuck it.* "I haven't played since school, but sure, I'll come take a look."

"Great." He sounded anything but happy about it.

"So, is it still okay to take Mack with us tomorrow?" I ventured.

Leroy glanced to where Mack lay, and his expression softened. "Yeah, fine."

I waited for more, but that was it. The man was nothing if not mule-headed. "Right, I'll get out of your hair, then." I called Mack to heel and headed for the bedroom, quietly fuming. Crush or not, there was no way I was staying with a guy who had issues about being touched by a gay man. I had enough going on without needing to deal with Leroy Madden's emotional baggage.

I added finding somewhere new to live to my weekend to-do list.

I threw myself on my bed to calm down and scrolled through my phone. There was a missed call from Bean, and I called him back.

"Hey, stranger." Bean's familiar voice boomed down the line and a wave of longing rolled through me.

A tall, thin, beanpole of a man, hence the nickname, Bean had a rumbling baritone that wouldn't have been out of place in an opera, but which in no way fitted his appearance. He'd been my number one right-hand man and there wasn't anything I wouldn't trust him with, on or off the boat. When Van had fucked me over, Bean had assumed the role of skipper on the next two-week trip and sent me off to Tinny's to lick my wounds, and I loved him like a brother. Bean meant home, the ocean, a life I'd never have again.

"Hey, you." After the fucked-up evening I'd had, I fought to keep the tremor from my voice. "Did you sink that boat of mine yet?"

He laughed and the phone almost shook in my hand. "You wish. Nah. Just thought I'd touch base before we head off tomorrow. You settled in?"

How the fuck to answer that? "I'll get there. Just feels a bit strange at the moment. Cora's son hasn't exactly been . . . welcoming."

"Fucker. You need me to come up there next layover and teach him a lesson?"

I tried to picture Leroy and Bean at each other's throats and decided I wouldn't want to bet on the outcome. Wolverine meets The Thin Man. It made me smile. And I said, "Nah, to be fair, no one warned him I was staying in his house, and the guy is a little prickly at best. Suffice to say I'll be looking for other accommodation."

Bean huffed. "Sounds like an idiot if you ask me, but no one's asking. Anyway, just thought I'd let you know, Laurie Smithson's looking for a new skipper to run his boat out of Christchurch, and I told him I'd pass it on. It wouldn't start for three months, so you've time to think, but it might be a good option if you need something."

It would, and my mind immediately started planning how I could work it. The thought of getting back on the ocean kindled that deep yearning in my belly. A fuckton better than staying where I wasn't wanted and twiddling my thumbs. But then I thought about Mum and all the other reasons I'd come up this way—to be closer to family, to try something different, and doubt crept in.

Bean continued. "I was thinking it could be a paycheque without all the hassle, you know? Maybe a good fit for now. Anyway, if you're interested, I'd get in touch. He said you'd be top of his list. You must miss being out like crazy. And man, you never let on just how much bullshit paperwork was involved with owning your own boat."

I laughed. "If I did, you'd never have bought it."

"Damn right." He went quiet for a minute. "And, ah, Van's been bitching around town about you taking Mack without telling him. Just thought you should know."

Jesus Christ. Anger rolled in my belly. Van was as good a place as any to hang my frustrations. "Yeah, he called. Any clue what's behind that bullshit because he's not fucking getting her?"

"No idea. Ewan's been chatting in the pub about some new business thing Van's getting into, but I'm not sure what that's got to do with Mack."

"For fuck's sake. Van couldn't run a damn business if it was given to him free. The man thinks waking up at ten with a coffee brought in to him in bed is an early start."

Bean snorted. "Truth. Anyway, just keeping your sorry arse up to date on the gossip. We miss you, man. I mean, I love having the boat and all, but we were a good team, right?"

My heart lurched in my throat. "A fucking great team, Bean. But it's yours now and you're gonna ace this. You were more than ready for your own boat. Say hi to everyone for me."

"Will do. And come visit soon. Don't make me come up there and get you. Or on second thought, maybe I will. Knock that Leroy guy's head into shape."

I laughed. "I might just take you up on that."

CHAPTER SIX

Leroy

I STOLE A SIDEWAYS GLANCE TO WHERE FOX LOUNGED IN THE passenger seat of my Hilux, his interested gaze soaking up the countryside. The worst of the Monday morning traffic was behind us and the driving was easy, not that you'd know it by my white-knuckled grip on the steering wheel.

Sister Sledge streamed through the speakers, Fox's fingers tapping away on one thickly muscled thigh wrapped in tight stonewashed denim. A fashionable rip mocked me from just above the knee, revealing the faintest glimpse of tanned skin and short dark hair, not that I was looking.

Yeah, right. I was soaking that shit up like sugar in hot coffee.

The universe was definitely fucking with me. Well, that and my mother who'd arrived for Sunday lunch with a surprisingly edible peach cobbler and what she called the 'best idea ever' for me to give Fox a lift into Whangarei the next day since I was already going. He wanted to check out some boats, but his car was still waiting on parts.

Fucking wonderful. Why he couldn't wait for his own vehicle to be fixed wasn't a question I was prepared to ask based on my mother's I-dare-you look. I'd caved and agreed.

I could've killed her. And by the constipated look on Fox's face at her suggestion, I was pretty sure he felt the same. It had been a long, long weekend and entirely my own damn fault. Other than forced interaction at work, rugby training, and Sunday lunch, I'd avoided Fox at all costs, and he'd been good enough to play along and pretend he hadn't noticed, other than a notable drop in temperature whenever he looked my way. I could hardly blame him for that. If only he knew that my epic arseholery stemmed from lust and not disgust.

And the Academy Award for epically fucking yourself goes to . . . yeah. Enough said.

Note to self: don't get tipsy around the guy. Without the benefit of way too many beers, we wouldn't have talked and got all chummy on the deck, and I wouldn't have realised that I maybe, *actually* liked the bastard, not just wanted to kiss him, or touch him, or have him touch me, or . . . *goddammit,* wait for the drum roll—fuck me.

I swallowed hard. Me fucking him would, of course, be marginally more acceptable to my brain, but who was I kidding? I'd spent the entire weekend thinking, fantasising, googling, watching, and yep, definitely him fucking me. Good God, the sooner he was out of my house the better. Still, it sounded like it wouldn't take much to get him to shift back down south, so I could only hope.

"You okay, Leroy?"

My gaze jerked his way. "Fine. I'm absolutely fine," I lied, because no, I didn't want to go there, or talk about it, or think about it, or do anything other than bury it as unsuccessfully as I'd done for the last five days, make that a year—my, doesn't time fly—because I'm chickenshit as all hell and my life is a fucking shitshow of irony.

Why now?

Why him?

Why . . . *this?*

Bisexual. I'd even practised saying it in front of the mirror, barely able to spit the word out as it sat huge and sour on my tongue. It wasn't that I hated the man-on-man part, because I was clearly on board with that in so very many, many Fox-shaped, lickable ways. It was more that the admission held an extremely unflattering mirror up to the jerk hypocrite that I'd been, and very likely still was, my entire life.

Whoever said sexuality was a choice, I needed that fucker's address and a suitably sized cactus to shove where the sun don't shine.

My head had been buried so far in the sand for so long that I had grit coming out my arse, and that shit had to stop. After my appalling behaviour in the kitchen, I'd sulked and pondered long and hard over the weekend and gotten more than my money's worth from my broadband provider. It all came with an uncomfortable realisation. The infatuation I had with Fox wasn't going anywhere, and that meant either making myself and everyone around me miserable or pulling it into the light and stop running. How had I completely missed this rather critical aspect of my nature?

And then it occurred to me, maybe I hadn't. I had the pieces, but nothing or no one had caused them to fall into place, until Fox.

I'd always noticed when a guy caught Judah's eye, always tried to see what he saw in them, and yeah, maybe that hadn't been as difficult as it should've been—the cut of a jaw, lay of a hip, swell of a rump. I'd appreciated, but because I hadn't lusted, I'd dismissed it as curiosity. And the fact I liked women, *wanted* women, made that dismissal easy. Not to mention I was all too aware of the way some of my schoolmates and others spoke about and treated Judah. Why would I risk a question that took me there?

Hell-bent on keeping well out of Fox's way, I'd worked out my frustrations in the side garden of the house, bewildered and shamed when Fox wordlessly produced a sandwich and coffee for my lunch. Then the bastard found another garden fork and got stuck into the pots on the covered veranda and my disgrace was complete. His careful distance and ongoing silence paid homage to the unspoken demilitarised zone that existed between us, and I couldn't find a way to bridge that without blurting the entire sorry story.

We were like toddlers in parallel play.

I'd gone so far as to dial Judah's number to ask his advice before cancelling and throwing my phone on the freshly clipped lawn and stalking away. I wasn't about to fuck up his honeymoon with my personal sexual identity crisis. Besides, what the hell was I going to say? *'Sorry little bro for pissing on you about your clear and present gayness for the last twenty-something years, but guess what? Surprii-iiiiise?'*

Yeah. Like that would go down well.

'Oh, and Mum, I know I was a bit of a jerk when you and Martha got together last year, but all is forgiven, right? And by the way, Martha, I want to fuck your son, so yeah, there's that.'

Jesus Christ.

I'd hoped the trip to pick up farm supplies would give a much-needed break from the cause of all these ground-shifting events. The man who'd consumed nearly every waking thought in my head over the interminable weekend and a fair few jerk-off sessions in the shower as well.

Not to mention said distraction had jogged to Saturday rugby training after refusing my clipped offer of a ride and arrived at the grounds looking hot and bothered, sweaty locks of hair plastered to his forehead, and so fucking tempting I almost choked on my mouth guard and Jon had needed to slap me on the back and make me sit down.

I'd spent the rest of training doing my best Houdini impersonation, avoiding tackling, or *being* tackled by Fox, or laying hands on him in any way at all. Which only meant I'd sucked big time on the field and everyone looked at me like I'd lost my fucking mind. If only they knew.

Fox, the bastard, remained cool as a cucumber and played pretty damn well for a guy who hadn't tied on a pair of boots since high school. But then, of course he bloody did. That's apparently how my life rolled at the moment. Coach thought Fox was the bee's knees and just what we needed and promptly offered him a position on the team, *my* team. Fox quickly agreed and then pointedly turned down my repeated offer of a ride home while everyone glanced between us with a barely disguised 'what the hell is up with you two' look.

Fuck. My. Life.

So yeah, the last thing I needed was yet *another* day in Fox's company, especially one with little more than a handbrake and a thin sheet of ice between us. Barring the training chess game antics, I hadn't been this physically close to Fox since the infamous incident in the kitchen when I'd popped an inconvenient boner simply because the guy stumbled into me. Oh, I hadn't mentioned that? How remiss.

Shoving my groin up against the cupboard had hidden the traitorous little shit, but I'd been mortified. I had an embarrassing history of usually needing at least a minute or two to get fully on board even with a woman ripe and ready under me. And yet Fox stumbles into me, and whoops, I'm primed to go. Which only went to prove how royally fucked I was. Even taking his hand to help him up from the lounger had sent butterflies zinging through me.

But two days of avoiding his spectacular arse, keeping half a boat length or a large empty room between us, and taking my dinner to the study each night on the pretext of working had accomplished zip.

I glanced again at those thick thighs and barely suppressed a second groan.

"Do you want me to switch stations?"

"What?" I blinked, confused.

"The music." Fox indicated to the radio. "Is it bugging you?"

"Oh. No." My cheeks burned. "It's fine."

He snorted and shook his head. "Of course it is. Everything is *fine*, isn't it Leroy? You're *fine*. I'm *fine*. The music is *fine*. The whole damn world is *fine*. But especially this fucked-up thing between us is . . . *fine*. God help me if those words come out of your mouth one more time, Leroy Madden, I'm not gonna be responsible for my actions."

I tried to ignore just how much I liked the sound of my name on his lips and focused instead on how I needed to put a lid on this. The idea of being bi might be slowly worming its way to acceptance somewhere in my brain, but Fox as a suitable subject for my first man crush was definitely not.

"What would you rather I said?"

"The truth would be a good start," he answered, turning on his hip to face me.

"About what?" I rolled my lying liar eyes. "I have zero idea what you're talking about." My pulse beat a wild rhythm in my throat, and I pulled out to pass a car. We weren't far from Whangarei, and I couldn't get there fast enough.

"About whatever the hell happened on Friday night," he pressed. "Whatever I did to turn what I thought was an enjoyable evening into a freeze-out, because against all odds, I *was* actually having a good time and I thought you were too. We were getting to know each other and, I thought, *maybe* putting last year behind us. Then we accidentally trip into each other, and you act like I passed on bubonic plague. Suddenly I'm persona non grata. Again. Does it really repulse you that much to be touched by a gay man? I have to say I'm surprised considering your brother—"

"What?" My gaze jerked to his. "No . . . I'm not . . . it wasn't that . . . I just . . . shit." I turned my gaze frontwards before I got us both killed.

His eyes burned holes in the side of my head. "Whatever. But just to be clear, let me allay any concerns you might have," he said flatly. "You don't interest me in that way, Leroy. Never have, never will. So you can just calm the fuck down."

I kept my eyes on the road and the rural landscape as his words sat sour in my belly. A checkerboard of neat farms flashed past sprinkled with the occasional run of hills planted in dense forestry. The remaining patches of lavish sub-tropical bush were held in check with seven-wire fences, like string around an exploding green bouquet, and herds of contented dairy cows, some sheltering under towering macrocarpa trees, grazed lazily on lush grass.

Everything was green as green, as far as the eye could see. Everything except the aching pit of black in my chest. *You don't interest me. You never have.*

It should've been good news, exactly what I needed to hear to shake this ridiculous fantasy playing out in my head.

But it didn't feel that way.

Silence filled the void between us while I scrambled for a reply. I'd been an idiot. Angsting over Fox and my attraction to him like a pathetic teenager. Worried about what giving in to it might mean, as if Fox was just hanging around waiting for me to jump up and tell him I wasn't straight. Hiding away like the slightest whiff of my confusion and he might just whisk me off to bed. Almost confessing to Judah, for Pete's sake.

And all the while Fox wasn't even fucking interested.

Shocker.

Of course the guy wasn't interested. Fox was a catch in anyone's book. Driven, sweet, experienced, and hot as hell—I let myself admit it. I, on the other hand, was a confused mess, sexually dull, terminally cranky, and with a business barely in the black.

A real fucking catch.

I'd been right to sit on my hands and do nothing.

Fox sighed and looked away, apparently giving up on getting an answer. Meanwhile, I focused on the heavy curtain of grey clouds gathered over the hills behind Whangarei and ran his words through my brain once again.

Not interested. It stung, but at the same time, in an odd way, he suddenly became safe to talk to.

"It wasn't you," I said quietly.

I felt the heat of his gaze as he turned, but he said nothing.

"What I mean is, it wasn't because you're gay." Kind of the truth. "I've had a lot on my mind, and you undeservedly copped the brunt of it." Definitely true. "I'm not good company at the best of times, as you've no doubt gathered. But you weren't wrong. Friday night *was* . . . nice."

He snorted. "I'll take that as high praise from you." But he looked sceptical. "So what happened? What changed to turn our *nice* evening into a freeze-out?"

I took a deep breath and picked the least explosive explanation I could muster without actually lying. "It was nothing *you* did." Kind of true. "I acted like a dick and I apologise. The mussel farm is . . . struggling. Nothing new there." I indicated and turned toward Whangarei harbour and the supply store. "It does okay, it's just not big enough to sustain both Mum and I long-term without major investment, which I don't have the money for. We need to expand or diversify into something like scallops or crayfish or live exports or value-added products."

He nodded. "I think diversification or value-added is key with a smaller farm of any description."

I knew he'd get it. "But it all costs. In Dad's day the business was much more lucrative. He had one of the first farms, and we have a pristine product from some of the cleanest waters in the world. But there's a lot more competition now—huge farms, big mechanisation, and tighter regulations. It only takes the slightest change in rainfall or soil runoff to shut us down for days or weeks at a time. Plus, Dad used to harvest on his own. But with tighter deadlines, equipment outlays, and more harvesting across the year to provide different forms of the product, we have to use contractors, which reduces our profit again."

"You and your mother are partners, right?"

"We work that way, but legally it's actually still in her name." I stopped for a red light and glanced over. Fox wore a thoughtful expression, the wheels in his business brain clicking over.

"That's damn difficult if you want to diversify," he finally said. "Not having the full authority you need to deal with suppliers, contractors, and banks if you wanted a loan. Does Cora know the bottom line? She doesn't work hands-on anymore, right?"

"Right. She knows we need to do *something*. Martha deals with the everyday accounts, but no one sees the whole picture except me, and Mum if we talk about it, which we haven't since she sold Morgan and Judah their land."

He nodded. "Have you thought about buying Cora out?"

"Of course I have, but I can't afford to. Between the mussel farm *and* the wharf and house, it's a huge outlay."

"How much land does the house have?"

"About three hectares after she sold that small block to Judah and Morgan last year. There's about a hectare in front, down to the bay, and then two more up behind. Most of that is scrub and bush along the headland, no real income potential."

"Two hectares is still a lot. Do you need it all?"

"I . . ." I hesitated. "I'm not sure what you mean?"

He shrugged. "Just that it's a lot of money to have sitting in land that neither of you are using."

"I guess. But it's a big part of this place."

He simply nodded, but I wondered what was going through his head. "Anyway, the farm isn't the only issue. I still have a student loan from uni, so . . ."

He cocked his head. "What did you study?"

The traffic light changed, and I was happy to duck those perceptive green eyes as we set off again. "Veterinary medicine."

His eyes popped. "Really? I would never have guessed that."

"Yeah, but I didn't finish. Dad died in my fourth year and I came home to run the farm. And should I be offended by your obvious surprise?"

"No, not at all. It just wasn't something I saw you doing. I don't even know why. Maybe because you seem so at home working in the sea," he said softly. "Do you regret having to leave?"

The port came into view at the bottom of the hill, and I pulled into the half-empty parking lot of AC Supplies. I switched off the engine and put my back to the door. "If you'd asked me at the time, I would've said yes. But looking back, I think it was the right move. I love animals, but the longer I spent in vet school, the more I realised there was a lot about the job itself that didn't suit me. I like working for myself, but dealing with clients all the time? Not so much. I'm not too fond of people in case you haven't noticed."

He chuckled. "Shocker."

My lips quirked up. "I guess I asked for that. It's not that I can't work with people, but I like being able to choose who I work with, and I like the quiet of the ocean, the rhythm of the work, being outside and not suffocating in an office. Lots of people would find what we do on the farm boring, but to me it's a soothing cycle, like the changing seasons."

His mouth curved up in a slow, knowing smile. "Exactly. It's been three months since I sold the boat, and some days I can hardly breathe, like there's not enough salt in the air, or the ground is too solid under my feet. Like there's an imprint on my heart that only matches the wings of a certain Southern Albatross that I'm convinced watched for our boat every time we passed west of Big South Cape Island, just so it could follow us. My dad talked about one that used to follow his catamaran for days. I think I got my love of the ocean from him."

"He died on a solo sail to Fiji, right?"

"Yeah. I was eighteen at the time. He hit the tail end of a cyclone that was supposed to fizzle out but got a second wind, and he didn't make it. They found the wreckage of his boat with him still tied aboard."

"I'm sorry." I wanted to reach for him, ask how he made it through that loss. Ask if he still heard his father's voice late at night when he doubted himself. "I guess we both know what it feels like to lose a father."

He studied me for a long minute. "I guess we do. And it's something our mothers share too. I don't know why I never thought of it before." He took a breath and stared at his hands. "It hit her hard, and a couple of years after he died, Mum left Dunedin and came up here to be closer to her sister in Auckland. But my dad was a sailor, and she would never have asked him to change that. Still, he wasn't a fisherman, so I'm not sure where I got that part from." He looked up. "Plus, give me an engine any day. The bigger the better."

We both laughed and the sound struck a chord deep in my balls, drawing my gaze to the way his green eyes sparkled to life, their weathered corners crinkling with merriment. Laughter suited him like a well-fitted coat, and for a second, I wondered how it would feel to put that smile there every day.

I looked away to watch an older man park his car and head for the store, umbrella unfolding against the slight drizzle. "My dad wasn't a fisherman either, not really. He knew boats since *his* dad was a keen fisherman, but in respect to the mussel farm, I think he just saw an opportunity for a business, whereas you obviously love fishing."

And there was that smile again, rich and inviting.

"I do." He leaned back against the door. "But commercial fishing wasn't exactly a vocation. It just seemed to be a good way to make a living from it. In reality, they have little in common beyond the general idea. We worked blue cod and crayfish and a range of other catch depending on the season. But fishing in the southern basin isn't for the faint-hearted—there's the weather, for one thing. The storms are like nothing you can imagine, and I sure won't miss the long stints away from home. I've gotten soft in my old age."

He chuckled and locked those bright green eyes on mine, and I was swimming out of my depth all over again. But for all of his humour, I wasn't convinced of his words. Everything about Fox screamed of a love of the wild ocean and there was a tightness to his eyes that far too closely resembled grief. I'd seen enough of it to know.

"It hurts, doesn't it? Being away from all that?" I asked, knowing the answer already.

He jolted, surprised, and then nodded. "I doubt anything beats the thrill of staring down the raw power of Mother Nature." He glanced over my shoulder to the sea.

"On a good day, with a blue sky, a favourable wind, and a myriad of marine life popping up to ogle us as we worked, it was pretty damn special, and you feel the privilege of that moment like a promise. Being at the mercy of an ocean that doesn't give a shit who or what you are, only that you exist on its whim for as long as it lets you. Or the roar of an impossible wind that breaches *everything*, chilling you to the bone in a second flat or icing your hands to the railing given half a chance. And that reliance on each other to survive and to get home." He turned back to face me. "It sounds crazy to love that, right?"

I didn't even need to think about it. "No. I think it's about the massiveness of life. It's this dance people like us do with nature, always knowing that nature holds the real power. It's only crazy if we start to believe that *we* hold that power or when we mess with the hand that's feeding us. When we get greedy or disrespectful. My business might not be as physically dangerous as yours was, but I get the awe and the sense of being 'allowed' to do what I do."

I couldn't hold the intense stare that came at my words, uncomfortably aware of the heat that inched across my cheeks.

"Just when I think I have you figured out, Leroy Madden, you go and surprise the fuck out of me." The words were soft, and my gaze flicked back to find a kind of fond affection in his expression that was entirely new.

And I liked it far, far too much. *You don't interest me that way.* I cleared my throat. "You must miss it badly."

He gave a half-shrug, the moment broken. "Yes and no. I miss the awe part, but there's a lot about the industry and its sustainability that was getting harder to live with. As much as I went above and beyond the guidelines to protect the fishery, plenty of others didn't. To me, it was good business sense. I'd lowered catches and eliminated unnecessary bycatch well beyond what was required. Most of the other fisherman found me . . . amusing, happy to settle for a more hit and miss approach to conservation. It's something I was struggling with even before Van forced me to sell, so maybe the timing was meant to be. A little like your vet school perhaps."

"And yet you're looking at game fishing?" I raised a brow, a little judgy maybe, but we were baring some embarrassing truths and I genuinely wanted to understand.

He rolled his eyes. "Fair point. There's a raft of issues with that, for sure. It's one of the reasons I didn't agree to anything before I trial a couple of Jeff's trips first, see how he works and how I feel about it. The offer was simply . . . convenient, and it *would* keep me on the ocean, but we'll see. He's asked me on a charter planned for two weeks from now. Would that work for you? I'd still like to help out on the farm if I can."

"You're not my employee, Fox. You don't need my permission. Do you think you'll still be around then?"

He stared at me, his jaw working. "If I'm welcome. I've been looking for other temporary work, but there's not much around at the moment. On the plus side, there's a commercial boat owner in Christchurch who's looking for a new skipper. It would be a good temporary fit, even if it meant moving again. I can't just tick along forever waiting for something to fall into my lap. And I don't want you to pay me, Leroy. You're doing enough having me stay. Besides, I like to be busy. So yes, I'll be free to help out, at least until I move into some new digs."

I shot him a sharp look. Move? What the hell did that mean?

He gave me a '*Come on, really?*' look, that I filed for later. "Well, I should have Kane trained by then, anyway, so it's all good."

"That's the guy coming to the house later?"

I nodded. "Cool, then I'll text Jeff and tell him we're on." He glanced back toward the Whangarei heads. "One thing I've taken from all the recent crap in my life is that it's the *sea* that runs through my veins, *not* the job, so I can be flexible how I get my fix. It's like you said, the ocean soothes something inside that's hard to put a name to, and your farm is doing just nicely in that regard, for now."

I stared because he so clearly fucking got it, we got each other. And for the most part, *no one* got me. Even Patrick, who loved his job, didn't speak of the sea in quite the same way. But Fox's words sent my pulse racing in my throat, spread the taste of the sea fresh across my tongue, and brought the call of gulls into my heart.

"I'm glad it's giving you that," I admitted. "It must be tough. I don't have quite the connection to the *deep* ocean that you obviously have. For me, it's the coastline, the way the land falls into the sea and that push-pull thing that happens. The lull and roll of the tide, like opening the door of a pantry, a tiny window to pilfer the goodies before it closes again. When I'm working the farm, I feel that rhythm, I'm part of that push and pull cycle. But when I was at university, it sat like this huge hole in my chest that I was forever pretending didn't exist."

"Why pretend?"

I sighed. "Because it's not an easy life. Because I thought I wanted to leave—that's what you did, you grew up and left, like Judah. Because I hate change. But mostly because I hated to admit I was wrong."

His lips quirked up. "Say it isn't so."

I snorted. "I'll give you a free ride on that one."

He looked about to say something, then changed his mind, and when I thought back on what I'd said, my cheeks flamed.

Thankfully he let it go. "So you're happy with your decision to come back and leave vet school?"

That was easy. "Yes, in the end. Although at the time, I was too busy being angry and pissed at Judah for not moving back to help. He was right not to, of course, but I brought a truckload of student debt back with me when I came."

"That had to suck," Fox sympathised. "Especially when you weren't going to use the qualification. The bank owned half the *Blue Swell*, my fishing boat, but at least that debt was connected to something I loved doing."

"I think that's why I was so resentful of Judah. Mum and Dad paid for everything he needed to get his passion all the way to Boston while I had to take a student loan just to study something that in the end wasn't right for me. It was petty, pointless stuff. Especially since

Judah didn't even know about my debt. Mum and Dad *had* planned to sell the farm when they retired and pay it off, but then Dad died, the business side of things got tight, and Mum needed the money."

"And then you found you actually *wanted* to work it, not sell it."

I shrugged. "That too."

"How much longer can it survive?"

The question didn't feel as intrusive as it should have. Fox had owned a business in a similar industry. He knew.

"Not long enough." The words gushed out like a confession and the relief of finally saying them almost brought me to tears. "A year, maybe two. Mum has no idea, nor does Martha. I've been leaning heavily on the rainy-day accounts lately that only I see."

"Shit."

My head fell back against the window. "Yeah."

A worried frown formed on Fox's brow and I wanted to reach across and run a fingertip across it.

I stopped myself.

You don't interest me that way.

CHAPTER SEVEN

Fox

I FOLLOWED LEROY INTO THE WAREHOUSE AND BUSIED MYSELF while he worked with an assistant to tick off his list of supplies. The place was jam-packed with anything and everything an aquaculture business could possibly need, and it was clear by the light-hearted bantering at the desk that Leroy knew the staff well.

It was strange seeing this side of him—relaxed and chatty—and I couldn't help but compare it to the guarded way he was with me most of the time. He was better than he thought at the schmoozing thing, even if he didn't like it, and I made a mental note to maybe tell him just that, now that we were apparently talking again. But the way he'd been so bloody careful not to come within spitting distance of me for two days—coolly polite and meticulously distant—still stung, and I wasn't sure I bought his explanation.

'Thanks for the meal, Fox.'

'You didn't have to make me lunch, Fox.'

'I'm heading to the study to do some work, Fox.'

'The invite still stands to go to training, Fox.' Like I needed his permission.

'Watch what you like, I'm going to bed, Fox.'

By the end of the weekend, I was one *Fox* comment away from throttling the dickhead. And so, when Cora suggested he take me window shopping for boats, I nearly refused on the principle alone. Stuck in a car for hours with someone who didn't want to be anywhere near me? No, thank you. But Cora, being Cora, insisted, and so I sucked it up, but the first half of the journey had been just as painful as predicted.

Until that conversation.

Leroy sharing stuff about his business? Private stuff? Hell, I hadn't seen that coming. Nor the way it made me want to haul him into my lap to calm the nervous bounce of his knee and kiss the worry from that beautiful face. Whatever the reason for his sudden openness, it thawed the wall between us enough for me to think I could maybe stay a while longer at the house. Which was just as well, as the local pickings when I'd looked were slim to none. In late February all the rentals were still busy with well-paying vacationers.

When I noticed a couple of attendants trolleying Leroy's purchases out to the parking lot, I made my way over to the service desk where he was talking with a gruff older man whose badge read Cole just under the word Manager.

"Just think about it, Leroy." Cole leaned against the back wall, his arms crossed, resting atop an ample belly. With busy grey eyes and a tangle of brown hair that didn't look like it had seen a comb in a month, he had a welcoming if somewhat unfocused smile, but the deep weathered lines that marked his face made it hard to nail an age. Late forties, I guessed.

"It's gonna be the next big thing," Cole said, earning my immediate interest. "The seafloor space is secured already, but you've got the opportunity to expand your own farm if you want to try it on your own rather than just invest. The co-culture between mussels and seaweed is almost perfect, but seaweed is way less labour intensive, so it's just a matter of setting it up, then you can forget about it till harvesting time. They're looking for investors now, Leroy. I wouldn't wait too long."

Leroy glanced my way, sighed, and waved me over. "Cole this is Fox, Martha's son. He had a commercial boat off Stewart Island, but he's recently moved up here."

Cole looked him over. "Did you bring the boat?"

"No. But I've got a mate with a charter business up here that I'm going to take a look at. Jeff Young?" I was interested to gauge local reaction to Jeff's business.

Cole's eyes lit up. "Yeah, I know Jeff. Good man. Took my brother and his family out a while back. They had a ball. Welcome to the area." His hand shot out and I accepted it.

"Cole's been trying to talk me into commercial seaweed farming for months," Leroy explained. "Like I have the money to invest in something like that."

"Maybe you've got more sense than this one?" Cole smiled broadly.

I chuckled. "I'm not really the farming type. Water's a little shallow for me. But maybe one day."

"It'll be too late by then," he huffed. "Now is the time—when it's just getting off the ground."

"You can't even confirm the market yet." Leroy shook his head. "That's way too risky for me."

"I'm sure people said that to your father back in the day as well," Cole said thoughtlessly. "If he'd listened to the naysayers, you wouldn't be in my store now, would you?"

Uh-oh.

Leroy's expression flattened and his gaze turned flinty. "Well, I'm not sure what you'd know about that, *Cole*, considering you barely knew—"

"What do people do with the seaweed?" I interrupted, shrugging off Leroy's glare. I knew that look and didn't want him throwing down between the filtration aisle and the mind-numbing display of hatchery shelving.

Cole continued unaware, waxing enthusiastic and seemingly happy to have an audience. "Well, the crazy thing is," he said in a decidedly conspiratorial tone, "the industries are in place *already*, but there's no reliable supply. There's soil additives and animal health products for a start—huge businesses on their own. They currently have to import the damn stuff since they can't get enough from the wild or beach wash-up. And then there's the buzz coming out of California about using seaweed in the exploding meat substitute market. It's a gaping hole just waiting for someone to fill it. I tell you, it's gonna be the next big thing."

Leroy narrowed his eyes. "Who says?"

Cole frowned. "Well, I mean, everyone," he blustered. "It's common knowledge. You only have to google it."

"Riiiight." Leroy collected his stuff from the desk. "If I had the money to spare, which I don't, I wouldn't be putting it in bloody seaweed. I'd expand the mussel farm."

Cole rolled his eyes. "You'd still be too small to compete with the big guys and you know it. Farms like yours can't survive," he said blithely. "They're dinosaurs. Diversify, Leroy, grow with the market."

Oh no you don't. I was next to Leroy before I was aware I'd even moved, bristling with a need uncomfortably close to protective. His gaze snapped me a warning and I froze. *What the hell was I doing?*

Meanwhile, Cole continued to bulldoze through Leroy's darkening mood, totally oblivious. If this was how he talked to his customers, it was a miracle he still had all his limbs and that not-so-pretty face. "The big farms have cornered the market," he droned. "There's no place for the little guy anymore. Everyone's selling to the major players and getting out. Maybe you should consider that too?" He frowned for a second, then burst into a smile. "Or get into seaweed."

For fuck's sake.

Leroy's stony expression paled, but he said nothing as an

awkward silence fell and realisation finally dawned in Cole's eyes and his cheeks fired bright red.

Halle-fucking-lujah.

"Of course, I didn't mean that *you* couldn't make it work, Leroy . . . your father—"

"We should be going," I said, catching a brief flicker of something between annoyance and gratitude in Leroy's eyes.

He reached for a bag of smaller purchases from the desk and turned for the door.

"Look, I'm sorry, Leroy." Cole stepped from behind the desk. "That was rude of me—"

"It was," I said quietly.

Leroy flashed me an angry look. "I don't need you to defend me, Fox."

"I know you don't."

He stared at me for a second, then turned to Cole. "I know you mean well, Cole, but I'm just trying to get through each month here, and your trite summary about what I should and shouldn't be doing without knowing a single thing about my business isn't welcome."

Cole flushed even deeper, if it was possible. "I know. Your Dad's farm—"

"*Leroy's* farm," I corrected, earning myself another angry Madden glare.

"Right." Cole looked between us. "*Leroy's* farm. But I stand by what I said about the other. Just think about it. I knew your dad. He came in here a lot, and I think he might've seen this as an opportunity as well."

Goddamn, the man.

Leroy's jaw ticked and the fist at his side clenched white. "You don't know anything about my father, not rea—"

"We should get going." I grabbed Leroy by the wrist and hauled him out of the warehouse before he went ballistic on the poor guy who I desperately wanted to believe was more ignorant than deliberately unkind.

"Let me go!" Leroy attempted to wrestle free of my grasp as we made it through the door and out to the parking lot. "Fox! Let. Me. Goooo."

I opened my grip and he staggered backwards, falling down on his arse. From there he shot me a murderous look—fierce blue eyes, gritted teeth, and all riled up like a cornered Tasmanian devil. He looked fucking adorable, and I might have even dared to say so if he didn't look two seconds away from skinning my balls.

He scrambled awkwardly to his feet and stalked over, not stopping until he was close enough for me to catch the lime of his cologne mixed with the vaporous salinity that lay on his skin as it did with all those who worked the sea. For a ridiculous minute, I wondered if he'd taste like a shot of tequila and almost leaned in to see.

Five inches shorter, he glared up at me, and it was all I could do not to smile. The man punched well above his weight in the cranky stakes, and I gave him ten points for balls to the wall grit.

"Is this because I dared touch you again?" I said evenly in a blatant attempt to deflect some of that piss and vinegar. "Because I think I saw some wet wipes in the back seat if you need to clean yourself."

His mouth dropped open. "What? No! Of course it bloody isn't." Then his gaze narrowed, and he stabbed his finger at my chest. "Very clever, but you can stop right there. I'm angry because you dragged me out of there like some toddler having a fucking tantrum."

I arched an amused brow and he glowered, saying, "Cole was way out of line."

"He was."

Leroy frowned. "Then why did you—"

"Because he didn't deserve what you were about to unleash on him."

"That wasn't your decision to—"

"Maybe not, but—"

He stabbed me hard with that finger again, but this time I

grabbed it, tucking it against my chest. "Enough." He tried to yank his hand back, but I held tight.

He hissed, "Cole was being an arsehole. He needed to know that." Leroy looked down, staring at our joined hands. We'd never touched like this before, and I wondered if he was going to freak out again. But he didn't try to wrest free, just stared.

"He *was* rude, yes," I agreed, and Leroy's gaze jerked back up. "But you're currently sitting on a powder keg of other shit that wasn't his doing. It was never going to be a fair fight, and sure, the man deserved a skirmish, but not fucking Armageddon."

Leroy's mouth opened like a fish, then closed again. "I'm not . . . I wasn't going to do anything of the sort." But his brow wrinkled in thought.

I raised a brow and the tips of his ears pinked. "Well, not Armageddon anyway." He looked down and scuffed the toe of his trainer on the asphalt. "Maybe just a small civil war." He held his free thumb and forefinger apart. "Just a teeny tiny one." A cute-as-fuck wicked grin tugged at his lips and, good lord, I was totally besotted.

Who was this guy?

I snorted and dropped his other hand, instantly missing the warmth. "Riiiight. Come on, Sugar Rae." I clapped him on the shoulder. "If you promise to keep your fists in your pocket, I'll buy you lunch. Then you can help me check out some boats."

He brightened considerably. "Now you're talking. How much have you got to spend?" He checked the load on the tray and then threw his bag in the back seat of the Hilux.

I shook my head. "Not enough. Suffice to say we'll be keeping our eyes firmly fixed on the bargain second-hand section. But today, I'm just looking. You got any local suggestions for lunch?"

A slow smile played at the corners of Leroy's mouth and I was struck again by the way such a small change smoothed that worried frown and lit up his whole face.

"Get in." He flicked his head. "You're in for a treat, but you're still buying."

"Of course I am."

Thirty minutes later Leroy pulled into a parking lot overlooking the Hatea River, which flowed through the centre of Whangarei township. The thick clouds and drizzle that had dominated the morning had thinned and broken apart, providing glimpses of a watery blue sky that promised a more settled afternoon. Two picnic tables were taken, but other than that, the place was quiet, bar a gaggle of geese who perked to attention with hopeful honks and cackles the minute we pulled in.

Leroy opened his door and reached in the back for the bulky brown paper bag that supposedly contained our lunch. He dangled it in front of my face, a shit-eating grin plastered on his face. "Hungry?"

I'm pretty sure I growled judging by his startled look. "What do you think?"

He'd disappeared with twenty dollars of my money behind a dodgy dry cleaner just off the main street in order to collect this mystery lunch but had adamantly refused to tell me what it was. The divine smell of hot meat and herbs had been driving me crazy ever since.

"Bastard." I made a grab for the bag, but Leroy was too quick, ducking out his door and jogging to an empty picnic table overlooking the swollen brown river. I tried not to follow the seductive bunching of his tight-muscled arse and failed. At the table he turned, held the bag aloft, and laughed, and I realised I hadn't even moved.

"Better hurry up," he called. "And get a towel from the back. The seats are wet. And bring the drinks."

I grabbed the cans of Lemon & Paeroa from the cup holders, threw the towel over my shoulder, and headed to where Leroy was unpacking a whole bunch of smaller bags onto the wooden table—a veritable feast.

The geese, sensing an opportunity, tottered their way over to form a noisy group at his feet.

"If you think you're getting fed before me, you've got another think coming." I clapped my hands and they waddled off in dribs and drabs like a slow month of Sundays.

"Obviously terrified," Leroy commented drily, then laughed as the final goose pooped on my shoe before joining his mates. "And also possessed of impeccable taste."

"Funny guy." I flashed him a mock glare while cleaning my shoe on the wet grass, then grabbed a seat on the bench opposite him. "Damn, that smells good. I'm gonna seriously lose my shit if you don't let me at some of that soon."

He reached into a bag and lobbed a ginormous pita my way. "Think fast."

I barely managed to get a hand on it. "Jesus."

He smirked and I stared at him, gobsmacked. "Who are you and what the hell have you done with my short-tempered friend?" I asked huffily. "I'm gonna need something a lot more serious than a soda to cope with a *playful* Leroy. I've barely gotten a handle on the arsehole version." I tugged one of the open bags closer to peer at its contents— a container loaded with a mountain of succulent meat smothered in some herby-looking sauce. It smelled out of this world. "Oh my god, this looks fucking delicious."

When he didn't answer, I glanced up to find his eyes pinned on mine, an odd expression on his face.

"What?" I frowned.

"Are we? Friends, I mean?"

Oh. I took a second to answer, searching for the right words since the ones 'I'd rather lay you down on this table and lick you into an orgasm really, really slowly' hardly seemed appropriate. "I think maybe we could be. Why? Is that something you'd be interested in? I won't be offended if you're not."

He studied me for a long minute, and I wondered about the need to think so hard about a simple offer of friendship. And not for the first time I thought I was missing something vital about the man.

"Yeah, I'd be interested," he finally said, his expression unreadable.

I snorted. "Jesus, don't get too excited, it'll go to my head."

A smile broke over his face. "Like I'd ever let that happen."

I laughed. "No doubt. Also, did you just make another joke?" I put a hand to my chest. "Be still my heart."

He threw a small wooden spoon at me. "Fucker." Then he ripped open the remaining bags and lined them up between us. "Go for it."

I mounded several forkfuls of meat and its accompaniments onto my pita.

"The guy who runs this Greek deli was born in Crete," Leroy explained, piling his own pita with fillings. "And this is hands down the best souvlaki I've ever tasted. Fair warning though—" He grinned at me. "—if you don't absolutely love it, I'm gonna have to ditch the whole friendship idea straight down the toilet. Just saying. Now, wrap your lips around that sucker and prepare to go to hea—" He froze mid-sentence with a horrified expression.

"I'll be kind and let that one go." I laughed until I realised he wasn't. "Lighten up, Leroy. It's funny. Friends, remember?" I waved between us. "It's allowed."

But when Leroy's gaze met mine, something flashed behind those electric blue eyes that would've shocked the hell out of me if I'd thought even for a minute it might be real. But then he dropped his chin and got busy eating his pita, and I was left to wonder if I was losing my mind.

Because I couldn't be right. I couldn't have just seen Leroy Madden looking at me like he wanted to eat *me* more than any damn thing in those brown paper bags.

It was well after three by the time we got back to the wharf in Painted Bay and started unloading the supplies. Mack exploded from the office to greet us in a tangled confusion of paws, ears and tail, and with a wet tongue that smelled suspiciously of cinnamon buns.

She circled our legs—her own mini maelstrom of excited delight, and I couldn't help the slight tug in my chest when Leroy fell to his knees and wrapped the bundle of canine happiness in a big hug. He'd done the same on the boat when he'd thought I wasn't looking the first time she came out. Why this complicated man didn't have a dog of his own, I couldn't understand, and the delighted surprise on our mothers' faces as they watched confirmed my suspicion that Leroy didn't show this side of himself often.

Putting their amusement aside, the two women badgered us with questions as we worked, as if getting to Whangarei required a day's journey by horse and not an easy hour by car. But it was kind of nice in its own way, and I realised how much I'd missed having family close.

Leroy left me to deal with the interrogation, and I finished by extolling the virtues of the 'Best Souvlaki in New Zealand,' noting the smile that flashed across his face at my words.

Cora's gaze sharpened and flicked between the two of us. "Leroy showed you to his favourite lunch haunt?" she asked, a smile playing on her lips. "Lucky you. Judah's been trying to wheedle that secret out of his brother since he got home."

"Really?" I cast a glance at Leroy who shrugged dismissively.

"He's way too easy to rile," he said, but his cheeks pinked none-theless, all of which left me feeling more than a little chuffed that he'd chosen to share it with me and a little confused as to why.

I was pretty sure Cora hadn't bought a scrap of the explanation either, but before she could call him on it, my mother intervened.

"So, how did the boat hunt go?" She grabbed the bag of smaller bits and pieces from the back seat and gestured for me to follow her into the office.

"It would help if I knew what sort of boat I'm actually going to need, but based on a first look, it's gonna be more expensive than I'd planned. No surprise there." I perched on the edge of her desk next to the incriminating half of a cinnamon bun. "You'll make her fat." I nodded at the pastry.

"Grandparents are allowed to spoil," she answered without even a hint of shame. "Keep going."

"There's nothing more to tell, only that I'm beginning to think I should've bought something down south where at least I know most of the dealers. It's a big investment. And I'm still not sure whether game fishing is the right move. Trouble is, I don't have a heap of other skills to fall back on."

"Rubbish." She threw the empty bag in the cupboard and patted my arm. "You've got a ton to offer. You'll figure it out," she said with faith I wished I had in myself. "Have you heard from Jeff?"

I nodded. "I'm going out with him and four clients in a couple of weeks. Just a day trip."

She smoothed the invoices from the day's purchases and stapled them. "Good. You'll soon know if it's the right move." She filed them in her inbox and continued without looking up. "You two seem to be getting along better."

I glanced out the open door to where Leroy stood in earnest conversation with his mother. "Yeah, I guess. He's a tough nut, but there's more there than meets the eye."

I felt her eyes on me and couldn't look for fear she would see exactly how drawn I was to Cora's son.

"I've always thought so too," she said, moving alongside to follow my gaze. "People think Judah is the more sensitive, but still water's run deep in that one."

"You may be right." I turned to find her watching me closely and changed the subject. "So, who is this Kane guy that's got everyone's knickers in a twist? Leroy's expression turns thunderous every time the man's name comes up."

She shrugged, her gaze dropping to the papers on her desk. "I think you need to make your own mind up about Kane when you meet him. It's not my story to tell."

"There seem to be very few stories around here that you *are* prepared to tell," I pointed out to her.

"Is that so?" She turned back to her desk and started shuffling papers.

"Mmm, all very mysterious, but I guess I'll find out soon enough. He's supposed to be coming to the homestead at four o'clock to meet with Leroy."

She shot me a look. "That should be interesting."

I waited, but she offered nothing more than a knowing smile. "You're the worst mother, you know that, right?"

"Aw, but you love me." She pinched my cheek.

"You ready, Fox?" Leroy shouted from outside.

I pushed off the desk. "See you tomorrow."

"Fox! Come on."

I rolled my eyes. "Gotta go." I left the office at a jog, settled Mack into the back seat of the Hilux, then jumped in beside Leroy. We hurtled up the hill, making it to the front door of the homestead bang on four to find a man sitting on the veranda steps with his arms wrapped around his knees and his head down.

I assumed it was Kane from Leroy's heavy sigh and the scowl that settled over his face. Curiouser and curiouser.

Why the hell employ someone you clearly didn't like?

CHAPTER EIGHT

Leroy

KANE LIFTED HIS HEAD AND I DID A DOUBLE TAKE. I COULDN'T remember the last time I'd seen him around town, but I was pretty sure he hadn't looked quite so . . . haggard . . . and thin. Gone was the cocky assurance I remembered from high school. Dark circles ringed his deep-blue eyes, his handsome face lined with worry, his expression a mix of nerves and steely resolve.

Although a bit lanky in his teenage years, Kane had always been strikingly attractive with his blond surfer looks and a sexy swagger, a combination that attracted more than his fair share of girls with minimal input on his part.

We locked eyes over the wheel of the Hilux, and I blew out a sigh.

"Should I make myself scarce?" Fox ran an appreciative eye over Kane, and I felt myself bristle.

"No. As long as you're helping out, you'll be working with him too." My gaze swept the sharp cut of Fox's jaw and the thick stubble that ran my mouth dry in seconds. "May as well meet the guy and get it over with."

He turned with a wry smile. "You make it sound like going to the dentist."

I kept my eyes on Kane. "You're not far off. Kane and I were in the same circle at school. We used to be friends."

"Used to be?"

I caught his eye. "Long story." I ran my palms down the front of my jeans and opened the door. By the time I got to the front step, Kane was on his feet and Mack circled him like a tasty dog treat. The dog was cheap as a brassy skirt.

"Hey, Leroy." Kane's tone was soft and unsure as he offered his hand.

I stared for a second before accepting. "Kane. This is Fox, Martha's son. He's helping me out for a bit. He'll be sitting in."

"Oh." Kane's gaze lingered on Fox and something slippery wound its way up my spine. "Nice to meet you, Fox."

"And you."

They shook hands, then Kane turned back to me. "Thanks for giving me this opportunity, Leroy."

"You can thank my mother." I let that sink in for a moment. "I'm still not sold on the idea."

Kane scuffed the ball of his foot on the deck and looked away. "Yeah, I figured as much."

I felt Fox's curious eyes on me and remembered his warning from the supply store. *A skirmish, not fucking Armageddon.* It almost made me smile, which was kind of a miracle in itself, considering. I wasn't sure exactly *where* Kane fell in that particular spectrum, but my mother wouldn't have put him under her wing without reason.

I blew out a sigh and walked past him up the steps. "Well, you better come in." I led the two of them into the house and down the wide hallway. Mack ran ahead clearing the house of any threats that might've found their way inside since her last patrol, and I was acutely aware of Fox's eyes still lingering on me. One thing I'd learned about Fox—the man missed nothing.

"Take a seat." I waved Kane toward the three couches set up in a U-shape around a coffee table piled high with aquaculture and sports magazines and a ton of remotes. "Beer?"

He shook his head. "Water is fine, thanks."

"Fox?" I threw a glance over my shoulder, marvelling at how the mood between the two of us had shifted over the course of a single day. I wasn't quite sure how to feel about the change, seeing as how it muddied the water that covered all my lines in the sand, not to mention there was zero chance I wouldn't fuck it up again, but for now, it was . . . nice.

"Yes, thanks." He threw open the windows and the doors to the deck before kicking off his shoes and taking those ridiculously sexy naked feet to the couch opposite Kane. If there was a train stop past lost cause, I was headed there at warp speed.

Mack ran like a demon into the backyard the minute the door opened to do . . . who knew what? Chase seagulls was apparently today's answer as I glanced through the kitchen window and smiled at her antics.

Fox chatted politely with Kane as I fixed our drinks, and I didn't miss the way Kane skilfully avoided answering any direct questions about his current situation. I put the tray of refreshments and a plate of brownies on the coffee table, hoping they were the product of Martha's hands and not my mother who could ruin a bakery item by simple act of reading the recipe.

Kane grabbed his water and a brownie from the tray, his hand shaking. Huh. I handed Fox his beer and our fingers brushed, and I nearly dropped the fucking thing in his lap. Yep, cool as a cucumber, that's me.

"Sorry," I muttered, refusing to meet his eye but not missing his amused snort.

I took a seat on the last couch, cementing my role as the third point on this awkward triangle, and watched Kane nibble on his brownie.

"This is really good," Kane said, raising the brownie in his hand.

"Well, that answers the question of who *didn't* bake it," I answered, taking a bite of my own and washing it down with a mouthful of beer.

"So, your mum's cooking still sucks?" A hint of a smile played at the corners of Kane's mouth, reminding me he'd spent more than a few weekends in this very room, suffering through my mother's attempts in the kitchen along with everyone else who visited.

"Yeah, well, time doesn't solve everything," I answered, the not-so-subtle reminder hanging like a sword between us in the thick silence that followed.

The smile slipped from Kane's face. He focused on the glass of water in his hand, and I took the opportunity to really look at him. At around six foot, he was thinner than I remembered but still looked capable enough to handle the graft on the boat with no trouble. He'd been working a farm, after all. But his eyes were skittish, his expression wary, and I couldn't get rid of the feeling he was hiding something.

"So, Mum said you guys have an organic farm further up the coast now," I pressed. "Must be why I haven't seen you around here much since you came back from university."

Kane looked up from his brownie, and I was struck again by the weariness in his eyes. "It's my dad's farm, not mine."

"Right." I continued to study him. "I admit I was kind of surprised to hear he sold the old Grange Road place though. I thought that was your grandfather's farm?"

Kane nodded. "It was, but money got a little tight after I left for uni."

He didn't expand and it wasn't my business. "You did an English degree, right? If I remember right, you always hated helping out on the farm."

His gaze slid to the window. "Yes, and yes. But there's not a lot of jobs to be had with an MA in English unless you want to teach, and . . . well, Dad needed me back here."

Jesus. Talk about pulling teeth. I shot a look to Fox whose raised brows mirrored my own frustration. "So, you've been working for your father ever since you came back?"

"Yes." Kane's gaze circled back to mine, but he added nothing more.

"And now you've left the farm?"

He blinked slowly. "Yes."

"Can I ask why? And also, why on earth you'd want to work on a bloody mussel farm if you don't even like general farming? I mean, it's still physical graft, and in addition, you get the unparalleled joy of being wet all day."

His jaw worked and he glanced at Fox before returning his attention to me. "I, um, needed a change."

Silence filled the room again and I wanted to punch something. *For fuck's sake.* Did the man want a job or not, because he wasn't exactly making this easy? In fact, there was something off about the whole conversation.

"I think I'll leave you two to chat." Fox got to his feet, shot me a pointed look, and headed for his room, closing the hall door behind him.

I took a deep breath and leaned forward, my elbows on my knees. "Okay, gloves off. The only reason you're sitting here, Kane, is because my mother asked me to give you a chance. You and I might've been friends in high school but based on what I've learned from Judah this last year, I'm not sure I ever knew you at all." I let that sink in, noting the way his six-foot frame almost folded in on itself.

His cheeks burned but he still said nothing.

I fell back on the couch and threw open my hands. "Jesus Christ, Kane. This isn't school anymore, this is my *business* we're talking about here, and Mum's. You have to give me more than fucking single word answers before I'm gonna trust you on my boat."

He flustered, gaze darting, pale cheeks reddening. "I'm sorry. I know. It's just . . . personal, that's all." He shoved his hands under his thighs and took a deep breath. "I've been on the farm all my fucking life, Leroy, and I'm just over it, okay? I want to do something different, *try* something different. And I need a job. Dad didn't exactly pay me a living wage; you know how he was."

I did know. Rufus Martin had always been a tight fucker.

"Right. So, I haven't exactly got a ton of savings. I need a job and I'm a hard worker. If that's not enough, then just forget about it. I don't know what else to tell you."

The truth would be a good start, but looking at Kane, I thought it unlikely I'd get that today. I tried to size him up, not sure what I was seeing. "Look, *if* I take you on, I need to be at least reasonably sure I won't have the police knocking at my door next week."

He startled. "Of course you won't. Jesus, Leroy."

"So, you're not in trouble, and you're . . . clean?"

I didn't miss the way his fist clenched in his lap, but then a resigned expression settled in its place. "*Yes,* I'm clean. And *no,* I'm not in any trouble that would bring the police to your door."

I shrugged unapologetically. "It had to be asked. We start early. It's a long drive here from up the coast."

"I'm staying locally . . . with a friend." His gaze dropped to his lap again, and that niggle in my belly grew. But there was nothing for it to land on.

I took a long swallow of beer as I thought about the whole conversation. "Okay."

"Okay?" He glanced up with a hopeful look.

I kept my voice steady, calm. "But we're not spending ten hours on a boat together every day with a huge fucking elephant in the room. I can't work like that. So before this job is finalised, we're going to talk about what the fuck you thought you were doing kicking my brother till his damn kidneys bled all those years ago."

Okay, maybe not so calm.

His face drained of colour and he fell back on the cushions, his hands shaking in his lap. "I . . . shit. I wasn't sure you knew. I'm . . . I'm so fucking sorry about—"

"Have you said that to Judah?" I growled, wanting to hear his side of what happened with my brother.

"I did. I mean I tried to last year."

"And what did he say?"

"Told me to fuck off, basically."

"Good for him. Jesus Christ, Kane, what the fuck was wrong with you, doing something like that?" My voice rose and he shrank back on the couch. "I knew you guys gave him a hard time—a fact about myself that sickens me now. I was a shitty fucking brother and I've got my own fences to mend with Judah, but I never, ever thought you would do *anything* like that. Judah might've been a pain in my butt at times, but he was my bloody brother, and that made him worth a dozen of you, not that I ever told him that. If I'd known what you did, I'd have fucking decked you where you stood. You do understand that, right? In fact, I'm tempted to do it now."

Kane's head bobbed up and down as he continued to stare at his hands. "I'm sorry. I'm sorry. I can't take it back, no matter how much I wish I could."

"Did anyone else attack him like that?" I needed to know, figuring Judah wouldn't tell me.

Kane shook his head. "Not that I know. And I didn't tell anyone what I did either. I was . . . *am* so fucking ashamed. There's no excuse, but I'd had a shitty week, and then Judah said something to me, and I just lost it."

"What did he say?"

His gaze slid to the window. "I, um, I don't remember now."

He was lying. "Something smart?" I rolled my eyes in abject disgust. "Like maybe standing up for himself, huh? You're right, there's no fucking excuse." I crossed the room in two seconds flat and stood over him. "He could've lost a kidney, you tosser, or a lot worse."

"I know, I know." Kane shrank into the couch. "And I'm sorry."

His eyes welled with an emotion I didn't have time for. "All I can do is keep saying it, to him, to you, anyone who needs to hear it."

"Does my mother know?" It was one way to find out.

He nodded.

My heart squeezed and I huffed an angry sigh. "Of course she bloody does."

"She needed to know before this idea of hers went any further."

"What did she say?"

"She was angry."

"No shit." I snorted. "And yet, here you are."

He shrugged. "I don't deserve to be."

"Damn right you don't. Judah isn't exactly pleased about this either."

Kane's eyes blew wide. "Judah knows already?"

"Of course he does. Do you think we'd be having this conversation if he didn't? I'm not about to choose you over my relationship with my brother, which is only just getting back on track."

"Of course not. I just didn't think . . ."

"No, you didn't. Can you imagine how difficult this is for him, how lucky you are to even get this chance?" I was shouting now, leaning over Kane who remained carefully still, his hands in his lap, not moving a muscle.

But I knew this wasn't simply about him. It was about *me* as well. About *my* guilt. About what *I'd* let happen. About what I'd done to my brother when he'd needed me. I knew all that, and still I couldn't stop.

"You should've told me, Kane. You've kept quiet about it all these years. Were you even going to tell me now if I hadn't brought it up?"

He sucked in a shaky breath. "I always thought Judah would tell you, but then when you never said anything—"

"You thought you'd got away with it?"

"No!" Misery flooded his eyes. "I *never* thought that way. But I didn't want to say anything in case Judah didn't want you to know. I'd figured I'd done enough damage. I never went near him again after that, I swear."

"How do I trust that?" I was dimly aware of my hands fisting.

"Leroy?" A warm palm landed on the small of my back and I spun to find Fox's face right there. Close.

Kissing distance.

"Don't do anything you might regret." His warm gaze levelled on mine.

Anger roared in my chest and I shoved his hand from where it rested on my waist. "Move. Back!"

His expression hardened and his gaze flicked to Kane for a second before landing back on me. "Maybe you should get some fresh air, calm down a little?"

"Maybe you should shut up about stuff you know nothing about," I snapped, but his unexpected appearance had broken through that veil of anger, and when I turned back, the fear and misery in Kane's eyes finally registered, and shame washed through me. I'd done that.

"Leroy?" Fox's voice fell soft in my ear. Close. Too fucking close.

"I think I should go. This was a bad idea." Kane scuttled to his feet and around the back of the couch, putting a barrier between us. "I never meant to make things worse. I just needed a job, but this isn't going to work."

"Leroy," Fox repeated. "Should I show Kane out?"

Yes. No. Dammit. "I don't need a minder," I spat, then instantly regretted the words because clearly, I bloody did.

Kane said nothing, just stood there, his weight shifting nervously from foot to foot. And the fact he hadn't already fled the house in the face of my fury told me everything I needed to know about just how much he needed the job.

Fuck. Fuck. Fuck.

A nose pressed into my hand and I glanced down to find Mack gazing up with those soft, soft eyes. Space opened in my throat enough to breathe.

"Be on the wharf tomorrow at six o'clock," I said with an icy calm-

ness. "Patrick will show you what to do. And I'll need your number."
I dug my phone from my pocket and shoved it at him.

Kane's panicked gaze shot to Fox for support. "I really don't think
this is a good idea."

"Just be there." I pushed my cell into his hand.

He fumbled a text, then tentatively handed my phone back like I
might snap him in two. It was tempting. "I really am grateful, Leroy,"
he said shakily. "And if Judah doesn't like it, I'll leave. No problem."

I snorted. "Oh, Judah *doesn't* like it, that I can guarantee you
already, and you're gonna have to deal with that. He also wanted me
to be really, really clear that you are to stay away from him. You see
him, you give him space, a *lot* of space, no questions. If he wants
anything to do with you, he'll make the first move, understand?"

He nodded. "Understood."

"Be sure that you do. See you tomorrow. Six sharp."

Fox waved Kane toward the hall. "Come on, I'll see you out."

When Fox got back, I hadn't moved and neither had Mack—the
warm reassurance of her body against my leg grounding me as I tried
to make sense of what the hell had just happened.

I hadn't meant to go off at Kane like that, I was just so tired of it
all. I wanted him to know that I was aware of exactly what he'd done.
Well, mission fucking accomplished, arsehole. So, why didn't I feel
good about it?

"Are you all right?" Fox reappeared at my shoulder and the clean
scent of the ocean filled my head. "I didn't mean to interfere. I just
heard the shouting and came to see if I could help."

"I didn't need your help." I turned to face him and damn, he
looked beautiful—and worried—and I wanted him so fucking much.
The anger roared back. "There were things that needed to be said
between us. Things that were no business of yours, not that it stopped
you."

His nostrils flared. "Now just wait a minute. I was only—"

"Only what?" I stepped into him, expecting him to move back,
but he held his ground, leaving barely a heartbeat between us. The

warmth rising from his body almost sucked the breath from my lungs. "Only sticking your nose where it didn't belong? Just because I poured out a few of my sorry financial woes doesn't mean you know *anything* about me or my life. Now, will you please just get out of my face and leave me alone? I can't fucking live like this. I need another beer." I shoved him aside and headed for the fridge.

He followed, stopping at the breakfast bar to watch me yank the door open. "I was just concerned."

"Whatever." I stared at the selection of beer, not recognising half the labels. Fox again, no doubt. I grabbed one at random and slammed the door shut, twisting off the cap and chucking it in the sink before taking a long, long guzzle.

A soft snort came from behind. "Feel better?"

I jerked my head around. "Why are you still here? And why the hell does my fridge look like I live in a fucking hipster's flat?" I brushed past and headed for the deck, barely able to stand myself. Even Mack skittered away, curling her warm body in a circle under the table, trying her best to look inconspicuous.

Neither of them deserved my temper, but Fox sure as hell made a convenient target for a lot of other reasons. I wanted him gone from my general vicinity as quickly as possible, and arsehole Leroy was the best way to ensure that happened.

But instead, he came after me, because of course he bloody did.

"You know, I wasn't joking at lunch," he said in the kind of soothing voice you might offer a rabid dog, and that made me want to stick a fistful of forks in my eyes, or his. It was a close call. The man had a serious streak of stubborn. "I really did think we had a shot at being friends."

I threw myself on a lounger and tried to ignore him.

He followed. "But you've got your head stuck as far up your arse as it was a year ago, so I guess that won't be happening anytime soon." His calm had vanished and the bastard inside of me smiled. "You're so bloody determined to push everyone away that you can't see when someone is genuinely trying to help. Well, don't worry, I don't stay where I'm not wanted. I'll pack my stuff and leave you in peace to sulk and pout at how difficult the world is. It seems to be what you're best at." He headed for the deck.

I hadn't realised I'd even thrown the bottle until the shattering of glass against the wall of the house registered in my brain. By then I was on my feet, hauling Fox around by his wrist.

"Who the hell are you to talk to me like that?" My hand landed on his chest, pushing him back. The flimsy tank hid nothing of the ample chest that lay beneath as I crowded him back against the glass of the open patio door. With only a whisper between us, the heat of his body fanned out across mine, sending my pulse thrumming.

He drew a sharp breath and went still, green eyes locked on mine, a million questions vying for attention in their depths. Good.

"What gives you the right to judge me?" I erupted through a red mist, my fingers curling and uncurling against that solid fucking flesh, every frustration of the last week surging through my body. "You're a guest in my fucking house, not that I had much choice in the matter. And now you're gonna do what? Leave and drop me in it? Tell our mothers I kicked you out?"

He gaped. "Jesus, Leroy, of course I wouldn't—"

"Confirm what an arsehole I am? Well, let me let you in on a little secret, Fox. They don't need any convincing, because I *am* an arsehole. I might be even better at that than sulking and pouting. Who knows? Jesus, it must've been hard work living with such a self-righteous, sanctimonious prick. No wonder your hus—" I slammed a hand over my mouth.

Shit. Shit. Shit.

But it was too late. Fox froze like cold steel against the glass, with my hand patting ridiculously at his chest like I could somehow magic the words back by the useless gesture.

"Oh, god. Oh, god, Fox, I'm so sorry." I crumbled against him, absorbing the heave of his stuttered breaths against my cheek, the rapid thud of his heart in my ear. "I'm so fucking sorry. I shouldn't have said that. And it's not true. Shit."

But he said nothing, taking my weight with his arms locked at his sides like a slab of granite. I should've stepped back but I was incapable of doing it, my fingers scratching at his tank, feeling the coarse rub of chest hair beneath, the heat of his body blanketing my front.

We stayed that way for seconds, minutes, until I felt the hard ridge of his cock nudge my belly, and every synapse in my body lit up.

"Leroy?" He swallowed hard, but still I didn't move, my own cock rising, aching, firm against his thigh. A sharp intake of breath was the only indication he was aware, and I knew the choice was mine.

I looked up slowly, the litany of easy lies silent on my tongue. I was done. I needed to know.

He lowered his gaze to mine just as slowly, breathing ragged. The pink tip of his tongue swept his lower lip, and I couldn't fucking look away.

"Leroy?" A hoarse whisper on his lips.

"Shhh. Please." I traced the line of his jaw with the tip of my finger, and he shuddered, his gaze shifting off my face for some distant point in the sky. His body fell soft, muscle by muscle in tacit agreement. I marvelled at the arc of his cheeks beneath my touch, the way the smoothness gave way into rough stubble.

Jesus Christ, how was this so sexy?

I dragged my fingers over his plump lips, tugging at the lower, pulling it down so I could slick my fingers on the inside, and then running them over my own lips as he dropped his gaze to watch me, transfixed, a groan of approval rumbling in his throat, the sound resonating hot in my balls as they tightened.

Then it was back to his face, the beauty spot beneath the lobe of his right ear that had taunted me for a year and then down and across the crease in his neck to his Adam's apple where I spread my hand around his throat and lightly squeezed, holding him firm against the glass. His breath hitched and his head fell back, eyelids fluttering closed, the deep flush of arousal on his face.

I paused to take the moment in. He looked . . . breathtaking—needy and flushed with arousal. *And just, damn.* I did that. *Me.*

I drew a trembling breath and relaxed my grip on his throat, my fingers moving down, grazing the ridge of his collarbone and across to the tip of his shoulder and the bulge of his bicep—large and hard and unmistakeably male. And so fucking hot. The hair on his skin woke up and he shivered. I smiled and leaned in, my hard cock searching for friction.

"Jesus Christ," he groaned, shifting against me, and I took a mental step back, reaching for that fear which had consumed me for a year, but . . . nothing. A man was rutting softly against me, and all I wanted to do was strip him bare and watch.

Not a no, then. More like a huge fucking yes. A yes to finally touching the man I'd fantasised about for twelve months. And Fox, quiet under my hands, opening himself to me, giving me this moment, because he knew.

Giving me permission, after everything I'd said. After the arsehole I'd been.

"Fox," I whispered, brushing a finger over his brow, and I could've sworn he whimpered.

His head tipped forward, eyes opening to mine, more black than green now—but wary, uncertain. "Leroy?"

I held his gaze even though it killed me. "Is this okay?"

He paused, then nodded. "Are you sure?"

"Shhh." I went up on my toes and finally, finally pressed my lips to his in answer, the warm, moist softness exploding in my body like a firecracker.

Oh god, how had I not known?

It was enough at first to taste the edges of his mouth, the reassuring salt on his skin as I brushed my lips into the corners of his smile and ran my hands around his neck to pull him down where I needed him. And he let me, enduring my fumbling exploration of this strange and beautiful new landscape without a word, just warm hands around my waist as he groaned and shuddered, rocking his hips so my dick rode the length of his thigh in a delicious slide.

Holy fucking shit. I cradled his face and ran the tip of my tongue along his lips as a low growl rumbled in his chest sending a shiver rolling over my skin. His mouth opened and I dipped inside for my first taste—beer, chocolate, and that ever-present hit of salt.

He pulled me tight against him, and I gasped as our cocks jammed together.

Fucking hell. I ground against him without even thinking, my tongue diving deep into his mouth, all polite niceties bowled aside. He felt so fucking good. Everything I'd imagined, hoped, and feared. I couldn't get close enough, deep enough, hard enough. Too many clothes, too awkward, too hot. I needed, needed—

Fox grabbed my arse in both hands and flipped our positions till I felt the cool glass at my back and him at my front. Him. All. Over. My. Body.

Oh god, *that*. I needed *that*.

He hoisted one of my thighs and I immediately got the message, wrapping both around his waist, hoping the glass would hold because I wasn't fucking moving. And all without breaking our kiss, awkward and fumbling until we locked position, and then . . . Jesus Christ . . . magic.

Then he suddenly stilled, his hot breath gusting on my face, and I opened my eyes to find the searing heat of his gaze less than a blink away, the question front and centre. Was I okay?

Was I? Fuck. Yes. No. Maybe. Jesus, I was and I wasn't, but none of that was helpful. And I wanted him regardless. I always had. I'd sort that shit out later. I tightened my grip around his neck and kissed him again, the only answer that made sense.

He groaned and the head of his cock shoved hard under my balls as he took over the kiss and proceeded to blow me the fuck away.

Tenderness left the room with its bags packed and I was kissed like I'd never been kissed in my life—Fox's tongue sweeping into my mouth and halfway down my fucking throat with barely a passing hello. Our teeth clashed more than once as I tried to assert . . . something, before finally throwing in the towel and giving myself over to Fox's thorough owning of my mouth. Not a corner was left unexplored and sounds I didn't even know I was capable of poured from my mouth into his.

He led. I followed, and that was fine by me, for now.

He rocked on his feet, canting his hips so the wide head of his cock hit just behind my balls every damn time. The tips of his clever fingers wrapped around my arse, dug through my board shorts and into my crease, unlocking every one of those fantasies I'd sealed away so very, very carefully. And holy fucking shit, every move, every dark and desperate nudge blew a galaxy of molten stars through my groin to explode in my belly, my dick throbbing and aching to come.

Then his lips peeled off mine and I mumbled some complaint, but when they found the sensitive arch of my neck, nuzzling, licking and nipping, any protest evaporated on my tongue.

"Fuuuuck," I huffed, the only word that made any sense as I squirmed for more friction, more *something*, anything, everything, while having zero idea what any of that meant—so very out of my depth. "I thought you didn't want me that way," I murmured against his hair as he rutted, his face buried in my neck.

"I lied," he groaned, thrusting up hard, and I was so fucking close.

"Leroy?" my mother's voice spilled through the house followed by the slam of the front door.

"Fuck," Fox cursed and immediately dropped me down, his wide eyes sweeping the interior of the house. He looked downright debauched, and I almost laughed as he shook his head, clearly struggling to drag his brain back from wherever it had gone while we'd been . . . occupied.

The same place as mine, I assumed, coming to my senses. I hauled my T-shirt out and over the tent in my boardshorts and split the shoulder seam in the process. *Shit.* I gave my dick a painful flick and flinched. *Goddammit.*

"Leroy?"

I shoved Fox away, none too gently, and he shot me a worried look. But his feelings weren't exactly high on my agenda with my mother seconds from discovering her 'straight' son in an inexplicably compromising position with her de-facto and very definitely gay, stepson—for fuck's sake—and him sporting an erection the size of Everest shoving at his fly.

I waved a finger at the offending appendage, as if he could somehow magic it away, and shot him a warning glance. He rolled his eyes and sauntered to the far side of the deck while I headed inside, sliding into a seat at the breakfast bar just seconds before my mother swept into the room, her arms piled high with Tupperware.

"Oh, there you are. I forgot to give you these earlier." She dumped the plastic containers on the countertop and brushed off her blouse. "Leftovers from Janice Devi's wedding yesterday. She figured you boys might enjoy them."

I popped the lid on the nearest and the rich scent of some spicy meat concoction set my mouth watering. The one underneath carried a mound of rice and some fragrant lentil mix, while the third held a selection of small cakes, chocolate chip cookies, and cinnamon donuts.

"Make sure to ring and thank her," she instructed.

"I will." I resealed the containers and started stacking them in the fridge, while my mother popped outside to say hello to Fox who looked far too relaxed considering what we'd just been doing.

How did he do that? Then again, I had utmost confidence in the power of my mother's presence to wane the most earnest erection.

She gave Fox a hug. He glanced over her shoulder and caught my eye. Then he winked, the jerk.

I almost lost an entire rogan josh on the floor, complete with a short stack of roti. I flattened my lips and glared back at him.

He . . . smiled.

A jiggle of nerves circled my belly and I mentally slapped myself. Fox wasn't a fool. I had to trust he'd keep that tasty mouth shut.

A few minutes later my mother wandered back and took a seat at the breakfast bar. "You should clean up that broken glass before Mack hurts herself," she said, watching me closely.

I didn't answer and she didn't push, opting to change the subject to what she really came about.

"So, how did it go with Kane?"

I rolled my eyes. "You've already called him, haven't you?"

She pouted. "I plead the fifth."

"We don't have the fifth, Mum."

"Well, I plead anything that's gonna get me out of trouble."

I sighed and leaned my elbows on the breakfast bar opposite her. "What did he say?"

"That you were angry about Judah, but that you'd agreed to trial him."

At least he hadn't thrown me under the bus. I tried not to feel grateful. "Kane mentioned he'd told you about the kick he gave Judah. That's assault, Mum. I have to say, I'm surprised you still wanted him after that."

Her brow furrowed. "He also told me he'd apologised to Judah last year, not that an apology makes up for anything. Your father and I didn't know half of what was going on. Judah only admitted to some name-calling. We worked with the school as best we could, but we should've done more. So yes, I *am* still furious about it, but Kane's not that kid anymore."

I waited, positive she knew a lot more than she was saying, but her expression made it clear that was all I was getting.

I blinked slowly and sighed. "It's still just a trial. And if Judah changes his mind and wants him gone, he's gone."

She pursed her lips. "That's only fair. You have my word, and I won't argue if it comes to that. Now, I have to get to the store. Martha needs paprika to finish dinner." She gathered her car keys and headed for the hall before turning back. "Oh, and one more thing." She eyeballed me. "You and I need to have a talk about the farm accounts. It's been too long."

With a heavy heart, I watched her disappear. Just what I fucking needed. Seconds later a shadow fell across my feet and I turned to find Fox leaning on the doorjamb, watching me with uncertain eyes.

"Can we talk?" he asked softly.

I closed my eyes and let my head drop back for a few seconds. Then I opened them and met his gaze as steady as I could manage. "I know you deserve answers, but I'm not sure I have them even for myself. All I can say is I'm sorry for what I said and for implying anything about your marriage. I didn't mean it and it wasn't true, and I *don't* want you to leave. And I'm sorry for losing my cool with Kane. He was a homophobic bully to Judah in high school, but I was just as guilty for letting it happen. It wasn't right, and I'll talk to him."

Fox nodded, still waiting.

I sucked in a breath and tried not to notice the way his lips still shone red and were kiss swollen. "And—" My gaze darted to where a smudge from my back still hung on the glass door. "I'm sorry I . . . kissed you. I shouldn't have done that. Whatever you're thinking about—" I waved my arm haplessly toward the deck. "—about *that*, I'm not . . . ready, Fox. I don't know if I'll ever be. Can we . . . oh god, I'm sorry, but can we just forget it happened, please?"

Fox stared with understanding and kindness I didn't deserve. But when he opened his mouth to reply, I couldn't face the certain pity in his eyes and left before he said anything to change my mind, but not before I caught the words—

"Well, I'm *not* sorry, Leroy Madden. Not for any of it. Not one bit."

Fourteen words to tuck away in a dusty corner of my heart, to hold close and think about when darkness fell on my empty bed.

CHAPTER NINE

2 weeks later

Fox

JEFF PILOTED THE RIVIERA FROM THE FLYBRIDGE BACK TOWARD Paihia wharf while I played fawning host and handed locally made craft beers to the two unappreciative men lounging and talking in the back of the boat. They studied the labels as if personally offended before taking a cautious sip and delivering a reluctant nod of approval.

It had been a scorcher of a day, the mercury reaching a record for the summer and barely enough wind to dry the sweat on your skin, and Jeff and I had suffered through eight long hours of it, pandering to the fickle needs of adult children who should've known better. My entire body, not to mention my temper, needed a good dousing of cold water.

It was six by the time we had Jeff's boat cleaned and locked away and I was on my way back to Painted Bay, my mind mulling over what I'd felt about the whole charter fishing experience. It didn't feel like a fit.

As a solo yachtie, my dad had known a lot about passion and risk, and the compromises needed to live the life you wanted. He'd been very clear on one thing. *"You can compromise on a lot, Fox, but never compromise on what feeds your soul or what drains it. Fight for one and run as fast as you can from the other."*

I was beginning to think this was one of the occasions I should run.

It wasn't about dealing with entitled and ungrateful clients, although that likely played a part—switching from commercial fishing to paid tourist guide had set my head spinning. But it was more about what I'd felt watching that majestic creature chased down and exhausted until the marlin had little choice but to throw in the towel. I'd known what to expect, of course. But watching it play out in living colour had been . . . unsettling.

The sparkling sight of it secured alongside the boat, its dark metallic-blue back shimmering in the bright sun, fading to a silvery-white on its belly with vertical stripes of pale blue that cut clean lines across its length, like a well-fitted Savile Row suit.

My heart had shuddered to a stop in my throat, flooded by that same sense of wrongness that had started to make itself known before I'd sold my own boat. Tag and release or not, I wasn't sure I could get past the look in that marlin's eyes.

Jesus Christ, I was becoming a sap. But for all that, I suspected my father might just agree with me, and that kind of mattered.

It was a nice time of day to be on the road. The early March sun was low in the sky, the first touch of autumn sparking reddish-gold on the trees and the shimmer of the day's heat still rising from the tarmac. Delta Goodrem crooned through my speakers, and I sank into the rhythmic hum of my tyres on the road—something I'd missed on the island where twenty kilometres of decent road summed up the entire driving experience.

My old truck had miraculously appeared in the homestead

driveway the previous week, and I was still chuckling at the familiar small-town service, so much like Oban that it came with a stab of homesickness. The keys had been left in the ignition, the invoice on the front seat with *All Done* written at the bottom and an arrow pointing to the bank account.

I hummed along with Delta and let my mind wander. No prizes where it went, because as hard as I tried, I couldn't shake the memory of that hot-as-fuck kiss with Leroy two weeks earlier.

Leroy, who according to everything I thought I knew, was straight as a die.

Leroy, who had been excruciatingly and infuriatingly polite with me ever since.

Leroy, who'd spent the last two weeks impressing me with his patience as he showed Kane the ropes, clearly trying to make up for his outburst.

And Leroy, who was always friendly enough on the boat but then painstakingly vigilant about keeping any alone time with me to the absolute minimum once we docked. Like some kind of will-o'-the-wisp, there'd be a smidgen of obligatory and shallow conversation while we prepped for dinner and ate. Then he'd help clear up, fluff a few cushions or do a load of washing, and then disappear to his study or bedroom as if he'd never been there at all.

Poof.

He'd even dodged a post-rugby training beer at the pub the previous week, citing overdue paperwork. I didn't believe him for a second. And there'd been no drinks on the deck, no snarky banter, zero laughter, and not a single chapter of worthwhile conversation beyond the grocery list and itemising the next day's work on the farm. Hell, even Mack at least earned a head scratch, a genuine smile, and a few 'good girls' thrown in for good measure.

Between Leroy and me, however, it was all civil and polite and so very fucking terrible, I wanted to scratch my eyes out. Because this was also the Leroy whose feather touch on my body and soft wonder in his eyes was damn near the hottest thing I'd experienced in my entire life.

The Leroy whose sweet taste I couldn't forget and who was the sole reason for the stripes my cock painted on the shower tiles every day.

The Leroy I wanted to throw over the nearest table and fuck until he screamed with pleasure and called my name.

So yeah, I might've had a singular focus since that one devastating kiss, a focus that was going to get me in deep, deep trouble. If I wasn't already there. Because as much as the man attracted me in far too many ways to confess, the last thing I needed was *any* relationship, but especially one playing tour guide for a budding gay or bisexual hottie who was so obviously struggling with the revelation and who would likely dump my sorry arse as soon as he'd finished experimenting.

Fuck that.

Add to the mix that he was a grumpy pain-in-the-neck, sometimes arsehole, and son to *my mother's girlfriend*—three words I never thought would come out of my mouth. The whole thing was a disaster in the making, and I needed to drop that seductive bag of snakes before it bit me in the arse and a dozen other places.

And speaking of pain-in-the-neck arseholes . . . I glanced at my phone and told Siri to call Tinny. We'd had a couple of unsatisfactory conversations where he'd said he was still working to fight the legal claim Van had forwarded, and it was enough to worry me. Even though Tinny had warned me, I'd naively expected the whole thing to somehow just go away.

He answered after a half-dozen rings, sounding breathless.

"Holy shit, don't tell me you're running?" I bit back a smile. Tinny loathed exercise with a passion he lacked for almost everything else, except his gorgeous wife, Violet, and the law. Laid-back had nothing on my best friend. "How quaint of you."

"If you mean am I *power walking* to save my skin, then yes." He choked out a laugh. "I'm late for dinner with Vi, who, as you well know, has the patience of a stampeding bull with a wasp up its butt."

I did know. The antithesis of Tinny, Violet had enough passion for the both of them, along with a penchant for throwing it around. "A delightfully graphic image. I'll make it quick then. I'd hate to be responsible for your untimely death."

He snorted. "No, you fucking wouldn't, cos then I couldn't bill you."

"You're right. I'll string it out as long as I can."

He chuckled, but I could tell he was still moving speedily by the slight gasp in his voice. He wasn't kidding about Violet.

"It's been two weeks, Tinny. Why is he doing this?"

Tinny sighed. "To fuck with you, of course. But what he's telling his lawyer is that he didn't know when you were leaving or that you intended to take Mack so far away. He was happy to have Mack stay with you while he had easy access, but now he wants her back or at least shared custody, and he's prepared to get a court order to make it happen.

"A court order! That fucking, cheating, lying bastard. Can he do that? Even though Mack was my dog before he ever came into my life?"

"I'm sorry, Fox, but yes, he's quite within his rights. He can also petition for it to begin now, and if you can't come to an agreement on how to move forward, the court will decide for you. That could delay proceedings by months, maybe as long as a year, although the court isn't too tolerant of protracted arguments about pets. But you also can't rely on a judge siding with you either. It's likely, but not certain. I hate being the bearer of bad news, but as your lawyer, I have to be clear on the risks and your options. Just know that if you decide to fight it in court, I *will* be there all the way for you."

"That little—"

"His arsehole lawyer says he's determined. Van couldn't have picked a better Pitbull divorce legal team if he tried. Which reminds me, I'm not a divorce lawyer. I told you that. Maybe you should think about changing."

"I want you. Jesus, Tinny, you're my friend."

"Which is precisely why—"

"No. I want you. I understand what you're saying. I get it."

Tinny sighed. "Okay, then you have to listen to me. And this is the bit where I ask you to please consider my future as a parent and not yell in my ear or pull my ample and exceptional balls through the nearest cell tower."

I wasn't sure I wanted to hear what was coming. "No promises. Also, not ample and definitely not exceptional, unless you've had some major work since last year's winter swim."

"You can talk." He laughed. "But before I cut you off my Christmas list, Van's slimy lawyer *has* indicated that Van *might* be willing to reconsider his claim for fair compensation for the loss of his beloved dog."

My jaw dropped. Even for Van, that was pretty damn low. "Compensation? Jesus, Tinny. Hasn't he bled me enough? What the hell is wrong with him?"

"Well, I might have done a little unlawyerly snooping of my own."

"In that case, I might give you *ample balls*, but that's as far as I'll go."

"Word in the community is that Van is needing money for some new business or maybe even to buy into Ewan's—"

"No!" I slammed my clenched fist on the wheel. "I'm not subsidising that arsehole any longer. He already got half the money from the sale of the boat and half what we had in the bank. Not to mention I bought him out of the house. And what the hell is wrong with Ewan? Why would he trust that sneaky little shit with any part of his business, especially after what he did to me?"

"Calm down. I understand that, but for all that you hate what happened, I think the idiot actually loves our fair-haired little Satan."

I snorted. "More fool him. I can't even feel sorry for him. In fact, a part of me hopes Van fleeces him as well. Seems only fair. So what's the plan?"

"I don't have much of one, I'm sorry. You really need to come back down here and try and work it out with him *before* the divorce settlement is due in court. You don't want this to fall to a judge to decide."

"Like hell—"

"Hear me out."

I sighed.

"Just to do some negotiating, maybe get an arbitrator in. You have a stronger claim than Van, and all the veterinary and council registration and paperwork is in your name. It should be enough, but it won't stop Van pushing it as far as he can if what he actually wants is more money. If you act like you're happy to let it go through the courts, that might worry him enough to push him to settle. But he could also call your bluff."

"Fuck."

"So you need to decide what *you're* prepared to do *if* he doesn't back down. Are you willing to share custody and fly Mack back and forth, or are you prepared to go the payout route?"

"That's fucking extortion," I huffed.

Tinny snorted. "Of course it bloody is, and I don't like it any more than you. But it's also perfectly legal. I'm just laying the facts down. It won't be the first time a family pet has been used like this, and there's nothing legally I can do to stop it. I'll keep pushing his lawyer for sense, but in the meantime be prepared for Van to ask to have Mack flown back down to satisfy his *time* with her."

"Can he do that?"

"If he gets his court order, then yes. And remember, worst-case scenario is that he could petition the court for Mack to remain on Stewart Island until a legal ruling on his ownership is decided. Have you thought about coming back down, just until the family court date? You still have your house, right? Then Van's access would be satisfied by your proximity, and once everything is settled, you'll know exactly where you stand. But at least you'll have Mack with you in the meantime and a chance to work a solution out with Van face to face."

I ignored my heart's immediate, yes. "Fuck, Tinny. It feels too much like giving in. But yeah, I can see how it could make things easier. I'll think about it. I'm just worried that I'll get down there and . . ."

"Not want to leave again?"

I sighed. "Yeah, that. It was hard enough the first time, and Bean said there's a skipper's job going in Christchurch."

"Really? Well, maybe that's a sign."

"Of what? Disappointing my mother after promising to spend some time with her? And coming up here was supposed to be a chance to do something different with my life, remember?"

He said nothing and I shook my head. "Okay, I admit it's tempting."

"Good. Just think about it, and stay positive. I think we've got this, but I can't promise. I'll keep in touch."

I sighed. "Thanks. And I miss you guys."

"Give me exceptional and I'll say I miss you too."

I laughed. "Pushing pedestrian at the most."

"Bitch."

"Bastard. But I do miss you."

"Ditto. Talk soon."

He hung up and I glared at the lengthening shadows on the road ahead. How could Van use Mack like that? For all that he'd been an arsehole over the last couple of years, he hadn't always been that way. Or had he? Maybe I just hadn't seen the signs or hadn't wanted to.

An image of Leroy and that kiss on his deck floated into focus once again and I groaned. I really fucking needed to put that behind me, for both our sakes. Leroy had been very clear that he wasn't ready and I needed to respect that. As gorgeous as he was, I sure as shit wasn't in the market for anything but a quick dirty fuck. And there was no way that person would ever be Leroy Madden. He didn't have one-night-stand written anywhere on him, and I sure as hell wasn't looking for more. Been there, never going back.

Maybe I should take Tinny's advice and go back south after all. It would certainly solve the Leroy thing.

But either way, I wasn't going to endure any more mind-numbing, banal civility either.

Leroy and I were going to have us a talk.

I found Leroy lounging on the deck with Mack asleep at his side, staring at the wide swathes of bronzed orange that pooled lazily on the barely rippling surface of Painted Bay, the sun doing its final slow waltz before dipping behind the hills at the back of the homestead. The sloping fields leading down to the beach were a picture of deep violet shadows, the caw of the seagulls and distant chug of an outboard the only sounds to break the stillness.

Hidden from view, I took a moment to drink my fill because damn, he looked beautiful. His short dark hair puffed in the light breeze, that solid tight body poured into dark blue boardies and a loose white singlet that showed off enough tanned skin to raise my pulse. He had a beer in one hand while the other gently played with the scruff of Mack's neck. The rest of him sprawled boneless, legs askew, head laid back, his expression peaceful and relaxed in a fashion I'd rarely seen, if ever.

It was a Leroy I barely knew.

The man from the kiss, I realised with a jolt.

The man who'd given himself over with nothing held back.

The man I hadn't caught a glimpse of since.

Mack caught my scent, scrambled to her feet with a chuff, and the moment was gone.

Leroy instantly tensed and turned to squint through the window. "Fox? That you?"

"Yes." I gave him a wave as Mack hurtled against my legs. "I'll grab a beer and join you." A look of almost panic crossed his face and I spoke before he could run . . . again. "Stay there, I'll bring you another."

He swung his legs over the edge of the lounger. "No, it's fine. I was going—"

"Stay there," I ordered. "If you move one muscle, so help me, Leroy, I will tie you to that bloody lounger."

He hesitated, then fell back. "Jesus Christ, keep your wig on. Whatever. But just one beer. I've got work to do."

Yeah, right. I ruffled Mack's fur and planted a kiss on her forehead. "Good to see you, girl. Did you have a good day with Uncle Leroy?"

"I heard that," Leroy said, a hint of a smile in the words.

"You were meant to. Did she behave?" I grabbed two beers and opened them in the sink, watching Leroy through the window. He'd stretched out, sunglasses now in place, no doubt to hide from me. I shook my head.

"Like an angel," he said. "She hung around Kane most of the day as if he'd been hired just for her pleasure. The guy does seem to have a way with animals. The farmer in him, I guess."

I carried the beers out and handed him one before collapsing into the other lounger. "And how is your new employee doing?"

He held up his bottle for me to clink, then took a guzzle. "Better than expected to be honest. Still keeping his head down and doing what he's asked, kind of like someone else I've had working with me recently, also a surprise." His eyes danced and my heart jumped in my chest. The tide had been out too long on one of those genuine smiles of his.

I snorted and raised my bottle in salute. "Glad to be of service."

And just like that, the grin slid from his face as if he'd suddenly remembered he wasn't supposed to be enjoying himself. He stared at the bottle in his hand and picked at the label. "He's loosening up a bit. I think he might've even cracked a joke today." He slipped his sunglasses off and looked up. "I finally apologised for going off on him, by the way. It took me two weeks, I know, but . . ."

I nodded. "No one's counting."

He studied me a moment longer, then looked away and things went quiet as we watched the long shadows slowly slip over the sand and onto the water on their trek across the bay. Mack rested her head on my leg and in a less than subtle move, nudged my hand.

I rubbed her back in long fluid strokes and she groaned in approval. Leroy's gaze followed my hand and I briefly wondered if we were thinking the same thing. Those minutes on the deck? Our hands on each other? The masochist in me wanted to hope.

"Van's contesting my ownership of Mack."

"What?" Leroy's gaze jerked up. "Jesus, Fox. Can he do that?"

I gave a half-shrug. "Apparently."

"What can you do?"

"My lawyer's working on it. He thinks I'd win if it went to court but that it might hold up the divorce for months, maybe longer. And in the meantime, I may have to share custody until it gets settled. And there's a chance that could be a permanent thing."

"Why, that little shit." Leroy said with feeling. "Mack's yours. Anyone can see that. You can't just let him do this."

"I don't intend to. But here's the kicker. Apparently, Van might consider dropping the claim *if* I increase his settlement."

Leroy's mouth hung open. "Holy shit. Who is this guy? And how the hell did you end up married to such an arsehole?"

An excellent question. "I think we've been here before, but to add a little more detail, Van was always high maintenance and a bit . . . precious. When we first met, he complained how his exes had all used him and how wonderful I was in comparison. Now, I suspect we exes could form a support group and swap war stories." I blew a weary sigh. "Still, there's nothing I can do except wait for Tinny to get back to me. He also suggested I should consider moving back down until it's settled. That way I can keep Mack with me."

"Is that something you'd want?" Leroy eyed me warily. "I know you love it down there."

I shrugged. "Yeah, I've been thinking that maybe I shouldn't have left the island when I did. Moving back would solve the Van problem for now, and at least I still have the house and that chance of a job if I needed it. After talking with Tinny, I called Laurie, the owner of the boat, and threw my name in the hat. He's keen but I'll have to make a decision soon. Still, it's not like there's anything else jumping up at me right now, is there?"

Silence fell and I continued to stroke Mack while Leroy turned a studied gaze to the sea. But I could hear his brain ticking over and a smile tugged at my lips. Sometimes, like now, he was easy to read— worry for Mack, fury at Van, and a surprising and touching concern for me. Other times, he was a closed and locked book with a Keep Out sign planted right in the middle of the front cover.

"Still, it seems a bit extreme," Leroy said, his expression guarded. "But I guess it's one solution."

I snorted. "I thought you'd be pleased to get rid of me."

He shrugged and took another slug of beer, his gaze fixed on the darkening waters. He spoke without turning. "So I'm guessing you weren't won over by the charter business today?"

"Hardly," I answered honestly.

Shadowy blue eyes turned my way.

I picked at the label on my bottle and grimaced. "Let me put it this way. It was a sweltering, long-arse trip with rich, annoying clients who showed zero respect for the fish. Tourist trophy seekers."

He pulled a face in sympathy. "Yikes."

"Pretty much. Add to that an inconvenient crisis of conscience that I'm still debating the source of, and no, it wasn't the best of days."

"Ouch. Sounds very . . . existential."

"Yeah, pretty much." I tugged the light windbreak over my head and rolled my shoulders to loosen all the bunched muscles still tight from working the gigantic fish. That left me in a loose singlet like Leroy, and I didn't have to look to feel the heat of his gaze as it brushed my skin, and, oh wonderful, I was getting hard. I dropped the windbreak into my lap and thought of the arseholes I'd had to wait on all day.

Yep, that did it.

"So what will you do?" he asked, turning back to the evening shadows that had dropped like a closing curtain over the bay.

I shrugged. "Jeff wants me to give it another go, but I'm undecided whether it's worth it. I think I'm gonna tell him, no. Maybe I'll grow bloody seaweed instead."

He snorted, then went quiet for a few seconds.

"Yeah, of course." He took a drink. "Well, you're welcome to work the farm for as long as you need," he said. "I could maybe even pay you."

I tried to keep the shock off my face as I stared at him, the slight flush on his cheeks lit by the soft glow from the kitchen. "You can't afford to put me on the books, Lee. We both know that." I wasn't sure who startled more at the shortened name, only that I was the first to look away. "Sorry, *Leroy*."

"No, it's, um, okay. It's just . . ." He hesitated, then shook his head. "It's fine. And you're right, I can't pay you anything like you're worth, but I could manage *something*. And whether you work for me or not, you're welcome to stay as long as you like." The flush deepened, his gaze jumping off mine as that familiar thick wall of tension rolled between us again.

I took a deep breath, swung my legs over the side of the lounger, and waited until Leroy looked at me. I arched a questioning brow and he immediately looked away. That was okay. I was in no hurry. I'd been battling marlin all day. Waiting out Leroy Madden would barely break a sweat.

After a few seconds, he rolled his eyes, but his gaze remained focused on some distant spot of night that didn't include me. "I don't want to talk about it, Fox."

Gotcha. "About what?"

He blinked slowly, then sighed and turned to put his feet on the deck. Our knees brushed and he quickly pushed the lounger back to put some space between us. "You know damn well what. I thought we'd agreed to forget about what happened and move on?"

Our eyes locked and my breathing stuttered. Jesus, he was gorgeous. Which was exactly why I needed to do this. "I agree we need to move on."

He looked . . . surprised and something else I couldn't name.

"But that's not what's happening, is it?"

He sagged, his gaze sliding to the deck. "Look, I apologised for the kiss. It won't happen again. I—"

"Lee, stop." I took his hand and he went still. "I don't want your apology. I enjoyed the kiss. It was . . . hot as hell if you must know."

He looked up in disbelief. "Riiight. You don't have to try and make me feel better."

I eyeballed him. "Have you looked at yourself in the mirror, lately? You're a gorgeous guy, Lee. And you're also pretty damn interesting underneath that fuck-off armour you polish every day. I'd have to be dead to not be attracted to you. I only said what I did because, well, because I thought you were straight and freaking out about me touching you."

He was staring, a solid notch in his brow. "You think I'm . . . gorgeous?"

I couldn't help a small smile. "You clearly don't agree."

He shook his head in a vague manner as if the question had never even occurred to him. "I mean, I guess I'm okay. I've never had trouble pulling a woman . . . when I needed to . . ."

A *woman*. It was a timely reminder. I squeezed his hand and his gaze jerked down in surprise that it was still clasped in mine. "You're a lot more than okay, Lee. Anyone, woman *or* man, would consider themselves lucky to get your attention."

An adorable flush crept up his neck, but he said nothing, just sat there shaking his head.

"I'm gonna take a wild guess that you haven't ever been with a man?" I watched his expression carefully.

He swallowed hard and shook his head. "You're . . . you're the first guy I've *ever* felt attracted to, like this."

Fuck. My dick stirred at the admission, but I scrubbed my hand across my jaw and schooled my expression.

"That's why I'm so angry with myself. *And* embarrassed."

I frowned. "There's no reason to—"

"For Chrissake, Fox, I'm thirty. How did I not know this about myself?" He pulled his hand free and got to his feet and paced. "I can look back and see a few signs, the guys I thought looked hot, although I wouldn't have used that word back then. The way I sometimes watched Judah with his boyfriends, pissed at how in your face he was about it all, but also . . . curious, I suppose. But I just put it down to having a gay brother, you know? Wanting to understand how he saw things. And because I liked girls, I ignored it. I was clueless."

"No, you were just you. It's not easy to sift through all that information as a teenager, especially since you liked girls as well."

"Judah caught hell in school. You knew that, right?" Lee groaned, still wearing a track in the deck. "His take-no-prisoners fabulousness made me so fucking uncomfortable. I was always telling him to tone it down."

"Do you think he pushed buttons inside you that you didn't want pushed?"

He paused and glanced my way. "Maybe, who knows?" He perched on the corner of the table and shot me a wry look. "Do you know when I was fifteen, Judah's room was full of posters of male ballet stars, and I remember sometimes standing in his doorway when he wasn't home, just looking at them. I told myself it was their athleticism, but if I was honest, I thought they were . . . beautiful, I suppose. But for all that, I can look back and see hints and whispers that I wasn't . . . *technically* straight."

I swallowed a smile, but he caught me and blushed.

"I know, I know. But the point is, although I might've been . . . *appreciative*, I've never actually been *sexually attracted* . . . to a guy." He paused as if debating with himself. "Until you." He threw his hands in the air. "There, I fucking said it. And to be honest, those two words don't even begin to describe what's been going on inside me."

The man was killing me, and with every fibre in my body, I wanted him to explain exactly what he meant, word for fucking word. But the misery that washed through those blue eyes as he spoke was plenty sobering. Lee might want me, but he didn't *want* to want me. And that was far too dangerous for my battered heart.

"Jesus, Fox, the way I treated Judah." Lee slid off the table and into a chair. "How can I tell him this now?"

"Whoa, whoa." I got to my feet and joined him, squatting at his side. "This is *your* story, Lee, not his. And there's no right or wrong time for finding out you're . . ." I waited with my hands open.

His head dropped back. "Bisexual, I suppose."

I nodded. "Okay, bisexual. You don't have to label yourself anything at all if you don't want, or you can change as you learn more about yourself. There are no rules here. Is that the first time you've said it out loud?" I cupped his cheek so he'd look at me.

"Other than to the mirror, which I have to say didn't appear too impressed at the time."

I chuckled and dropped my hand, noting the way his head followed for just a second. He looked . . . ragged, exhausted, like he hadn't slept well in weeks. Like he'd been fighting with himself. I fought the urge to haul him into my arms and tell all the arsehole homophobes responsible for the fear in that look to go fuck themselves. This shouldn't be so damn hard. It shouldn't rip you apart.

Instead, I started to talk. "I came out when I was fifteen."

Lee's gaze zeroed in on me.

"My parents were good about it. Dad took a little bit to get with the programme. He was just uncomfortable, I guess, out of his depth. He'd never even known another gay man. It was all new to him. But that didn't last long and then he was fine. Mum obviously understood, although the fact she never came out to *me* until last year tells a story of how difficult things were in her day. I guess I'd like to know more about that."

Leroy tentatively covered my hand with his calloused palm, and I was incredibly touched. After everything he'd said, everything he was feeling, the small gesture felt as huge as the sky that cloaked the deck. I glanced to where our rough skin met and smiled. Working men. Men of the sea.

"Well, it's good you can talk to her," he said softly.

I shrugged. "She did tell me that Cora's only the second woman she's felt that real tug of attraction to. Mostly it's been men. It doesn't have to be an equal split, and it can change and flux. People don't always understand that."

He nodded. "Morgan's mentioned that."

I slid my hand from under his, stood, and took a seat in the chair opposite. "Then maybe Morgan's a good person to talk with when you're ready. You know, we really should rename this place Bisexual Bay. What do you think? I mean, you, Morgan, Mum, Cora?"

He smiled, though it didn't quite reach his eyes. "Good luck getting that through local council. And I don't know so much about Morgan. He's a friend, but I wouldn't ask him to keep secrets from Judah, which means I'd have to tell Judah as well."

"I totally get that. But don't forget Morgan could be the voice of reason in Judah's ear. It could work in your favour if that's what you decide to do."

Lee frowned. "Maybe. So who was your first kiss?"

I smiled, remembering. "David. First kiss, first handjob, all on the same day."

Leroy laughed. "Wow, you don't waste time, huh?"

"His idea more than mine," I admitted. "But he wasn't out, and the next day he told all his friends *I* hit on *him* and he had to fight me off. Fucker. He was a bit like you, actually."

"Really good looking, then?"

"No. A mouthy little shit."

"Oh, fucking charming." The smile hit every reflected light in his evening-blue eyes and something in my chest pulled tight. God, he was beautiful like that.

"The next guy I kissed, I played it safe. Owen. Nerdy, cute, out, tiny, and sweet. It was good, but I kind of missed the arsehole factor." I winked and he laughed.

"Guess you do have a type then," he pointed out.

I snorted. "Maybe. But that wasn't what this was about. All I'm trying to say is that coming out isn't a race or competition. Talk when you're ready, or don't. Come out if you want to, or don't. Give yourself a break. This is big. Get comfortable with the idea first before you even think about coming out or not. And if so, to who and when. And my door is always open, any time. That's what friends are for. And that's what I'd like us to be if we're moving on. Not the stilted, polite crap of the last two weeks."

He stared at me with a soft, slightly sheepish look. "Sorry about that. I didn't know how to do . . . this. I was so fucking embarrassed. And I *am* sorry. Not about the kiss because you're right, it *was* hot." He grinned shyly and I wanted to frame the look in my mind, it was so fucking charming and so unlike the Lee most everybody knew.

"Good to know." I waggled my eyebrows.

His smile slid away. "Yeah, but it wasn't fair to you, at least not how it happened. And then I just ran the fuck away."

"Don't be sorry." I leaned forward on my elbows over the table. "You wanted to explore, to see if what you felt was real, and I was a convenient, safe opportunity right in front of you. It doesn't have to be more than that. So, moving on?"

After a second's hesitation, he nodded. "Moving on."

I nodded and pushed my chair back intending to leave him alone to think, but before I could move away, he grabbed my wrist and said, "But I want you to know it wasn't *just* an opportunity, Fox." His eyes glowed violet in the dim light. "And you weren't simply *convenient*. Like I said, I haven't been able to stop thinking about you since you ripped me a new one last year. Every time you came back to visit your mother, I couldn't keep my eyes off you. You're like this annoying song I can't get out of my brain."

I snorted. "I'll try to take that as a compliment."

He frowned. "You should. But that's *why* I was such an arsehole to you then and every other time, and *why* I was an arsehole when you arrived to stay. I didn't want to feel what I did—" His gaze flicked away then stole back. "—what I *do* about you."

Please stop.

He sighed. "I just wanted it to go away so I could get back to pretending that you don't make something inside me come alive."

Goddammit, he really, really needed to stop.

I dragged a breath around the solid lump in my throat while Leroy's gaze had me crawling out of my skin to touch him. "Leroy, you don't need to—"

"I'm not *discovering* my bisexuality just because an attractive gay man is in my space, Fox. You're not the first to be there. I spent three years at university. *You* are the *only* reason I'm thinking about it now, *at all*." He hit every word with intent. "And I want you to understand that's the real problem I'm facing here."

I did understand because I felt the same inexplicable pull. But I also wanted him to say it, to hear the words at least once. And so I kept quiet.

He shot me a look that said he was on to me, and then miraculously, he smiled. "I'm saying that I don't know if I *can* move on that simply. And that's my pathetic excuse for the last two weeks. You said you weren't sorry about what happened, and neither am I. Given the chance for a redo—"

He dropped his head back and stared at the starless sky for a moment before coming back to me.

"Given a redo, Fox, I'd have you naked in my bed, and to hell with every other fucking thing until I'd had my fill of you." He ended the sentence breathless and wide-eyed but with his gaze locked on mine like he just fucking dared me to look away, and my whole body caught on fire.

I could only stare at him, stunned, my mouth hanging open, which likely looked as attractive as it sounded. But when the silence dragged out and the right words didn't wondrously appear on my tongue, his expression clouded with uncertainty, then regret, and his cheeks flamed hot.

"Shit, shit, shit." He clenched his eyes for a second, then shoved his chair back and stood without looking at me. "I'm so sorry, Fox. I didn't mean to put you on the spot."

He brushed past and I let him go.

I didn't have an answer for him, for either of us. It was so fucking tempting to run after him, but I didn't want to start something I couldn't finish. Hell, I didn't want to start anything at all. I wasn't ready. I wasn't sure I'd ever be. I didn't even know if I was staying around. I didn't know what the hell I felt anymore, about anything.

All except for this strange, tender want in my heart, and a full cock rattling at the doors of its cage.

Son of a bitch.

So much for moving the fuck on.

CHAPTER TEN

Leroy

Do you need it all? Ever since that trip to the supply warehouse, Fox's question about the land around the homestead had been circling my brain, like now, as the *Green Lip* rocked gently in the lulling swell and I reapplied sun cream to my arms. There was an opportunity there, for sure, but would my mother go for it? I wasn't convinced.

I'd have to present her with more than just a vague idea, and for that I desperately wanted to talk with Fox, to pick his brain about what he'd meant. But yeah, things between us were hardly conducive to that kind of conversation. I could still barely look at him without heat creeping into my cheeks.

I reached for more sun cream and sent the bottle flying over the side of the boat. "Fucking, fuck, fuck!"

Three heads instantly jerked my way. "You okay?" Patrick called from the smaller boat, the *Cee Dee*—a take on my parents' names, Cora and Damien.

I gave them a thumbs up and sighed at the lie. It had been one of those days, beginning with a dream featuring he who shall not be named and a hard-on to rival the Matterhorn, and had gone downhill from there. I grabbed our long-handled net and fished the bottle out of the water before it floated away. If I didn't get my head in the game soon, I was gonna make a real mistake, one that actually mattered.

If only I'd kept my big mouth shut the other night, I wouldn't be such a mess now. If only I *had* moved on. But no. Instead, I'd told Fox just how embarrassingly hot I was for him. How I wanted him naked so I could do nasty, dirty things to him. I'd opted to blow the whole goddammed lid off that Pandora's box of mine and spent the last three days walking around with a permanent semi and a blazing face.

I was such an idiot. By the sound of it, he probably wasn't even staying. Every time he talked about Stewart Island, he had homesick written all over his damn face. He belonged there, he leaked the fact from every pore of his body. Hell, he'd kept his house down there. If that didn't say he was going back, nothing did.

And still I couldn't look at the man without stumbling over my tongue. And so I'd compensated the only way I knew how, by falling back on the snap-and-bite conversational strategy that had served me so well in the past to keep people away.

Until now.

Because Fox *knew*.

Because he couldn't be fooled anymore.

Because he'd been so damn nice about everything, I'd wanted to throw up . . . or fuck his face. It was a close call.

And because he'd started looking at me like he was two seconds away from eating me alive and I was so fucking on board with the idea, I was ready to baste myself inside and out, climb on the spit, and ask if he wanted fries with that.

None of it made sense. Because, what the hell would a gorgeous man like Fox—who could have anyone he chose—want with an inexperienced, bumbling, screwed-up man-on-man virgin like me? He might say he was hot for me, but who knew if he wasn't just throwing the poor, confused, way-out-of-his-depth newbie, probably bisexual *something*, a bone-r.

God, if only. Stuff of my fucking dreams.

But even if Fox *was* genuinely hot for me, I was hardly a prize, and I wasn't sure my heart would survive the battering when he inevitably *moved on.* God, I hated those two words. And when he did, we'd still have to see each other because . . . family. And I wasn't sure I could handle that.

I glanced up in time to see Fox heft a massive coil of rope onto his wide shoulders—those thick thighs shaking under the weight until he found his balance—and then carefully lowering it over the side onto the smaller boat so Patrick and Kane could ferry it out along the backbone of the mussel line. His skin glowed from the exertion, a sheen of sweat lay along the lines of every muscle, his dark locks hung over his face in a tangle of tempting ringlets, and his eyes laughed, happy as he worked.

Goddamn the man. A walking, breathing menace to my sanity.

I took the seat at the helm and discreetly adjusted myself.

Sensing an opportunity, Mack wandered across to nuzzle at my pocket and I slipped my fingers inside.

"She knows you've got treats in there." Fox walked past, a smaller coil of rope dangling from his shoulder.

"I certainly do not." I did my best to look appalled because meaningless banter was at least still within my capability. "That would be perilously close to buying her affection, and I have much higher standards than that." I withdrew my fingers and a liver-flavoured snack dropped to the deck. "Oops."

Mack pounced on it, and Fox gave a booming laugh. Then he raked a gaze over my body that set my skin on fire. "Us mere mortals can only aspire to such lofty peaks of moral fortitude as yourself," he said with a flourish of his free hand.

"I'm gonna need a dictionary," I commented drily.

"Strength and resilience," Kane called from the smaller boat.

I flipped him off. "Says the English major who's currently picking shellfish from ropes. You obviously aced your exams, tiger."

He laughed, and I watched for a minute as he helped Patrick feed out the rope to the usual barrage of questions. He'd loosened up considerably, more with the others than me, but we were making progress. I was beginning to catch glimpses of the boy I'd known in school, and it was both reassuring and troublesome. What the hell had happened to him?

In addition to the whole Fox fiasco, Judah and Morgan were due back in Painted Bay in the next day, and the knowledge was eating at me. With their return, Cora and Martha planned on resuming the open table Sunday lunch they so loved to host at the homestead. I made a mental note to check my mother wasn't planning to invite Kane. That would happen over my dead body. I couldn't imagine she'd be so tactless, but I wasn't leaving anything to chance.

Fox stepped up beside me and followed my gaze. The tangy scent of sweat mixed with fresh cologne and coconut sun cream did ridiculous things to my stomach.

"Are you worried?"

"About what?" I asked without turning.

"About Judah and Kane."

I snorted. "I'd be a bloody fool not to, don't you think? No matter what Judah says, he can't be okay about this, not really."

Fox elbowed me gently. "It was his decision, Lee. From what you've said, you gave him every opportunity to say no, but he agreed to try."

I leaned toward him, just a fraction, enough to catch the flare of the heat from his body. But in the process, I must've brushed his shoulder and he jumped like I'd burned him. But when he didn't move away, I let out the breath I'd been holding and relished the quiet intimacy of the moment and wondered what it meant, that he'd let me.

"Well, I'm here if you need to talk, you know that."

I swivelled my head to look up at him, my gaze lagging on all that tanned skin I'd been jonesing over. Remembering the way it felt under my hands, my lips. Remembering his smell and the thick line of his cock.

"Thanks," I said hoarsely. "Sorry I've been so wool-headed this week. I'm just a bit . . . well—"

"I know." He gave me a soft smile that curled my toes. "Me too."

Neither of us looked away, my gaze adrift in his—eyes the colour of the ocean, lighter at the margins, and much, much deeper than was safe for my heart. The moment was tender, wistful. For two people supposed to be moving on, I was pretty damn sure we hadn't even packed our bags.

"I, um, I think it will be okay. With Judah, I mean." I tore my gaze from his and put it back on the guys working the nursery lines from the *Cee Dee* about thirty metres away. "I meant what I said," I explained. "If Judah has *any* issues, Kane goes. I don't care how well he's doing. I'm putting my brother first this time."

I shot a quick glance up to find Fox still staring at me, an unreadable expression in place, and close, too close. A slight push up on my toes and I could—

He turned and grabbed the canvas bag that held everyone's water bottles, searching for a few seconds before handing me mine, then pulling out his own.

"You haven't been drinking enough," he said as if it was the most natural thing in the world for him to keep an eye on me. I nodded and finished it in a few swallows, as if it were equally natural that I should do as I was told, for fuck's sake. Fox finished his own water, then continued. "He's a good worker for someone who's never done anything like this before." He stowed my empty bottle back in the bag along with his own, then handed me a muesli bar.

"Like you," I pointed out, staring at the muesli bar and wondering what the fuck I was going to do about this stubborn crush on the man. "Also, what the hell is up with this?" I held the bar aloft.

He flushed. "What? You only had a half sandwich at lunch.

You're not hungry?" He went to grab the bar back, but I sidestepped his reach.

"I never said I didn't want it, just—" I shook my head. "You know what, it doesn't matter. Thank you." I peeled the wrapper back and took a bite. "It's good," I said through a mouthful of honeyed oats and sultanas. "I haven't had this one before."

"They were on special," he answered, munching on his own. "Thought we could branch out for a change."

We looked at each other and burst into laughter, spattering muesli bar all over the deck.

"Jesus, we sound like an old married couple." He wiped his mouth and took another bite.

We did, I realised with a jolt, and suddenly it didn't seem so funny anymore. As if he'd just thought the same thing, the smile slid from Fox's face and we finished the bars in silence before he headed to the stern to take care of any tools that needed stowing.

I called to the other boat, "Hey, Patrick." He looked up. "Get that anchor warp back in and drop the backbone. I'm calling it. Make sure Kane cuts the excess and brings it back in. I don't want any rope floating free to snag a passing motor."

Patrick gave a thumbs up and the two men went to work. I glanced to where Fox was working with a frown on his face and sighed. *What the hell was I going to do about him?*

"Leroy! Jesus, fuck, Leroy!"

My gaze jerked around to find Patrick waving frantically from the *Cee Dee*.

I ran to the side. "What happened?"

"Kane's hurt," Patrick shouted, getting down on his knees alongside a prostrate Kane. "He tripped in the rope coil and then tried to stop his fall. I think he's broken his wrist. I heard the snap. And he hit his head on the winch. He's out."

"I'll go." In two seconds Fox was out of his jeans and over the side, his red briefs sliding through the water between the two backbones of mussel lines—the passage too narrow for the *Green Lip* to navigate.

Patrick helped get him onboard, and a minute later Fox called back. "It's definitely broken, but he's conscious. Just a bit groggy."

I ran to the helm and radioed Martha with the news. The woman was rock solid in a crisis. "Can you get someone to meet us at Harry Roland's wharf? It's closer," I told her. "And let Harry know. By the time we get Kane back on board the *Green Lip*, we should be there in about fifteen minutes. It'll be quicker that way than trying to get an ambulance all the way out here."

"I will. Be safe."

I glanced to where Fox had the *Cee Dee* almost alongside and ran to meet them. He cut the engine and the small boat pitched in the roll of the wash. I dropped a section of the gunwale to make it easier to lift Kane on board, and Fox threw me a rope.

"Someone's meeting us at Harry's." I winched our side work platform level with the *Cee Dee*.

"Good thinking." Patrick helped an ashen Kane to his feet, and between them, with Fox's help, they got Kane safely on the platform and then up onto the boat.

"He took a solid hit on the winch." Patrick's voice shook.

"I'm fine," Kane protested, then winced. "Okay, it hurts like a fucking bitch, and I feel a bit woozy, but I'll live."

"Is he bleeding?" I asked, and Kane's eyes shot wide.

Patrick shook his head. "Nah. Tarp was covering it. Plus, his skull's too damn thick."

Kane looked relieved.

Fox gently lifted the man's injured arm to rest across his chest. "Keep it there," he insisted. Then he reinserted the section of gunwale while Patrick secured the smaller boat, and I got my first good look at Kane.

He was white as a sheet, swaying and cradling his arm like it was made of glass. The forearm was bent at an unnatural angle close to the wrist, the flesh below it bloated under tight blueish skin. I wrapped an arm around his waist and made him sit. He wobbled and almost fell, but I caught him just in time.

"Fucking hell." I stared at the shiny mottled skin covering his lower arm and my stomach started to roll. I'd never been great with blood or injuries. Even Judah's attacks still made me queasy, no matter how many I'd witnessed. "That's puffing up damn fast."

"Tell me about it." He grimaced and tried to ease himself into a more comfortable position while still holding his elbow to support his arm. I tried to help, but when he turned and caught his elbow on my hip, he howled in agony.

"Fuck, shit, I'm sorry." I dropped down, my hands on his knees. "Are you okay?"

After a few seconds, he unscrewed his eyes and drew a shuddering breath. "Let's not do that again, okay, Leroy?"

I huffed out a breath. "No argument from me. Stay there." I ran for the first aid kit, leaving Patrick to take point while Fox started the *Green Lip*'s engine.

"Let me." Fox reached for the box as soon as I returned. "You look a bit pale yourself, and I've had to deal with more than a few serious injuries on the boat when there wasn't any help close by. Is there a sling in there?"

"I'm okay."

"Let me do it, Lee." We locked eyes and eventually I nodded, more grateful than I was prepared to admit.

I turned to Patrick. "Get us going. I'll take over in a minute."

Patrick jumped for the helm and I stepped aside to let Fox take charge. He sat alongside Kane whose eyes were framed in tight lines of pain. Fox was still clad in nothing but his sopping red briefs that left little to the imagination. Dark wet curls graced his broad muscled chest, and beads of water ran in rivers off his olive skin. It was almost more than my thumping heart could handle.

"That break's too high for the wrist," Fox said quietly. "I think he's done his radius and ulna. And I don't like that swelling." He shot me a look. "How about you take over from Patrick. Get us where we need to go, and I'll do what I can here."

My gaze darted between Fox and Patrick. "I'm such a fucking wimp," I said, disgusted with myself.

"Hey." Fox sent me a reassuring look. "If I wasn't around, you'd manage just fine, Lee. Everybody here knows that."

I put my hand atop Fox's and squeezed. "Thanks." He nodded and went back to work on Kane.

Patrick turned and caught the exchange but I was past giving a fuck.

"You did a great job back there," I told Patrick, and his cheeks flushed. Then I patted Fox on the shoulder and headed to the helm. "Yell if you need me."

Harry met us at the wharf, and we manhandled a sluggish Kane off the boat and into the back seat of Harry's car.

"See you back home." I held Fox's gaze, a million unsaid things in that single look.

"Like hell." His jaw set in that determined way I'd grown used to. "I'll meet you at the hospital once Patrick and I get the boat berthed back in Painted Bay. You're gonna need a ride home. You sure you're okay?" His warm gaze burrowed into mine, undoing the knots of the day, one by one.

"Yeah . . . I'm . . . I'm fine."

He hesitated just a second, then pulled me into a hug, my body bursting alive at the brush of his hot skin on mine. "I'll be there as soon as I can."

"Thanks." I put every bit of gratitude into my expression that I could, then stepped away and added, a little too loudly, "And put some fucking clothes on."

Patrick chuckled and I just knew my cheeks were flaming. "He'll catch cold," I rushed to explain, glaring daggers at him.

Fox clapped Patrick on the shoulder and steered him toward the boat, shooting one last concerned look over his shoulder.

Oh yeah, we had this whole moving-on thing in the fucking bag.

CHAPTER ELEVEN

Leroy

X-rays showed unstable fractures of both Kane's distal ulna and radius. The fractured ulna was a clean break, the radius, not so much, and the displaced bone had compromised the blood flow to Kane's hand. They said we'd done the right thing getting him to hospital as quickly as we had. All from a simple fall.

Hours later, before he was taken for surgery to plate and screw the breaks, Kane thanked us and then proceeded to give a very long-winded and apologetic set of instructions, along with what I suspected was a significantly redacted explanation for them. He'd refused to let us call his father, saying he would do that himself and then sent us on our way.

Nothing was ever simple with Kane.

Ninety minutes later we arrived back at the homestead, one extra car and seven unexpected but cute-as-fuck kittens heavier. We'd found them at a remote beach about two kilometres from Painted Bay, in an old, dilapidated toilet block next to Kane's rust-bucket

Honda. Fox pulled his Explorer alongside the Honda and we stared at each other through the windows.

I could barely keep my eyes open, and we weren't done yet. It had been a long fucking day.

We met each other by the Explorer's passenger door and Fox smiled at me. "You did the right thing, you big softie."

We'd debated dropping the kittens to a woman I knew in town who rehomed strays, but I'd dismissed the idea quickly. "I'm not sure anyone has ever accused me of being that before."

There was another one of those small smiles. "Then they don't know you very well." He covered my hand with his, the heat of his palm like fire on my skin.

The comment wasn't as strange as it should've been considering the short time we'd known each other. Still, I slid my hand free before I did something I'd regret.

Mack bounded out of the house, took one look at the kittens, and came to an abrupt halt. Fox called and she approached cautiously, nose twitching, ears forward. Fox let her have a good sniff, and a few seconds later, she relaxed and we both breathed a sigh of relief.

He took the kittens inside while I headed up to the old bedsit and fossicked around for a box and a suitable litter tray substitute. Then I lugged everything back to the family room and set the box up with a cuddly blanket and a couple of soft toys I'd found shoved in a box labelled *Judah*—he could kill me later. And if I'd thought the blankets in storage were too smelly and had taken the throw off my own bed instead, well that was nobody's business but my own.

Fox took one look at it and burst into laughter. "Like I said, soft as bloody butter."

I shot him a glare. "Shut your mouth. Who knows how long the others had been in storage? They might've caught something." I stared him down. "It's a vet thing. You wouldn't understand."

He didn't even try to hide the smile. "Clearly."

Mack was in a protective-mumma-bear role, making it hard for us to even pick a kitten up without earning her frank and disapproving stare. So much so that Fox sent her to her mat to observe at a distance, and there she remained, whining softly.

We worked together to transform a couple of sheets of old plywood into a small makeshift cage and then placed the sleeping box and the fresh litter tray inside.

"I can't believe he's been living in his damn car," I repeated for the millionth time as we worked.

"You weren't to know, Lee. Let it go," Fox soothed yet again.

"I can't. I should've known something was up. I did, I guess. I just didn't push to find out what it was."

"I doubt he'd have told you. I mean he's been biking to work. No one suspected he wasn't staying with a friend in town like he'd intimated."

"Maybe. Maybe not." I had so many questions, I didn't know where to start. The kittens looked to be about eight weeks old, which meant they'd only been five when he'd first come to work for me, barely old enough to be away from their mother. Kane swore he'd found them in the parking lot when he got there, but I wasn't at all sure I believed him.

At least they were eating dry food. That was something.

"They could've stayed with Martha in the office," I grumbled. "He should've said something. Why didn't he tell us?"

"I suspect he didn't want to push his luck with a certain feisty boss." Fox arched a brow.

I ignored it. "There." I stood back to admire our handiwork. "Much better than putting them in a cold bathroom—your suggestion as I recall."

Fox snorted. "A perfectly reasonable one."

"Shows what you know. They need to stay warm, and this room has our smell. They'll be more relaxed, which means they'll cry less, and we'll sleep better. It makes sense."

He grinned. "Of course it does."

We watched as the kittens investigated their new home. They were pretty fucking adorable. And when one headed straight for the litter box to do its business, I considered that a win. "I don't think we should leave Mack with any access to them tonight. She seems good, but we can't be sure."

He was looking at me with that amused fondness in his eyes that made me jittery. "You'd have made a good vet," he said softly. "You have a way about you. You try to hide it, but animals always know."

"Maybe," I managed in a thick voice. "All except the part where I'd have to people all day."

He shrugged. "You're better at that than you think."

"I doubt that. God, I'm tired. It's nearly midnight. Let's feed them in the kitchen and then hit the sack."

We poured some of the kitten food from Kane's car into a couple of bowls on the kitchen floor, took the seven kittens from their kitty palace—two black, one ginger, and four tortoiseshell—and stood back. They attacked like hungry lions, and Fox gave a chuff of laughter.

A smile spread over my face. "We only ever had a couple of mousers when I was growing up. They stayed fat on the field mice and rarely came into the house. Watching these guys, I feel like I missed out."

He gave me a considered look, then sat on the floor with his back to the cupboard and his legs stretched out in front. "For a guy who wanted to be a vet, you weren't around many animals."

I leaned on the countertop with my arms crossed. "Dad had this big old German Shepherd, Dill. I loved that dog even though she only really had eyes for him. We used to sneak her food under the table whenever Mum cooked something particularly appalling." I flicked a look his way. "She was very fat."

Fox threw his head back and laughed. "I can imagine."

"You have no idea. You've only lived through a few meals. We had to survive years of it. When Dill died, Dad said he was too busy with the mussel farm to get another, but since a lot of my friends lived on farms, I was around animals plenty."

Fox raised a brow. "You've never thought of getting a dog since?"

"Too busy with the farm." My gaze drifted to Mack. "But maybe it's time. I've really enjoyed her being here."

Fox gave a soft smile. "She likes you too." He let out a slow breath. "Lee, I know I made light of it at the time, but I really *am* sorry for landing on you like we—"

"Don't." I held up a hand. "As much as I hate to admit it, my mother was probably right. Having someone around has been . . . nice, actually. I'm just glad I didn't completely screw things up."

"You didn't screw things—"

"It's kind of you to let me off the hook, but we both know that's not true. They should hang a warning sign around my neck —*Unlikely to ever get his shit together.*" My gaze dropped to the empty bowls and the seven kittens whose stomachs resembled miniature bowling balls.

"Lee, that's not true."

"I'm not fishing for sympathy." I stared until he looked away, and that huge trumpeting elephant lumbered back into the room. Because it didn't matter what I told myself, I took one look at Fox and my entire body screamed, yes.

"So, what are we going to do about Kane?" Fox changed the subject for which I was eternally grateful. "He'll be discharged in a couple of days."

I shrugged. We both knew Kane wasn't going back to his car, not with a litter of kittens, a broken arm, and my mother hovering in the background. But he couldn't stay in the homestead either. There was Judah to consider. He'd been good about the job, but this was something else entirely. I crossed to Fox and slid down beside him, skin brushing skin, the heat from his body washing over me.

He gave a curious look but said nothing.

"Any bright ideas how we handle it?" I asked, refusing to meet the question in his eyes.

He elbowed me gently. "We?"

I elbowed him back. "Friends, right?"

He laughed. "Well, *friend,* how about I take kitten babysitting and supply shopping tomorrow while you and Patrick handle the farm, and you figure out what we're going to do about Kane."

I focused on what seemed a good plan. "Yeah, okay. That works. And maybe try and book a vet appointment as well. I'll leave the name of the local guy."

"Done."

A couple of kittens stumbled food drunk against my ankles and then settled down to sleep. Three more had curled up in a tangled ball against the lip of the food plate, and the final two were heading for Fox. They made it as far as his hip before he scooped them to eye level in his big hands.

"You're just too damn beautiful for your own good." He nuzzled their fur, whispering kitten nonsense as they listened.

I reached a hand to stroke the nearest one, but Fox turned his head and my fingers brushed his lips instead. His eyes shot to mine, dark as night.

I should've pulled away, but I didn't. I should've used my brain, but I didn't. Instead, I kept my eyes off his and traced my fingertip over the plump softness of his lips, around and over and just dipping inside—they felt so fucking good.

He put the kittens in his lap and wrapped his fingers around mine, pressing the briefest of kisses to their tips before lowering them back to my thigh. "You, Leroy Madden, are also beautiful. But unlike these kittens, I'm pretty sure you *don't* know that, and so I'm telling you now."

A thin gasp fought past the ball of longing in my throat, and I finally looked up, looking for the lie, but Fox merely smiled.

Judah was beautiful. I'd heard my brother described that way all my life, and it was true. Judah *was* beautiful. But no one had ever called me that. *No one.*

I shook my head. "I don't need flattery, Fox."

He ran the back of his fingers down my cheek, once, then twice, examining my face like it was the most fascinating thing he'd ever seen. He might as well have torn my clothes off my body for the effect it had—every nerve electrified, the sizzle burning through my veins.

"I meant every word, Lee."

I jerked away. It was too much; the place he touched, too raw, too new.

He dropped his hand. "Sorry. I wasn't sure if—" He paused. "Why did you sit here, Lee? *Right* here?" He looked to the bare millimetres between us."

I didn't have an answer, or rather, we both knew what it was, and so I said nothing, my cheeks burning the truth without any help from my mouth.

He touched my hand with his fingertip. "Can I?"

I swallowed hard and nodded, and his fingers ran up my arm to the sensitive slope of my neck, trailing fire in their wake. His breath stuttered on the intake, but I couldn't look, couldn't risk what I might do if I actually saw what I hoped for in his eyes.

His thumb brushed my lower lip from one side to the other before pulling it down. I wanted to kiss it, lick it. I wanted to draw it into my mouth and suck hungrily. I wanted that and so much more, I could barely form the words to think it, let alone say it.

And so instead, I bit the inside of my cheek, avoided his gaze, and buried the want in sharp pain.

He gave a sad huff and dropped his hand. "You might fool a lot of people with that carefully bricked-up heart of yours, Lee, but that façade is paper-thin for anyone who bothers to take the time to *really* look. But you don't make it easy for them—you sure as hell didn't for me. But in case you still think you've got me fooled, I'm going to be really clear. I *see* you, Leroy Madden. You're a good man with a soft heart, a keen mind, and ten-foot walls of steel. Anyone worth their salt would be lucky and proud to be with you if you gave them even half a chance. *Anyone.*"

The words were so seductive. *He* was so seductive. To believe that even *my* rough edges could find a home without somebody wanting to file them down. But Fox didn't *really* know me, did he? *He couldn't.*

My gaze slid off those green eyes, so intent on unravelling the threads that knitted my raw and tender parts together. Strength mattered. The universe didn't spin your way just because you wanted it to. Watching Judah had taught me that. I'd failed him, thinking—wrongly—he could've made things so much easier on himself by not being So. Fucking. There. I knew how the world chewed you up if you weren't careful. You had to protect yourself, avoid drawing attention, fit in or stay out of the way. I'd watched Judah and not wanted to give my parents another kid who needed support.

Fox lifted my chin with his finger, and I blinked back the tears. He ran his thumb under my eye, and I clung to those fucking walls like a limpet.

"I think you feel everything deeply, Lee, far deeper than you let on, maybe even deeper than your brother. But where Judah uses those feelings in his dance, I don't think you trust yourself to know what to do with them. And so you bury them. But that doesn't mean you don't feel them to your bloody bones, Lee. And anyone who thinks otherwise doesn't really see you at all and isn't worth your time."

I swallowed hard. "You can't know that. But even if it was true, it doesn't make it any easier to open up."

He rolled his eyes. "Jesus, Lee, do you think I don't know what it's like to have a few trust issues? Do you think I don't wish I'd held some of myself back just so Van didn't have the power to eviscerate me quite as utterly as he did? It's not easy to give that power to another person, but when it works with the *right* person, man, that has to be magic."

I huffed in disbelief. "How can you say that? Van totally fucked you over."

Fox gave a wry smile. "He did, but there are never guarantees, right? Given a redo, would I do things differently? You'd think I'd have to say yes, right? But I'm not so sure."

I stared, wide-eyed. "You'd go through all that again? I don't fucking believe you."

He shrugged. "Believe what you want. But I reckon holding back is just as exhausting." He arched a brow. "You never even give yourself a chance that way. And I guess I *want* to believe what I've seen in other couples is possible for me too."

Morgan and Judah flashed through my mind.

"I hope I won't judge every other guy that comes along by Van's personal standard of fuckery, even though I'm not exactly chomping at the bit to try again anytime soon."

The timely reminder stung a little, which was ridiculous in and of itself. It wasn't like I had anything to offer even if something did happen between us.

"I'd like to think I have faith," he said. "And maybe you could too. Maybe you could take a risk someday. Let someone in, the *right* someone. You might know when you meet them. You deserve to be happy, Lee, and some lucky person deserves to have you in their life."

I wanted to believe him; I just didn't know if I could. "I've always thought I didn't need that in my life," I said. "That *special* someone that everyone talks about like you might just stumble on them one day while you're out picking up the milk, but I can't deny it's a nice fantasy." I drew a shaky breath. "And thank you. No one has ever said those things to me."

The tight lines around his eyes softened. "Then that's a shame." He cupped my cheek. "You deserve to hear every word, Lee, and a lot more."

I sat at his side, wanting it to be true, and in that moment, maybe it was. A thumb grazed my cheek and I wanted nothing more than to turn my face and lean into the touch. But before I could, he got to his feet and cool air filled the space where he'd been.

"I'm heading to bed." He gathered the kittens into a furball jumble in his big arms and carried them to their makeshift home accompanied by lots of soft mutterings. Then he locked all the doors as if he owned the place and walked back toward me, warm and bright and big in my life like I'd never expected, like he hadn't just exploded my world with his words.

"I'll check on them during the night," he said, fingers trailing softly across my hair. "Get some sleep, Lee. It was a big day." He called Mack to his side and was gone.

The click of his bedroom door seconds later gave me the quiet solitude I'd so jealously guarded all my life.

Which now felt empty and suffocating.

CHAPTER TWELVE

Fox

MACK SNORED ATOP THE PILE OF DIRTY WASHING, conveniently ignoring the sheepskin mat I'd paid over a hundred dollars for. I grumbled a good night on my way to the bathroom and received a slow rumbling fart in reply.

With the worst of the salt and grime washed from my skin, I cracked the window behind my bed and crawled between the sheets. Moonlight striped the covers as a cool breeze pushed at the curtains, and a morepork hooted from somewhere in the distance, along with the rhythmic brush of the waves on the sand. All else was still, a safe dark space for the thoughts in my head to slow their frenetic circling.

It had been a day. What a mess.

No wonder Lee was wound tighter than a two-dollar watch. It pulled at my heart, and I wanted to ease his burden far more than was good for me, far more than was safe. Especially with a complicated man who came with a mountain of issues.

This wasn't my house. Lee wasn't . . . *mine*. We weren't anything except friends, and even that was new . . . and tricky. *What in the hell was I thinking saying what I did?*

I might hope for a better relationship in the future, but Van *had* screwed with my head. Since he'd left, I'd only fucked a few guys. Never dated. Not wanted to. Not willing to . . . trust. Not yet. Not until the day I'd walked into this house a year ago and laid eyes on an angry young man with eyes the colour of a clear desert sky and a chip the size of the Titanic on his shoulders.

Somewhere in the house, a window slid in its sash and a door closed. Leroy's shower turned on and then off a few minutes later. Footsteps thudded softly down the hall and then back again, faded, and another door closed. I sighed and let my mind drift to the feel of a certain pair of soft lips on mine, hungry and curious. My cock stirred and I groaned and rolled onto my stomach to shut the fucker up.

I was still on my stomach when my eyes flicked open. The room was still hushed bar Mack's soft snores, but I felt the hot touch of Lee's eyes on my back like he'd shouted my name.

I turned and pushed up on one elbow. Lee didn't move, standing in the open doorway with his face half in shadow but with just enough moonlight bleeding through the shifting curtains to set my pulse thrumming. Dressed in dark sweats low on his hips, his hard, flat stomach pulling uncertain breaths in the play of shadow and light, he looked so fucking beautiful he stole my breath.

"I, um, knocked," he faltered, then rolled his eyes. "Like that gives me any right to open the door. I'm sorry. I just . . . I couldn't sleep. I was thinking about what you said." His gaze swept the room avoiding mine.

My heart kicked up. "What do you want, Lee?"

"I . . ." He fell against the doorjamb, exhausted—like he couldn't hold the weight any longer. "I should leave." But he didn't move.

The curtains blew apart, painting a stripe of weak grey light across my hips, and his gaze raked over my bare chest, eyes wide and black . . . hungry.

Come here. The words jumped on my tongue, but I bit them back. The breeze lulled and the curtains fell together, tipping the room back into shadow.

"What if it was you?" His voice shook, his face lost to shadow again. "What if *you* were that someone, Fox, the *right* someone I could take a risk on? Or at least, what if I thought you were?"

The right someone. *Dear God.* My toes curled on that crumbling lip of restraint.

I wanted to run a mile.

I wanted to grab him, protect him from the world, maybe even from . . . myself.

I could hurt this man. He could hurt me. And how the hell had that suddenly become possible?

Lee drew a bolder breath. "Does the idea frighten you, Fox?"

"It terrifies me."

He sagged a little. "That's good. Because I have no idea what I'm doing here. I have no idea what you want . . . or what I want, not really, or how to do . . . *anything.*" His voice trailed off.

"Come here." And there it was. Two little words with the power to fuck up my entire world. I lifted the sheet for Lee to join me and the curtains blew apart to light the way.

He stared at the empty space next to my body, hunger warring with fear and uncertainty on his face.

I said nothing. This was his decision.

He pushed off the jamb and made his way over. The mattress dipped under his weight as he sat. Not in. Not yet. Teetering.

I made fists with my hands so I didn't reach for all that skin pebbled in the cool air, or the wisps of dark hair on his chest, or that heavy stubble—so thick and rough my thighs burned at the thought.

Mack gave a soft whine as if she sensed the energy, the tension, all the unspoken words between us. I shot her a look. "Stay there." She stared for a few seconds, then dropped her head and settled.

Lee stretched a shaking hand and trailed a finger down my cheek. "What am I doing?"

"I don't know." My whole damn body shook.

He smiled, his finger still moving along my jaw and up the other side. "You are so fucking gorgeous, and I am so out of my depth. I shouldn't be here, Fox. We shouldn't be doing this."

I caught his hand in mine and placed a kiss on his palm. "Then walk away, Lee. I won't think any less of you. I don't want you to do something you'll regret."

"What about you?" He looked me in the eye. "Would you regret it?"

Would I? I considered my answer. "No. How could I regret anything I did with you?"

Moonlight washed over the frown on his face, and I rolled back to pull the curtain aside so I could see him better. He flinched and went to look away, but I cupped his cheek and brought him back. "I *want* to see you."

He smiled almost shyly, and my heart fucking melted in my chest. The man was killing me.

"I thought I was okay on my own." He moved his exploration to my chest, a single finger running down my sternum, tracking through the thick curls of hair. He glanced up. "And then you walked into this house a year ago and fucked everything up. I didn't know what to think. I still don't. I mean, I get that I'm bisexual whether I want to be or not . . ."

I raised a brow.

His cheeks darkened. "That sounds really bad, right? But I don't mean it that way. I know I'm attracted to both women and men, I get that, in theory. But *this*?" He flicked a finger between us. "This still . . . shocks me. *You* . . . shock me. The *power* of this shocks me."

Fingers lingered in the hollow of my throat and I swallowed. Instantly his gaze fixed on the movement, and he stared, fascinated, as if noticing it for the first time. I swallowed again and he ran the pads of his fingers over my Adam's apple and shivered.

"It's like I'm seeing things for the first time," he said thickly, his finger circling my throat. "How can something as simple as that be so fucking sexy?" He took a sharp breath and his gaze jerked upward to mine. "I thought I could accept being bi without needing to act on it. That this craving for you was just a . . . sign, to let me know. I've never felt a tug to any one person before, so why would you be any different? And if it came down to it, I could *choose* a woman, and I could live without all the fucking complications."

"Then maybe that's what you should do," I offered, not sure where the hell he was heading with all of this, only that my body was so fucking on board with whatever it *thought* it saw in his eyes, my skin was about to set itself on fire.

He rolled a lazy grin my way and then tapped my nose. "Oh, if only it was that easy." He rested on one elbow and ran his nose lightly up the side of my face, pausing at my hairline to take a deep breath. "You smell so fucking good. How do you do that? You smell like the sea and the earth, all at the same time."

"Lee?" I was so fucking turned on I didn't even know what I wanted him to say.

He kissed my forehead, his lips lingering for just a second before moving to my cheeks. First one, then the other, igniting a rush of heat through my body so powerful it stunned me. I shoved my hands under my hips before I grabbed him around the waist and rolled him under me.

He stared into my eyes from just a heartbeat away, a kind of wonder on his face, his breath liquid heat on my skin. "You feel it too, don't you?"

A single nod.

His mouth quirked up in pleasure and . . . relief, and I realised he hadn't picked up on how I'd felt, not really.

And so I gave him the words. "I do feel it. I have from the start, even if I didn't want to, just like you."

He ran a finger across my lips. "Dammit, Fox. You're buried so far under my skin, I can't even think without seeing your face or hearing your damn voice, no matter what I do. And so here I am."

He slowly brushed his lips across mine, soft and gentle, like he was treasuring every moment, like I was something to be savoured. Then the tip of his tongue slid across and I opened for him, inviting him inside, shuddering with pleasure as he dipped and tasted and drank me in.

I wanted Lee more than I'd wanted any man in a long, long time, but it was unnerving, neither of us sure about . . . anything. I dragged my head back into the game and pulled away, my hands cradling his face as he frowned. "Lee, I swear I want you, that you can trust me to try my best not to hurt you, but I can't promise—"

"I know." He pressed a finger to my lips. "I can't promise I won't go running for the hills tomorrow either. No promises, no lies, right?" He touched his lips again to mine. "All I can promise is that I want to try *this*, with *you*, tonight."

He threw the sheet back and straddled my hips, leaning over me, his elbows resting either side of my head. I slid my hands around the warm skin of his waist and sighed with pleasure.

He looked down to where I held him and smiled. "I've waited a long time for that." He looked back up and kissed me. "Every time you pulled a rope, worked a line, took the helm, made our lunch, whatever it was, I wanted those damn hands on me, just like this, skin on skin."

He laid himself out on top of me, slowly, carefully, eyes going wide in the moonlight as the hard line of his steely cock pushed tight against mine.

"Damn, Lee." I hadn't been so close to coming in my damn briefs in years.

"Man, this is some powerful shit." He breathed the words in wonder. "Is it always like this?"

Laughter bubbled from my throat. "That would be a hard no. Like, I-can't-remember-anything-quite-like-this no."

He snorted. "Good to know. Doesn't mean I won't be crap at this though. It wouldn't be the first time I disapp—"

"Shhh." I kissed his nose. "That's simply not possible." And I wanted five fucking minutes with whoever had dared tell him that. "There is no way on this earth that whatever we do tonight will be anything but amazing, Lee. I'm so fucking hot for you right now, you have no idea. You could do nothing but fuck my mouth with your tongue and I'll have a spectacular time."

A bright smile flashed across his face, then vanished just as quickly. "I want this so much, but I have no fucking idea. You might need to help me."

I drew him down until our lips met and then kissed him thoroughly, my fingers tunnelling his hair to the nape of his neck and holding him in place. He opened immediately, inviting my tongue to slide alongside his, the zing of his toothpaste making me smile against his lips as he almost devoured me.

He groaned and dropped his full weight onto my groin, grinding by instinct, quaking in my arms, and I was two seconds away from losing my load.

He wanted this. He wanted me. That was all I needed to know.

"Jesus, how can this feel so good?" He thrust harder.

And holy shit, I was gonna— "Stop talking." I flipped our positions to control the friction before I embarrassed myself.

His eyes flew wide. "Damn, that was hot."

I laughed. "Welcome to the world of two men, baby."

He froze and I thought about what I'd said and winced. "Sorry, I—"

"No." A slow grin stole over his face. "I like it. But I'd like your lips back on me more."

I snorted and did as he asked, feasting on the taste I'd craved since that first kiss. But he wasn't running this time, at least not right now. Tomorrow was another day.

He wrapped his legs around my waist, his heels digging into my arse, directing me down as we continued to kiss. But I needed us skin on skin.

I pushed free and tugged at his waistband. "Is this okay?"

He lifted his hips and had those sweats peeled off in a second flat, his cock thick and curved and dripping in the cool breeze. My mouth filled in a rush of want.

He threw the sweats aside and Mack groaned as they hit her in the face.

"Hang on." I leapt off the bed and bundled Mack into the hallway before shutting the door.

Lee watched me with a bemused smile. "Performance anxiety?"

"Shut up."

He laughed, making no attempt to hide his nakedness, which I found surprising.

"Take them off." He got to his elbows and signalled my briefs. "I want to see you too. I want to remember everything about tonight."

Remember. Warning bells sounded in my head. He was already assigning whatever this was to his past. I shoved the uncomfortable thought aside. So what if he was? It wasn't like I was looking for anything more either. No promises, right? If Lee wanted to remember, then I'd damn well give him something *to* remember.

And so I took my time, putting on a bit of a show, rolling my hips and thumbing down my briefs as slow as I could manage while at the same time turning to give Lee a good view of my arse, making him wait as I stepped free before turning back with a hand wrapped around my aching cock.

I was no stripper, but I could bring it when I had to for someone special. And Lee *was* special. *This* was special. Lee was about to share his body with a man for the first time, and I thought he was so fucking brave. What was going through his head as his gaze raked over my body?

"You okay?" I stalked closer.

"Huh?" His gaze jerked up from my bouncing cock as he licked his lips and stretched out his arms for me.

I guessed that answered that. I walked right into them and pushed him flat on the bed, licking stripes up the side of his throat and nibbling the soft curve of his neck. "I asked if you were okay?" Another lick, another nibble.

"Fine," he said, arching his neck to give me room to work. "Oh god. Totally fucking fine."

I pressed a line of kisses along his jaw, punctuating each with a few words. "Whatever you want . . . is what we do . . . but let's keep it simple. You want to stop, we stop. You want to rub off on me, fine. You wanna be jacked off, I'm your man. You want me to suck you dry, it will be totally and absolutely my fucking pleasure. And if you wanna fuck me?" I stopped and stared down at him. "I am totally, one hundred percent . . . down with that."

His mouth opened, then closed. "You'd let me do that?"

I took his lips in a slow, measured kiss. "Baby, I'm all yours."

He stared in disbelief. "Yes."

"Yes?" I grinned. "To what? I might need a few more specifics."

"Shit, sorry." He flustered. "Maybe not the last one, not first off. But . . ." He ran a finger across my mouth, then pushed it inside.

I closed my lips around the length and watched his eyes darken. Then I slid my lips back and popped off. "You want me to suck you?"

He drew a sharp breath and nodded. "Would that be okay?"

"Why don't you take a look at just how very, very okay I think that is." I lifted up to show my rigid cock leaking like a damn faucet.

I held my breath as he reached out and touched it, gently, his gaze shooting up for permission. I smiled, took his hand, and wrapped it all the way around. "I'm all yours," I whispered. "Anything you want. Does that feel good?"

He drew a ragged breath. "Better than good."

Then he started to stroke, slowly at first, then faster, harder, running his thumb over the head and dipping into the slit, staring at my cock in his hand with something like disbelief while I counted chickens and slugs and prayed I'd last the distance.

After a minute he found his rhythm and his gaze flicked back to mine, watching, adjusting, switching things up as I drew closer to that edge, my eyelids fluttering closed. If this was Lee nervous, I couldn't wait to see what he brought to the bedroom when he got his confidence.

"You're so fucking beautiful," he whispered. "I've been such an idiot."

"Jesus, I'm close." I groaned, wriggling from his grip. "I don't want to come just yet."

He looked surprised, then pleased. "Oh, right. So that was good, then?"

I snorted. "Yes. You're too fucking sexy for your own good." And I began to work my way down his body with my lips. He lifted up on his elbows to watch, his head falling back as I licked a swathe up and just into his pit and then down the underside of his arm.

"Holy fuck, how does that feel so good?" He lifted the other arm right off the bed and I obliged with a chuckle. "They never teach you that in sex ed."

I snorted and kept working his body, wanting to make this great for him, pulling out all my tricks. Groans of encouragement and murmurs of approval kept me on track. He was deliciously responsive. And when my tongue swiped his nipple, he almost arched off the bed.

"Holy fuck, yessss."

I chuckled, then sucked and licked until he babbled, my hand cupping his weighty balls, kneading and rolling as he fell back onto the bed and lost himself in the rising tide of sensations. And as he did, I delved lower and lower with my tongue, his fingers fisting my hair, guiding my mouth toward his jutting cock. I hovered over top, blowing a breath down its length, dark red with thick veins, a slight curve to the right, and a nest of dark hair at its base. I flicked my tongue lightly over its slick head and then swallowed it whole.

"Oh. My. Fucking. God." His head slammed back into the pillow and his back arched, ramming his cock down my throat.

I gagged, tears streaming.

He instantly dropped. "Shit. Oh my god, I'm so sorry."

"No." I grabbed his hips and took his cock back down. No one was going to take this moment from me. Leroy Madden at my mercy? It didn't get much better than that.

Concern flicked through his eyes, but when he saw me working my own cock, he got the message. I was just fine and dandy, thank you very much.

"Fuck, that's hot." He stayed up on his elbows to watch me jerk myself as I worked his dick.

I kept at it until a buzz hit the base of my spine and Lee had given up watching, strung out on the bed in a puddle of growling pleasure. I pulled off, slicked a finger, and ran its tip down his cock and over his balls to rest on his hole, adding just a smidge of pressure. Then I waited.

He tensed, then hissed, "Yesss. Please."

I smiled and popped through the tight band of muscle to dip inside, my gaze locked on his face for any sign he wasn't okay. But all I saw in those deep-blue eyes was need. At the second knuckle, his eyelids fluttered shut, and when I closed my mouth over his cock and crooked my finger slightly—

"Fuuuuuuuuuck!" His cock pulsed, come spilling down the back of my throat until it almost choked me. "Holy Jesus," he gasped.

I drank down every drop, greedy for more as Lee shuddered with a fresh wave, sucking him dry until he sank into the mattress, replete and boneless and hungry for air. Then I pulled off his softening cock and licked it clean, crawling up his body to press our lips together, careful to not push for entry. But he pulled me hard onto his mouth, plunging his tongue alongside mine to taste himself before pushing me away with a glint in his eye. "Finish on me, on my dick."

I stared at him. "Are you sure?"

"Fuck, yes. Do it."

Well okay, then. I smiled to myself thinking I shouldn't have been surprised that Leroy would prove to be as bossy in bed as he was out of it. The thought had me itching in all the right places.

I scrambled to my knees at his side, and half a dozen strokes was all it took to send ribbons of come over his spent cock. He stared long and hard at where it lay, and I wondered if this was the moment he'd shut down and run. If he'd crossed a line in his head.

Instead, I watched in amazement as he ran his fingers through the mess I'd made, tentatively at first and then smearing it all over his belly with his palm. And when he was done, he lifted his slick hand to his lips, ran his tongue all the way up the palm, and then held the fingers out for me to lick clean as he watched.

I was more than happy to oblige, holding his gaze, making sure to gather every last drop on my tongue. Then I used the sheet to clean the rest before crashing to the mattress and pulling him alongside, my arm wrapped around his shoulders just in case he had any thoughts of running away. He blew a long, satisfied sigh and settled against me.

I let him catch his breath, my fingers tracing slow circles on his shoulder. Then I nuzzled his hair. "So?"

He tilted his head back to look at me, cheeks flushed and looking thoroughly fucked. "I like mess." He gave a wry smile. "A lot of women don't. But the messier the better as far as I'm concerned."

I kissed his forehead. "Excellent news. I'll add it to the list."

"The list?"

"The *All the Ways to Get Lee Madden Hot and Bothered* list." I almost choked on the words as I heard them come out of my mouth. "Shit. That is, if you decide you want any more, I mean. Fuck."

He laughed and threw his leg over mine, wriggling closer. "That's gonna be a short list, since it appears all you need to do is put the name Fox Carmody at the top and the rest is history."

Did that mean . . . ? Something stilled in my chest at his words, something I wasn't prepared for. It felt suspiciously like hope. I shook it off and played with his choppy dark locks. "I wouldn't have taken you for a cuddler, Mr Madden."

"I wouldn't have taken you for a deep throat guru, Mr Carmody."

"It's a gift, what can I say?" I tightened my grip on his shoulder and rolled him closer. A comfortable silence filled the room as I continued to play with his hair, front to back, front to back.

His breathing slowed, his head heavy on my chest, and I might've thought he was asleep if it wasn't for the slow scratch of his nails on my chest, and I wondered what he was thinking.

It was an eerie calm, like the eye of an ocean storm. As if we'd lain in each other's arms a thousand times, and yet the feel of his skin on mine was brightly new and breathtaking.

Almost too breathtaking. Too . . . right.

I wasn't ready. *He* wasn't ready.

And yet here we were.

And that warning voice I'd so cavalierly ignored when I'd asked him into my bed came roaring back.

Someone was going to get hurt.

But for the first time, I thought it might be me.

CHAPTER THIRTEEN

Leroy

Fox tensed beneath my hand and I looked up. "What?"

He smiled and kissed my nose, but there was a wariness to his expression that hadn't been there earlier. "Just wondering what's going through your head. First time with another man and all."

Oh. "Expecting me to run, are you?" I ran my tongue over his chest hair, then snagged a few in my teeth and tugged.

"Ow." A frown creased his brow. "What was that for?"

"For not having more faith in me."

He grinned and smooshed my cheeks between his hands before planting a big sloppy kiss on my lips. "I'm sorry, but wasn't it you who said, no promises you wouldn't shoot through?"

"It was."

"So can you blame me?"

"Nope." The truth was, I was having enough trouble coming to terms with my reaction myself. Because Fuck. Me. Here I was, cuddled into a big brawny guy who'd just sucked my brains out through my dick and then come all over me, and what was I thinking? That I'd made a mistake? That I couldn't do this? That I needed to get out of this man's bed and back into my own as fast as possible?

Hell fucking no.

I was thinking I wanted more, a lot more. I wanted as much as I could get and fuck the whole damn world. I'd had good sex before, but nothing like this. So yeah, colour me just a little surprised. It might take some getting used to, but I was willing to give it the old college try.

And it wasn't just the sex. It was, quite possibly, very little to do with the sex at all. It was Fox. Fox was the difference. With him, I *felt* sexy. I felt important. I felt safe. With Fox, I was more than the farm, more than my dad's son. And I was more than a disappointing and angry brother.

"Hey." He pressed a kiss to my hair. "You know it's okay to freak out a little."

I rolled to my stomach and rested on my elbows, staring down at him. "But that's the crazy thing, Fox. I'm not. And I'm not sure why."

He smiled and brushed a lock of hair from my eyes, a flash of relief in those shadowy eyes. "I'm just that good," he said smugly. "I've always known this to be true."

I closed my teeth around his nipple and bit down.

"Ow." He pushed me away and covered his nipple with his hand, but I peeled it away and kissed the sting. His eyes darkened. "You are so fucking sexy."

"Come on." I shifted my focus to the window behind him and the layered greys of the garden outside. "As I recall, I sat there and did nothing while you sucked me down like a champ."

We wriggled onto our sides, facing each other.

He pressed his lips to mine and then to each of my eyelids. "Sexy isn't just what you do, it's in here." He tapped my heart. "And here." He tapped my forehead. "You turn me on just by being you, and I haven't a single doubt you'll blow my fucking mind when you turn that bossy side loose, Mr I Like It Messy. I can't wait to meet that guy between the sheets."

I drank in the words until it hurt too much, and my skin itched where his gaze stripped me raw. I tucked a long wave of sun-tipped hair behind his ear and whispered, "You barely know me."

"I know enough." He took my mouth in a lazy kiss that seemed to go on for days. Then he wriggled closer until our bodies touched chest to knee, and his cock stirred against mine. Shadow and light played across the weathered lines on his face—a history of sun and the harsh Southern Ocean winds.

Another draught of cool air breached the window and licked at our naked bodies, sending goosebumps the length of my arms.

Fox drew the sheet over my shoulder and tucked it in, a simple tender act that almost undid me more than the pleasure he'd drawn from my body. "Was it what you expected?"

"I'm not sure what I expected," I answered honestly. "I'll admit the sex was . . . different." I bit back a smile. "And I'll be sporting some spectacular beard burn—words I never thought would come out of my mouth."

He laughed.

"But it was kind of fucking amazing as well." I hooked his chin with my finger and pulled him in for a kiss.

"Oh really." His eyes danced over my face in that way he had that made me want to eat him up. "Do tell."

I took a deep breath and thought about it. "I felt . . . free, I guess. That's the easiest way to put it. I love the way your body feels so hard and solid against me, that you can move me around and that I don't have to lead. It was so hot. Everything I'd hoped it might be, and then more."

"Tell me about this *more?*"

Don't answer. It was the sensible option. And yet . . . "I felt safe, like I couldn't do anything wrong. That I wasn't going to disappoint you."

Something glistened in his eyes and he bridged the gap between us to place the gentlest of kisses on my lips. My hands found his hips and pulled him tight so he could feel what even the memory of him did to me. "Fucking hell, Fox. Is it wrong that I want you again? I can't seem to get enough."

His pupils flared, and his lips curved up in a slow, sexy smile. "Would you like to fuck me, Leroy Madden?"

I pretty much stopped breathing. I hadn't dared hope for a second offer since I'd refused the first, and I could only nod before adding in a small voice I hardly recognised, "Is that a trick question? Because damn, Fox, I think my dick went straight to heaven. But are you sure?"

He pressed a kiss to my nose. "I offered because I want you, Lee. I like it both ways, although I'm picky who I hand out invitations to. But yeah, I'll take your cock inside me any day, beautiful."

He straddled my hips and reached for the bedside table while I pondered the breathtaking possibility of his words and the equally terrifying thought of losing my load before I even got inside his tight hole. The one-armed stretch put Fox's nipple within licking distance and so I obliged. It would've been rude not to.

He almost jolted out of bed. "Jesus, warn a guy next time."

I waggled my eyebrows. "I think I'm starting to find nipples highly erotic. At least your nipples."

He snorted. "Good to know." He threw a condom and lube on the bed.

I stared at them. "Maybe this isn't such a good idea . . . I mean, I've only ever played around a little back there with women. Just fingers, you know?"

"Shhh." He silenced me with a kiss and then smiled softly. "It's not rocket science, baby. Tab A into slot B." He winked. "I think you've got this."

"But I . . . shit." My pulse hammered in my throat. "I want this to be good for you too." I closed my eyes, feeling like a complete jackass. "Jesus, listen to me. It's not like I haven't fucked anyone before."

He pried one of my eyes open, his gentle gaze soothing my nerves. "But this is big, right? I get that."

I opened both eyes and willed him to understand something I barely understood myself. "It's like there's no going back, no pretending after this."

"Do you want to go back? Because we can stop now."

Did I? "No." On that I was certain. "I want this." I ran my hand down his body to fist his cock. "I want you, Fox, so fucking much." The raw hunger in my voice gave me pause and I took a breath. "I might suck at this, but if you're willing to take the risk . . ."

"You? Inside *me*?" He grinned. "That has zero risk attached. There's no way that's gonna be anything but fucking amazing." He flicked the cap off the lube, squirted a good dollop out, and then, with our eyes locked, his hand disappeared between his legs and his eyes rolled back.

"Oh, damn." I lightly slapped his thigh. "Turn sideways so I can see." He turned and I shuffled around for a better look. Then I reached and shoved two fingers into his mouth as I watched, because . . . well fuck, who the hell knew why, but it felt amazing as he groaned with every thrust into his hole.

But it wasn't enough.

"Let me." I tugged his fingers from his arse, grabbed the lube and shoved at his hips. "Move your butt so I can get to you."

He laughed and repositioned himself on all fours in the middle of the bed. "Anything else I can help with?"

I slicked my fingers. "Why should you have all the fun? I like it messy, remember?"

He dropped his head and wiggled his butt. "Have at it."

He spread his legs and I pulled apart his cheeks, but the sight of that perfect, pink, slick, and oh-so-fucking-tiny hole, flanked by the lightest dusting of dark hair, brought me to a grinding halt. I glanced down at my thick, angry cock and winced. *Jesus.* How the hell was *that* gonna fit in there?

Fox chuckled. "You need a map back there?"

"Funny guy. Is there anything you don't li—"

"I'll let you know."

"Okay, yeah, cool. You do that." I reached a hand through his thighs and gave his heavy cock a few sharp tugs to slick him up while trying to slide my other fingers into that hot, softening hole without completely losing my shit.

"Fuuuuck," he groaned and dropped his forehead to the pillow as I fucked him with one hand while stroking him off with the other. It took a moment to get my rhythm because, hellooooo, cocks and holes.

Jacking another man felt odd, but not nearly as weird as it probably should've been, the solid weight of a dick in my hand, almost . . . comforting—a reminder Fox wanted me, that he thought I was sexy. And good God, wasn't that a fucking miracle?

"Um, Lee? Fair warning, you better fuck me soon or I'm not gonna last, which means you won't get to pop your topping cherry." His hole clenched around my fingers and a condom landed by my knee.

"Oh, right. Yeah, let's do that. But fuck, that was hot." My fingers slid free, but they were shaking so badly, it took three attempts to get the condom rolled on safely. I wanted Fox in a hundred ways I shouldn't, but in every way that mattered. And the sight of him spread like butter on the bed, just for me to take any way I wanted, his trust, his belief, and the enormity of what we were doing suddenly crashed through me.

I shuffled between his legs, cradled his hips in my hands, and dropped a series of soft kisses in a line across the small of his back.

He stilled and looked over his shoulder. "Lee?"

I met his gaze and smiled. "I just want to say thank you. For this."

He gave a crooked smile and wiggled his hips. "I can't fucking wait."

I ran a hand the length of his back and over the muscled swell of his arse, then slid my cock down his crease to rest against his hole.

He trembled and rocked back, nudging it into place.

I froze, my gaze caught on the point where our bodies met. This was it, a fantasy fulfilled, a year in the making. I breathed deep, steadied my hands on the hot skin of his waist, and pressed inside.

"Goddaaaaaaaamn. Jesus fucking Christ on a cracker," he muttered, slamming his fist into the mattress as I pushed through the ring of muscle, the hot furnace of his flesh wrapping around my cock to explode in my balls.

I jerked back. "Shit, sorr—"

"No!" He grabbed behind my thigh and tugged me back. "Don't stop. It's just been a while. I'll let you know. Keep going. Please."

I took him at his word and slowly slid home with Fox swearing every centimetre of the way, until he finally lapsed into sharp panting. And then I waited for his signal, struggling to endure the impossibly tight grip on my cock that threatened to send me over the edge before I got in a single stroke—my brain so scrambled I wasn't sure I could even remember how.

His hips rocked, just a fraction, and I dug my fingers in. "Jesus Christ, don't move," I snapped.

He snorted. "Got a problem back there?"

"Shut up. I'm doing fine. Just . . . don't move." I stroked his back, mapping the small spray of tiny dark moles just above his crease. "How is it possible for anything to be this tight? This is fucking paradise, Fox. To hell with golden sand and turquoise water, your arse beats all of that."

He snorted.

"Sonnets could be written about your hole," I rambled, any distraction to stop me nutting on the spot. "A stage show, maybe a musical—"

"Will you shut the hell up and just fuck me, please?" He glanced over his shoulder and pushed back, impaling my cock so deep I thought he might choke on it. "Right now."

"Oh. Right. Got it." I dislodged my cock from what I was pretty sure was his oesophagus and set about giving both of us what we wanted. I was at least familiar with the mechanics of this part, albeit the geography had shifted slightly. It wasn't pretty or coordinated, and it sure as shit wasn't slow, but judging by the noises coming from Fox's mouth, I had to assume he approved.

I'd like to think I made it to a minute, but I'm pretty sure it was less than half. Still, Fox was right there with me. And when I came like a fucking train in his arse, he was less than five seconds behind, back arched, fisting the sheets and with a low growling rumble in his throat that I'd remember to my dying day.

I collapsed over his back and made myself a promise to watch his face next time.

Next time.

Still buried to my balls, I trailed my fingers down his ribs and waited for my lungs to catch up with the distinct lack of oxygen in anything north of my dick. Beneath me, Fox hummed into his pillow —a soft contented sound that made me smile. My arms circled his waist as I tried to pull my brain back into my skull from whatever sun it was currently orbiting.

"What the hell was that?" I nibbled the curve of his shoulder as a cool breeze licked at my forehead.

"I think the technical term is a good dicking," he muttered. "But I think we need to repeat the experience as soon as possible just to be sure."

I snorted and licked at the tang of the sea on his skin. His taste. Mine too, I supposed. "You'll get no argument from me." I rested my cheek on his shoulder blade. "I think I might've gotten a little carried away. Do you need a Band-Aid somewhere?"

He barked out a laugh. "And where exactly do you think I might need this Band-Aid?"

"Well, I was thinking maybe here." I tapped the point where his neck met his shoulder. "Since my cock's so long and all."

"The perils of an overactive imagination."

"Oh, I don't know." I nibbled his shoulder. "Nothing I've ever imagined, dreamed, or fantasised even came close to what we've done tonight."

He stilled. "Me too. Kind of a surprise, huh?"

"In the best way." The words came out on a breath I didn't know I'd been holding—hoping, praying Fox felt anything close to what was unfolding in my heart. Maybe I was reading him wrong, hearing more in the words than was there, but I didn't think so.

He was the first to pull away, wiggling his bum. "Are you stuck? Should I call for help?"

I blew a breath through his hair, watching the way the moon-silvered ends wafted over his ear. "I like the way you feel." I gave a useless thrust with my almost soft cock, hoping the fire in my cheeks didn't shine too brightly in the light and shadows that crisscrossed his bed. "If I pull out, it might all disappear into a dream. As long as you're wrapped around me, I know it's real. I know it . . . happened."

He flattened his body on the bed and I went with him, easing my dick free and tying off the condom.

"It's real, Lee," he whispered, turning to his side and rolling me off him so we were eye to eye. "It happened. Possibly the most real thing I've had in a long time. And it doesn't have to be the last, not if you don't want it to be." He let the offer float between us. "Don't answer now. Just think about it."

"I'm not sure I need to," I said. "I'm waiting for the panic, but so far, nothing."

He smiled, warm and open. "You still get to take your time."

I ran a finger over his lips. "What if I don't want to? You might've only been here a few weeks, Fox, but this thing between us isn't really new, is it? You've been in my head for a year, whether I wanted you there or not."

He ran his gaze over my face. "And you in mine."

"So we've both done a lot of the 'is this a good thing or not' thinking shit. I haven't been fighting the bisexual part as much as I've been fighting going there with *you*. The no-going-back part of that equation."

A wariness crept into his eyes. "And now?"

He deserved an honest answer. "I still have concerns. It's not like you're a nameless one-night stand or some kind of experiment, is it?

We don't get to walk away from each other and leave it all behind. We have to find a way to survive whatever this is if everything goes tits up between us."

He winced. "We do. But neither of us made promises, Lee, and I still can't. My life is a mess as you well know, and you're not out, so we'd have to keep all that in mind. But I *offered* you tonight, to experiment if you like. I won't hold it against you if you don't want any—"

"Jesus, Fox, you're *not* an experiment. Never that. I wouldn't. This wasn't just about sex, at least not for me. Although I can't deny my cock's been stalking you for a year, but that's because the sexy bits were attached to *you*. It's *always* been about *you*. The sex was just the fucking Italian meringue on top of a delicious cake, which is also you . . . by the way . . . in case you missed the first dozen hammer hits to your head."

His lips quirked up. "Italian meringue, huh? That was very . . . specific."

I shrugged and pulled the sheet over our shoulders. "I happen to like Italian meringue. And feel free to throw me a life preserver before I drown. Anytime now would be good since I've just walked off an emotional plank here."

He bit back a smile and I hoped it was relief I saw in his face and not the pain of trying to work out how to let me down gently.

But he hadn't gone all stiff and prickly or pushed me out of his bed or rolled onto his back to stare at the ceiling and count the cracks, so those had to be good signs, right? Then again, I had zero clue how to read men. This touchy-feely stuff sucked. Being an angry arsehole had a lot going for it.

"Okay, so what is this, Lee? What do you see happening here? Bearing in mind the whole no-promises thing." He cradled my face and a wrinkle dipped between his brows.

I wanted to kiss it. I wanted to kiss him. I wanted too much, a whole lot more than I deserved, and with a man. Karma, right? How better for the universe to truly fuck with me?

"I, um . . ." My fists clenched, and I drew a ragged breath.

He ran a thumb under my eyes. "Okay, I need you to actually say the words, Lee. I need you to be really fucking clear about what you want."

I took a deep breath and buried my face in his neck, because this was never gonna happen with those penetrating eyes on me. He hummed and wrapped me in his arms, and from somewhere outside, the morepork called for its mate.

Oh god, oh god, oh god. "Okay, so, I might possibly, you know, given everything that's going on in my head, and the fact you've practically taken up residence there for over a year, and that what we just did may or may not have been the best fucking thing to happen to me since the price of mussels doubled when overseas markets—"

"Lee."

My eyes squeezed tight against the warmth of his skin. "Right. Well, against all odds, I might have . . . feelings, Fox, fucking inconvenient ones if you ask me, about you, *for* you. As in *us*-type feelings . . . stuff, maybe. Fucking hell, I'm crap at this. Like *not* an experiment, okay? Like . . . more, maybe a lot more." I sighed. "Yeah, mostly that last one, dammit. But I get the whole no-promises thing as well, on both sides, and I'm not asking for any."

He made a soft sound and his lips found my hair, my neck, my shoulder, my . . . heart, until I finally tipped my head back and gave him my mouth. Maybe for the last time, I didn't know.

A murmur of pleasure fell from his lips, and for a long minute, he lingered there, brushing his mouth over mine, his tongue slipping inside, tasting, searching, soft and kind and wanting, still wanting. And through it all, we kept our eyes open on each other, wary, uncertain. Which was fine by me. As long as we were kissing, he couldn't tell me how he didn't feel the same way as I did.

But it couldn't stay that way forever, and he eventually pulled back, our heads sharing a pillow, noses almost touching, his gaze intense on mine, searching for something. I wasn't sure what. My eyes dipped to that small beauty spot under his right ear. Much safer there.

He tipped my chin up until our eyes met again. "Shall I tell you about inconvenient feelings, Lee Madden?" He brushed the end of my nose with his and smiled. "Because right now, I'm fucking drowning in them."

And then he kissed me.

CHAPTER FOURTEEN

Fox

I woke to a cool and empty bed, squashed the panic in my chest, and went looking for Lee. He was elbow deep in suds at the kitchen sink, singing softly to Matchbox Twenty with his gaze fixed on Mack doing her morning patrol outside. I paused and took a moment to enjoy the view. His tightly muscled body clad only in a pair of my sweats, two sizes too big and hanging loose from his narrow hips, had my cock jumping in my boardshorts. I didn't know whether to be pleased or troubled by the depth of my visceral reaction.

The night. Lee. This *thing* between us was almost too much and certainly too soon, too . . . risky. And yet here we were. I wasn't about to back out even if I should. It was the best I'd felt in a long, long time, and for once, Stewart Island wasn't singing in my veins. Leroy Madden was.

A series of mewls took my attention to a sunny spot on the floor where the open patio doors led onto the deck. Someone had moved the kitten palace and a smile broke over my face. The man was such a softie.

We'd talked long into the early hours, wrapped in each other's arms until exhaustion finally took us. Lee had wanted to know all about Van, and I hadn't held back. Start to finish, he got the whole ugly truth including the fact I'd genuinely loved him. Lee had been quiet at that, but I wasn't about to lie. Loving Van was a part of my history, and whatever Lee and I were doing, whatever happened, that needed to be on the table.

We talked about losing our fathers and what it meant for us, how we missed them and why, and the gaping holes they left in our lives. A big difference had been the fact I'd taken inspiration from my father, whereas Lee seemed to have mostly taken on his responsibility. And as he opened up about his childhood, I felt that in some ways, he'd lost a part of his father *and* his mother much earlier. He talked about growing up on the fringes of his family, with his parents' lives consumed by the farm and with Judah's burgeoning talent and promising career.

But mostly he talked about Judah. How he'd let his brother down and the drive to make things right. He shouldered all the blame, which I didn't think he deserved. He'd played a part, for sure, but families were a complicated layering of relationships, and I hurt for the guilt he so obviously carried.

And we talked about this thing between us and how crazy we were. How we needed to take it slow. No pressure. No promises. No lies. No family dramas. No family *anything*, not yet. We weren't about to tell anyone. Lee was new to this, to men, to me. Who knew what he'd think in a day, a week, a month. And the hurt I carried from Van wasn't done with me yet.

Just the thought of trying anything with another guy should've been enough to have me packing my bags for down south—the easy solution. But when I looked at Lee, I wanted him, and not just in my bed, although the reality of that had blown my fucking mind. I'd never been anyone's first, especially not a grown man's very first touch of another man. I kind of loved that part, even if it was a reminder of how new this all was to Lee.

I had to trust he'd meant it when he said I wasn't an experiment, but would I be happy being Lee's first and not his last if it came to that? I wasn't so sure. The honest passion he brought to our bed, the need and wonder, the willingness to take a risk, for me, had unravelled my heart in ways I'd been completely unprepared for.

His desire and willingness to explore was as passionate as his anger had ever been. And something told me he'd love that way too. Lee did nothing halfway, and any man or woman lucky enough to earn his affection would know it to their quaking bones. Would it be an easy ride? Hell fucking no, it wouldn't. There'd be plenty of sparks and a few raging fires, good and bad. But you'd know you were loved without a scrap of doubt.

An image of Van popped into my head. It hadn't been that way for us. I'd presumed his feelings because I'd loved *him*, and we were *married*. Had I just seen what I wanted?

Watching Lee stack the washed plates one at a time, I realised his lover would never have to guess what Lee felt. Lee only knew one way—raw and honest, even when it hurt.

But I didn't want to hurt *him*. That above everything else. Nothing in my life was nailed down and Lee had a home, a business, a committed life here in Painted Bay, a place I barely knew. If something more sparked between us, could I see myself here for good, or even for a while? Painted Bay wasn't just a small town, it was a tiny speck on the coast. What business did it even lend itself to that wasn't already here? I'd come to be closer to family for a bit, but not necessarily to stay here forever. It seemed crazy to be thinking about all this so soon, but I didn't want to hurt Lee, and as he'd said, we had to survive whatever this was. There was no escaping that we were tied by family.

Jesus Christ. I didn't know what to do, other than I wasn't walking away no matter how much I should. I couldn't. And that set every damn alarm bell I possessed ringing in my head.

The music switched to Adele and Lee picked up the tempo, flicked his hips to the side, and hit a long, solid note, blaringly off-key.

I swallowed the laugh that bubbled up my throat. He might be awful, but he was all in, exactly the way he lived his life. He didn't jump easily, but it seemed when he did, he ignored the parachute and simply ran off the cliff.

I tiptoed across the room in my socks and slid my arms around his waist, pulling the hot skin of his back against me.

He startled and dropped a mug he was washing into the sink with a crash. "Jesus Christ, Fox. You scared the shit out of me."

"You left me naked in bed to do the dishes, sweetheart? I'm gonna try not to be offended by that." I dropped my chin to his shoulder and rode my very interested cock up his crease.

He froze with the sudsy cup in his hand, and I cursed my stupidity. "Shit, I'm sorry. I shouldn't have just assumed you'd be okay with—"

"No, it's fine." He spun, those wet hands circling my neck. "I like it. It's . . . weird, I guess. Not just that you're a guy, although that definitely grabs a weirdness factor or two, but more that it's *anyone* holding me, in my kitchen, in my house, but especially that it's *you*."

He went up on his toes and pressed a soft kiss to my lips. "I've been alone for so fucking long, Fox. It might take some getting used to, but I really love it when you touch me. And in case you didn't get the message last night—you and me? Hell, I'm like a kid on my first trip to Disneyland discovering the rides are way, way better than I ever imagined. We're on the same page about keeping this just between us, so I trust you."

"Disneyland, huh?" I grabbed his arse in both my hands and pulled him flush against me. "And do you have a favourite ride so far?"

He gave a sultry look, drew his bottom lip between his teeth, and melted my socks off my feet in two seconds flat. Who the fuck had told this man that he had no game?

"Well, Mr Carmody." He nudged his dick against mine. "I'll need to try *all* the attractions on offer before I can make an informed decision."

"Is that so?" I cupped his face and drew him in for a long kiss, tasting every one of the six hours he'd shared my bed, all the places our tongues had visited, and it still wasn't enough. '*I like it messy.*' Well so did I.

"Do I need to make a list?" I rested our foreheads together. "That way we can be really thorough."

"I approve of your organisational skills, Mr Carmody." Lee batted his lashes, making me laugh. "It's an important factor in any research project. And I think maybe we should start with . . . *this.*" He dropped through my arms to his knees, yanked my shorts off on the way, and had my cock down his throat before I could blink.

Holy fucking hell. My gaze swept the back yard just in case, but we were alone.

Stunningly uninhibited, Lee worked my dick with a sloppy, fervent enthusiasm, and all I could do was fist his short dark locks and hang on for the embarrassingly short ride.

"Jesus, Lee, I'm almost there." I pushed at his head. "Sweetheart, pull off if you don't—"

But he shrugged me off, and seconds later that rush of pleasure crescendoed in my body, and I exploded down Lee's throat with a loud groan, shuddering as he milked me dry, my thumb brushing his cheek as he worked and swallowed around my dick, eyes locked on mine.

I wasn't sure I'd ever seen anything as sexy in my life.

"Get up here." I tugged up my boardshorts, backed Lee against the stainless-steel fridge, and shoved my tongue as far down his throat as I could get it, savouring myself in his mouth, the taste and scent of both of us tangled on our skin—salt, sex, sweat, and the sweetness of this new thing growing between us.

"How are you not freaked out by all this?" I held his face in my hands and brushed our noses together.

He shrugged, a deep-rose creeping up his neck. "I don't know. I mean I've never been shy, just not particularly highly sexed. But with you—" He wrapped his arms around my neck. "Since the first time I saw you, things felt *different*. I want you like I've never wanted anyone. And now that I'm over the 'no way' part of that—" His eyes twinkled with mischief and I couldn't help but laugh. "—*now*, I just want *everything*."

I threw the back of my hand over my forehead. "I feel so objectified."

He laughed. "Well, if it'll make you feel any better, I'm more than happy to take a turn at being objectified." He pulled the cord on his sweats and dropped them to the floor. "Just saying."

His thick cock jutted proud, and saliva pooled in my mouth. I fell to my knees and licked a stripe up its length, keeping my eyes on his. "It's a tough job, but somebody has to do it."

He smirked. "Less talking, more sucking, Mr Carmody. I need to be at the wharf in thirty minutes."

I had him in the shower in ten.

By early afternoon, I'd made a good dent in the kitten to-do list. Saturday was normally Lee's accounts day, but he and Patrick needed to check things were secure after we'd left in such a hurry the day before. Plus, I had a feeling he needed a little space after last night.

I sure as hell needed some, if for nothing more than to calm the fuck down. One night together had blown my fucking mind, and I was still working through all the implications of starting a relationship with the newly rainbowed son of my mother's girlfriend. Complicated didn't even begin to cover it.

Kane had called from the hospital late morning to say the surgery had gone well but they were keeping him until Monday. Then he had to rest for three days before he could be up and about as long as he didn't use the arm—for six weeks.

My stomach sank, not sure how Lee was going to manage that particular trick on the boat, although somehow, I knew he would. He wouldn't see Kane without a wage. Lee was far more like his mother than he knew.

Kane sputtered and protested at the news he was going nowhere except into Lee's old bedsit above the garage for a few days. When I warned him he'd have to take his argument up with Leroy, Kane went quiet very quickly and we moved on to the topic of the kittens.

The vet had done the necessities and given them a clean bill of health, and Kane was good with a plan to start finding them homes. He wanted the black male for himself—Bostock or Bossy for short, apparently. Kind of apt since the kitten was a little warlock in the making.

It took a good couple of hours to clear the bedsit and get it habitable. It wasn't the Ritz, but it beat living in a shit heap of a car with a broken arm. I was hauling the bucket of cleaning equipment back into the laundry when my phone rang. I glanced at the caller ID with a sinking heart. The day had been going so well.

"Quit ignoring my calls."

"Good afternoon to you too, Van. How can I help you this fine Saturday?"

"You can start by answering your damn phone."

"Like now, you mean?"

"Don't be such a tool. Tinny said you're not answering his calls either."

News to me. I took a quick look and found three unanswered calls from the day before and a text. *Call me.*

Shit. Everything had been a mess since the accident. "Well, I'm answering now. I had an emergency yesterday. What do you want?"

"I want Mack. And I've got a court order that says we have to share her equal time. You've been gone more than a month, Fox, so I suggest you put her on a plane by the end of next week or—"

"Or what?"

"Fox, she's mine as much as yours."

"But that's where you've got it all wrong. She's mine, Van. She was mine before you came along, and she was still mine after you fucked my friend and left. What don't you understand about that?"

"I'm trying to be nice about this, Fox, but you're not making it easy."

"I hear a little more money might sweeten the pot. So much for the big love affair you have with my dog. It seems that's as easily bought as the one I thought you had with me."

"What? Who told you that?"

I said nothing.

He sighed. "I don't care what you heard. I love Mack as much as you. Taking her without telling me wasn't right."

Maybe. "You've got a damn nerve claiming the moral high ground after what you did to me."

Silence slammed down the line.

And when he finally spoke, it was in a much quieter voice, one I recognised from better times between us. "Please don't do this, Fox. Don't make me force you. I just want to see her."

I snorted. "And how the hell do you think you're going to force me? Go back to Ewan, Van. You got what you wanted. Leave Mack and me alone."

I hung up and called Tinny, barely managing a brief hello before laying into the poor guy about not doing enough to stop the court order.

"Back off, Fox. I tried to warn you yesterday if you'd only answered your damn phone. What did you want me to do?" He sounded righteously pissed off. "Chain the guy in my basement?"

"Yes. Exactly that. It would solve a lot of my problems."

"I'm sure." I heard the eye-roll rattle down the line. "He has a legal right, Fox. I warned you this could happen. Where were you yesterday?"

"One of the workers on the boat had an accident. Nothing major, it just ate up the afternoon at the ER with him."

"Is he okay?"

"He's got a broken arm, but he'll be fine."

"That's good then." He paused. "So, how's it all going?"

"You're changing the subject."

He snorted. "Not for long, I'm sure. Answer the question."

I thought of Lee and smiled. "It's been good. Complicated. Nice. I just need to decide what the hell I'm going to do for a living."

"You'll work it out. So who does the *complicated* part of that belong to?"

"I don't know what you mean."

"I'll ask again. Who is he?"

"What makes you think that word refers to a man?"

Tinny said nothing.

Goddamn, the man. As my best friend *and* lawyer, the combination left me two chances of fobbing him off—zero and none. "Okay, so there *might* be someone, a man, but it's just casual."

"A man? In under a month? That's mighty quick work for a guy who'd sworn off the troublesome creatures for a while."

Don't remind me. "Yeah, well, as I said, it's not serious."

"All right. You're entitled to have some fun. I get that Van jumped all over your trust, Fox, but you deserve to have a life. You deserve to find someone who'll treat you a lot better than that dickhead."

"This . . . this isn't like that, not really. As I said, it's just casual." Even I could hear the lie in my voice, and a sharp stab of guilt made me wince. *No promises.*

Tinny hesitated. "Okay, I won't push. But it's a start."

"Can we get back to Van, please? Is there *nothing* we can do to stop him?"

Tinny sighed. "Bar convincing him to see sense, not much. I've been in contact with a specialist divorce lawyer to check out your options, and I filed for an injunction, but I wouldn't hold out hope. The lawyer said that prior to the family court hearing itself and without evidence that Mack is unsafe in Van's care, a judge is likely to err on the side of caution and let the later hearing make the final decision. In the meantime, Van's got his court order and you flout it at your peril, Fox. That's your lawyer talking, not your best friend. Book Mack on a flight down here, and I'll make sure she gets back to you in a month. Or come back yourself."

"I'll think about it."

"Be smart about this, Fox. You don't want trouble just before a family court hearing on the divorce and Mack's long-term custody arrangements."

Fuck. "Okay, okay. I hear you."

"Make sure that you do. Let me know when you buy her ticket. And good luck with Mr Complicated and Nice."

———————

The back door slammed against the cupboard and the familiar sound of Lee's bag landing on the laundry floor made me smile. Seconds later he walked into the family room and broke into laughter. "Oh. My. God. You are too fucking cute." He made his way to the couch and perched next to my outstretched and exhausted body. I shuffled over to give him some room.

Mack barrelled up to lay a few doggy kisses on Lee's face before sniffing his crotch to ensure he was who he appeared to be and then giving him the full once-over sniff to vet his contacts and geographic high notes of the day.

"I don't see what's so funny." I glared, repositioning two of the kittens who'd found their way down the front of my T-shirt. Okay, so I might've put them there. But it was the only way to stop them digging their needle claws into my arms like some kind of human pin cushion. Once inside my tee, they'd immediately settled down to sleep, and everyone could relax. The rest of the brood were curled up in a line of furry full-stops, from my chest to my knees.

"They needed some attention," I explained. "I was merely doing my bit to make sure they're well socialised for whoever their long-term families will be."

"Of course you were." Lee bit back a smile and leaned down as if to kiss me, then hesitated. "Is this okay?" He pushed a few long strands of hair off my forehead.

"I've been waiting all day." I cupped his cheek and drew him down. He smiled against my lips, then slipped his tongue inside, and my day disappeared in the tangy taste of him. Was I falling hard and fast? Yes. Yes, I was.

"Sorry, I'm later than I thought."

"You had things to do. So did I. Let's agree to not do this dance. We both know what it's like running a business."

He nodded gratefully.

"So, are you . . . okay?" We both knew what I meant.

"More than okay." He stroked the closest kitten. "But it was good to have some time to think about things. You?" He locked eyes and I nodded.

"The same. No regrets."

He gave an almost shy smile. "That's good then." His cheeks brightened and his gaze drifted to the line of kittens down my body. "I'm very proud of you. Such dedication to their feline welfare."

"So you should be." I started handing him the kittens one by one. "I risked life and limb just to be here for them. Now it's your turn. I need to finish dinner."

"If I must." Lee stared at the mound of wriggling fur in his arms and fell sideways into my vacated spot. Mack stretched out on the floor alongside, her chin on the couch so she could watch the kittens stretch and settle again.

I bent down and ran my nose up his neck. "You smell good."

He snorted and tried to wrangle the kittens into some kind of order. "I smell of shellfish, sea, and sweat. Eau de mussel."

"Like I said, good."

He huffed. "You need to raise your standards."

I kissed him, holding his gaze. "My standards are exactly where they need to be."

A flush ran up his neck as he caught my gaze and held it. He looked, nervous. "Can I ask you something?"

I frowned. "This sounds ominous, but sure."

"Did you make a decision about that skipper's job?"

Oh. I frowned and pushed his dark choppy locks off his forehead to better see those wary blue eyes. *No promises. No lies.* "I thought I'd call him next week sometime. I was just waiting."

A nervous smile danced over his mouth, then was gone. "Yeah, of course. Makes sense."

I pulled him down and brushed my lips over his. "Taking it slow, right?"

He nodded, his cheeks dusky. "Taking it slow." He glanced toward the kitchen. "So, what's for dinner? You're pretty organised. I smell wine and cheese."

"Very good." I made my way into the kitchen. "Coq au vin and scalloped potatoes. I know it's only five, but I'm wrung out like a wet rag. If I didn't get it finished before I sat down, we'd be eating toast. But if you eat all your vegetables, I've got a special dessert I think you're gonna love."

He cocked his head and one of the kittens took it as an invitation to reposition on his shoulder. "Oh really?" He ran his cheek over the ball of fur. "Because I'm pretty hard to satisfy. It'll need to be . . . mouth-watering." He ran a pink tongue over his bottom lip and my cock did a little happy dance.

"Keep that up and you'll be getting nothing, because the dessert *thingy* will have risen and flopped before even getting out of the pan."

He laughed. "Well, we wouldn't want that, would we? I checked the bedsit before I came in, by the way. It looks amazing. Thank you."

"You're welcome. Terry and Hannah said to say hello. I pretty much emptied his store of cleaning supplies. I think I'll enjoy getting to know them better. He said to tell you they can't make Sunday lunch. Hannah has an early doctor appointment in Auckland on Monday and they're heading up tomorrow. He also took me aside and said he might be interested in one of the kittens for Hannah's birthday coming up. He mentioned she's been going through a bad patch with her arthritis since Christmas."

Lee nodded. "She needed both leg braces *and* her arm crutches for the wedding, but she still nailed the ring bearer job. And that's great news. We've got four of the blighters sorted into homes."

"Four?"

"Mum said they'd take one as well. And I have to say I'm kind of sold on this one for myself." He held up one of the tortoiseshell females who had become a favourite of mine as well. "I'm thinking, Prue. I knew a girl called Prue in high school."

I rolled my eyes. "Oh, wonderful. Just what I want to be reminded of every time I call her."

He sent me a look. "I really liked her . . . *dog*." He waggled his eyebrows and I laughed. "It was a beagle cross. Almost this exact colour. I couldn't tell you what Prue looked like."

I laughed. "You're a soft touch, Leroy Madden."

He fired me a heated look that curled my toes. "I wasn't last night."

I snorted and pointed my wooden spoon at him. "None of that. I'm trying to cook here."

He grinned and nuzzled the kitten before placing it back on his chest. "Judah and Morgan are home. I saw Morgan's truck parked outside the boathouse when I berthed."

I looked up and caught his worried look. "Did you tell him about Kane?"

He winced. "Seemed prudent to give them a quiet first night home. I just texted a welcome back."

I raised a brow.

"I know, I know. I just didn't want to spoil things, spoil tonight with you. Tomorrow is soon enough."

We shared a heated look, and I wasn't about to argue his reasoning. I set about finishing dinner instead while he bundled the kittens into their palace and headed for the shower.

By the time he returned, dinner was ready. But one look at him standing there in nothing but a pair of low-slung jeans and acres of flushed bare skin, looking downright fucking edible, with his hair wet and mussed, and water dripping down his chest—

"Here, right now," I ordered, dropping the serving spoon of cheesy potatoes back into the dish and throwing the tea towel into the sink. "You did that deliberately, you tart."

"Tart?" He sauntered toward me like he had all the time in the world, his expression reaching for seduction but failing to hide the nerves that lay just underneath, and I was reminded how very new this all was for him. But he was putting himself out there, and so fucking brave, I wanted to wrap him in my arms and tell him he'd had me from that first glare a year ago. The rest was just decoration.

"Not sure I've ever been called a tart before." He smirked, and he was lucky he was out of reach.

But as soon as he got close enough, I snagged his belt loop and jerked him against me. "Yes, *tart*." I ran my nose up the side of his neck and he shivered. Coconut and lime filled my head and desire pooled low and hot in my belly. "Sexy, wanton, teasing little tart," I whispered in his ear.

He pulled back to eyeball me. "My, my. You're bringing all the words out tonight."

I nibbled his ear lobe, then licked behind. "You have a smart mouth on you."

A hand wriggled between us to cup my groin. "Maybe you should do something about that."

His phone rang on the breakfast bar with the familiar ringtone of Cora, and I went to move away. The woman had impeccable timing, as usual.

"No you don't." Lee's grip tightened around my cock. "She can wait."

I arched a brow. "You know she'll just keep try—"

"She can wait." He reached over and flicked it to silent, then stepped back into me, kneading firmly.

I thrust into his hold and cursed softly, wanting him to know exactly what he did to me. "You make me want dangerous things, Lee. Things I'm not quite sure I'm ready for."

"I do?" He sounded genuinely surprised.

I caught his chin between my thumb and fingers and kissed those sweet lips, missing the salt that usually dusted them. "Yes, you do."

He frowned. "I just want to be enough for you. I know I'm new at this—"

I slammed my mouth over his to prove a point, not breaking the kiss until I felt him melt against me. "You are already enough. I've spent all day remembering how fucking hot you were on your knees for me. That smart mouth of yours wrapped around my cock. A fucking fantasy."

He drew a sharp breath, blue eyes darkening, confidence growing. "Any more fantasies you'd like to share?"

I grinned and put my lips next to his ear. "One or two. But I'd like to hear *yours* first." I wanted him centre stage.

He eyed me shamelessly, nerves settled. He flicked the buttons on his jeans and let them drop, revealing he was naked underneath—hard and dripping, and all I could do was stare. "See something you like?" he almost fucking purred, and that, plus the wicked look in his eyes, had me spinning my wheels.

I shoved the two casserole dishes back in the cooling oven, grabbed his hand, and tugged toward the hall.

"My room," he said, and I made a sharp left. He laughed. "In a hurry?"

"You have no fucking idea." I spun him onto his bed, its deep-blue cover striped by the late afternoon sun. My shorts and tank hit the floor seconds later, and after he produced some lube from his bedside table, I crawled up his body and fell into his eyes, wide and black with just the thinnest rim of blue at the margins.

"What do you want, Lee? Tell me and it's yours."

He cradled my face. "I want you. And I want to try you playing with my arse again."

I cocked a brow. "I'm sure I can manage that, just for research purposes, of course."

"Nothing too much. I don't know that I'm ready for *that* . . . quite yet. But I want to know if it's something I might want in the future . . ." His stare was intent, his cheeks flushed.

"Anything you want." I closed my mouth over his and he groaned into the kiss as I trailed my fingertips along his ribs and down that quivering belly to cup his balls, one finger stretched along his taint.

He arched up and threw his head back. "Jesus, yes, Fox." His thighs swept open. And he shoved the lube into my other hand. "Please."

Thirty minutes later, starfished and boneless in his bed, covered in lube and come and saliva, I figured he had his answer about whether he might like . . . more. My fingers and tongue had never left his arse and he'd finished with a shout to bring the walls down.

When he was done, I was so fucking turned on, I came on his chest with just a couple of tugs and his finger shoved up my arse. Then he got to his knees and licked my cock clean before dragging me into his shower where we made out under the steaming needles like a couple of randy teenagers.

Clean and somewhat dressed, we took our dinner to the deck and ate and talked and downed a couple of beers. Then I pulled Lee onto my lounger and into my arms, and we watched the sky turn a velvet blue behind the towering macrocarpas.

CHAPTER FIFTEEN

Leroy

MARTHA COOKED A MOUTH-WATERING BEEF ROAST FOR OUR reunion Sunday lunch, and afterwards, everyone retired to the deck where Judah held court, laughing and chatting about their honeymoon. He was relaxed, content, smiling, and so obviously well-loved, it caught at my heart—the two of them continuously reaching for the other to touch or kiss or share a look.

I found it impossible to look away.

Judah looked better than I'd seen him in a long time, and the realisation gave me pause. I'd always thought that once he got through high school, Judah had kind of landed on his feet—living the good life in a career he was born for, in a city he loved, making it big on the world stage and with a star-studded future ahead. Maybe I'd been wrong, because this Judah was an entirely new proposition, holding hands and sharing secret smiles with his husband.

But it wasn't only Judah who was different, I realised with an unwelcome jolt of awareness. For the first time, I was . . . jealous. Toe-curlingly and absurdly jealous. Only weeks ago, I'd have been happy for him but just as content that it wasn't me. Now? I glanced to Fox who was looking straight at me, because of course he bloody was. Now I wanted a taste of what Judah had.

Beside Morgan, Fox stood talking with Patrick while looking positively mouth-watering in a pair of dark shorts that clung to his muscled arse and a short-sleeved, bright-white tee that hugged those glorious fisherman biceps like it was painted on. The bastard wasn't going to know what hit him when everyone left and I finally got him alone. How dare he look so damn sexy when I couldn't touch him? Payback was going to be epic.

He smiled and I smiled back because all the best payback starts that way, right? I shook my head wondering what the hell had happened to me. Then Fox winked, and I realised *we* were doing that thing too. The *thing* that Judah and Morgan did. The shared-secrets *thing*.

And I suddenly knew exactly how much trouble I was in.

Fox frowned and I realised I was gaping unattractively.

"Okay?" he mouthed.

Patrick caught the question and turned my way. I quickly schooled my expression, but I doubted we were fooling him, not after yesterday. He had to know something was going on, but that didn't mean I was about to offer it to him on a plate.

I gave myself a solid mental slap and carried the tray of coffees to the outside table along with a fudge cake Fox had whipped up out of nowhere that morning while I was still fucked unconscious in bed. *Fucked* being the more generalised use of the term but one I was almost ready to make a lot more concrete and particular. Especially since I'd discovered the gobsmacking wonderland that was the human arse. Who would've guessed? John Mayer, take note.

I wasn't expecting the whole exploding galaxy of stars first time around bottoming—I really, *really* got the 'large peg in a much, much smaller hole' piece of the equation, but I was hoping for at least a nebula or two. What's more, I trusted Fox to get me there safely.

And wasn't that just a fucking miracle?

The man himself appeared at my elbow to slice and hand out the cake, every brush of his body an electric tingle that went straight to my balls. I was so focused on his unsettling presence and trying to control my reaction so I didn't blow our cover that I completely missed the direction the conversation had taken until I felt the burn of Judah's gaze when it landed on me.

"What the hell?" Judah growled. "Someone better explain right now why Kane needs to stay *here*?"

Someone meaning me, no doubt. *Fuck.* So much for the family reunion.

Patrick immediately pushed his chair back. Not one for confrontation was our Patrick.

"He's not staying in the house," I said evenly, holding Judah's angry stare. "Fox cleaned out the old bedsit. Plus, it's only for a few days, until he finds somewhere else. He can't sleep in his car, Judah. He's just had surgery and the accident happened on the damn boat, for fuck's sake. But if you really don't want him here, I'll find another solution." I took the plate with the slice of cake Fox handed me and slumped in my chair, ignoring it, appetite gone.

Judah pushed his own plate away. "Why should I give a damn about his injury or the fact he's been sleeping in his car? He's got his own bloody family. He didn't give a shit about me, did he?" He shot a pointed look at our mother. "The two of you cooked this whole thing up between you, didn't you?"

Martha's hand shot out to stay Patrick who looked about two seconds away from bolting. "Eat your cake, son. It'll be okay."

I winced, knowing that in Patrick's experience of his own family, that would've rarely been the case. But Martha's hand was a gentle soothe on Patrick's arm and he slowly relaxed.

I turned back to Judah. "Leave Mum out of it. She had no idea about the bedsit until yesterday. And we don't know about Kane's father, only that Kane's been living in his car." I slid my fork carefully next to my plate. "But I get it. You already agreed to him working for me, and that was big. You've every right to be pissed off."

Judah's lip curled. "Like I had any real choice about him working."

"You *did* have the choice," I shot back. "In fact, you had the final choice. If you'd said no, I wouldn't have even talked with him, Judah. You know that."

"Like my feelings ever meant anything to you, Leroy. You've thrown me under the bus too many times for me to trust anything you say."

The air rushed from my lungs like I'd been sucker-punched. All this time and we hadn't moved on at all. We were still in that place. "Wow. You know, this last year I'd thought . . . or at least I'd hoped . . ."

"What? That after everything you've done, we'd just slap each other on the back and walk off into the sun—"

"Judah!" My mother's face paled.

"What, Mum?" Judah turned on Cora. "You *know* what happened, or so I hear. How can you want to help him?"

"I do know what happened." She reached for Martha's hand. "But that was a long time ago, and people change, especially kids. Your brother has also changed. You *know* that. Or is it only *you* that's allowed to change?"

Judah blinked and started to protest, but Mum barrelled on.

"This is not Leroy's fault, Judah," she said flatly. "*I* asked him to take Kane on, but Leroy was adamant every step of the way that if you said no, that was it. He was angry with me for risking what he'd tried to build with you. He was on *your* side, Judah."

"He's never been on anyone's side but his own."

"That's enough." Fox pushed his chair back and put a hand on my shoulder, then quickly removed it. "Lee has been worried sick about what you were going to think of all this. I know because I overheard his conversation with Kane, and I had to step in to stop a fight on your behalf. The least you could do is listen."

My mother's gaze narrowed at the shortened name. I reached for Fox's arm, stunned that he would have my back so publicly, then realised that I shouldn't have been. "It's okay." I pulled him back into his seat.

Judah eyeballed Fox. "Keep out of this, Fox. This is family stuff."

Oh, hell no. I levelled a glare at my brother. "Fox *is* family. He's Martha's son. And he's been busting his guts on the farm for free to help us out this last month, to help Mum."

This time everyone looked, and I realised I was still holding on to Fox's arm. I quickly let go, adding, "He's only trying to help."

A flush made its way up Judah's throat and he hesitated, looking to Martha before nodding. "I'm sorry. That was rude."

She waved it away. "Already forgotten."

I caught Patrick's look of disbelief.

"Judah." Morgan's hand found his husband's arm. "Maybe just hear them out."

Judah turned, looking miserable, and I hated that we'd put him in this position. "Jesus, Morgan, you too? I thought at least *you'd* be on my side."

Morgan's expression softened. "I'm always on your side, sweetheart, you know that. I just need you to really think about exactly *what* side that is. Then I'll be there."

They stared at each other for a long minute until finally Judah leaned forward and pressed his lips to Morgan's. "I'm sorry. I know you're on my side."

Goddammit. I didn't want to cause trouble between Morgan and Judah. This was turning out to be the shitshow I'd thought, and I was done with it.

I pushed my chair back and stood. "Enough. I'll find somewhere else for Kane. He's not doing this to our family again. I'm sorry, Judah." I sidestepped both Fox and my mother and headed down the steps with Mack at my heels. I made it around the corner of the house to a bench on the covered veranda before I collapsed.

Mack curled at my feet with a soft whine as bile ran up the back of my throat. It was everything I'd feared, only worse. Because I'd been telling myself a lie. I'd achieved nothing with Judah. He hated me as much as ever.

I batted angrily at my eyes, but for once I didn't give a fuck, I just let myself feel. I should've said no to my mother. I knew it would blow up in my face. I'd gotten it so wrong with Judah so many fucking times. Jesus Christ, what chance did Fox and I have? Not to mention what Judah would say if and when I ever came out. A fucking disaster in the making.

"Mind if I sit?"

My gaze shot up to find Judah staring down at me. So fucking light on his feet, I'd never even heard him.

I shrugged and slid over, the bench creaking under our combined weight.

He stared out over the bay. The covered veranda had arguably the best view in the house, straight over the top of the old barn—Judah's new dance studio—and his and Morgan's boathouse to the ocean beyond. But there was no sun today, the sky heavy with clouds, a relief from the late summer sun, the bay a dull grey, as still as a grave. Perfect for my spiralling mood.

"So." Judah kept his eyes on the placid water. "I might've been a tad dramatic back there."

I couldn't help a small smile. "Is that you talking or Morgan?"

He gave a soft snort. "If I say Morgan, will you still accept my apology?"

"You don't owe me any apology. I should never have gone along with Mum. I'm sorry, Judah. I'll get Kane settled somewhere else and find some other work for him. I don't know what I was thinking."

He drew a slow breath and leaned back against the wide weatherboards of the house. "No, he can stay. I don't think it was really about him."

I turned to study him. "You don't have to—"

"I know I don't." He met my eyes with his own red-rimmed ones. "And maybe that's the point. I wanted to blame you, you and Mum. Then I didn't have to make my own decision. Because when I really think about it, I don't want to turn him away either. I guess I don't want to do to him what he did to me. And despite everything, I guess I trust Mum's judgement."

My eyes rolled so hard I was surprised they didn't tumble down my back and head down the hill for the wharf. "That might be a bridge too far." I elbowed him. "But are you sure about Kane, Judah? After what he did—"

"I know, and I can't say I'm thrilled about the idea, and the rules still stand. But I'm also not frightened of him. I'm still just bloody angry. So, until I'm ready, he needs to keep out of my way. One wrong word and he's gone." He eyed me pointedly.

I nodded. "Of course. But I'll find somewhere else for him by the end of the week."

Judah nodded. "Thanks. The crazy thing is, I do actually believe in second chances, that people can change. Maybe not everyone, but some. Of course, that's all well and good until it's my life that's involved, right?" He gave a smile that didn't quite reach his eyes.

"You know, until that day he kicked me, most of Kane's bullying was pretty low-key, just the usual snide comments and name-calling. I'd never been scared of him in that way. He just didn't have that vibe. Guess you never really know people. And afterwards, he just disappeared. Kept out of my way." He picked at a splinter of wood in the bench and then flicked it on the grass. "Mum says he's been working well the last few weeks."

Judah was trying, I could see that, and the squeeze on my heart eased a little. I badly wanted things between us to be better and hoped this was a good sign. "So far. Not sure what we'll do with him one-handed though. Drive the boat, I guess, if he's up to it."

He went quiet for a moment, then said, "You need to talk to Mum about the farm, Leroy."

I spun to face him. "What do you mean?"

He gave a sad smile. "I'm not oblivious, you know, and neither is Mum. I worked with you last year, I know things are tight. You need to buy her out and stop running it her way. I know you're itching to."

I blinked slowly, wondering just how obvious it was that the business was in trouble and how many people knew? All my suppliers for one. I sighed. "I can't afford to."

"Then find a way you can."

I shook my head. "It's not that easy."

He eyeballed me. "Nothing ever is. Ask me how I know that."

We both laughed. "Asshole."

"Dickhead."

"I have actually been thinking about a possible option. It's an idea Fox put in my head."

"Fox? Okaaaay." Judah looked unconvinced and more than a little surprised.

"Don't look like that. He's got a good brain for business. I just need to get it a little more solid before I raise it with her."

Judah gave a satisfied nod. "Good. See that you do."

"Hey, I'm the older brother, remember?"

"Like you ever let me forget." Judah's hand landed on mine and I jumped. "Wow, touchy." He smiled, a genuine one this time.

"Pffft. You've been on your honeymoon for a month. I know exactly where those hands have been, thank you very much."

He stared for a second, then threw back his head and laughed. "Fuck. Me. Look at you with the jokes. I think sharing a house with Fox has been good for you. Not to mention the man's pretty easy on the eyes. Shame all *those* attributes are lost on you. Which reminds me, 'a good brain for business'? I thought you couldn't stand him?"

I almost swallowed my tongue thinking of how very *not* lost the man's attributes were on me. "I, ah, didn't really know him, I guess. It's not like I gave him much of a chance, was it?"

"Maybe not. So, you two are getting along okay then? He had all guns blazing to defend you back there."

Oh boy. "Yep, fine. He's a good guy. And his dog's a sweetheart."

Judah stared at me for a second, then laughed. "Trust you to find the man's animal more interesting than the hottie himself."

"Yep, that's me."

"There's one more thing." He squeezed my hand and my heart leapt in my throat.

What now?

"I want to apologise for what I said back there, about us, about you. It was wrong. I promise I don't feel that way. I *do* trust you, and I should've made that clear. I know what happened with us was complicated. I've been thinking a lot about what it must've been like for you growing up with Mum and Dad so focused on me. I never once considered it might come at a price for you. I like what we are now, Leroy. I like having my brother back."

His eyes shone with tears and a huge weight shifted from my shoulders. "Me too." I pulled him into my arms and held on tight. "Me too."

We wandered back to join the others still waiting on the deck. Fox looked ready to jump out of his skin and Morgan was right there with him, his gaze raking over Judah, all prickly mumma bear. Fox stopped gnawing his fingernails and discreetly eyed the seat next to him. *Come here.*

"Do we need an ambulance?" Cora looked us over and nodded. "No? Good. Then I volunteer to collect Kane when he's discharged tomorrow and lay down the rules. And we'll get him another place to stay as soon as possible. Is that acceptable to you two?"

We both nodded.

"Excellent. Now, can we please finish our desserts? I want to do justice to the cake Fox made. Gotta love a man who can cook. You're damn lucky to have him staying, Leroy."

I couldn't meet Fox's eyes. "So he keeps telling me."

Everyone laughed, and under cover of the table, I pressed my thigh against Fox and he found my hand for a quick squeeze.

"I'll get more coffee." Martha planted a kiss on Cora's cheek, making her blush. "Patrick can help me." He immediately pushed back his chair and followed her inside.

"So, what did we miss?" Judah's gaze swept the table, landing on me for a quick smile, which I returned. It was a start.

Surprisingly it was Fox who answered. "Morgan has just raised a possible job opportunity for me."

I flicked my gaze to the big, brown-eyed man next to my brother. "Really?"

Morgan nodded. "We're currently down two commercial fishing observers in Northland. Fox could be a good fit. He'd have to apply and be interviewed of course. And then there's a three-week training, but he'd have a good chance and the next training is coming up soon."

I turned to Fox. "An observer?"

He looked interested, although maybe not excited. "Yeah. We carried them on the *Blue Swell* when we were asked. It's a requirement of the fishing licence and quota contracts. Observers monitor the catch, collect data, take samples, and generally ensure vessel compliance. They also watch for marine and bird interaction. Some of the skippers didn't like it, but I never had an issue, although it would be strange being on the other side, that's for sure."

Morgan slipped his arm around Judah's waist and pulled him close, and that deep yearning unfolded again in my chest. Then Fox's foot found the back of my calf and I almost smiled.

"I was explaining to Fox that it's not continuous employment," Morgan said. "They use short contracts to cover the seasonal demands, sometimes for just a few months. And it could require some long stints offshore. Two or three weeks at a time. Fox would have to be happy with that."

I turned to Fox. "And you'd be interested?" I was surprised. It seemed too . . . bureaucratic for his wild nature.

"Maybe. As a temporary fix. I know the business, which would give me some street cred with the boats. Plus, I'd be out on the ocean, I'd be earning, and I'd still have plenty of free time to plan the next business venture."

He was saying all the right words but I wasn't totally buying it. "I'd think it would be hard being back on the ocean, but not in your own boat and not in charge."

He held my gaze and I saw the uncertainty there. Was he considering this just for me? Because that was never going to work. It was hard to see Fox caged in a role like that.

"No, I'd be lying if I said I wouldn't struggle with that side of things," he answered honestly. "But it would give me some breathing room, and the shorter contract thing would actually suit me. As I said, it could be a temporary fix." He smiled but it didn't quite reach his eyes. "At least until I get into seaweed farming. I'm told it's the next big thing."

"Oh, for fuck's sake." I rolled my eyes, not missing the way he'd light-heartedly changed the subject. "Then *you* can get the next lot of supplies. Cole will be delighted, I'm sure." I explained the joke and we were all laughing by the time Martha and Patrick returned with the fresh coffee.

But my gaze remained on Fox and the way his wary one danced off mine, refusing to settle.

What the hell were we doing?

CHAPTER SIXTEEN

Leroy

I leaned against the window and drank my fill of the man sprawled sound asleep in my bed. I missed the way his warm body had wrapped around mine just minutes before, but I'd been hot and restless, and the open window beckoned. And all because I'd woken with a revelation.

I trusted Fox. Like *really* trusted Fox. Him and about three or four other people in the entire world. And it didn't matter which way I looked at it, turned it upside down, and shook the bejesus out of it, I still trusted him.

The realisation both awed and frightened me. Two weeks in, and I was far deeper into this whole relationship thing we were trying than I'd thought. Deeper and a fuckton more vulnerable. Me, who'd never had a girlfriend of any import in my entire life, was crushing hard, on a guy, like hard, hard. Like 'cut me a piece of his hair and put it in a locket' hard.

I had no clue where we were going or how the hell any of this was going to work out, but I trusted Fox to be there for the ride, even if we went down in flames. It was something I tried not to think about too hard even though it seemed the most likely outcome. Because as much as Fox seemed happy being with me for now, he still had no solid future plans beyond the chance at a temporary job, which wasn't exactly lighting him on fire whenever I mentioned it, and he certainly wasn't raising the subject himself.

Not to mention that barely two weeks before, he'd been tossing around the idea of turning round and moving back south until after the divorce was finalised, maybe even longer. To his house that he loved, on the island he loved, to his friends and crew, and to the chance of a better job—a job more suitable for his skills. And I wasn't stupid enough to think that had all just gone away because we were fucking.

I trusted Fox to be there for me and to be honest, but that didn't mean he was going to stay. The last thing he'd been looking for was another relationship, and especially not with me—a shiny newly out bisexual who didn't know his frot from his douche prep, and yes, I might've been doing some research.

And I saw that uncertainty in his expression when he didn't know I was watching—would I decide to pull the plug or find someone else? I didn't blame him. But I also didn't know how to make my certainty about *him* any clearer. And if I was honest, a piece of me had also wondered at first whether this thing between us *would* just burn out fast. If I'd tire of having someone in my space. Tire of having to keep watch on my naturally spiky temper.

But Fox never crowded me. And we had that domestic shit down pat, no arguments there. He almost always cooked, and I cleared, except when I felt in the mood to switch. He vacuumed, and I did the bathrooms. In the mornings, he made our lunches for the boat while I saw to the laundry, and then we both rode in my truck to the wharf. And so on, and ridiculously so on. It would've been nauseating if it wasn't so damn nice.

But Fox was like that Southern Albatross he talked about—the one that followed his boat. For now, Fox had landed on me, in

Painted Bay, but I couldn't shake the feeling that he'd be leaving again as well. This wasn't his home, no matter how much I wanted it to be.

Fox plucked at the covers in his sleep, his leg stretching from under the sweat-damp sheet to cool in the late afternoon breeze drifting through my bedroom, or more accurately, *our* bedroom as it had become by default over the last two weeks, ever since I'd first been introduced to the glory that was Fox's body.

Even Mack had joined the bedroom swapping party, finding a cool spot in my en suite to call her own at night. Hell, I'd have moved Fox's clothes into my wardrobe if it weren't for the need to keep this thing between us quiet.

His soft snore made me smile. He was so fucking beautiful, at peace and sated, his come dry on his belly from where I'd fucked him into the mattress. There went another load of sheets. We were gonna have to become smarter about that, like five loads of bed linen in a week wasn't going to raise flags. Trouble was, I'd found myself caring less and less about people finding out, and that wasn't smart.

I shook my head. How had this become my life? A man fucked out *by me* and asleep in *my* bed on a Saturday afternoon when I should've been working, and I couldn't be happier. You couldn't dream this shit up.

And more to the point, what the hell was I going to do if it came to a crashing end?

When Fox wasn't around, I missed his smile and droll commentary and the inevitable warning looks that told me to watch my mouth with Patrick and Kane when I got cranky and impatient. I'd been trying, really trying to learn from what he said about how he'd run his commercial operation, his crew, his *family* as he called them.

Being open didn't come easy for me, but with an occasional nudge and redirect from Fox, I was learning. And I was starting to have fun. I'd learned more about Patrick in the last three weeks than I had in the almost two years he'd been with me, and even Kane was slowly relaxing around me.

I glanced out the window to the back of the bedsit where Kane was still holed up after Judah had rejected Martha's discovery of a family in town who were looking for a boarder.

He's fine where he is as long as he keeps out of my way, Judah had said before walking off, and the two men had continued to pass each other like ships in the night ever since. I was pretty sure no words had been exchanged between them except the odd grunted greeting, and Judah remained cool whenever Kane's name came up, like the dodgy cousin you never talked about at the dinner table.

Go fucking figure. The only difference being my deduction of a small amount of rent from Kane's pay each week—like enough to pay Mack's monthly dog biscuit addiction and not much else.

For his part, Kane kept to himself and stayed out of the house. He found the remaining kittens good homes and got himself to and from the wharf each morning, turning down any offer of a ride. And he'd picked up the helmsman job with ease, even with only one useful arm.

Another snort from the bed grabbed my attention and my gaze trailed down those long-muscled limbs. Limbs that only an hour ago had been wrapped around my waist as I fucked him thoroughly. Fox was always generous with his arse, offering it to me at the drop of a hat or any other article of clothing that happened to fall off between us on a regular basis.

But I was getting more than a little curious to be on the receiving end of the fucking for a change. Fox had a beautiful cock—another sentence I never imagined coming out of my mouth—and I loved when he fingered me. Not to mention, his rimming skills were down-right filthy. I was getting much more adventurous, and curious, about *everything* to do with that particular part of my anatomy, and I also wanted that intimacy. I wanted to understand that look that exploded in Fox's eyes when I slid into him. I craved to know.

He snuffled and one eyelid opened. "You're creeping me out. Come back to bed." He rolled to his back and lifted the sheet. My gaze swept up those long legs and thick thighs, my cock plumping.

He threw me a filthy look. "Go on. You know you want to. You're still all naked and gorgeous."

"Don't tempt me." I sauntered across, making sure he had a good view. Even though I wasn't shy about my body, I'd never flaunted it, but over these last two weeks, I'd come to accept that Fox loved looking at me. Hell, he told me often enough, and it was hard to ignore how his body responded. He'd have me naked all day if he could, and the feeling was mutual. It was heady stuff.

I'd just made it to the bed when Fox's phone buzzed on the bedside table, and he reached for it. I caught the flash of the name before he opened the text. Laurie Smithson, the guy with the skipper's job down south. *Shit.* Try as I might, I couldn't stop a ball of disappointment clench in my throat.

Fox caught my eye and I read the apology there. But there was really nothing for him to apologise for. *No promises. No lies.*

"Still haggling about the skipper's job?" I asked, trying to keep my voice neutral when he finally looked up from reading the text.

He blew out a sigh. "In a way. I did tell him I didn't think it would work, but he's not giving up without a fight. I have another month to make my mind up, apparently."

Damn. I folded my arms to stop my hands from shaking. "Then maybe you should take a look."

His gaze jerked to mine. "Why would you say that?"

"Fox, I'm not stupid. It's a good job. Maybe the best one for you right now. I don't want you turning it down just for me."

"Who said it was just for you?"

I drew a slow breath. "Are you telling me you'd have turned it down so quickly if we weren't—" I flicked a hand between us. "—doing this? Fox, you had . . . *have* a whole life down there. You said yourself when you first got here that you didn't know where you'd end up."

He studied me, his jaw working, and I had my answer before he even spoke. "Okay, yes, I'd probably have seriously considered the skipper role because it's a good job, but that *was* before you. I like what we're doing, Lee. I like *us*. I want to try this. And I left that life for a reason."

But you didn't really want to leave it, did you? You ran, but you kept your roots there, your house. What am I against all that? Still, I trusted Fox and I had to believe that he wasn't just protecting me.

"Just please don't stay here if you need to be somewhere else," I said bluntly. "I won't be responsible for holding you back, and I won't blame you if you leave. You have a life to rebuild, I get that." But even as the words came out my heart was screaming, *don't go.*

He reached for me. "You're *not* holding me back. I want to be here."

He was so earnest, and it went some way to reassuring me. "Okay," I said, my voice a little shaky. "Just make sure you make the right choices for you, not because of me. If you want to go down, then do it. Maybe the distance thing wouldn't be so bad at the moment." *Liar.* "I mean I'm not even out, right, and you'd be coming back to see your mu—"

"Shush." He pulled me onto the bed and into his arms, drawing me close. "I'm not going anywhere right now. And if I do decide to take another look at the job, we'll talk about it then, both of us. Deal?"

I sighed and nodded, burying my face in his neck. "Deal." It would have to do.

He kissed my hair. "Good, then maybe we can find something less depressing to do with our time." His free hand trailed down my body, leaving fire in its wake as always happened whenever Fox touched me.

I pushed back off his chest and wriggled to free myself. "Oi, we have training this evening, remember? And Mack needs a walk, plus we have to eat."

He pouted adorably and I couldn't resist snagging that mouth for a kiss, happy to shove away all those doubts that clouded my time with him. But I'd been played. The instant our lips touched, his arms swept around my waist and I found myself flat on my back with a six-foot-three, green-eyed mountain of solid muscle grinding against me.

Well, damn. Being manhandled in bed had become my number one fetish and the bastard knew it. I was rock hard in an instant.

"You were saying?" He peppered my face with kisses while thrusting against me.

"Nothing." I kissed him back. "Absolutely nothing. Down a bit— there! Shit! Fucking hell!" My head fell back as his mouth landed on my throat, then moved lower to my chest, my armpits, my nipples. I liked it rough around there and Fox knew it. All teeth and lips and tongue, biting and sucking until I knew I'd look like a fucking chessboard and have to wear a high-neck T-shirt for days.

I raised my head and my hands found that spectacular arse to hold on to. "Yessss," I muttered in his hair. "Come on, Fox, almost th—"

"Leroy? Fox?" The front door slammed. "Anyone home?"

"Goddammit!" I had the bedroom lock flicked in two seconds flat, not entirely sure how I got there. But when I turned to put my back against the cool timber, I saw Fox hanging off the side of the bed, almost strangled in the sheet that stretched between us like a taut rope. *Oops.*

"I thought you bolted the front door?" I whispered.

"Me?" Fox threw me a what-the-fuck look. "I thought you did? Does she never knock?" He struggled to untangle himself.

"Sorry, sorry." I unwound the sheet from my hips to give him some slack. "Stay here. I'll go see what she wants."

"Leroy?" From the family room this time.

"Hang on," I shouted, stumbling over the sheet, which was still caught around one ankle, almost sending Fox into hysterics. "I just got out of the shower. Won't be a minute."

Fox's gaze raked over the state of my very *unwashed* body, and I threw the sheet over his face because he deserved it.

"Shut up. I'm winging it here," I whisper-growled.

He chuckled and lay back with his hands behind his head to watch as I scrambled into a pair of shorts and a tank.

I flipped him off, then pointed at the dried pool of come on his stomach. "And for fuck's sake, get rid of that if you come out. I'll close the hall door so you can pretend you came from your own room."

"Oh." His mouth curved up in a wicked smile. "That would be the room that your mother just walked past. The one with the open door. The very *empty* room. That one?"

"Don't be a smart arse. I'm doing my best here." I hit the bathroom to check the mirror and— "Holy Jesus." I looked like I'd just walked out of a brothel after a very long night. I sniffed myself. Make that a long week. I tried to run my fingers through my hair, but they snagged on stuff I didn't even want to think about.

I stared at my reflection and my face sagged. "I am so totally screwed."

Fox appeared behind me in the mirror and planted a kiss on my neck. "You'll be fine. Lift your arms."

"What?"

He looked in the mirror and I followed his gaze. Fuck. I had bite marks all over my chest and—I lifted an arm—dear Jesus, my armpits as well. And I'd chosen a tank? Of course I bloody had.

Fox slid my tank off, replacing it with a modest black T-shirt.

Then he fixed my hair, spritzed me with cologne, which to be honest was likely to clue my mother in before anything else, and pointed me toward the door. "Go get 'em, tiger." He smacked me on the butt and gave me a push.

I spun and took his face in my hands and kissed him. "Thank you."

Delight danced in his eyes and he returned a more lingering smooch. Then he pulled back and straightened my clothes before giving me a final thumbs up. "You've got this, baby. She'll never guess."

After a quick peck on my mother's cheek, I headed for the coffee maker to avoid her astute gaze while at the same time keeping my woefully odorous body at a distance. Epic fail.

She sidled alongside, put her back to the counter, and folded her arms. "Sooooo, you and Fox?"

The empty mug I'd been holding shattered on the floor. "Shit." I stared at the broken bits of china and tried not to panic.

"Mmm." She patted my shoulder. "You finish the coffees and I'll clean up." She headed for the laundry, her choppy brunette bob bouncing merrily as if the world hadn't just taken a sharp dive down a rainbow rabbit hole. "Then you can answer my question."

Something I had zero intention of doing. "I've no idea what you're on about." I stepped over the mess and went back to making our coffee. "We're getting along much better, that's all. You should be pleased. Jesus, Mum, what sort of question is that? You know I'm not —" I stopped the lie dead on my tongue, not completely sure why but pretty certain it had something to do with the naked man who'd recently taken up residence in my bedroom.

Omission was one thing, but lying about what Fox meant to me suddenly seemed all kinds of wrong. If I was serious about Fox, I needed to start showing him, or I might risk losing him altogether. I didn't have much to offer, but I had that.

My mother looked at me, a shrewd and quiet knowing in her eyes, and then she sighed. "You're whatever you are, Leroy. And you're my son. I love you. That will never change. I haven't always shown you exactly how much, and that's on me. It could be a girl, but I wasn't born yesterday. I know what I saw when Fox defended you at lunch that day, the ease between the two of you, the way you watched him, and—" Her gaze dropped to my throat and she smiled. "That neck's just a little too low, sweetheart."

My hand immediately went to the exact spot Fox had marked me, and I was pretty sure my entire body sucked in on itself like a burst beach ball and went up in hell flames of mortification. "Oh, dear God." I hauled the neck of my T-shirt higher.

"Shush." She took over the coffee and waved me to a seat at the table. And just like that, a year rolled away and we were still sharing the house. "I didn't need a love bite to tell me, Leroy. You're *different* around him. Lighter somehow. You've laughed more these last few weeks than I've seen since you were a child. And he's . . . protective of you. Believe it or not, I think you need that. You've been alone for too long, too used to thinking you have to do it all. You deserve to be looked after. I hope he does that. You hardly need my approval, but you have it no matter what."

I swallowed hard, caught between shock and relief. "Please don't say anything. It's only been a couple of weeks."

"I'd never do that." She slid my coffee cup across the table and settled those blue eyes on mine. "But he's had your attention for a lot longer, hasn't he?"

How the hell did parents do that?

"Oh, I watched the two of you dance around each other last year, all puffed-out chests and angry stares. You had me hot and bothered just watching you."

She had to be joking. "What? We did nothing of the sort. I couldn't stand him back then."

She arched those well-plucked brows of hers and I snorted.

"Okay, maybe not that, exactly, but he unsettled me, Mum. He still does. Ugh." I banged my forehead twice on the table and she chuckled. "I knew I was attracted to him, but—"

"It made you angry."

I slid down in my seat. "Yeah. I didn't want to feel that, especially for him. I hardly need any more demands in my life. And I'd watched Judah all those years." I shook my head. "It was confusing."

She raised her cup to mine and clinked. "Here's to being hit over the head by an inconvenient love hammer later in life."

I'd almost forgotten. "Was it the same for you with Martha?"

She took a second to answer. "Yes and no. I knew she had feelings for me—little things she did, the occasional glance, that sort of thing—but I felt no attraction to her in that way until after your father died, well after, when I started taking notice in a quite different way." She gave a coy smile and sipped her coffee. "But once I knew, it was me who started the ball rolling. Age can be a good thing that way. It comes with a good dollop of not giving a flying fuck anymore. Is this thing between you and Fox serious?"

I took a long swallow of coffee and thought hard before I answered. "To be honest, I don't know. I mean, it's not like I have a lot of experience in any of this, Mum. I barely got my training wheels off with women, let alone men."

She shook her head. "Nope, I'm not buying. You don't jump into anything easily, son. I think you do know."

I narrowed my gaze. "Get out of my head."

She sat back with her hands up. "Fair enough."

We sipped our coffees in silence for a moment and I thought about my mother and how damn brave she'd been.

"Okay, so I think maybe it *is* serious." It was barely a whisper. "At least it is for me. But I'm not entirely sure what Fox feels. His life is pretty up and down right now, and he wasn't looking for a relationship."

"Neither were you."

"I know. But I don't want to assume anything. I'm . . ." I blew out a shaky sigh that rattled my heart. "Jesus, I'm scared, Mum. Holy shit, how is it even possible I'm saying something like that?"

She rested a hand over mine and squeezed. "Because he's touched your heart, son, and I for one couldn't be happier about that. I was beginning to wonder if anyone could break through to it."

I gave her my best eye-roll. "Wow. Thanks for the vote of confidence."

She laughed. "True, nonetheless. Still, there are never any guarantees, but based on what I know about Fox, he's a measured man. He wouldn't be doing this—not with you and not after what his ex-husband did to him—if he wasn't sufficiently interested."

"Sufficiently." I shook my head. "You couldn't come up with a more encouraging word?"

She shrugged. "I can't read the man's mind. Sometimes you just have to take a chance."

"But what about Judah? He's gonna hate this."

"Judah will deal with whatever happens. He might bitch and moan and yell, and I'd expect a hard time for the rest of your life if I was you, but he'll cope."

I flipped my hand to lace fingers with her. "I wish I was so sure. But can we please drop this, and you can tell me why exactly you're here in my kitchen interrupting what you damn well know you were interrupting."

She slid me a sly grin and waggled her brows. "I knew it. He's in your bedroom, isn't he?"

"Good God. No. We are not having this conversation. Just because you and Martha like to wave your freak flag around with little regard for your children—"

"The woman is a sexy beast, what can I say?"

"N.O. No! Now, why are you here?"

Her expression grew serious. "I'm here because you've been avoiding having a conversation about the farm finances."

I gaped. "And so you thought it would be a good idea to simply turn up and ambush me with no time to prepare and an hour before I'm due at rugby training?"

She fired me a shit-eating grin. "Pretty much exactly my plan. It's the only way I can nail you down."

"I can't do this now."

"Yes, you can. The farm can't support both of us, Leroy, and it doesn't need to. I'm holding you back. No, don't look like that. I know it and you know it. I think everyone knows it. The farm is stuck. It needs to grow, or something. But I know you won't take any risks while my name is on the business, and you need to. It's time the place was yours."

For a second, I couldn't breathe. Everything I wanted for my business future came down to the next few minutes. I forced out a breath and sighed. It was time. "All right, let's talk. But promise you'll hear me out before you answer."

A slow smile crept over her face. "You have an idea, don't you?"

I gave a sharp nod. "Maybe."

She sat back. "Okay, I'm listening."

I calmed my heart. "Yes, the farm needs to grow or diversify, and yes I have ideas about that." My lips quirked. "Maybe even ridiculous ideas. But I won't risk anything of yours on gut feelings and I have nothing to put up for the loan other than the farm itself, which is barely scraping by, and I still have the remains of my student debt to pay off."

She pulled a face. "Your father and I should have managed that much better. You didn't deserve to be landed with that, not after coming back to run the farm."

"You couldn't predict the market would drop, Mum."

"That's not what I meant, and you know it."

I did. But there was little point digging up old wounds. "Judah needed your help. You made the right decision."

"That's good of you to say, but you're wrong. You needed us too. We were just a little tunnel-visioned at the time to see it, and that's on us."

"Um, sorry to interrupt—oh, hi, Cora." Fox gave a cute little wave from the doorway, his face scrubbed and shining. I rolled my eyes. He wasn't fooling anyone. He still looked freshly fucked and practically purring. "I thought I'd take Mack for a walk, Lee. Anything you want from the store?"

"Hello, Fox." My mother eyed him up and down and I booted her under the table. "What?" She fired me an innocent look. "I was only going to say how nice and clean he looked."

Fox hesitated, his gaze flicking between us. "Okaaaaay. Thanks? It was a hot day, right?"

"So I've heard." Mum's eyes danced.

"Oh. My. God. She knows, Fox. You can drop the act."

"She knows?" His gaze darted anxiously between us, then

settled. "Oh, thank Christ for that." He made his way over and squeezed into the chair next to me. "Are things . . . okay?"

Cora reached across to pat his hand. "They're fine. And I won't say anything to Mattie or anyone else about the two of you, rest assured. Although, if I've picked up the vibe, your mother is bound to notice something sooner rather than later."

Fox shot a worried look my way. "We were going to wait for a bit to see if . . ." He trailed off and my heart stuttered in my chest. "Well, to see what happens, I guess."

I reached for his hand and gave it a squeeze. "We still can. This is for us to decide, no one else, right?"

"Right." He nodded and stood. "Then I'll leave you to it. I'll check with Kane if he needs anything picked up. Be back soon." He bent to kiss me, but I pulled away. I wasn't even sure why. Habit? Fear? He hesitated, then squeezed my shoulder and headed for the door.

But I got there before him. "I'm so sorry." I pressed my lips to his and he cupped my cheek to hold me there. "It's going to take a bit of time to get used to all this," I told him. "But I want this. Be patient with me."

"Always." He kissed me again and then left, calling to Mack on his way out.

I took my seat at the table and tried to ignore my mother's broad smile. "Stop preening," I grumbled.

"I will if you tell me about this damn plan of yours."

And so I did.

CHAPTER SEVENTEEN

Fox

"Okay, I've waited long enough. Spit it out." I tugged off my thick woollen rugby socks and threw them toward the laundry, missing by a good metre. Fuck it. They could stay there. But Mack immediately pounced, strutting around the room with the smelly things hanging out of her mouth like she'd won the damn lottery.

I'd felt Lee's eyes on me the whole ninety minutes of training. He was excited about something, but he refused to tell me what until we got home, said he didn't want to be rushed.

"Spit what out?" He slid me a sideways grin and I flicked him on the forehead. "Ow. Okay, okay, but I want your business brain in gear because I need your honest opinion. I've been working on an idea to buy the farm, and Mum . . . shit, she actually likes it. And really it was your idea, so . . ."

Mine? And also, Leroy Madden was asking for *my* opinion, my *business* opinion? *Holy shit.* Lee never asked anyone for anything, especially for an opinion and especially about something as important to him as this. Something gushy almost made its way out of my mouth, but I hauled it back at the last minute and cleared my throat.

"You okay?" Lee grabbed his packet of fish and chips that we'd picked up on the way home, tore a hole in the top, squidged some sauce through the hole, put his fingers inside, and snagged a few chips —because he rolled that way.

"I'm fine." I reached for my own packet, laid the fish to one side, stacked the potato fritters in a corner, and poured the sauce into a neat pool, just so. We'd attempted to share a single packet once. Never again. The man was a monster. "So, tell me about this plan of yours and how it's my idea?"

He turned sideways on the couch and stretched his legs toward my lap, tapping my thigh with his big toe. I lifted my fish and chips, and he slid his feet underneath, the move so unconscious you'd think we'd been living together for years. And something about that idea sat really, really well in my chest.

"Okay, so the *your* idea part is about that question you asked me outside the supply place in Whangarei about whether I needed all that land?" he said. "That got me thinking."

I frowned. "Still not following."

"Well, I've still got some student debt, right?"

I nodded, munching on my fritter.

"And the farm is in Mum's name, so I have no real equity to offer a bank in order to buy her out."

I nodded again and dunked my fritter in some sauce.

"So, I had an idea how to solve both those problems. I suggested to Mum that she sell me the homestead, but only including the single hectare of land down to the beach and the wharf facilities. And that she let me have it at a heavily discounted price so I'd have plenty of equity to leverage the loan I need for expansion."

"How low are we talking?"

"I've left that to her, but after we talked, she suggested a few hundred thousand."

My jaw dropped. "But it has to be worth well over a million with the land and the business. Probably closer to two. Why would she do that?"

"Hear me out. And remember, she did the same for Judah and Morgan with the land, the boatshed, and the old barn. They got that package for a song, just enough to float the farm a bit longer."

I shoved a few chips in my mouth. "Okay, keep going."

"So, Mum would keep the remaining two hectares that run behind the macrocarpas and along the headland. There are at least four or five large sections in that if someone wanted to divide it or sell it as one big parcel. Land like that is scarce in this area, especially with those views. It would be worth a fortune. Mum would easily get enough to set herself up for the rest of her life, without needing any more from me. Plus, she wouldn't be at risk if the business went under."

"It won't go under. And if you started charging the commercial vessels the berthing rates you should, it'll help your cashflow even more."

I grimaced. "Yeah, they've had it sweet for years. There's a lot we have to do to meet council and marine bylaws for that side of the business, and their contracts nowhere near cover that. I could double them and still undercut nearly everyone else. But Mum hated the thought of raising the rates. She's known the guys for years."

"But the business needs to catch up. It's time, Lee. You can do this."

"So you think it's a good idea then?"

"And your Mum's on board?"

"She was almost more excited than me. I was worried she'd be too sentimental about it, but she wasn't in the least. She said her life was with Martha now and going in a different direction, and she just wanted to see me successful. Of course, we have to make sure we can actually do it, especially the part about selling the back plot of land. We need to check any restrictions on that, but even if they won't let a developer divide it further, land like that around these areas with those views would still sell for more than enough to see Mum nicely set up. She's off to talk to the lawyers and start making enquiries next week."

I pulled Lee's empty fish and chip parcel from his hands and put it with mine on the coffee table, then hauled him into my lap. He came eagerly, bright blue eyes dancing in excitement.

"If your mother is okay about it, then I think it's a bloody brilliant idea. You clever, clever man." I circled my hands around his trim waist. "Everyone wins, so hell yes, you should do it."

"Yes!" He fist-pumped the air and then wriggled in my lap with a sly look on his face. "And since it all came from that one question you sparked in my brain, I'm feeling in an extremely grateful mood."

I groaned and grabbed his hips, pulling him down harder. "And exactly how grateful would that be?"

"*Very* grateful." He gave a sly smile. "My, my, whatever do we have here, Mr Carmody?" He shoved a hand down my rugby shorts and fisted my thickening cock. "I think *someone* wants to come out and play."

I chuckled. "*Someone* has just endured ninety minutes of training and had his balls squashed numerous times by Lachie Carmichael's haul-up on the back of my shorts in scrum practice. In its current state, *someone* would be lucky to manage a handshake without falling asleep on the job."

"Oh, I don't know so much." Lee gave my cock a few slow strokes and the bastard began to rise to the occasion. "Although, I guess you *are* quite a few years older than me, and I've heard about these kind of age-related performance . . . *issues*. So, I guess I'll manage just fine with my own hand." He tapped a thoughtful finger to his chin. "Or maybe I could trial that anal plug I ordered ten days ago. Yeah. I probably don't need your cock at all."

I grabbed his finger and held it. "I do not have performance *issues*, you little toad. And also, what fucking anal plug?"

He smiled but said nothing.

I shoved him off my lap and onto his back, then climbed up his body until we were eye to eye. "No anal plug goes anywhere near you unless my fingers are attached to it, are we clear?"

He grinned. "Perfectly." But his expression seemed uncertain, and I was jolted, as always, by this unexpectedly vulnerable side. A precious peek behind the curtains. "I was going to tell you about it," he said softly. "But when it arrived, I felt a bit ridiculous."

"Ridiculous?"

A blush stole over his cheeks. "I feel like I don't know myself when I'm around you, and I'm still trying to process what that means. I feel like I've fallen down some rabbit hole. I've never been interested in toys. Hell, I've never needed much sex for that matter. And if you'd told me a couple of months ago, that I'd be ordering an anal plug, I'd have laughed in your face."

"But you're not laughing now." I brushed his choppy dark hair off his face. I wanted to see those beautiful eyes. "Something about the idea of it attracts you?"

He nodded.

I brushed my lips across his. "There is *nothing* ridiculous in finding what turns you on. And I don't give a shit what you thought about sex before, only what you think about it now, with me. What makes *you* hot makes *me* hot. Giving you pleasure, watching you go over that edge is the biggest fucking turn-on."

He studied me for a moment, his blush deepening. Then he reached for a stray lock of my hair and spun it around his finger, avoiding my gaze. "Did you do stuff like that with . . . him? With Van?"

Oh. I tapped his cheek and turned his gaze back to mine. "Some. Not plugs. He liked to be blindfolded sometimes, have his hands tied, that was about it. Sex was . . . different between us, not like it is with you."

"Of course. I guess that makes sense." He blinked hard and looked away. "I mean, I know you loved him—"

"That's not what I meant. Look at me."

His gaze slowly tracked back, but there was a wariness there.

"This thing—" I moved a finger between us, wanting to make what I was about to say, crystal clear. "—is special. Yes, I did love Van, once. But I'm with you now, and I don't want to be anywhere else. These last weeks with you have been the most frustrating, wonderful, and amazing weeks I've had in a long, long time. Years, in fact. And I'm not lying when I say the sex has been spectacular. But it's not just about sex."

"Okaaaay." The uncertainty was back.

I smoothed his brow with my finger and kissed his nose. "The sex is so good because it's you. Van isn't in my head anymore, not in that way. You've cornered every damn neurone currently available up there. I might've been attracted to you a year ago, but through all the bitching and anger and miscommunication and now finally this, that attraction has grown into so much more. I'm here because this is where I *want* to be. And *I'm* scared too. Jesus, Lee, I'm only just getting clear of a failed marriage. I wasn't looking for this. And I certainly wasn't expecting you."

"And yet here I am." He smiled thinly.

"Here we both are." I kissed him softly. "And I'm not about to walk away unless you want me to. And just so you know, I've decided to apply for the observer training."

"Really?" he asked softly. And something sparked in his eyes. Relief maybe. "And you came to this decision during training? And it had nothing to do with our earlier conversation, of course."

My cheeks heated. "Smart arse. Look, I'm not saying it's exactly what I want, but there's no harm in starting the process, right? They still might turn me down. I just want to . . . try." *To stop that wary look that I hate seeing in your eyes. To show you how much I want this.*

He took a breath, keeping his gaze fixed on me. "And the other job?"

I gave a half-shrug. *No promises. No lies.* "Let's see how this application goes first."

He nodded. "Fair enough."

We both knew I could've shut Laurie down for good, but we also both knew how new and fresh this thing between us was, even if it mostly felt like so much more. I wanted to believe in us, in him, and I did. But then I thought I'd been sure about Van at the time. It was hard to trust my judgement anymore. What if Lee changed his mind and it blew up in our faces and I needed to get out of here? I was too far gone to be around Lee and not have him.

He shivered in my arms and a hand slid around my neck. "It's okay. Trust isn't easy, right?" He held my gaze. "I'm here because I want to be too, Fox. And not because I'm experimenting. I'm here because it's *you*. I think I tried to dislike you so much because a part of me recognised the very real danger you represented, the changes I was going to have to make. But I'm done fighting. This thing is good between us, the best I've ever had, and I'm not walking away either."

The tightness in my chest I'd been carrying for weeks unknotted and slid free, and I pressed my lips to his, the kiss tender and warm and filled with something fresh and possible and still a little fragile. And when we were done, he rested his forehead on mine.

"Have you decided what you're going to do about Mack?"

It wasn't the first time he'd asked, and I still didn't have an answer. "I'm working on it. We have a family court date coming up, so if we can't reach an out-of-court agreement before then, I guess they'll decide."

His frown formed under my own brow. "Damn, Fox. That seems bloody risky to leave it to the court. Are you sure you shouldn't go down and talk face to face?"

No, because if I go down . . . if I leave here . . .

A frown dipped between Lee's eyes as he waited for my answer.

"No," I finally said. "Not unless I have to. I don't want to get into everything with Van again. I'm tired of the arguments, and that's what it'll turn into. Plus, I've been thinking maybe I should just pay him out."

Lee's eyes popped. "Wow. Do you think he'd go for that? You said it seemed like he genuinely missed her."

"To be honest I don't know what to think. He keeps texting me to fly her down, but—"

Lee pulled back and cradled my face, his gaze fixed on mine. "I understand. She's part of you."

I nodded, eyes brimming. "She's the only good thing I took out of that fucking marriage. She was mine before Van came along, and all the way through she's been with me. She's family. But I know that by not sorting this out soon, I could lose. I feel paralysed. It's ridiculous, right?"

"Shhh." He put a finger to my lips. "It's not ridiculous. You love her."

I fixed on those brilliant blue orbs, and a flood of feelings passed between us that had nothing to do with Mack.

Lee cleared his throat. "But you need to make a decision, Fox. You'll beat yourself up if you don't even try to settle things before the hearing."

"I know."

"Good." He ran a line of kisses over my cheeks. "Now, not to change the subject or anything, but about this plug thingy? Would you perhaps be interested in investigating its potential sometime . . . soon?"

I snorted, welcoming the shift of mood. "Absolutely. I'm down with whatever floats your boat."

He licked his lips. "Yeah, that catalogue was . . . fascinating."

"Oh really? Tell me more."

"Well, this particular plug just so happens to come with a . . . battery." He ran the tip of his tongue over his lips and garnered my full attention.

"A battery, you say?" I rasped.

He waggled his eyebrows. "Mm-hmm. And a . . . remote."

My pulse thrummed in my neck. "And where might this instrument currently reside?"

He gave a Cheshire smile. "It's currently *residing* in my bedside table."

"Right. So maybe we should check on it. Make sure it's still there, just in case."

He shoved his face right up in mine, his hot breath fanning my cheeks, the scent of dirt and sweat and fish and chips inexplicably sexy. "I think that's an excellent idea."

"You do realise that as soon as we start, your mother is going to walk in or phone or something? Our erect cocks seem to act as some kind of summoning spell," I cautioned.

He tugged my lower lip between his teeth, then let it go. "The word mother is never again to fall from your lips while I have my hand wrapped around your cock, got it?"

"Then I suggest you find some other way to keep my mouth busy."

His lips curved up in a wicked smile. "Oh, I think I might have just what you need."

CHAPTER EIGHTEEN

Fox

"Hey, Leroy," Kane called from the supply shed across from the wharf office. "Do you want me to fuel the *Green Lip* up for tomorrow? She's getting a bit low if we want to finish seeding those nursery lines. It'll take us most of the day."

"Good idea," I answered for Lee who was still on the phone with the harvesting company. "Patrick's here if you need him." Patrick immediately set down the coffee he was juggling and got up to help, but Kane waved the offer aside and I gestured for Patrick to stay.

Kane was still restricted to helming and not much else, but he was doing a great job. His arm was a lot stronger with the physio, but it would still be a few weeks before he could start using it. He likely shouldn't be doing what he was, but he was insistent on working in any way he could. He managed the boat one-handed just fine around the farm, as long as someone else got us there and back. He wasn't earning a full wage, but he was learning, and I'd been more than surprised at Lee's patience.

With the phone in one hand and a coffee in the other, Lee rolled his eyes my way. "I *know* that building weather system is supposed to pass to the north, but I still want them harvested before. On Tuesday, like you promised. I can't afford to wait another week. It's too risky. And I've had that spot for over a month."

Lee's jaw ticked in annoyance as he listened to the response over the phone.

"That's not my problem. Why should I give up my spot just because you screwed up your calendar?"

Patrick glanced my way, concern etched across his face. It was the last thing we needed. Patrick's trip to Wellington for his brother's graduation had been planned on the assumption the harvest would be done the day before he left, and Lee refused to let him cancel.

Lee's lips set in a thin line from whatever the guy on the other end was saying, and then he slammed the phone down. "Goddammit! If we had a better choice of harvesting contractor, I'd drop Colin tomorrow. Says he double booked us with Lionel's farm, and since Lionel is closer to Colin's current location, he's going to do that farm first."

"But we had him fucking booked." Patrick fumed.

"Tell him that. He said it would cost too much to come up here, only to have to turn around and go back, and didn't I understand that he ran a fine profit margin? Like I fucking don't! To hell with the fact that we had to wait as it was. We should've had those mussels out a week ago. They'll be at size limit already. Son of a bitch!" Lee kicked the rubbish bin into the wall, making everyone jump. It hit the floor with a clatter spewing balled-up paper and a mix of ice cream wrappers from one end of the office to the other.

He stared at the bin like it had personally offended him and then at my mother who'd seen it coming and rolled her chair smartly out of the way. His cheeks stained pink. "Sorry, Martha."

She patted his hand. "Go home and have a beer, Leroy. Nothing you can do to change it now. So, where's Mack today?"

"Home. Her stomach wasn't happy with the worming tablet last night. Figured we could do without the repercussions of *that* on the boat." I retrieved the bin, gathered the spilled contents back inside, and set it back down under Martha's desk. I rested a hand on Lee's shoulder as I passed. "Come on, Cristiano Ronaldo. Let's go home."

Martha huffed, Patrick snorted, and Lee shot daggers at them both. Then he visibly deflated. "Fine. But I want some damn kettle chips with that beer. None of those healthy seed cracker things you keep trying to make me eat." He fired a glare my way.

I bit back a smile. In an attempt to improve our diet for the coming rugby season, I'd cleaned the cupboards of junk and crap. "If you're referring to my take on Jamie's Christmas snap crackers, I feel personally attacked. You can say all you want about how your diet didn't need improving, but for the record, gravy is not a beverage. We have to eat to win, slugger." I punched his arm, which earned me a furious scowl. "It's for the team, right?"

He rolled his eyes. "We're in the Northland fucking social league, not taking to the paddock against England. And *for the record*, gravy is so a beverage. It pours, ergo it's a beverage. Well, except for the one you made last week that refused to leave the jug even when upended. That was definitely more of an adhesive. Could've given Superglue a run for its money."

"Enough." I gave him a shove. "I can't listen to your lies a minute longer." I nodded at Patrick watching with a huge smile on his face. "Go home, Tricky. We'll see you tomorrow."

"See what we have to put up with?" Patrick eyed Martha as he pushed off his seat. "I don't earn near enough to deal with this shit."

Martha laughed. "See you tomorrow, son."

Once Patrick was gone, I felt the heat of my mother's curious gaze land on my face, and I felt a twinge of guilt for not telling her about Lee yet. Lee had left the decision to me, but like so many other things piling up in my life lately, I hadn't found the right time.

I clapped Lee on the shoulder in a manly, bro kind of way, which only made him laugh since he knew exactly what I was doing. "Come on, let's get that beer. And just because I feel sorry for you, you can have some kettle chips. Besides, I figure there's a celebration in order."

"What?" He pulled up short and eyed me suspiciously. "Celebrate what?"

I waggled my eyebrows. "Celebrate me passing the observer interview."

"Oh. My. God." He whacked me on the arm and I let out an embarrassing yelp. But the sudden brightness in his eyes warmed my heart and made me smile. I'd wanted to surprise him.

"You never mentioned an interview." His gaze narrowed. "Is that where you went yesterday when you said you were looking at a boat?"

I gave a half-shrug. "It might have been. I'm not saying either way."

He switched his attention to Martha. "Did you know?"

Her face broke into a wide grin. "I refuse to incriminate myself."

"Riiiight. You'll keep," he said to her, and then whacked me again on the arm. "Tricky bastard. But you got it?"

I held up my hands. "I passed the *interview*. They're going to send me a pile of forms I have to sign, and I need to pass the training, but yes, I've been offered a place."

"Yesss! That deserves at least two packets of chips, and you're buying." He grabbed his bag and sprinted for the door, only to come to an abrupt halt when Judah stuck his head inside, cheeks flushed from running.

"Hey, can one of you give me a hand for a minute? The tap in the main studio bathroom is spraying water *again,* and much though I hate to admit it, you guys are much better at that shit than me or Morgan. God love the man, but he's useless with a spanner. And I swear there's a damn poltergeist in that class. It happens every time I have them."

I caught sight of Kane behind Judah, shifting nervously from foot to foot, keeping his distance. Judah followed my gaze and turned his head. He gave a curt nod loaded with enough ice to regenerate a glacier or two. "Kane."

"Um, hi, Judah. Go ahead, I'll wait."

Judah turned back and rolled his eyes. "So, someone, please?"

Leroy looked my way. "You or me?"

I hesitated. If I let Lee go, it would give me a prime opportunity to talk to my mother alone. I thought I even saw a flash of hope in her expression. Then I remembered I'd be telling her that I was fucking her girlfriend's son and ran chicken instead.

"Let's both go," I said. "If Morgan's tried already, it could be seriously screwed."

Judah huffed a laugh. "Ain't that the truth."

Lee looked over his brother's shoulder to Kane still hovering in the distance. "Go home, Kane. We're done for the day."

Kane scuttled off to his car like the hounds of hell were on his tail, and Judah followed his departure with just the hint of a smile on his lips.

Thirty minutes later we were finally driving up the hill.

Lee waved a hand toward the studio as we passed. "You know, I love Morgan. He's a brother on the rugby field, and the man can grow a veggie garden to die for, but he doesn't have a single DIY bone in his damn body. Lord knows what he thought he was doing with that bloody sink. It looked like a snakes and ladders board underneath. Now on to more important things, like do we have to go to the store for those kettle chips? I'm gonna be mighty pissed if we get home to find there are none there. There will be consequences."

I slid a hand onto his thigh, and he moved it a little north until he had it lodged over his dick. I gave a squeeze and he wriggled contentedly. "I may have one or two hidden away," I admitted. "Although I'm intrigued by the whole consequences thing. Maybe I should keep them secret."

He spun in his seat and glared. "I fucking knew you had a stash. Where?"

I shot him a look of disbelief. "You've got to be joking. Like I'm telling you that."

He turned into the driveway, grumbling something that sounded a lot like a sexual threat, and I laughed. Bring it on.

"It's my damn house. If you've hidden something, I've got a right to— Whose car is that?"

I jerked my head to the passenger window and my heart stuttered in my chest.

"And who is that?"

"Oh, fucking hell. Jesus Christ."

"I somehow don't think so." Lee frowned at the handsome blond man sitting on his front step with Mack staring up at him like he'd hung the bloody moon. He got to his feet, brushed his hands down the front of his skinny jeans, and folded his arms. A dog lead hung from his hand.

Lee's gaze shot to mine. "Fox?"

"Buckle up, sweetheart. You're about to meet my ex."

Slim and impeccably dressed, as always, Van oozed that feisty confidence that had drawn me from the beginning. Van was always a handful, something I'd initially found exciting and sexy. He looked determined, but when he saw me through the windscreen, a flash of uncertainty crossed his face. It vanished just as quickly, however, and his lips set in a thin line.

"Do you want me to leave?" Lee's voice was steady, but I could tell he was thrown by the whole ex thing—his gaze raking over Van as if trying to understand.

And I got it. The two were as different as could be. I didn't need to think long. "No. Stay, please. Just maybe give us a little space."

He nodded and squeezed my hand. "I'll sit at the end of the deck. But fair warning, Fox, if that fucker even looks at you sideways, I won't be responsible for my actions."

I couldn't help but smile. "My hero." I cupped Lee's face and drew him in for a thorough kiss, right in front of my ex. He looked surprised but also more than a little pleased. I'd let Van know that I'd moved on and that Lee was mine, and the thunderous look on Van's face said it all.

Van let me come to him, his hand resting on Mack's head, making his own point. But his gaze tracked Lee's every movement from the truck to the chair at the end of the deck. "Who's the hottie?" His lip curled. "You don't waste much time, do you?"

"I'm gonna pretend I didn't hear that," I shot back, taking a seat on the step and calling Mack to my side. "You have zero right to make any comment on my *single* dating life considering your own track record. At least I waited until I was out of our marriage."

"So you say," Van huffed, eyeing the step. "So we're doing this out here, are we? Not even going to be civil about it?"

"Yep. I'm way past civil where you're concerned, and I'm not having you put one foot inside that house, not if you're here for the reason I think you are."

Van glared for a second, then sat with a grumbling sigh. "Whatever. You can be such an arsehole."

I said nothing.

"Fox? You okay?" Kane called from halfway down the stairs of his bedsit. "He was here when I got home. Wouldn't say what for or even give his name, just said he'd wait. Do you need him gone?"

"What the fuck is this?" Van glanced between Kane and Lee. "Do you really need protection from little old me, Fox? Are you scared you might still feel something for me?"

"Get over yourself, Van." I waved Kane off and he disappeared back up into the bedsit. "You're barely a blip on my radar these days. The only thing I feel for you is contempt and a great deal of relief."

At the end of the deck, Lee snorted.

Van shot him a dagger look.

I added, "You burned any feelings I had for you a long time ago. The sooner I'm shot of you completely, the better. So, how about we get this over with. I take it you're here about Mack?"

Van reached a hand to where Mack sat between us and my trai-torous dog gave it a lick. She and I were going to have words.

"She loves me, don't you girl? You've missed me," he crooned, and I wanted to slap him.

"She saw you around Oban town nearly every fucking day, Van. I've only been gone a bit over a month. It's hardly the great reunion."

Van stared at me. "Why do you have to be like this?" He slid closer along the step until we were almost touching. "We used to be really good together. We had some great times." He turned his gaze to where Lee sat, ears flapping like a damn elephant.

"Don't play games," I warned and slid away to put more space between us. "I know you too well, and I have zero interest in you *or* your feelings."

He sighed and his gaze narrowed. "She's coming back with me, Fox. I have the court order in my pocket. You either let me take her now, or I'll get the local cop to enforce it. I have a flight booked tomorrow and a dog carrier in the car. You can have her back in a month, which is damn generous considering you made me fly up here to get her."

The last thing I wanted was to get Jon involved. "You're not going anywhere until I talk to Tinny."

He waved a hand. "Be my guest. You can do what you like. Won't change anything."

I pulled out my phone and after a few rings Tinny picked up. I walked off a way so Van couldn't overhear, but I needn't have both-ered. As much as Tinny was pissed about how Van had gone about it, there was nothing he could do, and he already had a copy of the court order. The injunction was refused. My best bet was to keep on good enough speaking terms with Van to get this settled without court, and a slap-down fight wasn't likely to achieve that.

Then he reminded me, "I told you so."

Fucker. It wasn't what I wanted to hear but he was right, and when I ended the call Tinny's answer must've been obvious on my face, judging by the smug look Van wore.

"He told you I'm right, didn't he?" Van said evenly. "So how about you stop fucking me around and just let me take her? Don't make this harder than it is, Fox."

"Harder for who, Van?" I shook my head. "Mack's gonna hate it. Why are you doing this? I get that you like her, maybe even love her, but she's *my* dog. You've taken enough, don't you think, and destroyed our marriage? Do you really need to fight me for Mack as well? Do you want to hurt me that badly? What the fuck did I ever do to you except mistakenly trust you?" I couldn't stop the break in my voice.

Lee was there in a second, his warm hand on my shoulder, his gaze cold as ice on Van who scrambled to his feet and stepped back, clearly sizing Lee up. I got to my feet as well, sniffing trouble brewing.

Van refocused his attention on me. "I'm not trying to hurt you, Fox. I just want what I'm entitled to. I miss her, and she obviously misses me." He reached out a hand and Mack shoved her head under it for a pat.

Damn dog.

"She hasn't missed you, arsehole," Lee scoffed. "She treats the fucking postman like that."

I choked out a laugh. God, I loved him. And then it suddenly hit me. I *did* love him. I *did*.

Damn, when did that happen?

Van shot Lee a killing look that Lee held without the slightest flinch. Van had no idea what he'd taken on. Lee could eat him for breakfast.

At length, Van gave up and turned back to me. "Look, you'll get her back in a month. You have to come down for the court date anyway, if you want to argue your case, that is." He rolled his eyes and bile rose in my throat.

"You know, I've only just realised how lucky I am to be shot of you, Van. You actually did me a huge favour fucking my friend. What a waste of my time you were. Ewan's welcome to you."

Van visibly winced and I wasn't proud of the pleasure it gave me. *Fuck it.* Yes, I bloody was.

His expression turned sour, distorting all those charming waifish features in something decidedly unpleasant. "Likewise. I should've held out for someone a lot better from the start."

Lee pushed forward. "Why you little bitch—"

"Touch me and I'll have you for assault," Van sneered, taking another step back and putting Mack between himself and Lee. "I think I should maybe push to keep Mack on the island permanently. Not sure I can trust you to uphold your end of any shared custody agreement, Fox, at least not based on recent behaviour." His gaze shot to Lee, and he smirked. "You kept our house down there, right?" The question might've been for me but Van's gaze was pinned on Lee who visibly winced at the word *our.*

It was everything he already feared about me, and I wanted to punch Van for that alone.

"Says it all, really," Van continued, clearly enjoying Lee's discomfort. "You've kept your options open, Fox. You didn't actually want to leave, did you? I have to admit I was surprised. You were never a mainlander, and *anyone* who knows you well enough knows that. Your heart's always been down south. Nothing's gonna change that. Ever. You could never be happy up here. You're just playing fucking games."

Beside me, Lee drew a sharp breath.

"Enough." I was over Van's fuckery. "Shut your mou—"

"No." Lee's hand slid over my fist and held it firmly. He stepped in close, the solid weight of his body steadying me. "Don't give him what he wants, baby. He's not worth it. Show us the damn court order." He reached an open hand to Van.

They held a staring match for a few seconds, then Van produced the paper from his pocket. Lee took it. I didn't even want to look.

"Seems genuine," he said glancing my way before throwing the paper back in Van's face.

Van stooped to pick it up, then turned his back to Lee. "I'm staying at the Wanderer Motel in Whangarei if you want to talk . . . alone."

Lee tensed.

I couldn't fucking believe it. "I've got nothing to say to you, Van, so just piss off before I change my mind about letting Mack go."

"Like you have a choice." He shrugged. "Still, it's your loss. I've got food in the car. I'll text you when she gets home safely."

I was in his face before I knew it, Lee's hand holding me back. "That's not her fucking home, you bastard."

Van shrugged but his hands were shaking. "It is, at least for the next month. Enjoy your—" He looked to Lee. "—whatever. And a word of advice for *you*." He held Lee's gaze. "Don't expect too much from this guy. He doesn't give a shit about anything except his work. You'll soon tire of being left alone, just like I did. Until one day he'll just leave altogether and come back where he belongs."

Lee muscled forward. "That's where you're wrong, dickhead. Because I *don't* get left alone. We work *together*. It's a fucking dream. You made a big fucking mistake letting him go, but he's mine now, so you can fuck off back to that hole you crawled out of. Men who can't keep it in their pants aren't worth a second look, and they never change."

Van's cheeks flamed bright. "Believe what you want, you'll soon learn the truth." But his voice was shaking, and I wanted to haul Lee into my arms and kiss the fuck out of him.

"Put your bitch on a leash next time, Fox." Van threw a look Lee's way and then headed for his car, calling Mack.

Mack stayed where she was, confused, her gaze shifting between Van and me. *'Dad? What do you want? Do I go, Dad?'* I almost broke down and dragged her inside the house, but I didn't want her to sense my panic and stress more than she already did, and so I waved a hand toward where Van was waiting by his car. "Off you go, girl."

She hesitated, nudging my leg, and I was done holding back. I squatted in front and hauled her close. Lee quickly joined me, peppering Mack's muzzle with desperate kisses and whispering promises in harsh choking breaths.

Then he slid an arm around my waist and held tight as I buried my face in Mack's neck, tears running down my face, willing her to understand just how much she meant to me. That I wasn't sending her away. That I loved her. That I'd come for her. That she'd be okay. But not at all sure that *I* would.

"Be a good girl, sweetheart," I whispered into her fur, Lee's hand warm and heavy on my back. "It's not for long. I'll see you soon. I promise I'm coming to get you. I promise."

I gave her a gentle push toward Van, my hands trembling, my heart ripping apart. She leaned back as if sensing something wasn't right. But then Van crouched and called her over, a treat held out in his hand. Mack looked between us and I nudged her again.

"Go on, baby girl. I'll come get you soon."

She relaxed a little and wandered across to take the offered treat. Van opened the back door and enticed her inside with even more. She looked back once then jumped in. He shut the door and my heart lurched.

Oh god, oh god, this is really happening.

I thought Van would simply drive off, smug and satisfied. But when he got to the driver's door, he looked up, and whatever he saw on my face made him hesitate.

"I promise I'll look after her." He held my gaze. "You can trust me on that much at least, Fox." And then he got in the car and drove out the gate with Mack's head craned out the rear window, staring back, barking frantically, and clearly wondering what the hell was going on.

As soon as they were out of sight, my knees gave way and Lee caught me as I slumped back down on the step. He wrapped his arms around my shoulders and drew my head against his chest.

"It's okay, baby," he whispered into my hair, his voice cut and choking. "We'll get her back, you'll see." He rocked me against him. "We'll get her back."

I slipped my arms around his waist and hung on tight, my chest heaving like someone had reached inside and yanked out my heart. The first time in eight years I'd been without my constant companion, the one who'd got me through all Van's fuckery. The only one who'd mattered when he left, and I felt like half my heart had been torn from my chest.

After a few minutes, Lee stood and took my hand. "Let's get you inside and into a warm bath." He helped me to my feet. "Hopefully that worming tab is still doing its thing and she shits all over his bloody motel room."

He ran me a bath in the huge old clawfoot in his en suite, grabbed a couple of beers while I stripped, and then climbed in behind me, wrapping me in his strong arms and shoving a beer into my hand.

"Drink this and let me wash you." He picked up the sponge and doused it in his coconut body wash. "At the risk of repeating myself again, what the fuck did you ever see in that wanker?"

I couldn't answer, just drank my beer and let Lee wash me head to foot. His strong fingers worked the suds through my hair, massaging my scalp, kneading through the pain and loss to ground me in his care. When he was done, he pulled me back into his arms and held me tight while I hoped and prayed that Mack hadn't thought I'd just abandoned her.

And when the water raised goosebumps on our arms, Lee dried me in a warm towel, bundled me into bed, and rocked me to sleep in his arms, the big spoon to my little for once.

CHAPTER NINETEEN

Leroy

I MANOEUVRED THE *CEE DEE* ALONGSIDE THE *GREEN LIP* AND tied up. The early autumn day, although bright and blue-skied had that pre-storm feel about it, close and hot and still. But a soft breeze had just circled in from the east and a few scattered whitecaps were beginning to build. And in the ocean itself, unsettled water simmered just below the calm green skin, currents tugging at the ropes as we worked—a gentle reminder of the system that was churning the oceans just north of the country.

My gaze landed on Fox in the back of the boat as he tended to the equipment, muscles taut and corded, his expression far too serious. I sighed. He hid it well, but he'd sunk pretty low in those first days after Van had left with Mack. He'd been withdrawn, quiet, and irritable—so unlike his usual self, I'd been worried.

But Van, the dickhead, had been oddly considerate, maintaining a steady stream of texts and photos to Fox's phone, and slowly, day by day, Fox had surfaced from his funk. Almost a week down the track and he was back to smiling again, even managing a few jokes, or at least he was trying for my sake. The last thing I wanted was to be grateful to his little shit of an ex, but I kind of was.

But I knew Fox missed Mack like he'd lost a limb, the fact was etched in deep lines on his face, and it pulled at my heart to a degree I could barely admit. In the short time we'd been together, the three of us, *four* including the more recent addition of our kitten, Prue—had become this strange family unit. And if *I* missed Mack, God knew what Fox had to be feeling.

After that first day, I'd hoped he'd talk to me about it. But a week on and he was still avoiding the subject and I didn't want to pressure him. His sleep was restless and broken, and the observer training application forms remained on the breakfast bar waiting to be posted —another thing he hadn't mentioned since Mack had left. But he accepted every hug I offered like it was made of gold, so that had to mean something, right?

I couldn't deny that meeting Van had unnerved me. He didn't say anything I didn't already know, of course—that Fox loved down south, loved it enough to keep his house there, regardless of all the shit that had happened to him in that tiny community. But now Mack was down there too. And if Van got shared custody, Fox would continue to be tied to the place, maybe even more than he was now.

Did I stack up against all that? Who the fuck knew? Not me. I only knew that it was eating at my nerves like battery acid.

Plus, Van and I couldn't have been more different, and I didn't know how to put that together and make sense of it. Fox had fallen in love and married Van, and he'd evidently been happy until Van fucked it up. So what the hell did he see in me? We looked nothing alike, and our personalities seemed equally opposed, so what the fuck? If Fox was drawn to vivacious and sassy, then I was so far from that, I may as well have been born on a different fucking planet.

I wanted to believe he'd found something in me that was equally attractive and not freak out like the insecure little shit that I apparently was. Not sure how good a job I was doing, hence the picnic I had secretly planned and brought on board. A little bribery? Maybe.

Was I hoping to wow Fox with my as yet unexplored romantic side? You betcha. I wasn't above a little distraction and enticement, and it was time to clear the air one way or another.

I intended to rebalance those scales and level the playing field. I wanted Fox to know exactly where I stood. And I needed something from him to reassure me we were still in this thing together. He missed Mack and I got that, but *I* was still here, and I needed that to mean something, dammit.

"That's it," I called over the gunwale from the *Cee Dee*, then climbed on board. "We've tied down everything we can, just in case. It'll have to be enough. Those forecasters better be right, not that we can do anything about it now. I vote we go enjoy the last nice day we might see for a while."

Patrick flashed me a knowing smirk, and Kane ducked his chin to hide his laugh. But Fox spun around like he'd been bitten by a snake.

"Tell me there are pigs in the air," he called back. "Or that hell has just ordered a metric ton of puffer jackets, because otherwise—" He stepped up and peered into my eyes. "—you're sick, aren't you? Dying of some rare disease that makes you want to have fun and do nice things for people."

Kane's shoulders shook harder.

"I'm fine." I shoved him aside. "Arsehole. And I *do* nice things . . . occasionally?"

Kane broke into a fit of coughing and disappeared below deck while Patrick found a spot on the horizon suddenly absorbing.

"Oh, go fuck yourselves," I griped. "And as for you." I eyeballed Fox. "Do you want to see some more of the local coast or not? Tricky's flying down to his brother's graduation this evening, and so he and Sugar offered to take the boat back and leave us the *Cee Dee*. So, if you stop being a dick about it, I'll take you on a tiki tour of my home coast."

Kane reddened at the nickname Fox had landed him with, but it was kind of fitting. Sugar. Kane. The fact he hated it meant I tried to use it as much as possible.

Fox stared at me like I'd lost my mind, and a hand landed on my forehead. He made a sizzling noise and jerked it back. "Really, really sick."

"I'm *not* that bad."

Fox glanced at Patrick and they both answered along with Kane from below deck, "Yes you are."

"Ungrateful minions. Now stop being a dick, Silver, and grab your duffel before I leave you behind."

Fox glared and I simply waggled my brows. He hated the nickname *I'd* come up with for him, complaining that he was nowhere old enough for silver fox material. I'd promptly snagged a couple of grey hairs from his head, which had earned me a most robust and enjoyable fucking later that day. He'd promptly announced a new rule: nicknames were only to be used on the boat. I was more than happy to oblige since he'd landed me with Prickles. *Bastard.*

Fox headed below deck to get his gear, still shaking his head but with a happy smile tugging at his lips, and Patrick gave me a discreet thumbs up. I'd told him and Kane about my plan, fobbing it off as a thank you for all his help. I knew I wasn't fooling Patrick, even though he'd said nothing directly to me, but I swear Kane had to be the most oblivious guy on the damn planet.

One positive to come out of Patrick's awareness that something was going on between Fox and me was that he'd stopped sitting as close as humanly possible to Fox at lunch, and the flirting had all but disappeared. That meant I wasn't forced to consider killing him at least twice a day, and in some strange way, his tacit approval felt good.

Which meant two people knew about Fox and me, and the world still turned. How about that? I'd hoped to talk to Judah as well, but I kind of wanted Fox's go-ahead first, and he'd been strangely silent on that matter, along with everything else in recent days. Plus, I knew he hadn't talked with his mother either, and yeah, that bothered me more than I wanted to admit.

I hauled the chilly bin of goodies I'd stashed under a tarp at the back and loaded it into the boat.

Kane appeared from below deck. "You need me to do anything this afternoon? I'll help Tricky restock, but then I'm free."

"Can you supervise the kids for a play?" The kids being Kane's kitten, Bossy, and Prue, the torty female that we'd kept, yes, *we*. Fox *and* me. Hence the afternoon's agenda. What to do about the gorgeous man I'd shared a bed with for the last few weeks and who didn't look to be leaving it anytime soon, or so I hoped?

Kane immediately brightened. "Yeah, Bossy could do with some girl time since the others have all gone to their new homes, and they both miss Mack."

They did and it stabbed at my heart just a little more. "Thanks. That'll be a big help. And you should take him to visit the store sometime. Hannah says she thinks Poppy is lonely as well."

"Will do."

Another two weeks and Kane would start light duties, and I couldn't wait. I had no idea how Patrick and I had survived without the extra help, but I was guessing I'd run him into the ground, the same as I'd done to myself. Then again, Fox worked for a wage that may as well have been nothing but was the only one he'd accept, and Kane cost me a lot less than Patrick, who could run the entire operation given half a chance. And that was something we were working on. Maybe one of these days Fox and I could even take a weekend off.

Fox and I. Nerves jangled in my belly.

I had everything ready when the man himself reappeared with his duffel over his shoulder and climbed down into the smaller boat.

"I'm all yours." He fired me a wink, and a few seconds later we were on our way.

Excitement bubbled in my chest as we raced between the run of small islands that dotted this part of the coastline. I'd never once played hooky from the farm, ever, and I almost giggled like a kid bunking school. It felt . . . good.

"So, is this a kidnapping?" Fox's arms slid around my waist from behind, his chin landing on my shoulder as I pushed the throttle.

I turned for a quick check, but the tiny island hid us nicely from view of the farm. I relaxed and leaned into the warmth of Fox's hard body, a body I'd gotten to know in all its glorious detail. How on earth we still had energy to work the farm each day after our exploits between the sheets at night was beyond me. I craved him under me as often as I could, and we'd made a good dent in my fantasy list of sexual checkboxes.

I aimed to tick another off today.

Fox pulled me flush, his larger body wrapping around mine like a hot cocoon. I loved when he did this. I felt protected and cherished. And he did it a lot, maybe because he'd guessed that in those moments, I felt the least alone. And I could even believe he wanted to look after me as much as I did him. And it was getting harder and harder to pretend I was doing anything other than falling in love with Fox Carmody.

He'd pulled a jersey over his T-shirt against the brisk wind trolling from the east, but the ridge of his hard cock wasn't remotely hidden by those paper-thin boardshorts he still wore.

"Mmmm, you feel good." He ground against me.

I chuckled and shoved my arse back, feeling him nudge into my crease. "I always feel good, according to you."

He laughed. "That's because you always do. So, what's the destination, baby? How excited should I be?"

I turned and pressed my lips to his. "Oh, I think you should be very excited. I know I am."

"Is that right?" He looked amused. "Who are you and what have you done with my sweet, grumpy boyfriend? You *never* finish early."

"I did today." My gaze briefly swept his before returning to the ocean ahead, but if he'd realised what he'd said, it didn't show on his face. We'd never used the boyfriend word, and I tried not to get excited. I swallowed hard and let it go.

He continued, "You've told me often enough you don't do surprises."

I chuckled. "It's different if I'm the surprise *giver*. Besides, it's good payback because, believe me, you are just one big surprise."

"Mmmm, I smell a rat, but I like where this is going, so I'm all in."

Cute enough segue. I eased back on the throttle and spun in his arms, making sure to lock eyes. My hands slid around his neck. "So am I. With *you*. All in, all the way. I just wanted you to know."

His eyes widened and he immediately leaned behind me to flick the throttle again. The boat slowed and rode the pressure wave to a rolling stop. Then he pushed me up against the dash.

"Say that again." He cradled my face and lowered his lips to mine, once, then twice. "Say it."

I swallowed hard. "I'm all in, Fox, with you. And I can't believe those words are coming out of my mouth." I could barely hold his gaze, hoping but not sure of what I'd find there. "I don't know when it happened, but this isn't going away for me. I think I maybe even knew at the start that it would end up here—"

"Lee—"

"I know you're just out of a marriage, and you weren't looking for another relationship, and your head is all tied up with Mack and Van and your divorce and a new career, and you and I together is the worst fucking idea in the universe, and I'm nothing like Van, and Painted Bay isn't Stewart Island, but none of that seems to matter to my head." I sucked in a breath, aware of his thumb brushing my cheek.

"I like you, Fox. More than like. I like *us*. I like how I am with you. I like you in my bed and in my house and in my life. And would you please just fucking say something before I make a worse fool of myself? I know you might not feel the same, and that's okay. Well, it's really not—" I dropped my gaze to where I was fisting his sweater. "—but I need to have some idea, *now*, before we go any further." I sighed and flopped against his chest. "Oh god, I actually just said all that, didn't I?"

He chuckled. "Yes. Now, are you done?" His lips nuzzled the top of my head.

"Burnt to a fucking cinder," I muttered against the wool of his jersey.

"So can *I* say something now?"

"Please."

"Okay. Well, how about you look at me for a start?"

"Do I have to?"

"Yes."

I tipped my head back until we were face to face.

"That's better." He pressed a soft kiss to each of my eyelids, no small miracle with the boat shifting in the lumpy swell.

"I have to say if you're about to let me down and dump my sorry arse, you're being particularly cruel about it," I grumbled, once again dropping my chin.

He laughed and once again tipped it back up. "I'm not about to let you down. If anything, I'm worried you might come to your senses soon and realise you've made a mistake choosing my sorry arse. But before I say anything else, let me pick up on one thing you said somewhere in all of that. Yes, you and Van are almost complete opposites, but for me that's nothing but a positive thing, and I'm sorry if I haven't made that clear. And I'm also sorry that I've been such a prick since Van took Mack."

"It's fi—"

"No, it's fucking not. I should've talked to you. I don't want you to be anything other than what you are, Lee Madden, because that person means *everything* to me. And so, to answer your question, I'm *all in* as well—with you, with *us*. Between our mothers and your brother, it's like a bloody soap opera, but I'm here and I'm not going anywhere. Not if you want me."

I stared into those deep green pools and beamed. "I've never wanted anything or anyone more." I went up on my toes to let him know just how much I meant every word and . . . completely missed as the boat lurched under my feet and planted my lips somewhere west of his throat, leaving me spitting up merino.

"Fucking hell." I pushed him away, batting my fingers over my tongue to free the nasty fibres while he snorted in laughter.

"I hate you." I shoved him onto the passenger seat. "And will you stop laughing at me?"

He tried, until he saw me still spluttering, and cracked up all over again.

"That's it." I stabbed a finger at his chest. "This tiki tour is officially over. Back to the farm for you. And FYI, the closest you're gonna get to sex in the immediate future is watching Bossy lick his balls. You've cooked your goose, sunshine."

He grabbed my hands and pulled me over to him. "Oh no, say it isn't so. Not the goose."

"Idiot." I straddled his lap and shut him up with a geographically correct kiss this time, and his arms swept around me as he owned my mouth along with every other fucking part of my body that wasn't tied down.

"And you don't hate me," he said when he finally pulled back, something in his voice stilling the breath in my chest. "I actually hope you're falling in love with me, Leroy Madden. Kind of like I'm doing with you."

I froze, my heart jumping in my chest, my gaze locked on his, searching for the lie. But the truth was all there on his face, everything he felt open for me to read like a letter in his eyes—every word as real as the ocean rolling beneath us. "You're falling in love with me?" I breathed the words like a wish.

"No, baby." He smiled and put his lips against my ear. "I'm already in love with you."

I was pretty sure we made it to the tiny bay I'd chosen for our picnic on autopilot. I had no memory of getting there, just the warmth of

Fox's hand around mine the entire trip. It made up for the chill in my bones over being such an absolute arsehole.

Why hadn't I said it back? Why hadn't I said I loved him?

The tiny inlet sat at the north end of the unpopulated island, and mid-week, there was no one there. Just as I'd hoped. We ran the boat ashore and secured it before spreading a blanket on the golden sand and unpacking the picnic I'd managed to throw together that morning without being rumbled by Fox.

We stripped down to our shorts, slathered on some sunscreen, and went for a quick swim in the incoming tide. I made sure to surreptitiously give myself a thorough wash where it counted, while Fox fooled around like a seal in the waves, and then we headed back up to the rug and ate our picnic to the accompaniment of a few squawking, ever-hopeful gulls, and with just a few cotton wool clouds dusted over a blue sky. The warm slide into autumn was my favourite time of year, although with Fox at my side, Fox, who apparently loved me, I barely noticed.

The conversation was easy, as always, no indication that I'd just done the dickiest thing imaginable by not telling the man I loved that I loved him back after he'd been brave enough to take that chance with me.

He didn't seem concerned, but I was.

But I'd been caught out. Because for all that I'd hoped, I hadn't dared believe. Because this kind of thing didn't happen, not to me— thirty years and not even a long-term girlfriend. Maybe even partly because it was a man saying it, although the gorgeous guy sharing my bed on a nightly basis was a decent heads-up that I was over those initial nerves.

"Lee?"

"Yeah?" I turned to face him. "Sorry, I was daydreaming."

He smiled. "I was asking what you and your mum had decided about a time frame for the business changeover? I thought I heard you talking before we left?"

I nodded absently. "She's thinking a couple of months, but we're meeting with her lawyer next week. That's *if* we survive Sunday lunch that she's apparently cooking this week."

He snorted. "There's always that."

"It's your mother's fault for coming down with a cold."

"I'll be sure to tell her."

I reached for his hand. "How's Mack? Have you heard today?" I was always wary to bring the subject up in case it drove Fox's mood downhill.

He pulled his 'I don't want to talk about it' face. "Let's not spoil the picnic."

I sighed. "You can't just ignore your feelings, Fox."

He stared at me, an amused glint in his eye. "It's worked quite well for me so far. Besides, look who's talking."

"Okay, okay. But this conversation isn't over."

He gave a sly smile. "I never dreamed it was."

I held the container of crackers out. "Want some more? I think there's some Brie left as well."

He shook his head. "I'm wonderfully stuffed. Or, wait a minute, maybe just some cheese."

"Okay, good. Excellent." I waited as he sliced a piece of Brie. Then I put the container aside, patted the lid like a nutcase, and pulled my balls back down from where they'd been hiding. "So . . ." I spun back around and frowned at the large mouthful of cheese he was intent upon chewing. *Too bad.* "I, um, I think I love you too."

He paused mid-chew.

"I mean, I *do* love you. I do . . . already. I'm pretty sure, anyway."

He swallowed the cheese, clearly straining a little at the effort.

"I don't know why I didn't say it before. Well, I do, I guess. I was surprised, you know, that you said it first. Well, surprised you loved me, actually. I mean, I hoped, but . . . Fuck, I'm making a fucking mess of this." I fell back on the blanket with a hand over my face. "I'm just sorry I didn't say it back, that's all. It wasn't because I didn't feel the same, because I do . . . feel the same. Ugh."

He pried my fingers from my face and loomed over me. "It's not a competition, baby. You get there in your own time."

A waft of excellent French Brie assailed my nostrils.

"I know it's not a competition." I screwed my eyes shut. "But I *do* love you. And I should've said it back. I so fucking suck at this stuff, Fox. I warned you."

"Hey." He kissed my lips, my nose, my forehead. "You've said it now, and I feel so bloody lucky that you feel that way about me."

I opened my eyes one at a time to find him smiling at me. "You do?"

"I do, and can I suggest moving on to celebrating the moment in the age-old wise and venerable tradition of fucking each other's brains out?" He threw his hat on the sand and belly crawled up my body until we were nose to nose.

"So, was that cheese good?" I smiled up at him and his cheeks flamed.

"Shit. Do I need to rinse my mouth?"

I bit back a smile. "Of course not."

"Oh fuck, I do, don't I? Hang on." He grabbed the water bottle and rinsed while I laughed. "Okay, ready." He cradled my face in his hands and leant in for a kiss. At the last second, I threw him aside.

"Hold that thought." I slipped out from under his body and reached for the picnic basket.

"That's not quite how I saw that playing out." Fox fell onto his back and stretched out an arm to snag my shorts. "Get back here."

"Just a minute—here." I turned and shoved lube and a condom into his hand.

He stared at them, a slow sexy smile playing on his lips. "You pack for every occasion. I'm impressed."

I straddled his hips and slid my hands over the coarse hair on his chest that I loved so much. His cock swelled and my own rose to meet it.

"I've never actually been fucked on a beach," he said with a wry smile, his hands running up my bare arms, pebbling the skin. "This'll be a first."

"Oh really?" I circled both his nipples, feeling them harden under my fingertips. "Sorry to disappoint, but I'm about to tick that off before you for once."

He went still, eyes dark. "You wanna run that by me again, baby?"

Not really. I took a breath. "I want you to fuck me on this beach, Fox. I'm ready. I've been ready for a while now. I want you inside me, and I want it today. Can you do that for me?"

Next thing, I was on my back with Fox lying the length of me, hard as a rock in his shorts. "Oh yeah. I can do that, sweetheart, *if* you're sure. We can take it nice and slow, but you call the shots. You want to stop at any point, and we stop, okay? You've got nothing to prove. I'm happy with exactly what we've been doing."

God, I loved him. "I know. But I trust you to make it good. I'm not expecting it to be all sunshine and rainbows, not first time around, but we've played around down there long enough. I'm ready, and I want you."

He leaned down and sank his mouth over mine in a deep kiss, our tongues sweeping together as we slowly made out, no rush, no pressure, just two men with all the time in the world to get things right. Then he mapped every inch of my body with his hands and lips, dialling up the heat as he stripped my shorts from my body and set about burning my world. And all I could do was shiver and gasp.

But he kept his promise, teasing and fucking me with his fingers, rimming me until I couldn't take it any longer—until I got all pissy and threatened to finish myself off if he didn't get a wriggle on. But he knew what he was doing, whereas I didn't have a clue what was coming, and so I trusted him—every stretch slow and thorough as he opened me gently, the hissing sting as he added fingers one at a time lost in languorous kisses. And when things ratcheted up, he moved down my body and swallowed my cock deep into his throat, his fingers still working my arse, and I saw stars.

By the time he breached my hole with the head of that thick cock of his, I was desperate to feel him inside me, slick and loose and right on the edge.

But that first long burn still sucked the breath from my lungs, the slicing stretch so much more than I'd ever imagined, and my cock took a moment to reconsider the wisdom of the venture and flagged. But the pain passed, and Fox slowly pressed home, centimetre by centimetre, until he was finally fully seated. My breath came in short gasps and long groans and the world tipped on its axis and . . . wow.

Just fucking wow.

Impossible pressure, too much, so full, too full, but not enough. But more than anything it was his closeness, so close, so fucking intimate. Fox inside me, so far inside, so deep, I'd been right to wait. Having him like this, every nerve in my body zeroed in on the intrusion, the sweeps of feeling, his breath on my neck, his restraint, his power, my . . . vulnerability. It blew my fucking mind.

"Move. Goddammit, Fox, move." I shouted in his ear.

He pulled up with a smile. "Ready?"

I nodded frantically. "Okay. Hang on, beautiful."

He started out slow, and it still hurt just a little, the stretch, the angles, until at some point it just didn't anymore. And then I wanted him faster and harder while all the time he watched my face, watched and smiled, and I'd have sworn his eyes were fucking leaking. Then he stuttered, his thrusts wilder, his head thrown back, and I was so fucking close.

He pounded and thrust and I couldn't get enough, angling my body so he caught me just right, and when the heat of his spill flooded the condom in my arse and he pushed and groaned with his mouth wide open on my shoulder, I was just a second behind, my body erupting in a wave of pleasure that came from God knew where, somewhere new, the same but different, deeper.

And when we were both done, sated and boneless, I wrapped my legs around his waist and whispered in his ear, "I love you."

CHAPTER TWENTY

Fox

"Fox, wake up!"

We'd hunkered down in the homestead all day as the edge of the storm whipped the top of the North Island. Lee was doing God knew what in his study, and I'd been out cold on the couch with Prue stretched across my thighs.

"What?" I shot bolt upright at Lee's voice, Prue shot vertically in the air, and the empty ice cream bowl perched precariously on my chest took a hard turn to the right and fell to the floor in front of some Netflix documentary on solar eclipses I'd been watching sometime never.

"Shit, Lee, you gave me a heart attack."

He snorted and eyed the broken bowl. "I'd have to race that Everest-sized serving of chocolate chunk you just demolished for that privilege, Mr Your Body Is A Temple—not."

I winced and had to admit that my healthy eating enterprise had taken a back seat lately to my self-indulgent pity party. "It's milk. It's good for you." I was still musing the mess on the floor when a thick cable jersey and cyclone-worthy raincoat and trousers landed on my chest.

"Riiiight. Get dressed. You'll need those." Lee disappeared into the kitchen and banged around in the fridge, throwing stuff into his duffel before grabbing a dustpan and brush and clearing the broken bowl. "For fuck's sake, hurry up, will you?"

"Are you going to tell me what's got your knickers in a twist, or is it a secret?" I shoved my legs into the waterproofs and got to my feet. Prue yowled like a demon. "Goddammit!" I immediately sprang to the side. "Sorry, girl. Didn't see you there."

I stroked her silky coat, then tackled getting my arms into the jacket. A gust rattled the glass in the old sash windows, and I jumped. "Holy hell, that wind's picked up. How long have I been asleep?"

"A good hour. And yes, we're at gale force with gusts over forty knots in places." Lee planted my heavy boots and a pair of thick socks at my feet and began lacing his own. "Harry called to say he was collecting the last of his crayfish pots after the forecast changed and saw one of our backbones floating free in the channel. It must have broken its anchor warp at one end. That's over a hundred metres unsecured. If the other end goes, we'll lose it completely and it sounds like the main harvest section for next week."

"Oh, fuck!" I slammed my feet into my boots, suddenly wide awake.

"My thoughts exactly. He did what he could, but it was too heavy for his boat to pull and he said the channel was starting to cut up nasty. I called the met office, and they said the edge of the cyclone wasn't pushing as far west as they'd hoped, which means we're gonna cop the lower half at least. They're putting out the marine warnings now. Dammit, Fox, if I lose that harvest . . ."

"I know, I know."

"It won't matter if Mum sells me the farm, there won't be a fucking business to run. How the hell did the warp break lose?"

"No point worrying about that now. Let's just fix it. I'll let Kane know what's going on."

"Fine, but I don't want the mums worrying unnecessarily. They'll just get on our case. Same with Judah. Kane can man the communications and it'll keep him out of the way. I can't be worrying about him one-handed out there. Plus, that gives us a safety net if we get in trouble. You and I can manage with the *Green Lip*. Tell him to keep his cell close and also check with the marine radio in here."

"Will do. I'll meet you at the truck. And feed Prue or she'll be raiding that damn pantry again."

Twenty minutes later, we got the *Cee Dee* secured to the wharf so we could leave her and were heading out. A booming black sky hung full and heavy as far as you could see, lit silver from the occasional flash of lightning, and in a few minutes, we'd left the relative shelter of Painted Bay for an angry, boiling sea.

"Holy fuck," I shouted into a sudden punch of wind, grabbing for a handhold and planting my feet as a huge swell rolled under the boat, pitching it sideways before righting it again. "Where the fuck did this come from? I expect this shit down south, and a lot worse, but I thought you guys were soft, shallow floaters up here?" I sent Lee a wink and he laughed.

"You're such a fucking arrogant prick," he shouted back as he expertly manoeuvred the big boat through the heaving seas. "We get weather too, you know. Tropical cyclones aren't all piña coladas and waving palm trees."

Another wave thumped us from the side, and I scrambled for a footing. He laughed and I slapped him on the back before leaning in for a kiss. "Fuck yeah, baby!" My pulse pounded in my ears, my lungs gasping. "I haven't been in a decent storm for months."

He shot me a look, eyes bright and adrenaline-fuelled. "Me neither. People will think we're crazy, but it's a blast, right?" He leaned forward, squinting to see through the sheeting rain. "As long as we get that damn line secured again."

We sobered a little at that, and I took a few seconds to duck below deck and call Kane to let him know we were heading out. I could barely keep my feet, and the creaking hull and pounding waves overwhelmed everything else, but he got the gist and we agreed to switch to marine radio. I headed back on deck.

"So what's the plan?" I moved to Lee's back, our lifejackets bumping, but at least I could hear. I snaked an arm around his waist, and he leaned back against me. It felt strangely intimate, a shared touch in the middle of a hot and angry storm, and I took a second to take it in—the two of us riding squalls, working together, laughing, making it happen, and I wanted more. I wanted us like this forever.

He leaned his head back so I could hear him. "It's too rough to do more than a patch job, but we have to try," he shouted. "We'll never get it back on its concrete anchor block in this, so I'm gonna try and tie it to the neighbouring backbone and hope that's enough to keep it out of trouble."

It was a good plan. "I'll get the rope ready."

He turned his head to kiss me. "Be careful."

I felt eyes hot on my back as I weaved my way to the stern, flung from one handhold to the next until I made it to where the long ropes were stored. Then I chose the best for the job, hoisted it over my shoulder, and then lunged my way back up to the helm while trying not to get thrown over the side.

Lee alternated trying to steer through the pelting rain and keeping an eye on me until I was safe. I made it back to the helm, grabbed his chin, and planted a fierce kiss on his lips.

When I let him go, he laughed at me, eyes black and wild, water dripping from his hair and lashes, his hood hanging useless down his back, every inch of him sodden from the neck up. He looked absolutely mesmerising.

"You look like you wanna fuck me," he shouted into the wind as the boat rose and crashed into the next trough.

"Like you wouldn't believe," I shouted back, getting all up in his face. "So let's save these bloody mussels and then all bets are off."

"You got it." He drove the boat into the next swell, and we tipped vertically before thumping down once again. The gales were fuelling the current, whipping the sea into a dangerous cauldron. But on the next crest, a flash of lightning lit up the backbone floats of the mussel farm and we were almost there.

"Look!" Lee shouted, pointing to a line of floats at right angles to the rest. "I'll get in as close as I can, but I'll have to take a wide arc so we don't get anything caught in the motor. The dropper ropes could be lying sideways just under the water. We'll never see them."

"Okay." I peered into the gloom. "You handle the boat. You've got a much better touch with her than me. I'll look after securing the line."

Lee nodded, then fisted my coat and pulled me in. "You be bloody careful. If you fall in and drown, I'm gonna net you up and then kill you again with my own hands, understand?"

I laughed. "Understood."

"Good boy." He gently slapped my soaking cheek, then set about trying to keep the *Green Lip* on course as a huge wall of water broke over the front and nearly slammed us both into the deck. Seawater choked my throat, and I coughed and gasped for air.

"You okay?" he yelled, scrambling for a foothold.

I looked up from where I'd been thrown to my knees on the deck with a huge grin on my face. "Did I tell you how much I loved this shit?"

He laughed and kicked at me with his boot. "Get going, you idiot."

It took four attempts and nearly an hour before we had the end of the backbone float line secured to the boat. Then all we had to do was drag it to its neighbouring backbone and try to tie it on.

From what we could tell from the *Green Lip*'s spotlights, which were only just short of useless in the pissing rain blowing sideways and the rollercoaster waves, a few of the drop lines had taken a hammering and lost some of their precious cargo. But for the most part, the clusters of mussels visible on the few others that I could actually see in the almost dark were still holding on. If we could get the backbone secured and stop the currents and surges from doing any more damage, we had a chance of saving the harvest.

"I'm going . . . as close . . . need to watch stern . . . anchor line . . . watch out," Lee shouted, half his words lost to the noisy squall so I had to fill in the gaps.

The *Green Lip* was really too big to get in close without risk of snagging the backbone anchor line, but Lee did his best. That said, I figured I needed to be ready to take an unplanned dip if we missed our target or got snagged. I was hoping to avoid it, although I may as well have already been in for a dunk considering how bloody wet I was. Wet skin under wet cotton, under wet wool, under wet oilskin— just plain fucking soaking wet.

A flash lit up the sky and seconds later thunder crashed overhead, the sound splitting my head. Closer than the last. We weren't out of this yet. Bloody weather forecasters. I wanted to get a few of them out from their desks and onto this boat—see if their accuracy improved any.

"A little more." I waved my arm at Lee. I couldn't even see the orange float at the end of the secured backbone, let alone attempt to tie the broken one to it. *Goddammit.* I kept a tight hold of the gunwale and leaned over the pitching black depths as Lee inched closer and closer.

"Stop!" I yelled, throwing up my arm as I caught sight of the anchor warp angling into the sea only metres from the *Green Lip*'s stern. Lee instantly powered up and cranked the boat out of the way before trying another approach. I watched from the stern, guiding him in with my arm, the wind throwing my voice somewhere out to sea.

As soon as we were close enough, I signalled him to stop, which was easier said than done. Keeping position was a bitch, but somehow, he managed. And while he fought to give me a chance, I somehow got the dragline I'd tied to the damaged backbone for the purpose of towing the thing, untied and secured, to the other backbone which remained safely anchored. I wasn't sure I still had all my freezing fingers, and who knew if it would hold, but it was the best we could do.

As soon as I was done, I signalled Lee to head to safer water and the boat lurched forward. I made my way up to the helm and grabbed him in my arms. "We fucking did it!" I shouted over his shoulder, and he turned with a grin from ear to ear like a kid in a toy shop.

"Radio Kane, we're coming in."

I grabbed the radio and told Kane we were headed back. He said he'd put the coffee on. "Don't bother," I told him, winking at Lee. "We'll be heading straight to bed. I'll let you know when we're safely back at the wharf."

"Do that." Kane signed off, and Lee turned for Painted Bay, fighting the bouldering waves every step of the turn.

I yelled next to his ear. "I'll go below for some water and chocolate bars. We need to stay fuelled."

He nodded. "Just what I need, more fucking water."

I kissed his sopping-wet nose. "Have I told you how much I love your grumpy pants?"

He tried and failed to hide a smile and I headed below deck, mission accomplished.

In under a minute I had the water bottles tucked under my arm, and I almost had my hands on the chocolate bars we kept stashed in the cupboard when everything in the cabin went dark. My shoulder slammed into the opposite wall, the water bottles jettisoning like torpedoes from my hands, and the chocolate bars, along with everything else in the cupboard, crashed to the floor, the container of coffee catching my forehead on its journey past.

"Shit, shit, shit!" I shouted to no one as something screamed in the engine room, metal on metal, and the cabin lights flickered on and off like a carnival sideshow.

That didn't sound good.

The boat's engine gunned free, the *Green Lip* airborne and floating just for a second before slamming down on another rising swell, and I lost a metre of height as the upward and downward forces crashed together.

"Fox!" Lee called down. "Fox, are you okay?" The boat lurched alarmingly, and I scrambled back on deck.

"Yeah, just."

His eyes widened and he grabbed my shoulder. "Shit, you're bleeding. Come here."

I reached my fingers to my forehead and they came away black in the sputtering light of the dash. "It's just a nick. Damn coffee tin. What the fuck happened?"

"We got caught between two opposing waves. It dumped us sideways. I'm gonna try again."

I grabbed his arm. "What's that?"

"I said, I'm gonna try—"

"No. What's that noise? Something's off in the engine room. Listen."

He did and his brows crunched. "Shit."

"I think we should take a look—"

The lights on the dash flickered and went out, quickly followed by the spot, and we were plunged into a black so deep, I couldn't even see Lee's face. Then lightning lit up the sky and his eyes were fixed wide on mine.

"Can you try and keep her steady while I check the engine?" he asked, calm and focused, the working Lee.

"Of course."

And he was gone. The electrics came and went in random fashion, and I ran possibilities through my head, none of which were good. The engine plugged along, but it didn't sound right, and every time I rode the throttle a little to reposition her, it lagged like there was nothing there.

A few minutes later, Lee appeared above deck wearing a sombre look. "The engine's running way too hot," he shouted. "The cooling system's not working properly, and I'm not sure why. Plus there's oil leaking from somewhere, but the boat's rolling too much for me to track it. We can't risk heading back like this."

"What do you suggest?" He was the expert in this area, not me.

He took a second to think as another blaze of lightning lit up the rolling shell of the ocean like some galactic black hole. And in the ghostly reflection off its surface, I caught the concern and uncertainty in his eyes. I cupped his cheek in one hand. "You know this coast. I'll follow you anywhere. I trust your instincts."

He held my gaze, then gave a sharp nod and took over the helm. "Let's hope she holds together long enough to get us there."

I stood behind him again, one arm circling his waist, the other hand clenched around a handhold. "You've got this, sweetheart."

He angled his head to the side so I could hear him. "There's a small cove just up the coast with nor-easterly protection. Enough to ride the storm out. It'll be rough as guts, but we should be safe. I'm not abandoning my boat, Fox, not without a fight."

I kissed his cheek. "Then we won't. But if it gets too dangerous, I'll drag your sorry arse onto that shore if I have to tie you up in one of your own nursery ropes."

He grinned. "Promises, promises. You better let Kane know while the radio's working. The way this night is going, the battery will probably cark it as well. Tell him, Flounder Cove."

I gawped at him. "Really? We're taking our limping boat to a place named Flounder Cove?"

He slipped me a sideways eye-roll as water poured from the tight line of his jaw. "Have a little faith." He tried to throttle into the next wave and the boat miraculously held together, although the burgeoning smell of oil was hardly reassuring.

Kane was determined to call the coastguard, arguing until I managed to get him to hold off with the promise that if he didn't hear from us in the next thirty minutes, he could go ahead.

But Lee was a skilled skipper, and he nursed the *Green Lip* against the bullying storm with an expert hand. Battered by thunder and lightning, rogue swells, and pounding seas, we slowly pushed through. The navigation was spotty at best, the electrics flickering constantly, and I knew Lee was mostly getting us there by instinct and local knowledge. I left him to it, keeping silent at his back. I'd meant what I said. I trusted him.

Twenty endless minutes later we limped around a bluff and into another world. Maybe not as calm as we'd hoped, but manageable, good enough. Lee took the boat as close as he could to where a large curving bluff blocked the worst of the gales, and together we got her anchored and secure. Then we hunkered down in the cabin as best we could in the rolling seas, and radioed Kane to try and borrow Jon's boat to bring breakfast and a tool kit in the morning. It was a lot more powerful than the *Cee Dee*.

Kane said he'd add it to the list right under the shotgun he was going to shoot us with for giving him a heart attack and the contract offering him a raise.

"That man's settling in nicely." Lee climbed toward me through the wrecked cabin, naked bar a pair of bright blue briefs and a dry blanket around his shoulders. Our wet clothes were hanging in the engine room to try and at least stop them dripping. We'd freeze if we wore them any longer.

Lee crawled up my body to where I'd managed to make a kind of bed on top of a bunch of tarpaulins and nestled beside me. "Now, I believe you mentioned something about fucking me when you had the night's storm in your eyes." He kissed my throat as the tide rolled beneath us.

"Really?" I arched a brow. "The way our luck's gone tonight, the boat would lurch at the wrong time and I'd end up impaled though the hull, stuck forever in Flounder Bay."

He laughed. "I'm sure the dolphins would enjoy playing with the strange-looking fish."

I tweaked his nipple. "Fuck you. A seal, at very least."

He snorted. "Come here and spoon me, it's been a very harrowing night."

I turned on my side and pulled him close.

He looked over his shoulder and softly kissed me. "I love you, Fox Carmody."

I kissed him, sliding my tongue inside. He tasted of the ocean. "I love you too, Lee Madden. At least tonight your snoring won't keep me awake."

He chuckled and kicked my shin. "Good luck with that. I can out-snore a fucking hurricane, sweetheart."

And I believed it.

Our bare skin kindled enough heat under the protection of the canvas to keep us warm as the wind wailed and the boat rocked and lightning lit up the cabin every other minute. If we got an hour of sleep, it would be a bloody miracle.

CHAPTER TWENTY-ONE

Leroy

"Leroy? Are you in there?"

I peeled an eyelid open, taking a second to wonder where the fuck I was and what hellish lump of concrete had found its way into my mattress. My eyes landed on the pushed aside tarpaulin, and Fox's naked limbs wrapped tight around my body.

"Leroy!" The voice outside dropped like a blade into familiar and horrifying focus, and enough ice water hit my brain to wake the living dead.

Judah.

"Fox," I hissed, trying to keep my voice down. "Fox, you have to let me go." I wriggled, but the grip of steel around my waist refused to budge. *Goddammit.*

He groaned, arched his hips, and his morning wood launched into my crease. "Mmm. But you feel good." He murmured against the back of my neck and a hand found my panicked cock.

I determined to kill him, slowly and extremely painfully.

Feet made their way across the deck and the handle on the hatch rattled.

"Fox!" I kicked his shins, and his eyes finally sprang open. "Ow! What the—"

"Judah's here." I hissed.

"What? Shit!" He made a grab for the tarp just as daylight broke through the hatch and feet appeared on the steps. If there was a god, they had to be laughing their damn head off right about now.

I slid from under the tarp, trying to create at least a little distance, but that was as good as it got. Judah's worried face appeared in the cabin and he launched himself at me, pinning me to him in the bear hug to end all bear hugs.

"Jesus Christ, Leroy. You stupid, fucking idiot. What the hell did you think you were doing going out in that storm? You could've gotten yourself killed, both of you."

I froze as Judah's tears wet my shoulder, chastened that I hadn't thought to call and warn him before we left. Being accountable . . . to anyone other than maybe my mother was new. But Judah obviously cared, and that was inexplicably kind of wonderful. I glanced at Fox, who wore a soft smile as if reading my thoughts.

I slid my arms around Judah. "I'm sorry. I didn't think. I'm not used to—"

"Then get used to it." He pulled back and cupped my cheeks. "Thank Christ Kane had enough brains to let us know after you'd anchored somewhere safe."

"He did?" That surprised me on a number of levels.

"I'm sorry, Leroy, but I was worried," Kane explained, flicking glances between Fox and me like the lightbulb had suddenly gone on. "You okay, Fox?"

Fox nodded. "I'm fine."

"You did the right thing," I told Kane over Judah's shoulder. Then I jerked my head to where a motor was rumbling outside. "Morgan?"

Judah nodded. "Jon was fine lending his boat, he's busy with the storm damage. But Morgan wasn't about to let me come get you without him, or let Kane drive with his arm. It's stopped raining, but the seas are still pretty damn messy, and there's shit all over the place, logs and branches, and you can't see a thing with all the silt in the water. Plus, I might've had an attack yesterday morning." He shrugged. "It was probably the drop in atmospheric pressure. I'm realising that's a thing with me. I'm fine, but you know Morgan. He worries."

I was impossibly touched, finally noticing the pallor in his face and the exhaustion in his eyes. But he'd come for me. I'd been such a fool about him. "Judah, you shouldn't have taken the risk."

"I'm fine. And for fuck's sake, you're my brother, Leroy. What the hell else was I going to do? But I'd keep a low profile around Morgan for a bit if I was you. He's not too impressed by your stunt."

"It wasn't a stunt." I stepped back, a gust of wind licking down from the open hatch to remind me I was in nothing but my briefs. I grabbed my wet jersey and held it against my chest. "If I'd lost that harvest, we would've been in real trouble."

"I know. But it wasn't as important as you." Now that he'd let me go, he seemed to suddenly clue into the fact I was standing there all but naked. "Jesus Christ, you'll bloody freeze. Kane had sense enough to pack some dry clothes for you both, just in case." He shot a small smile Kane's way, which gave me pause. It must've shown on my face because he said, "Last night earned him a few Brownie points, that's all."

Kane flushed and held out a bag. "They're dry," he said. "I'm sorry, but I had to look around a bit to find them." The implication clear. He'd found all Fox's clothes in my room.

Shit. I tried not to look at Fox. Guess we'd outed ourselves to my second employee. "Thanks." I held Kane's eyes and his cheeks blazed bright. I threw the wet jersey aside and dug into the bag for something warm.

Judah immediately grabbed my wrist and held my arm out. "Jesus Christ. Are you seeing someone, Leroy?"

"What?"

"I'm gonna check with Morgan." Kane was up those stairs and gone in a second.

About the same time, I glanced down at my chest and caught the soft groan of misery in Fox's throat. *Fuck. Fuck. Fuck.* I was still covered in bite marks from our picnic the day before. Fox's bite marks. I'd completely bloody forgotten.

"You've been pretty damn sneaky about it." Judah smiled. "I'm impressed. So, who is she?"

I could've lied, but I wasn't going to. I'd screwed up enough with Judah already. Nothing was going to make this any better, but it could sure as hell get a lot worse. I looked to Fox.

He gave a half-shrug and a small smile. *It's up to you. I'll still be here.*

Judah's gaze shifted between us and he frowned. "Lee? What the hell's going on?"

"Wait a minute." I wasn't going to do this practically naked. I pulled on the shirt and the sweats Kane had brought and then tossed the bag to Fox who did the same.

Judah drew a sharp breath at the equally impressive scratch marks I'd made on Fox's back. "Holy fucking cow." His focus jerked back to me. "You mean he—you two—" He shook his head in shock. "Son of a bitch. You and Fox? Martha's bloody son." He shoved me back into the table and Fox immediately jumped between us.

I held a hand up. "It's okay, Fox."

Fox stepped back, but not far. And he kept a wary eye on Judah.

"No, it is not fucking okay," Judah fumed. "You're straight. Or at least you were the last thirty years of your life. What the hell's going on, Leroy?" He swung on Fox. "Did you—"

I grabbed his arm as he lunged.

"He didn't do anything I didn't want, Judah, so calm the fuck down. This is none of your business."

Perhaps not the best thing to say, and Fox drew a sharp breath.

Judah rounded on me. "Not my business? After you throwing me under the bus my entire life for being, in your words, 'too fucking gay for your own good.' And then you start fucking a man and I'm supposed to just smile and say, welcome to the club, brother? I don't fucking think so! How long has this been going on?"

"What's going on?" Morgan appeared behind Judah.

"Stay out of this, Morgan," Judah snapped. "My big brother has been fucking Fox, and we're all just finding out about it now and supposed to like it. How long, Leroy? And how long have you known you were gay, dammit? Did you know in high school? Did you know when you were standing back and watching them call me names? Did you know even then? You owe me some fucking answers!"

"He doesn't *owe* you any answers, Judah, at least not about most of those questions." Fox stepped between us and Morgan took his place alongside Judah in some kind of stand-off. It would've been laughable if it wasn't so gut-wrenchingly real and upsetting. Everything I'd been afraid of thrown at me on a silver platter, and it was my own damn fault.

Fox went on. "You know as well as I do, Judah, that no one has to come out to anyone else's timetable but their own. Leroy's story is his, just like yours is yours. You've admitted you knew nothing about him regarding this, so why not give him the respect you'd give anyone else."

"Who the hell are you to lecture me?" Judah stepped so close I could smell his shampoo, and I was vaguely aware of Morgan's restraining hand on his arm, the concern cutting deep lines in his face.

"I'm his *boyfriend*, Judah." Fox said it so clearly, so simply, as if it was the most natural thing in the world, as if it didn't just pin my heart to his shadow.

Judah's jaw fell open, and he fired me a disbelieving look as Fox continued. "I don't give a shit if you're his brother, Judah, you'll back off and speak to Lee civilly, or you won't fucking speak to him at all, understand?"

My hand found the warm skin of Fox's lower back and I slipped it around his waist and stepped to his side. "It's okay." I kissed his shoulder, Judah's eyes bugging out of his face as he watched. "I might not owe Judah, but I'll answer some of his questions at least."

Fox hesitated, then stepped aside, just a little. I dropped my arm and took his hand instead, with Judah watching the movement like it cut him to the core.

"I'm bi, not gay." I was shocked at how calm I sounded. "And I didn't have any clue about it, not really, not until Fox came along. I believed I was straight all through high school. I've never been head over heels over any girl, but yeah, I like them."

I squeezed Fox's hand and he returned it. "Maybe at some level I was aware, who knows? That's possibly why your out-and-proud stance made me so uncomfortable, but I really can't say. Either way, it was an arsehole thing to say to you regardless of what was going through my head, and I'm not giving any excuses."

"Damn right." Judah threw out his chin in challenge, and Morgan slipped an arm around his waist.

I suddenly remembered what my mother had said about Morgan being able to talk to Judah after the fact, and I hoped like hell she was right. Because there was nothing but pain and hurt and a belligerent 'fuck you' in my brother's eyes. And I really didn't blame him.

I took a breath and ploughed on. "When I first met Fox last year, I was shocked by my reaction to him, appalled even."

Judah's lip curled and Fox gave my hand another squeeze. "I tried to hate him, tried to ignore what he made me feel every time we met after that, but I couldn't get him out of my head. And when he came to stay. . ." I glanced up at Fox and he smiled. "I wasn't looking for him, Judah. I wasn't wondering or questioning, it just happened, and in the end, I couldn't run away from him either." But I caught a level of anger in my brother's eyes I'd never seen before.

"So, what?" he spat. "You're experimenting with Fox? Does Fox understand that? Does he know that you're maybe just trying him on for size? Satisfying your curiosity at his expense like so many other straight boys do. Breaking our bloody hearts like they were cheap toys—"

"Judah!" The shock in Morgan's voice cut through Judah's tirade like a blade, and Judah spun, looking ready to unleash on his husband as well before thinking better of it and sagging against him instead.

Too shaken to reply, I let Fox turn me against his chest and bury his lips in my hair. I tilted my head and cupped his cheek, desperate for him to believe me. "You're *not* an experiment and I'm *not* playing games. I wouldn't do that to you."

"I know, Lee." He kissed me fleetingly. "I know. You have nothing to prove to me." It was his eyes more than his words that reassured me—deep green pools of kindness.

Judah wouldn't look at me, but I caught Morgan's quick nod, and it gave me courage to ask a few questions of my own. "Maybe I've got no right after everything I've done to you in the past, Judah, but let me ask you something. Why, when I find out I'm bisexual and act on it, it's only experimenting? When you knew you were gay, you *dated*. And why am I only *curious*, but you're allowed to be serious? And why are you able to have a boyfriend you're committed to, while I only get to have a fuck partner that I'm clearly going to leave?"

I didn't expect an answer and I wasn't disappointed. Judah never even acknowledged the questions.

"I'll be in the boat with Kane," he said. That Judah was opting to be alone with Kane rather than talk with me, said everything I needed to know about Judah's opinion.

Morgan let Judah go with sad eyes before pulling me into a brief hug. There was another hug for Fox, who was clearly surprised but returned it.

"He needs time." Morgan glanced to the hatch, although the worry in his eyes spoke volumes to the fact he wasn't quite as sure about that as he'd have us believe. "And it's too rough to do anything more with the *Green Lip* today. If you're happy to leave her here, let's make sure she's secure and get something big enough to tow her tomorrow."

I wasn't happy about it, but there was little choice. And she was in less danger than if we tried to get her back as things stood weather-wise.

But it was a long, silent trip home, with Fox's arms around my waist the only thing keeping me upright. Judah refused to even look at me, and for all that Fox had my back, there was a look on his face that I'd never seen before.

Fear and resignation.

Martha and Cora met the boat and fed us hot coffee and donuts in the wharf office with the heater going. Well, all except for Judah and Morgan who disappeared to the boathouse with barely a nod. No one said a word about the snub, but there was obvious concern on our mothers' faces, and after Kane finished his coffee, he disappeared out of there lickety-split, back to the homestead.

Cora directed a pointed look at Fox that needed zero interpretation. *Talk to your mother.* Then she headed for the boathouse where I figured she wasn't going to get much joy from Judah either. That left Fox, Martha, and me, and I was gone a minute later, telling Fox I'd see him back at the house. His expression as I left was full of apology and an odd yearning.

I didn't even want to think what that meant.

I'd been home about half an hour when Jon called to offer me his boat if I needed it while the *Green Lip* was being fixed. It was a lot bigger than the *Cee Dee* and I was incredibly grateful. I didn't think the engine problems on the *Green Lip* were that major, but she'd likely be out of action for a couple of days at the very least, and I couldn't afford to be stuck with just a gofer boat. I needed that anchor line fixed before the harvester arrived.

I'd only just hung up when Patrick called to say he was booked on the first flight in the morning. He'd heard the news from Kane and was on his way to his brother's graduation but wouldn't stay the extra nights he'd planned. I tried to change his mind, but he was having none of it, and I was again struck by how lucky I was to have him. When Patrick asked how I was doing and was Fox okay, I knew Kane had been talking. I couldn't even find the energy to be angry. Patrick hoped things would work out for us, and I was so choked up I could barely get the thank you out.

Next on the list was another mussel farmer I knew from just north of Whangarei. He had a boat big enough to safely tow the *Green Lip* back to the wharf and was more than happy to help out a fellow small operator. It was the way things were done in Northland. We arranged for him to be there the next morning, weather permitting.

I ended that call feeling like I was finally getting things done, but when Fox dragged his weary body inside twenty minutes later and collapsed on the couch, eyes red-rimmed and haunted and barely meeting my gaze, a pit the size of a small star opened in my stomach.

"Talk to me." I sat beside him, needing to touch him, to make him look at me. "Was your mum okay . . . about us?"

He sighed. "Yes and no. Cautiously happy but concerned as well. About us, and about Judah."

"Cautiously happy. Jesus, I am so tired of living my life like there's a fucking sword above our heads," I grumbled.

He drew me down and kissed me like he might never get the chance again. "How are *you?*" he asked, his eyes full of concern.

I shrugged. "Okay, I guess. Numb, probably. My mind is spinning so fast, I don't even know where to start." I stabbed at his chest with my finger. "So if even just for a fucking second you're thinking of finishing things between us like that gloomy fucking kiss implied, I will end you now, do you understand me?"

He snorted and fought back a smile. "Do you know how much I love you right now?" He played with my hair and cupped my face in his hand. "And no, I am not finishing anything between us. But something became really clear to me this morning."

"That my brother is a self-righteous dick?"

He gave a soft laugh. "Well, other than that, of course."

"He was right to be angry." I fell forward on Fox's chest. "I hurt him back then, and I'm not sure I can ever make that up to him. I should've talked to him sooner."

Fox threaded his fingers through my hair. "I never want to come between you, and I hate that this has happened. You've done your best to heal a lot this last year. Maybe it's Judah's turn. Still, I know how important your relationship with your brother is for *you,* and for this whole family, actually. And I also know this thing with us isn't going to help that."

"But—"

"Shhh." He put a finger to my lips. "You need time, Lee. Time to work things out with Judah, and I have to clean up my personal mess as well. I've been avoiding confronting Van, avoiding seeing Ewan, avoiding getting this thing with Mack finished in case I don't get what I want. But I realised this morning that you and I can't move on without all that being sorted out. I need to put the whole sorry mess of my marriage behind me so that *we* have a chance." He cradled my face, his thumbs stroking my cheeks.

"You're going back south, aren't you?" The words broke from my lips in a whisper, and his eyes filled.

"Just until the family court process is done, or until I can get an agreement with Van about Mack. And until things are better here for you and Judah. I won't be the one responsible for ruining everything you've achieved."

An icy chill ran through me. "Will you talk to Laurie about the job?"

He blinked slowly. "Not unless you and I talk about it first. I promise."

I drew a shaky breath. It was something, at least. And I wanted to believe him, that it wasn't for good, that he wouldn't be tempted to stay. But a part of me kept hearing Van's words in my ears. Fox *had* kept his options open. A house in a place he loved. A good job *if* he changed his mind. Van's bitter words—that Fox had never been a mainlander, that his heart would always reside in the deep south—drilled a fiery hole in my brain that wouldn't be ignored.

If Fox left, would he ever come back?

Did I have enough of his heart to bring him home?

I wanted to believe.

"Don't look at me like that." He stroked my cheek. "I'm coming back, baby. No matter how long it takes, I'm coming back. Let's just do this one step at a time."

I sighed and fell into his arms, understanding at some level he was right. For us to have a chance, we needed the best foundation we could muster. We had to trust and hope and clean the slates.

And so, for the rest of the day, we worked quietly side by side in the house. Fox called Tinny and made arrangements to leave early the next day and packed. I organised my boat mechanic and the supplies I'd need to fix the damage to the farm and watched him pack.

And then, after Fox cooked me dinner and the rain finally stopped, we shared a beer rugged-up on our favourite lounger on the deck, under a dark brooding sky almost bereft of stars, and Fox led me to our bedroom where he fucked me slowly and agonisingly sweetly until I came on a soft gasp and a damp pillow.

He cleaned me so damn tenderly, I almost lost my shit then and there. And when he was done, he pulled me into his side, wrapped me up in his arms and held me until the soft grey light of morning filtered into our room. He slipped from our bed with a brief kiss to my shoulder while I pretended to sleep, listening to him shower as I choked back the tears.

But he wasn't fooled. Wrapped in just a towel, he came back to bed and covered my body with his, holding me in his arms and pressing me into the mattress as he covered my face in kisses. As if I needed the reminder of his raw beauty and the weight of him in my life, of the anchor he'd become, the Fox-shaped hole that I wasn't sure I'd survive if he didn't keep his promise and come home, to *our* home.

We talked quietly as he came and went from the bedroom

packing his bag, moving those piles of clothes from the bedroom floor that had driven me up the wall for weeks. Chatted like it was any other fucking day, and I could barely stop myself from screaming in frustration at the bald insanity of it all.

I wanted to yell at him not to go. I wanted to tell him I trusted him to come back. I wanted him to fall to his knees and say he'd changed his mind and decided to stay and that everything else could go to hell—that he couldn't bear to walk out that door.

I trusted he meant what he said, at least now. But a squirming niggle in my gut worried that when he got back to his old home, the place he'd loved for so long, that maybe what we had together wouldn't stack up enough to bring him back?

I wanted to say too much, to hurt him for doing this, for leaving me with nothing decided, the familiar sting of anger so fucking reassuring on my tongue. I wanted to tear into him, tell him I regretted ever getting into his bed, regretted all those soft words I'd spoken, yell until he finally understood just how much I felt for him, how the not knowing what might happen between us was ripping me apart.

And in that moment, his gaze shot to mine, like he knew. He came over and drew me into his arms and took my lips in a slow, achingly sweet kiss that drew the threads of rage from my mouth and let them fall, lost in faith I wasn't sure I really had.

And when he was done, he placed a final kiss on my forehead, smiled and ran his thumb over my mouth, and then left the room with "I love you" on his lips.

Seconds later, the front door closed, and soon after that his Explorer roared to life.

I listened until the sound of the engine drifted, lost in the morning's grey light.

Then when all was finally quiet, I curled on my side and let the tears fall.

CHAPTER TWENTY-TWO

Fox

Tᴉɴɴʏ ᴘɪᴄᴋᴇᴅ ᴍᴇ ᴜᴘ ꜰʀᴏᴍ ᴛʜᴇ ᴀɪʀᴘᴏʀᴛ ɪɴ Iɴᴠᴇʀᴄᴀʀɢɪʟʟ ᴀɴᴅ I spent the night catching up with him and his wife. I was grateful for the chance to take a deep breath and just be among friends. I told them everything: about Lee, about Judah, the mussel farm, my mum, Cora, the storm. Everything.

I was a mess. The adrenaline crash after the storm, our disastrous outing by Judah, and then leaving Lee the very next day had left me raw and unmoored. And although I'd left most of my clothes at the homestead, the look in Lee's eyes when I'd left told me he wasn't at all sure I was coming back, and I hated that he felt so uncertain. And yet didn't I have questions as well? Wasn't that also why I was down here?

They listened in silence, but then Violet wanted to know more about Lee. "Bugger the rest," she said. She wanted to know about the man who'd stolen my heart. I'd headed north less than three months before, cynical and unsure I'd ever trust another man, let alone fall in love.

"The man who changed that was a man worth knowing," she'd said, and I couldn't disagree. "A man you should be careful about walking away from too quickly," she'd also warned.

And so later that night in the spare room where I'd spent many nights after Van had left me, I thought about her words and knew I didn't want to walk away. But I also had to know. I had to face my past and choose to leave it this time, choose to change my future.

I called Bean to organise a few beers with the old crew once I hit Stewart Island. They were berthed after a stint offshore and couldn't wait to see me. I thought about that. And then I thought about Patrick and Kane and Judah and Morgan and all the people I'd met in Painted Bay.

Then I called Lee, wanting to talk, to tell him what I was feeling, how much I missed him, how much more I loved him. But the call went to voicemail, and all I could do was send him a text and worry.

Instead of sleeping, I chewed over what the next day would bring. What it would feel like to set foot on the island again. To face those speculative stares, the whispered comments, the pitying looks, and to meet Van on his home turf with the support of his community behind him. And I remembered my mother's words from our short conversation after the storm.

"You have to decide if Lee's worth what you need to give up in order to have him, son."

"I don't know what you mean, Mum. There's nothing left to give up."

"Isn't there?" She studied me in the way mothers did when you couldn't see what was right in front of you. "Why did you keep the house?"

"Because I wasn't ready to sell? I might use it as a vacation crib one day, who knows?"

Her brow arched meaningfully. "Really? You'd holiday in the place where Van and his family lived? It's a tiny town, Fox.

Seems you could find a lot of other more relaxing places to spend time."

"I know. But I love it there. Dammit, Mum, he took everything from me. The house is the only thing left. Maybe I should've sold it, but I bought it before I met him, and it meant something to me. My first home, a sign, a symbol if you like. And I wanted something left to show I'd even been there. I loved him once. I'd imagined our whole lives spent in that town, on that ocean. I know you never trusted him, but I did. I fucking did, and he blew through that trust like a wrecking ball."

She held me as I wept about all the dreams I'd lost and about trying to hold on to something through it all, anything. And I thought about Van's challenge to Lee outside the homestead that day, that I would always go back, that I was a southerner to my core. And he'd been right, at least back when he'd known me, when I'd loved him.

Only he wasn't right any longer. He didn't know what I'd found in Painted Bay. I'd only dreamed of going back down south until the moment Leroy Madden had kissed me. And in that one moment, everything changed. Now, Lee was my home, not down south, not a place, but a man.

"This thing between you sounds serious." She stepped back and dried my wet cheeks with her sleeve.

"Very much. He's not . . . he's not what people think. And he's so fucking scared of letting people in. Of needing someone. Or asking . . . for anything. It's like he has to do it all on his own."

"I know." She smiled softly. "I knew him as a teenager, don't forget. But he's changing. Leroy's a good man. I can see how this might work for you both."

"Can you? Because so far we've done nothing but make a total mess of everything."

"Pfft. We don't get to choose the timing or who we fall for. Look at me and Cora. I was pining after a blissfully married straight woman for years. Anyone would've called me crazy for even dreaming. The universe is a strange place, Fox. All you can do is listen as best you can, put your glasses on, and try and follow your heart. The rest is a crapshoot."

I snorted. "That's not quite the reassurance I was hoping for."

I woke the next day to a text from Lee. ***I miss you too. Good luck with everything.***

To the point, I supposed, but was it too much to hope for a little more . . . something? Still, he had a lot going on with the repairs to the *Green Lip* and the farm, and I shouldn't have been so damn needy anyway.

After some hastily organised just-in-case legal paperwork, courtesy of Tinny, and a phone call to a surprised Van to warn him of my imminent arrival, I landed back on the island and sucked in my first breath of clean southern air—salty and cold—my heart still racing from the spectacular view of Oban on our approach. A chocolate-box gathering of painted houses set haphazardly into the hills that bordered the sweeping beauty of Horseshoe Bay.

I could've opted for the short ferry ride, but Jerry, the pilot, was the brother of one of my old crew, and when I checked to see if he was making a supply run to the island that day, he'd told me to get my butt aboard or he'd take it as a personal insult. It was the kind of insider tightness that I'd missed, and I carried a small pocket of worry that I'd arrive in Oban and feel that same sense of loss all over again. But as we'd set down on the runway, the only ache I felt was for Lee, his arms and the clean scent of his skin.

"A shame you didn't have the same capacity to surprise me when we were together." Van led me to his car having shocked me speechless by meeting the tiny plane on its arrival.

I chuffed in amusement. "As I remember it, you had every second of my home time scheduled to within an inch of its life—plans to get off the island, to go out for dinner with friends, a list of things I had to fix. There was never a spare moment *left* to surprise you with *anything*. And even when I tried to do something special, you seemed to find something to complain about. It wasn't worth the grief."

He put his seat belt on and stared at me. "You should've said something."

I turned away. "I did."

He pulled into the driveway of our old house and my heart leapt at the sight of Mack inside at the patio door. I spun in my seat, shocked that Van would do that for me, but he simply shrugged.

"You can have her for the night," he said flatly. "I'll pick her up tomorrow. I put some essentials in the fridge, and Joanie at the store made up a box to see you through a few days. I've got things to do today, so I was thinking tomorrow lunchtime, if you want to talk, that is. I'll come here, unless you'd rather come to our—"

"Here will be fine. Thanks for Mack." I looked to the house where Mack was leaping at the door, howling with excitement. "It means a lot."

He shrugged. "No problem. I told you I wasn't trying to hurt you, Fox. She missed you."

I was surprised at the admission and not so secretly delighted. I grabbed my bag and watched Van drive off before turning to stare at the cottage that had been my home, and then *our* home. I remembered the pain of leaving, the ache in my soul on that last day. But as my gaze swept the tidy front yard and crisply painted front door that I'd spent days restoring, the only thing in my heart was an image of wide plank floors, a massive family dining table, a deck under the stars, and eyes so blue I could fly in them.

Leroy

Fox had only been gone a couple hours, and the most I'd achieved was to shift from my bed to the dining table, trying to ignore the empty place where the training application had been and whatever the fuck that meant. I hadn't even dressed, and my tow was arriving at the wharf to pick me up in under an hour. There were a million things I should've been doing and zero motivation to do any of them.

Luckily, Kane spotted my mood the minute he knocked on my door at seven to see what needed doing. And when I'd just waved him off with a cryptic, "I'll call you later," he'd ignored me and called Morgan. The two of them had then made a quick reconnaissance trip to Flounder Cove while I was still feeling sorry for myself. On their return, they reassured me the boat was fine and the cove calm.

Once I quit being mortified, I could've kissed them.

Patrick would catch the afternoon flight, and I should've had a work plan ready to go, but the blank paper had been staring at me for over an hour. The only things circling my brain were Judah's words of condemnation along with Fox's words of goodbye, and neither of them was getting me anywhere.

I wanted Fox back here with me, now. I needed him here. It wasn't because I couldn't cope. I'd been on my own a long time and I'd get through anything I had to. I'd survive. But I wanted him here with me.

Trust him. He promised.

But the homestead was now too big, too empty without his larger-than-life presence. Had it really only been two months since I'd found him making a damn sandwich in my kitchen and I'd hoped he'd piss off and stop fucking with my nice little world? Now I wanted him back in my bed and fucking *me*. My how times had changed. His smile, his touch, his solid presence in my life, his belief in me. I missed every single second of it.

But with half his stuff still sitting in piles on my bedroom floor and in my drawers, I had to believe he was coming back. And that meant I had to do my part. Fox had gone to sort his shit out and I needed to do the same. When he was done, I wanted to be damn sure there was nothing in the way of him coming back. And if that meant Judah and I took a hit in our bridge building, so be it. Judah was a stubborn son of a bitch, but so was I. We had that much in common. I loved my brother, but I wasn't about to lose Fox to make everything nice with Judah.

But I hadn't told Fox that, had I?

I got my pathetic arse off the chair and into the shower. As soon as the *Green Lip* was berthed safely, Judah and I were gonna have a little come-to-Jesus talk.

Four hours later, the *Green Lip* was safely back at the wharf, and the mechanic was taking stock of the damage with Kane hot on his heels. Patrick would be about to board his flight, and I was knocking on Judah's door . . . loudly.

"Hold your bloody horses." The door swung open to reveal Judah in a pair of his favourite dance leggings and a tank, the sheen of perspiration a clue to the fact he'd been working at his barre. "Oh, it's you." He lifted his tank to wipe the beads of sweat from his face and I was immediately struck by his pallor. That, and the dull, hollow look in his eyes. In fact, he looked remarkably like the reflection I'd seen in my own bathroom mirror that morning.

His gaze darted over my face, and he scowled as if he hadn't found what he'd hoped. "I guess you should come inside, or you could just fuck off. Either is good with me." He walked away, leaving the door open.

Well, okay then.

"I don't have to come in," I answered evenly, ignoring his drama. "I'll happily take door number two, just tell me to go. Your choice. I just thought it would be good to talk. Talk, *not* shout. And maybe a bit of listening on both sides could help as well."

He studied me for a second, then his lips quirked. "Touché. Just stop sounding like my damn husband, will you? *Traitor* that he is."

"I heard that." Morgan appeared from the bedroom in his fishery officer uniform.

"Hey, Morgan. Thanks again for checking on the *Green Lip* this morning."

Judah rounded on his husband. "So that's what you were doing?" He glared. "I thought you were helping a friend with some storm damage."

Morgan sailed past to press a kiss to Judah's lips and turn my brother's glare into a soft smile. "I was. Leroy *is* my friend, and he was that long before you and I met, sweetheart. I also remember him not being too happy when we got together, either. And yet here we are." He arched a brow.

Judah huffed. "Very sneaky. I'll see you when you're done." He pulled Morgan in for a second, longer kiss, and then Morgan gathered his bag and shot me a wink on his way out.

"No breaking anything," he said before closing the door and leaving a thick blanket of awkwardness in his wake.

"I can go if you'd rather," I offered. "If you really don't want me here. I love you Judah, but I'm not giving Fox up, not for you, not for anyone. You need to understand that." *And not for a damned island either.*

His jaw worked for a bit and then his shoulders sagged. "Oh, for fuck's sake, take a seat. Morgan will skin me alive if we don't sort this out, and I suppose he's right. Just don't tell him I said that. He's smug enough as it is. I'll make coffee. That always makes things better, right?"

I took a seat at the breakfast bar and watched Judah work, graceful in everything he did, as always. The man could probably take a shit and have it look like he was dancing *Swan Lake*. Go figure.

"So, do you love him?" Judah asked, keeping his back to me. "Fox, I mean."

I didn't hesitate. "Yes, very much."

"Bugger." Judah positioned a cup and flicked on the espresso maker. Then he turned and put his back to the countertop. "Now I really do feel like a heel." He sighed and his cheeks pinked.

I blinked hard. Judah didn't blush or get embarrassed, ever.

"Okay." He locked eyes. "I'm sorry for what I said about you experimenting and the whole being-curious thing." He rolled his eyes. "Man, Morgan ripped me a new one about that when we got back, if that makes you feel any better. You'd have thought I was single-handedly responsible for the whole bi-erasure movement." He turned and swapped cups, then set the machine going again. He handed me the first espresso along with a carton of milk.

"It does." I smiled and he looked up. "Make me feel better, as it happens."

He snorted. "Yeah, I figured it would."

I added a splash of milk to my coffee while Judah doctored his own with sugar. I figured it was my turn.

"You're not the only one with an apology to offer," I said. "I should've told you sooner, but I'd had my head up my arse for a long time. And Fox and I only slept together for the first time the night before you got home, the day Kane was hurt. It wasn't planned, it just happened. I'd spent so long running from the idea, and it was still all so new."

He laughed. "So that's why he had your back at lunch that day and why you were so cagey about him. Jesus, I should've guessed something was up. You never let anyone do that without tearing a strip off them for trying to help."

Oh. "I don't?"

He eyeballed me. "No, you don't, Mr I Can Handle Anything So Stay the Fuck Away."

Wow. But also . . . true. "Yeah well, I kissed him the first week and then ran away for two weeks, not literally, just . . . you know. I was such a mess, I'm surprised he didn't give up on me right then."

"So he didn't know you were bi?" Judah's expression was soft, almost fond.

"Well, the kiss probably gave it away, but before then, no. I barely had my head around the idea myself."

"So you had no idea when we were in school, no inkling?" He left it at that and all the loaded shit that went with it.

"No, at least not consciously." And I told him all the tiny hints I could recognise in hindsight and how the last year after meeting Fox had done a number on me until I finally accepted I was bi.

He listened and then talked about when he knew he was gay, who he'd crushed on, and how it had been for him dealing with all the fallout of being gay in a small town. He omitted my role in all that, and I hoped that meant all wasn't lost between us. He also spoke about the artistic director he'd been fucking when he found he had Meniere's and how the fucker had dropped him like a stone when he knew Judah wouldn't dance professionally anymore.

"But you sure got me beat at one thing," he finished.

"Oh really?" I found that hard to believe. Judah had lived a rich and flamboyant life. I couldn't imagine anything I did topping that.

"I might've fucked a few men in my time and then married your friend, *big brother*. But you, you little hussy, are fucking your almost stepbrother, and I'm so fucking proud of you. Look how far you've come from the little homophobic dirtbag you were in school."

We both laughed, and I knew in that minute we were gonna be okay. We had a lot of stuff to sort out, but we'd get there.

Judah's expression sobered. "I heard Fox flew back south."

I finished my coffee and slid the cup away. "He has loose ends to tie up. We decided to clean house before we started on this thing between us long-term."

"And was I a loose end?"

Yes. I smiled. "No, you're a fucking knot."

He laughed. "So, long-term, huh? That's pretty damn fast."

I met his shrewd gaze. "Maybe. But it's been brewing a year. And it's what I want. Him too, I hope."

"You hope?"

"Stop repeating everything I say." I pushed my chair back and walked to the glass wall that looked down the old boat ramp and out across the bay. "He says he does. It's me who's nervous. I know how much he loves it down there. It's his home and he never really wanted to leave in the first place. He still has his house there, Judah, and now his ex has taken Mack back down, and if they can't reach an agreement, then Fox has to stay for the hearing, and he has all these friends there, and then there's this job he's been off—"

"Stop, stop, for Christ's sake." Judah blew out a sigh and followed me to the glass. "That's a hell of a laundry list of worry you're spewing there. You said, *he says* he feels the same. Does that mean you don't believe him?"

Did I? "Yes, I believe him. I'm just . . . worried, I guess." My gaze slid sideways to the ripples on the receding tide.

The warmth of Judah's hand rested on my shoulder. "About what?"

I swallowed hard. "I'm worried that I'm not enough." My voice choked. "Not enough to bring him back. Maybe not enough to keep him here."

Judah's arms slipped around my waist from behind, something he'd never done before. We'd never been touchy-feely that way. "Well, let me tell you something, brother. You're more than enough for any man or woman, Leroy, and don't you forget it. You're stubborn and generous, and pig-headed and loyal, and even warm and funny if you let yourself be. I might have disliked you for a long time, but I've always loved you as a brother, and I always saw your qualities. And I think Fox sees you even clearer than I ever did, maybe clearer than Mum. I can tell by the way he looks at you. Which begs the question of why the fuck you're still here when he's down there?"

I shook my head and leaned back just a little. Judah took my weight. It felt strange, this closeness between us. Strange but good. "I can't leave. I've got all the repairs to sort out, and Fox needs to do this on his own."

"Does he? I'm not so sure about that. I think Fox already knows you're enough. I think it's you who needs convincing. So why not go convince yourself? Patrick is back in a couple of hours, right?"

I nodded and Judah stepped around in front of me.

"I've watched him, Leroy. Hell, I've worked with him. That man could give you a run for your money on that farm. Why not give him a chance to show it?"

"But the *Green Lip*—"

"Will be fine under Tricky's supervision." He laughed at my look of surprise. "What? You didn't think I knew about the nicknames . . . Prickles?"

I elbowed him in the ribs. "Shut up."

Judah's hand landed on my shoulder. "What's going on in that hamster-wheel brain of yours?"

I drew a shaky breath. "What if Fox decides I'm too much trouble? What if he really doesn't want to leave but comes back for me and we don't make it? I'm not sure I'd survive seeing him as part of this family and not . . . having him." I choked on the last.

Judah cupped my cheek with a tenderness I'd never had directed at me. "I get how it's safer to hide yourself away on the mussel farm with your boat and an overdraft and pretend no one else could possibly understand your life, the hours, the uncertainty. But in many ways, that was my life too, Leroy. You don't have a monopoly on that. The right person won't add to your load, they'll lighten it. But you're never gonna find them if you don't take a risk. Maybe stop closing doors and try opening a few."

"But Patrick's never done any of this on his own."

"Maybe not, but he's quite capable. He has Jon's boat, and he has Kane. Morgan and I can help if we're needed. Why not go see the island that means so much to him? It's something you should know about him."

I bit back the automatic no and took a breath. *Could I really just go and leave the farm in Patrick's hands? Go to Fox? Go and be at his side while he went through something difficult, just as he'd done for me?*

"Can you organise my tickets while I pack a bag?"

Judah beamed. "Hell yeah, I can."

CHAPTER TWENTY-THREE

Fox

IT WAS A PERFECT MORNING ON THE ISLAND, THE KIND THAT might make a man wish he'd never left. Blue skies, a few puffy clouds, and just a light breeze to ruffle your hair and draw a deep sigh of wonder. If you weren't a local, you could be lulled into thinking it would be a great idea to move here.

And maybe it would.

Provided you realised that the jailbait weather was in fact a sneaky lie designed to hide the fact that Stewart Island was the last stop before Antarctica—nothing to break those howling winds and frigid temperatures when they decided to pay a visit. Which they did, all too often for comfort unless you really loved the place, which *I* did.

But as I drank my coffee on the back deck with Mack asleep on my feet and watched the recreational fishermen launching their boats down at the wharf, my thoughts were on none of those things.

They were on the phone in my hand, the man I loved, and the long and erratic text conversation we were having. I'd wanted to reassure him again that I was coming home, tell him all the things circling my brain. *Home.* Twenty-four hours on the island had been all it had taken. I maybe knew before I even got off that plane. *Home.* The word sat easy in my heart because that's what Lee, the homestead, and Painted Bay had come to mean to me. Not this island, not my house, which now felt empty and cold and devoid of the most important part of my life, a man I loved more than anything. Not my business, which was gone and which I realised I didn't want to recreate. I didn't want to look back. I wanted to move past the person I'd been and stretch my wings into something different.

I'd wanted to tell Lee all those things, but he was being strangely evasive. Cagey as fuck and unwilling to engage to the point where it almost stung.

I texted, **This is ridiculous. We haven't talked since I left. I'm gonna call.**

No. I'm with the mechanic. The boat will be ready tomorrow. It's still go for the harvest. And I talked with Judah.

Now that was news. **How'd it go?**

Better than I thought. I'll tell you when we can talk properly. How long will you be staying?

Goddammit. I needed more than that. **I don't know. Depends on Van. If he doesn't agree to anything beforehand then I'll stay till the court hearing at least.**

Okay.

Okay?

Have you seen him?

He met the plane, go figure. That met with radio silence. I added, **I didn't ask him to do that. He let me have Mack for the night.**

More silence, dots coming and going on the screen before finally, **Send me a pic of her.**

I did.

She looks good. Was she pleased to see you?

She went crazy. Wouldn't let me out of her sight. Slept on the bed all night.

I told you she'd miss you.

I stared out over Horseshoe Bay, its water bursting bright with the deep blue of the sky above. It might be one of the prettiest sights in New Zealand, but another bay had wormed its way into my heart, along with a stroppy, prickly, dark-haired, blue-eyed beauty.

I texted, *I'm coming back, Lee. I love you.*

I know. I love you too. I just hate that he's there and I'm not.

I did too.

Is it nice being back?

A loaded question. *Yes and no. I love this place but the first thing I thought when I landed was that I wanted to be back with you.*

A longer pause this time.

I texted, *I'm coming home Lee.*

Say it again.

Say what?

Home.

I smiled. *I'm coming home.*

———

"Knock, knock," Van called from the front door, and I told him to come through to the deck. He appeared a few seconds later and Mack immediately ran to welcome him. I really was going to have to have serious words with my dog.

Van dropped to his knees and gave Mack a hug. She groaned and flopped onto her back.

"She's such a slut for a belly rub." Van laughed and obliged Mack with a vigorous scruffing.

While he was occupied, I took a minute to really look at him, look without the anger he usually stirred in me. He seemed . . . tired and a little pale, his delicate features less perky than usual, his brown eyes wary.

I shook my head. It wasn't my concern. "You want a coffee?"

He looked surprised, then nodded.

I got to my feet. "I'll bring it out. Maybe a bit of fresh air will be good for the conversation."

He rolled his eyes but kept scratching. "I expected you to bring Tinny. The man's like a Rottweiler with a law degree."

I snorted. "He wanted to be here, believe me. But I'm hopeful we can work this out. What about you? No Ewan? No lawyer?"

Van pulled a face. "My lawyer's not happy, but he's agreed to let me talk. And Ewan . . . well you know why he's not here."

I did. Our friendship had been dealt a death blow that neither of us wanted to face. I left to make Van a coffee and refresh my own. Watching the two of them through the kitchen window, I wondered about the lawyer comment, then let it go. You never knew with Van.

Mack licked at Van's face and batted his hand to keep him scratching. A small niggle of guilt snagged in my chest. Van did love Mack in his own slightly selfish way, I'd known that, even if my anger wouldn't let me admit it. And yes, I might've taken her from the island knowing it would hurt him. So sue me. Didn't mean I wanted to share her with him long-term, but I couldn't deny they had a relationship. And I wasn't leaving the island without a solution to the problem one way or another.

If Van couldn't be *encouraged* to give Mack up to me, then I'd agree to share her with him. Anything to finalise the divorce and start a new life with Lee. But I knew my preference, and that was for getting Van out of my life for good. I didn't want to have to keep a relationship open with him simply because of Mack if I could possibly help it. Tinny wasn't so sure about my decision, but he understood.

Van and I took seats on opposite sides of the picnic table and I handed Van his mug—the one that had always been his. I hadn't even thought, just automatically reached for it. He smiled as he took it, and I wished I swapped it out when I realised.

"So, why did you decide to come back now?" he asked, wrapping his hands around the mug for warmth. "The hearing's not for a few more weeks."

I turned to make sure there was no misunderstanding. "You know why. I want this thing with Mack settled between us, without court, the sooner the better. And once that's done, I'm going to sell this house and shift everything north. I want to move on with my life. There's nothing here for me now."

Van was quiet for a few seconds, although he looked surprised. "You're selling everything up for *him?*"

"If you mean for Lee, then yes," I replied evenly. "I want that. I want him. I don't want anything left here."

Van blinked slowly, then looked away. "Wow. I didn't think things were that serious."

I ignored his comment. "I don't want to drag this through the court if we can avoid it. You should be happy. This is what you've been hoping for, right? Forcing me to settle. What's it going to take? Money? Or do you really want Mack? Do you really want to take her from me? Fucked if I know at this point, Van. I've given up guessing what the hell you want anymore. Seems I was wrong for our entire married life, so why would I be right now?"

He rolled his mug between his palms on the table. "You make it sound so fucking dirty, but all I want is to be able to start something of my own. It's not about money. It's about security. You should understand that. You were always on at me about making something of my business. Well, I'm trying to."

"*I* should understand *you?* That's rich. You cheated on me, lied about it, socially ostracised and drove me out of here, and then came back for my livelihood as well. And now you want my dog? How the fuck can I understand *you?*"

His gaze slid to the distant shape of the South Island on the horizon. "I shouldn't have lied about you cheating."

I gaped, stunned at the admission. "Then why the hell did you?"

He spun back to face me. "You know why. My whole family lives here, Fox. Mum would've been devastated. What was I supposed to do?"

"Not fucking lie about it, for a start," I fumed. "Out of everything you did, *that* was the thing that hurt the most, Van. Marriages fail, affairs happen, but to turn it around as if it were my fucking fault? I really didn't think you'd stoop that low."

He paled a little. "Well, I did. I'm sorry."

Not nearly sorry enough for my liking.

"But I was entitled to half the business," he said without a blink of apology. "Don't forget, I'm starting over too. What if Ewan and I don't work out?"

I stared at him. *Don't ask. Don't ask.* "Are you two having problems?" *Goddammit.*

Van's gaze slid sideways to the sea. "Not *problems.* We're just . . .different, in lots of ways." He faced me again. "And don't look so fucking smug. It's nothing we can't work out."

Yeah, good luck with that. But I didn't say that. Instead, I threw up my hands. "Hey, nothing to do with me. But maybe keep it in your pants this time while you do." Yeah, that was just too damn tempting and his eye roll said it all.

"Fuck off. It's more that my business isn't exactly a money spinner yet," he added. "And I want to pull my weight financially."

More like *Ewan* wants you to. I barely held back a grin. "You'd earn a lot more if you put in the hours."

He shot me a filthy look. "Do you ever get sick of being right all the damn time? It's so fucking annoying."

I shoved aside the memory of Lee's angry words that night on the deck which accused me of much the same thing and spat back, "Is this the part where you tell me how fucking Ewan for a year was my fault, because if it is, then this is going to be a short conversation?" My phone buzzed in my pocket, but I ignored it.

He shook his head. "No. I'm not saying it was all your fault, just that your standards are impossible to live up to, that's all. Ewan is . . . easier, I guess. He looks after me."

And there it was. My phone blew up in my pocket again.

Van sighed. "Do you need to get that?"

"No. It's fine. And as I recall, you liked a bit of verbal sparring, being kept on your toes. We had some *energetic* fights as I remember."

Van smiled. "And some equally energetic make up sex."

He wasn't wrong, but it didn't hold a candle to what I had with Lee.

Van looked away. "I do like a good fight, you're right, but things are much less complicated with Ewan. With you, it was like living with Captain Fucking America."

I rolled my eyes, not about to touch that with a barge pole. "You know, back in the day, *I* wanted you happy as well, Van. I just didn't understand why that had to include me giving up the life I loved."

"But you're prepared to give it up for *him*, right? No more ocean ways for you anymore."

I frowned as the truth of that hit home because I *was* prepared to give up everything for Lee, whatever it took, not that I was going to tell Van that. Instead I said, "The difference being Lee would never ask me to. Besides, I have no life down here anymore."

"You could if you wanted." He threw me a sideways glance that was hard to read but definitely on the suggestive side.

I stared at him, not sure if I was reading things right. "What the hell are you saying?"

"Just that." He shrugged. "You *could* come back. We were good once, if you remember, you even said it yourself. And Ewan might be consider . . .opening things up." He held my gaze.

Holy shit. "Jesus Christ, Van." I shook my head. "Whatever you're suggesting, I'm not interested."

He stared at me long enough to make me wonder if I'd really even heard what I thought I had. "You love him, then?"

I didn't even hesitate. "I do, but I'm not discussing Lee with you."

He huffed. "I bet you discussed me with him."

I couldn't hold back the laugh. "Damn right I did, but I'm here to talk about Mack. Can we just get this over with, please? How much do you want?"

"It's not about money."

"Of course it bloody is. You don't want her. And if by some miracle it is about Mack, then let's settle that now." I gripped the cup tighter in my shaking hands.

This was the moment I called Van's bluff. '*He has to believe you,*' Tinny had said as I'd practised in front of him.

"I'm not leaving till this is done one way or the other, Van. So, how much do you want? Or if we're going to share Mack, I'd rather she wasn't flying too frequently. So let's agree to maybe every two months?" My heart hurt just to think about it. "This is your last chance. If you let this go to court, the deal is off the table. There will be no more money above your entitlement. I'll agree to splitting custody. All you'll get is Mack."

He ran his fingers through his hair, complete bewilderment on his face along with a touch of panic. "Jesus, Fox. You'd really do that? Agree to share her just so you can get back to that *guy* and a mainland life you always swore you hated?"

"Yes. Yes, I would. And funnily enough, I don't hate it at all. I love it because I love Lee and he's there."

"Fuck. Me." Van shoved his coffee cup aside and leaned back in his chair, shaking his head and looking anything but happy.

I waited him out, finishing the dregs of my coffee.

"Twenty-five thousand."

I choked and spat coffee across the table. "Fucking hell. You've got to be joking. Is that your fucking lawyer talking? Because I know you're not that crazy."

Van's jaw clenched. "No. He told me to ask for more."

"Well come down from those clouds because that's never happening. You know what I got for the boat, and I also need something to start again, you arsehole."

"That's not my problem."

"It is if I make you go to court, because then you'll get nothing above what you're legally owed. You do realise what you're doing is blackmail, right?"

His lip curled. "And what are you doing? It's the same thing."

My mouth opened but I closed it again and took a breath. *'Don't lose it.'* Tinny's words. "You know what, I'm gonna let that go. Ten thousand above the already agreed settlement."

"Ten?" What the fuck am I going to do with ten? It won't even buy me a new car."

I pushed my chair back from the table and Mack leapt up from her spot in the sun to come over. "You don't need a new car. You already took mine, remember?"

His cheeks pinked. "Whatever. Twenty."

"Twelve."

"Eighteen."

"Fifteen, and that's it. That's as high as I'll go." Tinny had baulked at even that, but I was done with this shit.

Van stared, his jaw working as he studied my face with those pretty little eyes of his. Eyes that now turned my stomach. I held firm, reminding myself why I was doing this, how pissed off I was for needing to do it at all. The court could very well make me split custody, and Van might insist just to mess with me for not paying him out. It was the last thing I wanted. Fifteen thousand to get his face out of my life? Hell yeah, that was worth it. I'd still have enough to start again.

"Okay, fifteen," he grumbled, and it was all I could do not to punch the air with a hell yeah.

Holy fuck. I'd done it. "Stay there." I scrambled to my feet. "I've got the paperwork inside."

He rolled his eyes. "Of course you bloody do. Maybe I should call my lawyer first though."

I swung around to face him, fear coiling in my belly as I tried not to show the panic on my face. "Go ahead."

He eyeballed me for a minute and all I could do was pray. Then he shrugged. "Nah, go on. He can tear a strip off me later. I want this over with too." He called to Mack and she ran across to be suitably adored and fussed over.

I left them to it and ran inside to get the papers Tinny had drawn up and call Mark, our local JP, to witness our signatures. Tinny had warned Mark the day before and he said he'd be at my house in five minutes—the benefit to living on a tiny island. Thirty minutes later everything was signed and sealed, and Mark had gone on his way, along with my promise to shout him a steak in the pub the following night.

I couldn't keep the smile off my face as I handed Van his copy of the agreement and walked mine over to the countertop in the kitchen.

Van shook his head. "So, are you fucking happy now?"

"Blissfully," I answered. "You out of my life forever? What's there not to be happy about? Still, I guess I should say thank you. You didn't have to sign."

"No, I didn't." He eyed me pointedly, then stretched back in his chair and sighed. "But I wasn't lying about Mack. I do miss her. And I was pissed you took off without saying anything, although fuck knows what I would've done with her every two months, to be honest. From the minute I got her back here, I spent half my bloody time fetching her down from this house. I'd find her asleep on the deck or on your front step. It didn't matter if Ewan and I were home or not, she'd disappear up here. Pissed me off. Anyway, Ewan's promised me a puppy of my own."

I barely held back the eye-roll. Ewan was an idiot, and he was welcome to Van for as long as he could hold on to him, which I was betting wouldn't be long.

Van got to his feet and ran his palms down the front of his skinny jeans. "So that's it. Our lawyers can finish up and we're done. So, unless you want me to hang around . . . for old times' sake . . ." He held my gaze, but I wasn't going there, and eventually he shrugged. "Then I'm guessing it's time for me to move on as well."

"I'm all for that." Lee's pissy, wonderful voice came over my shoulder and I spun to find him walking toward me, duffle in hand, and looking drop-dead gorgeous.

"Lee!" I jumped to my feet. "What . . . but . . . how in the hell did you get here?"

Lee's face split in a wide grin. "I believe it's called a ferry, baby." He dropped his bag and ran past Van without a single acknowledgement, laying a fiercely possessive and hot-as-all-hell kiss on my lips.

I returned it with enthusiasm, then crushed him to my chest and whispered in his ear, "You're fucking evil, and I love it."

Mack ran circles around our legs, barking and whining until Lee finally gave in and dropped to his knees for a good tongue licking.

Van watched on with a sour look.

My heart still jumped in my chest. Lee was here? For me? He'd left the farm and came down here for me—*oh shit*—the farm, the storm. "But what about the boat and the damage to—"

"It's fine." Lee got to his feet. "Patrick's got it all in hand."

Fine? In hand? Who the hell was this guy?

"You know, you should really have more faith in people." He gave me a smug grin. "Patrick's quite capable."

Little shit. I hoped my expression conveyed exactly what I had planned for that smart mouth of his the minute we were alone. And judging by the way his eyes darkened and his cheeks brightened, I figured I'd nailed it.

His gaze slid off mine and swept over the view. "Nice spot you've got here, baby." Then he turned to Van. "Ah, Van. I'd say it's good to see you, but I'd be lying."

Van rolled his eyes. "Lee, what a surprise."

"That's Leroy to you. And it shouldn't be a surprise. My place is here with Fox."

Fucking hell. Be still my heart.

Van added a second eye-roll. "Been eavesdropping, have you?"

Lee grinned. "I didn't want to disturb the legalities, so I waited. Thank you, for Fox's sake. I personally think it's more than you deserve, but that's just me." He looked my way. "Shall I wait inside?"

I shook my head.

"No. Van is just leaving, aren't you Van?"

"Apparently, I am."

Lee snorted. "Don't let the gate hit you on the way out."

"Oh, and I intend being in the pub tomorrow night," I told Van. "With my old crew and anyone else who's still speaking to me on the island. I might be setting a few rumours straight as well. Just saying. You might want to steer clear."

"Yeah." Lee slid his hand under my shirt while keeping his eyes on Van. "I'm gonna make sure certain truths get a little loud airing."

"Oh, for fuck's sake." Van's lip curled. "Like they'll believe you over their hometown son? Do your worst. I'm out of this madhouse."

"You do that." Lee smiled up at me. "I've got a man to take to bed. Six foot three, eyes like the ocean, and fucks like a trooper. You were an idiot to let him go."

Dear God. I glanced down to check I hadn't been pissed on as well.

Lee and Van eyeballed each other, and I had to hand it to Lee. Van wasn't often at a loss for words, but for a few seconds, all he did was stare. Then he grabbed his keys and got to his feet. "You two fucking deserve each other," he said.

Lee hummed and kissed me on the cheek. "I couldn't agree more."

Another staring match and then Van turned to me. "Walk me out?"

I glanced at Lee who reluctantly nodded. "I'll wait inside."

I kissed him soundly and then followed Van around to the front of the house with Mack padding at my heels.

"You've got yourself a firecracker there," Van remarked when we got to his car. "Got a temper on him too. I'm not sure you can handle him?"

I glanced back at the house, where I was damn sure Lee was keeping an eye on things, and chuckled. "Man, I hope not. He's a lot more fun that way."

Van snorted and got in his car. "For what it's worth, for all the good times we had, I wish you luck. I think you're gonna need it."

I laughed. "Nah, see, that's the thing, Van. With Lee, I don't need luck, I only need him." I slapped my hand on the top of his car and watched him leave, Mack at my side.

Leroy

When Van drove off, I ran to the back deck and pretended to be admiring the view so it wouldn't look like I'd been snooping. But when Fox found me, he just laughed and ruffled my hair and I figured I'd been rumbled, dammit.

"You're so cute when you're trying to look innocent," he said. "You can't lie to fucking save yourself, sweetheart, and I love that about you."

"Sorry, not sorry," I said as he swept me into his arms and sat me on the outdoor table for a long and thorough debauching that involved a lot of tongue and a considerable amount of grabbing at sexy bits, which I was more than okay with. "I did try to call, you know?"

He glanced at his phone and finally registered the missed calls he'd ignored earlier. "Sorry, we were talking."

I smoothed the frown lines on his forehead. "So I found out. I, um, happened to see the contract on the counter while you were seeing Van off."

"Oh you did, did you?" He smiled. "What do you think?"

Loaded fucking question. Humbled, shocked, pissed at Van, and hugely thankful. But also ashamed that I'd ever doubted him. "I know you didn't do it just for me, but I'm kind of blown away."

"I wanted to make sure we had nothing holding us back, and if that meant a little financial pain to make sure Van was kicked to the curb, it was worth it, just to be sure. You, *we* are far more important than money."

Us. We. Man, I loved the sound of that. I'd been a total idiot. I took a deep breath and let it out slowly. "I'm not proud of the fact, but I confess I was worried that you might not come back. The house. The island. Your friends. I just wasn't sure, you know? And I wanted you to know how serious I was. That I wanted to change, to let go a little, to take a risk as someone once told me. That I was willing to do what it took to make sure we had the best chance of working."

He smiled and kissed my forehead. "If I'm honest, I wasn't entirely sure how I'd feel about being back, myself. But I knew the minute I set foot here that my time was done. Actually, I knew before that. I completed my training application and posted it at the airport. The *only* place I want to be is with you. You're my home, Lee. And Painted Bay is my home because *you're* there. Oceans and places don't make a home. People you love do that. And I love you. I wanted to tell you all this when I was trying to make you call me earlier. Which reminds me . . . you said you were with the mechanic?" He raised a brow. "I fucking knew you were up to something."

"See, I *can* lie." I stabbed a finger at his chest.

"I couldn't see your face," he reminded me.

"Well, I wanted to surprise you," I said, my cheeks burning. "Good surprise or nasty surprise?"

He cradled my face and drew me close to whisper in my ear, "The very best surprise. I can't believe you're here, and I'm so fucking happy." He pulled back to eyeball me. "But what about the boat and the harvest? Are you sure Patrick will be okay? There's change and then there's *change*."

I laughed, slightly hysterically. "God knows. I'm trying not to think about it, or I'll lose my fucking mind. I wrote the most detailed list known to humanity, and Mum and Martha and Judah can help with any questions. Plus, I have unlimited minutes on my call plan." I sent Fox a crooked smile but struggled to hold that shrewd gaze because the truth was, I was barely holding my shit together. But I was trying, and I knew Fox saw all of that and more.

"You talk to him as much as you need to. I'll understand, you know that."

And the thing was, I absolutely knew he would. I trusted him. He was there for me, whatever it took, and wasn't that a fucking miracle.

"I am so fucking proud of you," he said, and my cheeks burned brighter. Was that a gay thing or a bi thing because fuck if I'd ever blushed so much in my entire life. "So just how hard was it to walk away?"

"You don't even want to know," I grumbled, then held his eyes and tunnelled my fingers through all those beautiful long waves, corkscrewed from the salt and damp in the air. "And it's not over yet. I nearly had a panic attack in the motel in Invercargill. Holy shit, that city is a damn freezer, and it's barely autumn. How do you people live down here?" He leaned forward and I kissed his forehead. "But leaving was also the easiest thing I've ever done," I added. "If that makes any sense, although I needed Judah to kick my arse first."

"Judah?" He frowned, and I traced the furrowed line between his eyebrows down his nose to his lips, his skin warm, the angles of his face achingly familiar. And mine to touch for as long as I wanted.

"I'll tell you later," I said softly. "But suffice to say, as far as the farm is concerned, Patrick appears to have things in hand for now, although I may still have a meltdown or two over the next few days, so be gentle with me?"

He smiled with so much care and affection in those green eyes that my breath stuttered in my chest. How was this possible? How had I found myself in this place and with this man? How was I so fucking lucky?

"You did all this for *me*." He nuzzled his nose against my cheek and then ran it up into my hair, breathing me in all the way before pulling back, the sound going straight to my balls. Then he cupped my cheek and looked at me hard. "You can bet your little porcupine quills that I'll be gentle with you. I still can't believe you're even here."

I snorted and turned my face to take his thumb into my mouth, enjoying the way his nostrils flared before I let it go. "Neither can I. Although I have to say it was worth it just to see that look on fuckface."

Fox threw his head back and laughed. "Still, he signed the contract, so I can't hate him completely."

"Good for you. I'll happily detest him enough for the both of us."

He shook his head. "That's what I love about you. Always seeing the best in people. He thinks you're a firecracker, by the way."

I gaped. "Bastard. I'm a fucking block of C-4 at the very least."

"This is true." He smoothed my ruffled feathers. "But you're *my* fucking block of C-4."

"Damn right, I am." I put his hand on my dick while at the same time unzipping his jeans. "And this gorgeous bastard is my fuse."

He stared down at his cock bulging through his open fly. "How the fuck did you manage that?"

"Magic." I thrust against his hand to get him back on point.

He cupped my arse and tugged me closer. "Damn, you feel good."

"Mmm. More." I leaned back and kicked my hips up so our dicks brushed.

He hissed and unzipped me for a better grip. "Fuck, Lee."

"Exactly. Can we take this in—" I bucked up. "No, not—more to the—yesssss!"

"Jesus, Lee." He grunted. "How long . . . are you here?" He

pulled back to look at me, face flushed, cock leaking, and my mouth fucking watered to have him.

"A week?" I panted, hoping he was okay with that. "I want you to show me your favourite things. The places you love. I want to know this southern side of you. On the flight down, I looked up the Maori name for Stewart Island. *Rakiura.* Glowing skies. Because of the Southern Lights, right? It's a pretty name."

He nodded and I trailed my fingers down his cheek and tugged on his hair. "I want you to take me to the local pub and kiss me, Fox—say fuck you to all the people who doubted you. I want to know the ones you like and the ones who turned on you so I can name and shame. I want to meet your old crew and hear embarrassing stories about you. And I want to meet Tinny and his wife and anyone else who's important to you. And I want to ask them to come visit."

He stared, a lopsided grin on his face and his eyes dancing. I'd have given him anything in that moment, and I *knew*.

"I want this time with you, Fox. I'm not good at this kind of thing, and I need to be better. I *want* to be better. I want a life with you, a proper one. Not one where I'm exhausted and angry all the time. You make me laugh, and when I'm with you, I see things differently. I'm lighter . . . I'm a better person."

He leaned in and brushed his lips over mine. "Just know I don't need this other person you talk about. I only need you, as you are. I'll love you any way you come. And I don't deserve you, Leroy Madden."

"Quite possibly." I grinned and smoothed the front of his T-shirt and patted his chest. "But we can work on that part." I attempted my best version of a come-hither look and he snorted with laughter. I whacked him on the arm. "Fuck you too."

He winked. "Any time, baby." Then he kissed me, and his tongue slid inside to deliver another hit of that taste I couldn't get enough of, sending my heart thumping in my chest and my cock raging.

"Fox." I pulled back, but he growled and chased my lips. I pushed him away. "No, Fox. Fox!"

"Huh?" He blinked dazedly, leaning back.

"Jesus, Fox, enough with the kissing already. You need to fuck me, now, as in right now!" I shoved him away, hauled my jersey over my head, and began tugging at my shirt and jeans. "Fucking goddammit, pig in a piss tank, who makes these bloody things?" A button went flying as I finally got them to my thighs, and Fox grabbed my hand.

"Hang on." He hauled me up and threw me over his shoulder, my arse flying in the cold southern breeze, which was kind of . . . *damn* . . . fucking erotic. I reached down and made a grab for his arse, but he slapped my butt. "Leave it alone, you trollop." Then he ducked through the glass slider and into the house.

We might have even made it to the bedroom if it wasn't for Mack, who decided at that moment to run in front and almost send both of us flying.

"Son of a bitch!" Fox stumbled, slamming me into the kitchen wall, and I promptly got the giggles.

"Put me down, you idiot."

"No. Mack, mat!" Fox shouted, and the poor dog slunk away while I couldn't stop laughing.

"Perhaps I should carry you?" I choked out as he tried to steady me on his shoulders. "Age and all that."

"Shut up," he grumbled before nearly taking my head off as he staggered through the bedroom door and dropped me to the mattress with a lot less grace than I'd have hoped. "Thank Christ for that." He landed on his knees on the floor beside me, swearing and complaining as he hauled my jeans down my legs.

Still howling with laughter, I watched as he circled my jeans and briefs above his head and let them fly off into the wall.

"Thank fuck for that." He crawled up my body, breathless, until we were finally face to face. "Permission to come on board?" he asked, green eyes twinkling.

"Permission granted, handsome." I bussed his nose. "Always."

EPILOGUE

Two months later

Leroy

ARMS SLID AROUND MY WAIST, AND THE KNIFE IN MY HAND made a jagged slice through the lamb roast, almost taking my finger with it.

"Goddammit, Fox!" I spun in his arms, waving the blade in the air. "You have got to stop fucking doing that. How are you so damn quiet? I *never* hear you."

He smiled and plucked the knife carefully from my fingers before sliding it onto the countertop. Then he pulled me flush against him, his big body wrapped around me like a thick blanket, and something inside quieted as it always did in his arms. We could be frantic in bed or snoozing on the couch, but the stillness remained. No matter what my body was doing, when I was close to Fox, my soul was at rest—the feeling still so new it caught me unawares most every time.

"I need you," he whispered against my lips, glancing at the clock on the wall. "We have time."

"Oh we do, do we?" I smiled against his lips as he kissed me, his tongue sliding inside for a brief reconnaissance. I was almost convinced. My cock was certainly on board with the idea, but then I thought of my mother's appalling timing and— "We told them noon, baby, and it's twenty to. How lucky do you really feel?"

"Cancel lunch." He buried his face in my neck and nibbled a line to my shoulder. "Tell them Mack's eaten Prue or the mussels are lonely or whatever the fuck you want. I want to do dirty, dirty things to you."

I snorted and reached for his thick cock pressing into me. "The mussels are lonely? Really? That's the best you could come up wi—"

"Oh my fucking god. I am never, *ever* going to get used to this." Judah sailed into the family room, placed a bowl of his almost famous recipe for ambrosia on the dining table, and then glared at us.

Fox's head fell to my shoulder. "Jesus Christ, what is it with your bloody family?"

Judah put his hands on his hips and struck a pose. "I'm done. I want my straight brother back. At least I never found *him* dry humping in the kitchen. Morgan, I'm gonna need to visit that weird friend of yours again for a cleansing. My healthy aura is completely fucked. Also, I might be just a teensy bit turned on, and holy shit, that is just so fucking wrong on so many levels."

Morgan kissed his husband on the cheek. "Dramatic much? But yeah, I can work with that other scenario . . . later." He slapped Judah's arse and took a seat at the breakfast bar. Then he tapped the next-door chair and Judah almost leapt onto it.

I winked at Fox. They could be pretty damn cute together.

"Oh. My. God. Can you please pull your shirt down over your . . . thingy." Judah waved a frantic hand my direction.

I glanced down and . . . oops.

Fox tugged my shirt over my boardshorts and gave me a kiss. "Hold that thought. Do you need any help to finish?"

I shook my head. "You set the table, that's enough. Go talk." Judah and I had cooked the Sunday lunch for a change, and since Fox cooked pretty much every other day, I wanted to give him the day off.

Fox joined them at the breakfast bar, and he and Morgan immediately started chatting about Fox's impending contract, while Judah busied himself with Prue who was clawing her way up his jeans looking for attention.

Fox had sailed through his observer training—no surprise there—and was a few days out from boarding his first vessel in his new official role. It meant two weeks at sea, and although he tried to hide his excitement, it was written in every sparkle of those green eyes. The chance to once again be out on the deep ocean had lit a fire in his belly, and I was so fucking thrilled for him. I would miss him, but I had plenty to do while he was gone, including a much-needed spruce-up of our bedroom that Fox knew nothing about.

His furniture had arrived from down south, but I refused to have anything that might've even touched Van anywhere near my house, and especially not in our bedroom. My pig-headedness on the subject had earned me a million-watt smile and a thorough fucking. I hadn't decided which I liked most at the time.

In the meantime, I'd been stashing furniture and paint at Mum and Martha's cottage for the last two weeks, and Jam from the collectable store in Painted Bay had helped me with colours after I'd called in to look at some of his stuff. I wanted things that would go with the age of the house, and Jam, as it turned out, had an eye for decorating. We got on pretty well. *Look at me being all friendly and sociable and shit.*

"We're here, so you can start." Mum and Martha breezed into the room, quickly followed by Patrick who immediately joined the others at the breakfast bar.

The only one missing was Kane, no doubt having his own lunch up in the bedsit with his growing menagerie, including a nest of motherless starlings he was doing his best to keep alive. The man was a magnet for lost creatures.

Judah had advanced communication between them to at least a decent hello and even the occasional wave or nod of the head, but that was about it. An invite to lunch was still a ways off.

Mum sidled over and pecked me on the cheek. "Mmm, that looks good. So, how are our favourite, bestest boys?"

At the breakfast bar, Judah narrowed his gaze. "And exactly *which* boys would you be referring to?"

"All of you, of course." She ambled over to deliver a kiss to Judah's cheek. "You know I don't have favourites."

Judah and I shared a look and an eye-roll. Things were good between us and getting better. I figured if we could laugh about stuff like our mother's determined obliviousness regarding her early parenting, things were looking up.

Martha shot me a knowing wink and pulled my mother into a kiss. "Behave yourself, woman."

Cora waggled her eyebrows. "Like hell."

Judah groaned, Fox swore, and my chin fell forward on my chest.

Then as one voice we said, "Rules," and pointed to the printout on the fridge which read *Absolutely no public woman-on-woman canoodling allowed at the homestead in front of genetically related persons.*

Both Cora and Martha laughed. "We never agreed to that. Besides, we're always interrupting you lot with your hands all over each other."

"Well, you wouldn't if you'd bloody knock for a change."

"Where would be the fun in that?" Martha teased. "Come on, Fox, pour your mother a wine."

Mum joined me back in the kitchen. "Are you ready for the lawyers on Wednesday?"

I nodded. "The loan approval is set. We just need to get the surveyors to get cracking with the boundary change proposals. Then we can adjust the titles and it's all go."

"Good. And I hear you're thinking about seaweed?"

I groaned and shot Fox the evil eye. He caught it and laughed. "Goddammit, Fox has been talking, hasn't he?"

My mother smiled. "I thought you hated the idea?"

I plated the lamb while my mother drained the peas. "I did. But you know Fox. He's had a bee in his bonnet about it ever since Cole raised the subject. And he's done a ton of research. Turns out, seaweed farming might just be the next big thing." I pulled a face and my mother laughed.

"But I'm not going to rush in. Fox wanted to sink some of his money into a joint venture, but I said no, not yet. It's too soon. Especially after what Van did to his business. I want to make sure anything we do in the future is all laid out properly in a contract, for both our sakes. I don't want any questions or old regrets in his head, especially since we're still so new."

She patted my arm. "There's no one answer to these things. Find the way that works for you and to hell with what anyone else says." She turned to the noisy conversation happening at the breakfast bar. "Judah, is your friend still planning on coming up this month?"

"What friend?" I turned to my brother.

"Abe. He's a choreographer I know from Wellington. Nice guy. I asked him to help me develop an idea I have for a mid-year performance with the kids. If we can build enough confidence in them with that, then maybe we can tackle a Christmas review. I'm okay on short routines, but something like this needs a few more skills. He's hoping to take some vacation time either before or after, but he'll be here for a couple of weeks. He's staying with Mum and Martha."

I looked to my mother. "You barely have the room." My gaze flicked to Fox who nodded.

"He can stay with us, if that's okay with Judah?"

"Of course it is. Thanks." Judah's eyes were soft on mine.

"Maybe he can do something with Lee's two left feet," Fox quipped, and I lobbed a tea towel at his head.

"Shut up. For a guy who doesn't know his shimmy from his moonwalk, you have an awful lot to say for yourself."

Terry and Hannah arrived just as we were about to sit down, Hannah looking more comfortable on her canes than she had in months having started a new drug that seemed to be helping her arthritic pain better than the last. I really hoped it kept working, because at ten years old, she was way too young to have to deal with that shit. But even though *she* looked better, Terry's face was cut with deep lines and exhaustion in his eyes I'd never seen before.

"I haven't been sleeping well," he brushed off my concern and promptly changed the conversation.

Lunch was rowdy, with three different conversations going at once and a lot of shit-talking. Halfway through I took a minute to sit back and really look around the table. Not five months before these lunches had been nothing more than a chore, and I'd have been counting down the minutes until everyone left and I could get back to the farm or on to my books—irritated with the conversation and the interruption to my peace and quiet.

Today the only thing I wanted to get *onto* was Fox's dick. Everything else could wait.

And these lunches had become a time I enjoyed. A time with my family. My *growing* family. I looked to Fox and across to Patrick, who'd proved himself an indispensable and reliable farm manager. I'd even officially changed his title to match, although the pay increment was minimal. But I'd made the announcement over a previous family lunch, and he'd been chuffed as anything.

As if he'd read my mind, Fox's hand found my thigh and he leaned in close. "I love you."

I couldn't stop the smile that lit up my face, and I turned and kissed him soundly on the lips. "I love you too."

We let the others clean up and headed to the deck and some much-needed fresh air. Out of sight of the kitchen, Fox crowded me against the railing, his front to my back, and ran his hands under my shirt and across my belly, making me shiver.

"It's a beautiful afternoon." He rested his chin on my shoulder, his breath fanning hot against my neck as we stared across the outgoing tide of Painted Bay. "But not nearly as beautiful as you."

I turned my head and kissed his cheek. Enough of a breeze stirred off the water to puff those dark, sun-tipped locks off his shoulders, but not enough to put a chill on his skin. A cloudless sapphire sky saw to that, the thin winter sun doing its best to put a smile on everyone's face.

"You're such a smooth talker." I smiled and turned back to the view, snuggling deeper into his arms.

A dozen or so people were head down and bum up, digging for pipis in the exposed sandy seabed, hats on against the beat of the afternoon sun, even in early winter. Others sat with their legs dangling off the edge of the pier, rods in patient hands, hope baiting the lines that stretched out into the bay with the current.

Fox's hold tightened, and I leaned back into his embrace, folding my arms over his at my waist.

After a few quiet moments, his hand slipped free and took mine. And as he kissed my neck and ran his lips up to my ear, something sharp and cool slipped onto my finger.

My gaze jerked down to see a broken ring of shell hanging from my left ring finger. I spun to face him. "Fox?"

He smiled and took my chin between his thumb and forefinger. "This is a promise, sweetheart. I know it's only been five months, and neither of us is sure about any formal bits of paper in our future. But it seemed to me we were both sure about one thing. *Us.*"

He cradled my face, his lips just a breath away, and I was lost in the deep ocean of his eyes.

"I love you, Leroy Madden. I love this place, I love this life we're just starting to build, and after my last relationship, I think that's something of a fucking miracle, to be honest. And so this is my promise to you that I'm not going anywhere. That I want this. I want you. More than I've ever wanted anything in my life. And I want to replace this shell with a ring when you're ready—no ceremony attached unless we decide we want one down the track. But I want this on your finger, if you'll take it? If you feel the same."

I couldn't speak, I could barely think, my heart stunned in disbelief.

He grinned and tipped my chin up. "That mouth's wide enough to have a better chance of catching a fish than anyone down on that wharf."

"Shit, sorry." I licked my lips. "And yes, fuck yes. All of that and more. Have you got another of those things in your pocket?" I was tugging at his jeans when he put his hand in front of my eyes and opened his fist to reveal a second shell.

I sent him a sly grin. "You were very sure of yourself, mister."

He blew a slow breath and I suddenly saw the nerves he'd hidden so well. "No, I wasn't. I just hoped."

I grabbed the shell ring and set it on his finger, but it caught on the knuckle and wouldn't budge. I muttered and swore and stuck it on his little finger instead. "Finger like your cock. Too bloody big for its own good."

He snorted and brushed the back of his fingers down my cheek. "So beautiful."

I looked him in the eye. "Yes, I want this, and I want a ring. But I want *mine* on *your* finger as well. I love you, Fox Carmody. I want this life and I want you. Now, put your lips on me before I decide *to hell with an audience* and bend you over this railing to show you exactly just how much I want you."

He threw his head back and laughed, and then he kissed me like he'd been waiting his whole life just to have the chance.

I kissed him back, all in, nothing held back, knowing exactly how he felt.

Thank you for taking the time to read

ON BOARD
Painted Bay 2

If you enjoyed Fox and Leroy's story please consider taking the time to do a review in Amazon or your favourite review spot. Reviews are a huge help for spreading the word. Thank you so much.

Don't miss the next book in the series:

IN STEP
Painted Bay 3
(coming 2022)

MORE BY JAY HOGAN

AUCKLAND MED SERIES

First Impressions

Crossing the Touchline

Up Close and Personal

Against the Grain

You Are Cordially Invited

SOUTHERN LIGHTS SERIES

Powder and Pavlova

Tamarillo Tart

Flat Whites and Chocolate Fish

Pinot and Pineapple Lumps

PAINTED BAY SERIES

Off Balance
(Romance Writers New Zealand 2021 Romance Book of the Year Award)

On Board

In Step

(coming 2022)

STYLE SERIES

Flare

(coming late 2021)

STANDALONE

Unguarded

(Written as part of Sarina Bowen's World of
True North—Vino & Veritas Series and published by Heart Eyes Press)

Digging Deep
(2020 Lambda Literary Finalist)

.

ABOUT THE AUTHOR

JAY IS A 2020 LAMBDA LITERARY AWARD FINALIST AND THE WINNER OF ROMANCE WRITERS NEW ZEALAND 2021 ROMANCE BOOK OF THE YEAR AWARD FOR HER BOOK, OFF BALANCE.

She is a New Zealand author writing in MM romance and romantic suspense primarily set in New Zealand. She writes character driven romances with lots of humour, a good dose of reality and a splash of angst. She's travelled extensively, lived in many countries, and in a past life she was a critical care nurse and counsellor. Jay is owned by a huge Maine Coon cat and a gorgeous Cocker Spaniel.

Join Jay's reader's group Hogan's Hangout for updates, promotions, her current writing projects and special releases.

Sign up to her newsletter HERE
Or visit her website HERE.

CPSIA information can be obtained
at www.ICGtesting.com
Printed in the USA
BVHW041338140921
616731BV00011B/180